Praise for Geek Mafia!

"The story is gripping as anything, and the characters are likable and funny and charming. I adore caper stories, and this stands with the best of them, a geeky version of The Sting... this is one hell of a book."

—Cory Doctrow, BoingBoing.net

* * *

"Unputdownable...highly recommended"

—Seth Godin, Bestselling Author

* * *

"Twists and turns will leave you guessing many of the time who is really scamming who. Dakan is able to write a 320 page book that is over all too soon."

—410Media.com

* * *

"Geek Mafia ain't just any book...the kid's got chops, the book's getting props, and the price is right. We bought one."

—Vladimir Cole, Joystiq.com

* * *

"A fast, fun novel from author Rick Dakan. One is reminded that living a sheltered, regimented life can be oh so boring and dull. It's time to get 'Off-the-Grid' and experience freedom in a whole new way! A highly recommended read!"

—USABookNews.com

GEEK MAFIA

PM

GEEK MAFIA

Rick Dakan

PM

GEEK MAFIA, Third Edition
By Rick Dakan

ISBN: 978-1-60486-006-1
Library of Congress Control Number: 2007906968

Copyright © 2008 Rick Dakan
This edition copyright © 2008 PM Press
All Rights Reserved

PM Press
PO Box 23912
Oakland, CA 94623
www.pmpress.org

Design and illustrations: Austin McKinley
Cover: John Yates
Interior layout: Courtney Utt
Copy Editor: Anthony Salveggi

Printed in the USA, on acid-free, recycled paper.

This work is licensed under the Creative Commons Atrribution-Noncommercial-No Derivative Works 3.0 License. To view a copy of this license, visit http://creativecommons.org/
licenses/by-nc-nd/3.0/ or send a letter to Creative Commons, 543 Howard Street, 5th Floor,
San Francisco, California, 94105, USA.

This is a work of fiction. All characters in this book are fictional and events portrayed in this
book are either products of the author's imagination or used fictitiously.

Acknowledgements & Dedication

First and foremost, this book is dedicated to mom and dad. Without their support and love none of this would've been possible.

Thanks to everyone who helped me with early drafts of this book and for all their helpful comments and careful criticisms: Karen and Stephen Dakan, Alan Dakan, Austin McKinley, Neil Hendrick, Becky Woomer, Laurie Roberts, Rebecca Stultz, Poz, Charles Salzberg, and Michael Neff. All of you gave valuable insights and your support helped me see this thing through to the end (which is really just the beginning.) And if you enjoyed reading my bubbling here, you can read my babbles every day at

rickdakan.com.

Chapter 01

PAUL Reynolds crisscrossed his sketchbook with furious strokes, filling the pages with images of the vengeance he would take on his former co-workers at Fear and Loading Games. He'd founded the company three years back, and, just a few hours ago, his partners and erstwhile friends had fired him without cause or warning. He concentrated hard as his pen brought to life demonic figures from one of the best-selling comics he'd created, scythe-wielding cyber-men called Myrmidons who tore into surprised computer programmers with fangs and claws. Elsewhere on the page, computers assembled themselves into 21st-century Golems, rising up against traitorous CEOs and producers to crush them to bloody pulp as they cowered beneath their desks. Sitting at the bar in Señor Goldstein's Mexican Restaurant in San Jose, California, Paul's own artwork engaged him for the first time in months, maybe years. Under other circumstances, that would have made him happy. But today's circumstances allowed only two emotions: despair and a burning desire for revenge. Not wanting to succumb to the former, and not quite wanting to find a gun and go back to the office, he instead drew.

He had turned to a fresh page and begun to sketch his most elaborate revenge-scheme yet when a woman walked into his line of vision. There were four or five other women in the restaurant already (most of them employees), but this one stood out. This one would've stood out anywhere. Her hair, cut short and spiky, was dyed a magenta so bright it nearly glowed. She wore a tight black t-shirt, baggy olive drab shorts that hung on shapely hips, and heavy black boots with two-inch thick soles. She had a faded black messenger bag slung across her chest, the strap pressing between her breasts. If Paul had to guess, she wasn't wearing a bra. She definitely wasn't your average Silicon Valley techie on an early lunch break, and certainly not a restaurant employee.

Grateful for the distraction, Paul focused on the newcomer, chilling his anger for a moment with a swift sip of margarita and melted ice. He ran a hand through his fine brown hair, brushed a few wrinkles out of his Green Lantern t-shirt, and sucked in his bit of beer belly before he turned back to the sketchbook and kept drawing. He didn't care what his pen pushed onto the page as long as he looked busy. As far as Paul was concerned, a sad man sitting at a bar before noon was not someone with whom striking young women with ruby hair engaged in random conversation. However, as past experience in many a coffee house and dive bar had taught him, a scruffy artist sketching away when normal folks should be working often attracted all kinds of interesting attention. And so, he sketched.

"I'm here to speak with the manager," the woman said to the bartender.

"Yeah, he's here," the bartender replied and skulked off to find the boss.

The girl leaned forward onto the bar, drumming a random beat on the wood with her knuckles while she looked around the room. Paul, who'd been watching out of the corner of his eye, took the noise as an excuse to glance over at her. She was looking right back at him, smiling.

"Hey," she said.

"Hey," he replied. He gave a smile, but inside he was suddenly embarrassed by the attention. He didn't want to hit on girls. He wanted to get drunk and figure out if there was any way he could avoid his looming fate. But he hadn't dated anyone in over a year, and some urges—and some women—refused to be ignored.

"What're you working on there?" she asked.

"Oh, just doodling you know," he said as he looked down at the page. He'd sketched the outline of a hydra-like monster with five heads and ten tentacles. Four of the heads were laughing as the tentacles strangled the fifth. "I'm a… I'm a comic-book artist."

Was that true? Was he no longer a videogame designer then, just like that?

"Really? Very cool."

"Thanks"

"But tell me something," she said as she came over and claimed the bar stool next to his. She smelled like soap and shampoo, clean and fresh. "Are you really a comic-book artist or are you, like, a comic-book artist in waiting?"

"What?"

"You know, you meet guys all the time in bars or Starbucks or wherever who carry around their notebooks and sketchpads and say they're writers or artists. But really they're waiters or clerks or something." She paused to put a reassuring hand on his forearm. Her touch was warm and the feel of her flesh gave him a little internal twitch of arousal. "Not that there's anything wrong with that or anything. I'm all kinds of things in my head that I'm not actually in real life."

"No, no, I'm the real deal. I'm even published. Hell, I used to even get paid decent money for doing it."

"But not anymore?"

"Well no. I've moved up in the world, or at least my paycheck has."

"Sold out, huh?"

"Sold out, yeah. I left comics a few years ago and helped start a computer game company. I've been the lead designer on a game called Metropolis 2.0." He rubbed the tattoo on his arm, the company logo as he had designed it. Back in his apartment, Paul still had that first sketchbook from five years back when he'd scribbled those early doodles. Doodles that grew into the forthcoming online computer game that PC Gamer magazine had hailed as "the most anticipated release of next year." By contrast, his personal anticipation for the game had taken a precipitous nosedive in the last few hours.

She nodded in approval. "Very cool. Is it out yet?"

"Not yet. Comes out in August."

"So tell me something else..." she started to say, but just then the bartender returned, interrupting her thought.

"I'm sorry, the manager's at the bank or something," the bartender said. "Do you want to leave a message?"

The pink-haired woman eyed the bartender for a moment and then looked back at Paul and winked. "How long do you think he'll be?"

"I dunno, fifteen minutes maybe? He should be back before the lunch rush."

"Ok, I'll wait for him." The bartender nodded and started to turn away, but she reached across the bar and tugged on his sleeve. "While I'm waiting, can I have a shot of Sauza and another margarita for my friend here?" She eyed Paul once more. Again, the wink. "Make that two margaritas and two shots. I've got to catch up."

"Sure thing."

Now she turned back to Paul, who had to admit that an already bizarre day had suddenly taken a strange new twist—but at least it was finally turning in the right direction. "Ok, so what were we talking about?" she asked.

"You wanted me to tell you something."

"Oh yeah! Right, I got it now. So," she said again, "Tell me something. Why did you say you're a comic book artist when you're a computer game designer? I mean, these days that's just as cool as being an artist, maybe cooler 'cause it means you probably actually make a decent living and can buy a girl a drink."

Paul looked down at his hydra sketch, a monster attacking itself. "Well, I guess because I've just been told I'm going to be fired tomorrow."

"Oh, yeah, well, that sucks. Good thing I'm buying this round of drinks then, huh? Even a better thing that I ordered those shots." She reached into her shorts' pocket and pulled out a weather-beaten black leather wallet. Paul caught a glimpse of red panties as the weight of her hand in her pocket pushed her shorts off their perch on her hip. "Speaking of which, here's my man now."

The bartender had arrived with the drinks. He spread them out before Paul and his new friend—a shot and a margarita each, saying "Sixteen dollars even." She pulled out a twenty and handed it to him and then picked up both shot glasses, giving one to Paul.

"Here's to getting fired and fuck the fucks who swung the axe."

"I'll drink to that," said Paul, and he did in one fiery gulp. He surprised himself by not coughing and sputtering as the liquor burned its way down his throat. He chased it with a sip of his margarita and then said, "But enough about that shit," anger and sadness blooming again, despite the pretty girl. Time to change the subject. "What're you here for, looking for a job?"

She made an utterly dismissive noise in the back of her throat. "Hardly. No, I'm here to make a deal." She opened up her shoulder bag and drew out a pair of small plastic figurines. They were little mariachi performers, with guitars. "Novelty salt and pepper shakers," she said. "They're all the rage with the jet set this season."

"You sell those?" Paul asked, surprised.

"Something like that," she replied with a smirk and took another sip of her drink. She quickly wiped her hand off on her shorts and then held it out to Paul. "Hi, by the way, I'm Chloe."

"Paul," he said, shaking her hand and looking her in the eyes for the first time. Deep green. She smiled back at him, full of enthusiasm. "Nice to meet you."

"Nice to meet you too, Paul. Go ahead and keep the little guys." She gestured to the figurines. "Think of them as my gift to you. May they keep you company in whatever your new endeavor might be." She raised a toast and they clinked glasses and drank.

Paul smiled—his first genuine smile all day if memory served. "I'm honored. Thanks." The two of them took the awkward moment of silence that followed to continue sipping. "So," he finally said, "What're you and your micro-mariachis doing here?"

Chloe put her drink down and said, "Oh, we're just out for a stroll, taking in the sights. No, actually I'm hoping the restaurant will let me put 'em on the tables for a day. I'm doing market research for the company that makes them. See if people think they're cute or annoying."

"How're they doing so far?"

"So far so good actually." Something over Paul's shoulder caught her attention as she spoke and her gaze drifted toward the front door. "This is my last stop before I take a break for lunch. And if I'm not mistaken, the guy I need to speak with just walked in the door. Will you excuse me a minute?"

"Sure."

"Watch my drink. Actually, order us another round." Chloe stalked across the restaurant to intercept the manager. Paul's gaze followed her as she walked and he decided pretty much right then and there that he was smitten. She seemed perfect, and he couldn't wait to find out how, as would undoubtedly be the case, she wasn't actually perfect at all. For now though, Paul ordered another round of drinks and watched her chat with the manager. He seemed dubious at first, in a hurry to get ready for the noonday rush. But she charmed him over quick, and then handed him a pair of shakers to look at. He smiled a few times and laughed loud enough for Paul to hear from across the room when she pointed to some apparently funny idiosyncrasy about the pepper mariachi. They chatted a few more minutes before shaking hands and parting ways with a smile.

She stopped midway between the manager and the bar and pulled a cell phone from her pocket. She moved it about the room trying to get a signal and then dialed it. She talked for a few minutes and shut the phone before coming back over to Paul, dusting her hands in the universal sign of accomplishment. "Done and done."

"Good work. He seemed to go for it pretty quick," said Paul.

"Oh, the guys are always easy, especially restaurant managers. They usually don't give a damn. As long as he's not a slave to some corporate overlord who decides decor or some crazy shit like that, then it's usually cool." She sat back down next to him again and downed the last of her drink just as the next round arrived. "Actually, he claimed to have remembered me from somewhere—although he didn't know where. Whatever. He said yes, and that's all the matters."

"You are pretty memorable."

"You think so? I dunno, maybe you're right."

"Trust me, you definitely make a memorable first impression."

She raised her glass to toast him. "Yep, that's what your mom said last night anyway."

"Really," Paul said, feigning indignity, "Wow, I can't believe my mom said that." He paused for dramatic effect. "After all, she was so tired after working your mom over, she said she fell right asleep when she got home."

Chloe laughed, more because Paul had played back at her than because what he said was funny. She adopted a British accent for a moment. "Well played, old chap, well played." Then, voice back to normal, "You're all right, Paul. Most people wouldn't pull the mom card that fast. Especially if they knew me and knew my mom died of breast cancer last year."

Paul was horror stricken. Was she serious? She couldn't be serious right? He started to apologize. "Oh, that's… I'm sorry. I…"

"I'm just fuckin' with you, kiddo," she said, laughing. "No worries. Mom's fine and livin' large in the suburbs."

Paul laughed along with her, although his had a tinge of nervousness that he tried to conceal. Who the hell was this woman? Still, he'd decided he officially had a crush on her now, and he wasn't about to let a bizarre sense of humor dissuade him from a much-needed distraction. So what if she made jokes about her mom dying of cancer? At least she was making them to him.

"You know, Chloe, you've got a pretty fucked up sense of humor," Paul said. "I like that in a woman."

"Hold your horses there, sport. Let's not get into what you like inside women yet—we just met after all." This sudden sexual spin on his comment conjured up a couple of graphic images he couldn't have ignored even if he'd wanted to, which he didn't.

Chloe stared at Paul for a long moment with something he hoped was attraction, or at least interest. Then her phone buzzed and she looked briefly at the display screen before turning her gaze back on him. "Paul, have you had lunch yet?" she asked.

"No, not yet," he said, liking the direction things were headed now.

"Well, I skipped breakfast and, quite frankly, I'm feelin' a bit more buzz from these drinks than I'd expected. I need to get some food in me."

"You want to get a table?" Paul asked, motioning toward the restaurant section.

Chloe dropped a wad of bills on the bar as she stood up. "This place? No fucking way. It's over-priced, under-spiced slop." She walked right past Paul toward the door, and he struggled to sweep up his sketchbook and belongings as he followed her.

"We're going to my place."

Chapter 02

CHLOE'S house reminded Paul of a cross between a used bookstore, a computer repair shop and a college dorm. A wall of bookcases dominated the living room, each shelf crammed with two, sometimes three layers of books, videotapes, CDs and DVDs. More stacks of books and magazines stood in every corner. Paul was certain they would have taken over all the other flat spaces as well, were it not for the half-assembled computers and three dusty old monitors occupying the coffee table, end tables and everything in between. The only semi-open spaces were around the two couches that faced each other from across the room. A large red-and-black checkered blanket covered one of them, while the other was cracked but still serviceable brown leather. Thrift store purchases both, Paul thought.

"The computer stuff belongs to one of my roommates," Chloe said. "She's always fiddling with those things to get better performance or whatever. The books are mostly mine or my other roommate, Kurt's. Come on into the kitchen and we'll rustle up a sandwich."

Paul followed her back into the open kitchen area, which (given that he was ostensibly here to have lunch) he was relieved to see was clean. There was clutter in there certainly, but no dirty dishes or leftover food-stuffs appeared in evidence. Along the left wall was a cheap, plastic patio table with long wooden benches on each side and miss-matched chairs at either end. Newspapers, books and a laptop occupied most of its surface area, but the end closest to Paul seemed clear enough to see actual use as a place for dining.

"Is peanut butter OK?" she asked, motioning him toward one of the chairs.

"Sure," he said and sat down at the table. As she started to prepare a couple of peanut butter sandwiches on white bread she said asked, "So, tell me Paul, why are you getting fired tomorrow?"

"I'm not really entirely sure," he replied, although this was a stalling tactic. He knew pretty well why he was getting fired; he just didn't quite know how to put it into words. It'd only been a couple of hours since his high-school friend and CEO had told him what was happening. "I mean, they gave me reasons, but they're not really reasons. They're not things I did wrong."

"What does that mean? They didn't like your looks?"

"Yeah, basically," stated Paul. "More to the point, they didn't like the look of how I was doing things. What I mean is, I'm not a tech guy, right? I'm an artist and a writer. I'm used to working at home and scribbling away and meeting my deadlines. So when I helped start this company, I figured it would be mostly the same. I figured I'd sit in my office and do my work and hit my deadlines and go to my meetings and all that."

"But you didn't do that?" asked Chloe as she placed a plate with a sandwich in front of him and went back to the refrigerator.

"No, that's exactly what I did, which was part of the problem."

"Do you want a beer or a coke or something?" she asked.

"Coke's fine."

Chloe brought back two cokes and set them down on the table before taking a seat next to Paul. "So, wait. How was doing your job a problem?"

"I don't work like a programmer," he said. "I don't sit and draw or write for twelve or fourteen hours at a stretch like they program. I can't do it. My brain is done long before then. Four hours of writing in a day and I don't have anything left to say. There's nothing there. Alternately, I can draw for about twice that long. Sure, I can do more—a lot more if there's a deadline or it really needs to be done, but then I'm wiped. I'm no good for anything for the next few days."

"And your buddies at work thought you were slacking off because you weren't putting in the same kinds of hours," she said. "Basically, they fired you for being a lazy clock-watcher. That's the only reason?"

"Well, that and the fact that I probably pissed a whole bunch of them off even though I didn't mean to."

"Yeah, well, that'd do it. What were you doing to make everyone hate you?"

"I don't think it was everyone—just some of them. To be honest, I don't have a reputation for listening to other people's ideas." Paul stopped her before she could comment, "And yeah, yeah, that would be bad if it were true, but really it's not. I do listen to other people's ideas. I like to listen to them. But if the ideas aren't good, I'm not going to use them just to make people feel good."

"Besides," he continued, anger creeping into his voice. "They hired me for my ideas. The game itself was my idea, based on my comic book. And of course I listened to other people's thoughts. But I had the vision and, I can tell you this for sure, no one else there had anything remotely resembling a vision."

She'd nodded, her expression sympathetic. "OK, Paul, I think I get the overall picture. In a nutshell, they fucked you over."

"Yeah," he said. Saying it all out loud to her made had him angry again. Angry at what they'd done to him. Angry and betrayed and…

"I do have one question though," Chloe said, interrupting his angry reverie.

"Shoot," he said.

"You're talking in the past tense, like you've been fired already, but earlier you said you're getting fired tomorrow. What's up with that? Most people I know who get fired are shown the door right away. Why wait twenty-four hours?"

"Oh, I thought I explained that," answered Paul. "They can't fire me. I mean, they can't just walk in and tell me to leave. I'm one of the founders. I own nine percent of the company and I'm on the Board of Directors. They have to actually vote me out."

"Really?" asked Chloe, a spark of renewed interest in her voice.

"Yep. Like I said, this whole project—the whole reason for this company—was my idea."

"So the vote hasn't happened yet right?" she asked. "How do you know you're going to get voted out?"

"Well, there are only five of us on the board, and the others all told me today how they'd vote. They wanted to have a meeting right then and do it, but I'm entitled to twenty-four hour's notice, and I said I wanted it."

"Why?"

"I dunno really. I was just so shocked. I had no idea they were even thinking about doing something like this. Really. No idea at all. And I'm sort of prone to doing rash things—you know, getting angry and stuff. I knew if I went into a meeting right then I'd blow up. I might hurt somebody or get in more trouble. Some part of me was smart enough to say, 'Hey, just get out of here.' So that's what I did."

"That makes sense," she said. "I'd for sure have yelled and screamed and broke something. Or someone."

"Those feelings came later—once I was in my car." Paul looked down at his sandwich. This job, this company, had been his big break, his chance to do something that tons of people would see and enjoy. He was supposed to come out of this a millionaire. He'd never have to work again if he didn't want to. But they'd kicked him out—some of them good friends of his. They'd stolen his idea and kicked him out.

That morning, as he'd sat there in his car outside the office, he'd contemplated just throwing it in gear and driving straight through the plate glass door at the front of the office, just flooring it and putting his trust in the airbags to save him. Or not. Whatever. Paul didn't think he could have done it, but he really wished he had. He wished he had it in him to be so grief stricken that he didn't care what the consequences for his revenge were. But he did care. He was worried about his future. And for that he felt like a coward.

"And then you did the only logical thing under the circumstances," Chloe said. "You went and got a drink."

"Yes I did."

"But are you sure they're going to vote you out tomorrow?"

"Oh yeah, they made that real clear. They already offered me two month's severance, which is more than they have to. Plus I still own whatever stock I've vested."

"That sucks," Chloe sympathized. "But that last part's good though, right? You still own part of the company, so if the game takes off, you should make some money."

"Yeah," said Paul, but he didn't sound convinced.

Neither, it turns out, was Chloe. "Of course there's probably a bunch of different ways they can screw you on that right? Like in the movie business where people get a percentage of the profits but no movie ever really makes any profits because of accounting tricks and whatever. I'm sure game companies do the same shit."

"Yeah," Paul hadn't had this particular depressing thought until now. "I doubt they'll pay out dividends or anything as long as I'm sitting on nine percent of the stock."

"You know what, Paul? They've got you bent over good. They're giving it to you in the ass and all that's left to negotiate is who's going to do the moving back and forth."

"I hadn't thought of it that way. Thanks for the image."

"Have you ever been fucked in the ass, Paul?" she asked, her voice dead serious.

"You mean before today?" he asked, not sure what she was driving at.

"No, I mean actually fucked in your actual ass."

"I can't say I have, no," he laughed. OK, this is weird, he thought.

"I didn't think so." She leaned closer in, her face just a foot or so away from his now. "And would you like to be fucked in the ass?"

"Um… no. It's not on my list of things I want to experience."

"You have a list? What's on the list?"

"Well, I, ummm…"

"We'll come back to the list. You're wondering what the hell my point is, right?"

"Um, yeah. Definitely."

"Here's the deal, Paul." She put her hands over his where they rested on the kitchen table. Again, the touch of her skin on made him squirm on the inside—squirm in a good way. "You've just been fucked over so bad you wanna scream. Hell, you probably already did scream. But now it's time to pick yourself up and move on. Either that or get used to being the bitch, right?"

No matter how in lust with her he was right now, he sure as hell wasn't about to let her do anything to or put anything in his ass. Well, probably not. But he didn't think that things were heading that direction.

"You don't sound convinced," she said.

"Well, I'm new to this." He smiled. "Be gentle, it's my first time."

"Don't worry, you'll learn fast." She took her hands off his, making him immediately miss her touch, but she needed them to slice through the air and emphasize her final point. "You know what's better, Paul? Better than lying there and taking it like a bitch? I'll tell you. It's much better to be the one who does the fucking. Which is why I'm gonna help you Paul. I'm gonna help you fuck those bastards 'til they can't walk straight for a year."

"Sounds good," Paul agreed. "But how can you help me?"

"What kind of help do you need?" she replied. "I've got a lot of hidden talents, but I can't come up with the solution for you. You have to know what to ask for."

"I think I need a lawyer more than anything."

"OK, say I'm a lawyer. What then?"

"You're a lawyer?"

"We'll pretend I'm a lawyer. What would a lawyer do for you?"

Paul thought about this. What would a lawyer do for him? In his experience, not much. Real life lawyers tended to hem and haw and beat around the bush. They seldom gave straight answers and they were never the go-for-the-throat sharks you see in the movies. "Actually, what I really need is someone like a TV lawyer," he said. "Someone to go in there and threaten the whole lot of them into giving me what I want. Make them afraid of being in court for the next decade. But that sounds like it would cost a lot of money and probably wouldn't actually work."

"And what is it you want, Paul?" asked Chloe. "Do you want your job back?"

"No, not anymore. I'm pissed at being fired, but I could never work with them again. No, I want what I'm due. I've got my stock, but that won't be worth anything for years, if ever. I'd really prefer to just have that money now and leave those fuckers behind forever."

"Hmmmm," mused Chloe.

"Hmmmm?" asked Paul.

"I'm beginning to see a plan. A brilliant plan." She smiled wide. "Ab-so-fucking-lutely brilliant. A way to make them pay you every last cent you're owed and make them do it tomorrow. Truth is, it's really your plan. And believe me, it's a very, very good one. At least it will be once we finish coming up with it. But first I have to ask you some questions."

Paul had a skeptical look on his face. "Okaaay," he said. "What do you need to know?"

"Do you still have a key to the office and the security codes and all that?"

"Yes," replied Paul.

"Great," she said as she pulled her cell phone from her pocket and started dialing. "What time does everyone go home?"

"It's hard to say," said Paul. "Most of the people leave around seven or eight, but a couple of the programmers stay until midnight or later." He watched as she held the phone to her ear. "Who're you calling?"

"I'm getting the gang together. We can't do this on our own. Gotta have the whole crew."

Then she was talking into the phone, leaving a message for someone named Raff. After that, she made four or five other calls while Paul just sat there. He wondered who these people were and if one of them was Chloe's boyfriend (or girlfriend for that matter). If she had a boy/girlfriend at all. She never told any of the people what was going on—just that they needed to get over to the house by six and that they had a job to do tonight.

"One more thing Paul," added Chloe when she hung up on the last member of this mysterious gang. "I need you to tell me everything you can about your company's lawyers and your partners' legal experience."

Chapter 03

PAUL knew that the plan was insane and probably illegal. Certainly the stuff he'd been helping Chloe and her gang of followers do for the last few hours was technically illegal. He'd asked them why they were helping him, what did they hope to gain. They'd told him that this is what they did for fun. Chloe assured him that they "lived for this kinda shit." OK, fine. He could sort of see that. Once he was there, helping them come up with the plan and then actually carrying it out, it sure as hell was exciting—probably the most exciting thing he'd ever done.

Now that he was home and alone with his misgivings and paranoia, it all seemed like a really stupid idea. If it weren't for Chloe and her mesmerizing enthusiasm, there's no doubt that he wouldn't be doing this at all. But it was too late now. Or was it?

It was five in the morning when Paul got back to his apartment. He'd told Chloe that he wanted to get a few hours sleep before the big meeting, but he now realized that there was no way he was going to be able to relax. When he'd stepped out the door twenty-two hours earlier, he'd still had his job and was looking forward to showing the rest of the art team his new designs for some of the higher-level monsters he wanted to add to the game. "Screw that," he thought. "They're my monsters now. I'll use them somewhere else."

It could never work. How could it? Right then and there Paul decided that he was going to call the whole thing off. It wasn't too late. They hadn't done anything yet that wasn't reversible. No one had been hurt. No money had changed hands. No one had been lied to. If he called it off right now, he could just move on and try and put the whole, sorry state of affairs behind him.

He sat down on the couch, the sole piece of furniture in his living room aside from the TV, and started to dial Chloe's number. Then he stopped. "No," he thought. "Not yet. Think about this for a minute. It might work. And if it does work, you're set. Everything you want out of this shitty situation."

Paul decided to make himself a pot of coffee and take a nice long, hot shower. He was supposed to meet Chloe at the office at 9 a.m. sharp. If he called her at home in a few hours, he could talk things through with her again and, if he wanted to call them off, he could.

As he stood in the shower, he wondered again why they were helping him. They were thrill seekers, sure. But this wasn't skydiving or even graffiti. It was, in a way, theft or extortion, or possibly fraud. There might be serious jail time on the line. But Chloe, with her uncanny confidence, had assured him they'd be fine. That it wasn't nearly as bad as it sounded. Not nearly as against the law as Paul thought it probably should be. She'd called some lawyer friend (did she say former lawyer or former friend?) and run some of the stuff by him. "Be cool," she'd said. Everything would work itself out. He almost believed her.

He decided to dress professionally for this final confrontation and would've put on a suit, but he didn't own one. He didn't even have a tie. In fact, he wasn't entirely sure he'd still remember how to tie one if he did. It'd been ten years since he worked at Barnes and Noble and had to wear ties. They didn't even make the clerks do that anymore, he'd noticed. He had a white button-down shirt that had been hanging in his closet since before his friend Matt's wedding. He'd had it cleaned for the occasion and then forgotten to pack it. He found a relatively clean pair of khakis to go with it—his dress blacks were balled up in the corner and covered in carpet lint.

By 6:30 in the morning he was dressed and ready, his squeaky leather dress shoes pinching his toes. Looking in the mirror, he decided that he had been right about dressing for the occasion. He wanted to face his accusers with dignity and professionalism, even if he did decide to call the plan off. He'd go over it again with Chloe, let her convince him or not. Then he'd decide. But when he called her, he only got voice mail. He left a message asking her to call him back, but somehow he didn't expect to hear from her. Maybe she was the one who'd gotten cold feet.

Not wanting to sit still and not wanting to eat, Paul just got in his car and drove the freeways for an hour, listening to Air America, but not really paying any attention. The liberal radio network usually got him good and fired up with leftist indignation, brought on by the right wing's latest outrages, but today it flowed right over him. It had a calming effect nonetheless, keeping his thoughts from obsessing on what he was apparently about to do.

He arrived on the street where his office sat at 8:30, but pulled into a parking lot halfway up the block. From there he could see the office parking lot, and he could tell that Chloe wasn't there yet. But Greg, his friend and CEO (Former friend? Former CEO?) was there and so was Jerry, the game's producer. Frank, the lead programmer, wasn't there yet, but Paul would've been surprised if he had been. Frank seldom came in before 11:00 on a normal day (and Paul knew he hadn't left last night until close to midnight), so making a 9 a.m. meeting was always tough for him. Also M.I.A. was Evan, the art director. There was one other car in the lot, which Paul recognized as belonging to the company's lawyer.

He sat and watched and listened, waiting for the rest of them to arrive. Evan sped into the parking lot about five minutes later, and Paul watched him go inside. Paul had ducked down when he saw Evan pull onto the street, though if Evan had bothered to glance over he might have recognized Paul's car. "Oh well," he thought, "it won't really make much difference." By 8:55 there was still no sign of Frank. More alarming, there was no sign of Chloe. He checked his voicemail, but no one had called.

Shit! he thought. What the hell is this about? He couldn't believe she was late. For a fraction of a moment, he wondered if maybe he'd imagined the whole thing. Maybe there was no Chloe. Maybe he was having a breakdown and had dreamed up the woman, the gang, the plan—everything. But no, that didn't seem too plausible. Odds were she'd probably just chickened out. Or maybe she'd been playing him all along. Either of those would make more sense than her actually going through with the plan they'd come up with together.

Paul started his car and drove the two hundred feet to his soon-to-be former office. Just as he was getting out, he heard screeching tires from the street behind him. Chloe? No, it was Frank's red Miata. Oh well. Paul and the lead programmer saw each other, but both decided it would be more comfortable to pretend they hadn't. He went on inside and avoided any awkward parking lot confrontations.

The conference room was back and to the right, in a corner of the office hardly ever visited. Paul's stomach fluttered and bile crept up into his throat. He felt sweat trickle down the small of his back even though the office was refrigerator cold. This was going to suck, he realized. At least Chloe had given him one thing—he'd spent the last twenty hours planning his revenge and flirting with a pretty girl instead of obsessing about his fate. He was somehow grateful that he'd only have a few minutes of feeling this shitty anticipation before the axe fell.

Everyone but Frank and Paul already had seats at the makeshift conference table (really four smaller tables pushed together to form one big surface). The company's mousy lawyer, Marie Woods, sat in the seat Paul usually took for himself at these meetings. That's a sign if ever there was one, he thought.

"Hey Paul," said Greg. He'd also dressed up for the occasion, wearing a yellow tie and too-large blue blazer over his plump frame.

"Hey," signaled Paul. He realized he'd forgotten his notebook and wanted to go back into the car and get it. But it was too late; no turning back now. "Hey Evan, Jerry." The two other men nodded to him. Evan said something inaudible into his thick beard that might have been hello. Paul thought that Frank should have been inside by now. The meeting should be getting started, but Paul guessed that the fucker had stopped to check his e-mail first, as always.

Jerry, dressed in khakis and a polo shirt with the company logo on it, tried to lighten the mood. "Your Buccaneers are shaping up pretty well, huh?" Paul's hometown team had traded for a star running back over the weekend. "This could be their year."

"Yep," said Paul. What the hell was he talking about? The two of them had always talked sports—it was their only real common bond, but really, was this the time? Just trying to kill the silence Paul supposed. Fuck that. He took a seat and stared down at his hands, wishing again for his notebook so he could at least pretend to be busy.

Finally, Frank came in, thin, short and wiry with a shaven head and an unkempt goatee. He brushed past where Paul sat without saying a word and took his place at the table. "Hey," he said to Greg, who just nodded at him.

"Are you ready, Paul?" asked Greg. "Yesterday you said something about getting a lawyer?"

"Um," mumbled Paul. "I guess I'm ready. Whatever." He didn't even look up from his hands as he talked. "Let's just get on with it."

"Ok," said Greg, his voice sad, although Paul wasn't sure why. If he was sad, he shouldn't have fired him. "We all know why we're here, but we have to do this the right way to make it official. I'm going to ask Marie to run the meeting so we can make sure we cover all the legal bases."

He stopped and looked up from his notes. There was a knocking sound coming from somewhere. It had to be the front door, which locked automatically.

"All right, first, for the record we need to make a note of who's here…" announced the lawyer, but the knocking had become pounding and Paul interrupted her.

"I think there's someone at the door," said Paul.

"Whoever it is can wait," chimed in Evan, speaking for the first time. Paul knew Evan hated confrontation—all four of them did. They preferred to whisper and complain in private rather than actually telling someone they had a problem with them. Evan no doubt wanted this to be over as quickly as possible.

Marie was about to continue, but Paul stopped her. "I should check. It might be… um… it might be my representative." Part of the plan was that he wasn't supposed to actually call her his lawyer. Was it Chloe? No FedEx guy would pound that long and hard.

"I thought you said you didn't have representation," said Greg, looking both confused and a little worried.

"Well, I wasn't sure she'd…" the pounding grew even louder. They could hear the glass door shaking in its frame.

"I'll let him in," said Frank, springing up from his seat and heading out the conference room door. A few seconds later they heard muffled voices and then Frank came scurrying back into the room, a startled look on his face.

Chloe came in a moment later, although Paul hardly recognized her.

"Sorry I'm late," she said, slamming her leather briefcase down on the table next to Paul. "You haven't fired him yet, have you?"

Chapter 04

FOR a moment, Paul wasn't even sure who had walked into the room. Chloe had totally transformed herself since he'd last seen her. She wore a wig for starters, and a very good one. It was light brown and shoulder length. It looked so natural that if he didn't know she had much shorter hair, he would have guessed that she had dyed it. But it was the outfit that made the change. She wore a well-tailored, very professional, woman's gray skirt/blazer combo with a yellow silk blouse. Her wrist sported what looked to Paul's uneducated eye like an expensive and fashionable gold lady's watch from which he thought he detected a glint of diamond. In short, she looked just like the high priced lawyer she was supposed to be. She was certainly the best-dressed person in the room.

Chloe reached across the table to shake Greg's hand, stretching forward as she did so. Paul watched Greg glance down at her cleavage while he shook her hand. "I'm Rachel Roth, here on behalf of Mr. Paul Reynolds."

"Hi," said Greg. "I'm Greg Driscol, and this is…"

"I know the rogues gallery here," said Chloe cutting Greg off and looking around at the assembled board members. "I've learned all about you gentlemen."

Marie stood up and shook Chloe's hand. "Marie Cooper, from Johnson, Myers and Wick. Nice to meet you," she said. "OK, we've got the intros down, shall we get on with the dirty business?"

"Um, sure," Greg said as he sat back down. "I was just about to turn things over to Marie."

The plan was now in action and so far so good. But Paul knew that this was a crucial moment. Chloe didn't really know the law—just a few points that her friend had helped her out with. She couldn't let the real lawyer take over the meeting. Her dramatic, unexpected entrance had them off guard, and Paul hoped she seized the moment and pressed on.

Chloe stepped up to the plate right on cue. "Yeah, you know what? Before I let Marie here get going, there are some things I need to go over with you. I think they might have a real bearing on how matters proceed from this point on."

"Okaaaay…" said Greg. "I suppose that's fine." Paul had heard Greg say a hundred times that he never liked to go into a meeting he didn't already know the outcome of. He was going to hate this one. The CEO looked to Marie for support, and she just kind of shrugged, whatever that meant.

"First things first, I want to let you know that Paul here is more than willing to resign his seat on the board. We realize this situation just isn't working out the way we'd hoped, and so it's time for the two parties to go their separate ways." That seemed to comfort them.

"So, all we have to do now is figure out what Paul gets out of the deal," she continued. "I mean, this whole project was his idea, and he does own a sizable chunk of stock. I tell, you guys wouldn't even be here if it weren't for him, right?" No one said anything. "So we figure he's owed something for his time and trouble."

Greg didn't seem to like where this was going. "We've offered Paul two months' severance and, of course, he gets to keep all the stock he's vested."

"Huh," scoffed Chloe. "Yeah, as you say, of course he gets to keep the stock he's vested. He already owns that. Not much you can do there, so that's not really a concession. Now giving him the rest of the stock he was supposed to vest if he'd stayed on. That would be a concession."

"I'm afraid that's not on the table," said Greg.

"Yeah, no way," interjected Frank. Paul wasn't surprised to hear this. They'd never gotten along very well, and Frank was always worried about the bottom line (something Paul had kind of admired until right now).

"That's fine, that's fine," she continued. "Don't get your panties in a bunch, boys. We just want what's ours." She fished around in her brief-case for something and then looked up. "No, that's not even right. Paul wants out. He wants to go bye-bye and leave you behind him like a bad dream. Thus, he's willing to sell what's his to you."

"You want us to buy out his stock?" asked Greg.

"Yep."

"Why would we do that? It's not worth anything yet," replied Greg.

"Is that what you tell your investors, Greg?" asked Chloe.

"I tell them that it's not worth anything yet. It has potential value."

"But you sure paid a lot for it, didn't you, Greg?" said Chloe, looking at the piece of paper she'd fished out. "You paid two and a half mil for your shares."

"That's because I'm an investor, and I believe in this game," he said. Greg had made money—a lot of money, selling his first startup to a much bigger conglomerate. He and Paul had been friends in high school and, when Greg said he was interested in maybe getting into computer games, Paul suggested doing one based on his comic-book series. Thus, the company had been born.

"You're not the only one," stated Chloe. "Didn't PC Gamer rate it the most anticipated online game of next year?"

"Yes, one of the most anticipated. I think we were number three."

"And didn't GameSpot.com just last week do a glowing, four-part preview of the game, calling it the most innovative game world to come along in years?"

"Yes," agreed Greg.

"What's your point with all this?" asked Frank.

"Just that the game is looking like it could be a big hit," said Chloe, "Which is in large part because of Paul's ideas. So the way we see it…"

"Listen." Now it was Greg's turn to interrupt. "None of this is why we're here today. There's no way we're going to buy Paul out. We've got no reason to. We've made a fair offer, and if the company ever does get sold, then Paul will probably do very well for himself."

"Yes," said Chloe. "In the long run that may be true, but who the hell cares about that? We're talking the short run here. We're talking about Paul getting fired for no real reason at all."

"We don't need a reason," said Frank, which was true, and the smart thing to say. Chloe had hoped to get them to say something—anything she could use against them to show discrimination or lack of cause. But they didn't need a reason, and they were smart enough not to give one.

"Yeah, you just don't like him. Fine, we can handle that. Paul doesn't like you much either, but that doesn't matter. The truth is, if the game does well, or even just ok, there are going to be bonuses and raises around here, right? Probably tens, maybe hundreds of thousands of dollars each. But bonuses only go to those of you still drawing paychecks. You could pay out all the profits like that, and Paul would never see a dime. His stock would be worthless to him."

"There are limits to how much…" added Marie, finally trying to get in on the conversation.

"I know, I know. There are limits. But we both know that good lawyers and CPAs or whatever can find loopholes and shit." Chloe went back into her briefcase for another document. "You guys don't like Paul. You probably like him even less now that you've met me. So I'm betting that if you get a chance, you'll screw him."

She tossed a stack of stapled documents out onto the table.

"What's this?" asked Greg, picking up one of the packets of papers.

"It's our proposal." Chloe just stood and watched as the four board members and their lawyer took a moment to read it over.

"No fucking way," said Frank. "You want us to pay him $850,000? Even if we had that kind of money—which we don't—there's no fucking way we'd give it to him." He turned to talk directly to Paul. "What do you think you've done to deserve this, huh? You go home at five—or earlier—every day. You don't have any technical skills. You don't have any experience. You're a pain in the ass."

"C'mon Frank," said Greg. "Calm down a second." Then he turned back to Chloe, shaking his head. "As I said, Paul's gotten plenty out of his time here and…"

"No Greg," Chloe insisted. "We don't think he has gotten plenty. We think he's short about $850,000."

"This is silly," declared Greg. "We really don't have that kind of money to spend on this nonsense. As Paul knows, we've got a little over a half a million in the bank, and we need every penny of it to pay salaries until we ship this game."

"You've got the money, Greg." Chloe smiled, reading from the paper she'd just taken from her briefcase. "According to your tax records, you should have something like seventeen million in the bank. Plus the two houses and the condo in Florida."

"Even if that's true," said Greg, who Paul knew never liked to talk about how much money he had, "why would I want to buy out Paul for that much? I already own thirty percent of this company, that's more than enough."

"Don't you have confidence in your little game here?" asked Chloe.

"It doesn't matter. As you pointed out, I've got a lot of money. I don't really need more, and me giving Paul $850,000 isn't going to make the game any better or help business. There's no up side for me." Greg shifted his gaze to Paul. "I'm sorry, man, but I'm not giving you any more money." Paul just stared back at him, trying to not smile or sneer. Greg had no idea what was coming.

"See, Greg, that's where you're wrong," declared Chloe. She had a stack of four folders in her hand, and she pointed at Greg with them to emphasize her point. "In fact, it's very much in your company's best interest to make Paul happy right now. Because if Paul's happy, then he and I are just gonna go away. You'll never hear from us again."

"You're going to sue us?" said Frank, quick to pick up the subtext. "You've got no standing. We don't need a reason to fire you." Frank turned to the company, Marie, for confirmation. "Isn't that right?"

"That's correct. The company does not have to show cause for termination," the lawyer stated.

Chloe hadn't looked at either of them during the exchange; she'd kept her entire attention focused on Greg. "I'm not prepared to say whether or not I agree with that," she said, "but I'm sure Marie here can also tell you that just because you don't think we have standing, that doesn't mean we can't sue you. We will, sure as fuck, sue the hell out of you."

Marie kind of shrugged again; at least that's what Paul thought of it as. It was as noncommittal a motion as he could imagine. As he'd told Chloe, Marie was a contract lawyer, not a trial lawyer. She was solid on the details but not very good with the confrontation thing. Plus, she had the annoying lawyerly habit of never saying anything was one hundred percent sure. She always hedged her bets and gave caveats on her advice. "It's possible," she told Greg. "They can certainly bring suit, although it's unlikely they'll get very far with it."

"But hey," said Chloe, "It's all billable hours for your firm, right? What do you guys charge? $300 an hour for something like this?" Marie didn't deign to answer.

"You won't win," said Greg. "I've been down this road before, this exact same road with my first company. You'll cost us some money, but it'll cost Paul money, too. After all, he's paying you right?"

"What?" said Chloe, sounding distracted. She'd started reading something from inside one of her files.

"I just pointed out that Paul's got to pay you, too. He'll lose this case and it will cost him a lot of money and, I happen to know, Paul doesn't have a lot in the way of savings, does he?"

"Nope," said Chloe. "He seems pretty stupid about money, you're right. But that's OK; I'm not charging him anything for this. This is a freebie."

"Are you a friend of his uncle or something?" asked Greg, a little confused now.

"Oh no, nothing like that. Never met the man. No, you see, Paul here gives great head. I mean GREAT head. He goes down like nobody's business. Better even than most women I know. So I figured I owed him. Plus, I wanna keep him around, and if he doesn't get his much deserved payoff, he might leave and move back to Florida." Even Paul was shocked when she said this. The rest of them were knocked back on their heels.

Greg had the presence of mind to close his mouth after his jaw had dropped. Marie blushed and looked down at her notes and the other three followed suit. Chloe continued before they could regroup from that particular set of visuals she'd conjured up for them.

"And I've got plenty of time and energy to spend on you guys. There will be a wrongful termination lawsuit, I can promise you that, but it's only the beginning, just the tip of the iceberg. Because you see, Paul here's a major stockholder in this company. He's vested 8.5 percent of it, which certainly gives him standing to protest any kind of financial mismanagement. And from what Paul tells me, there's a fair amount of that going on around here."

Chloe paused to deal her files out around the table. There was one for each of the other four founders and one for her. Marie didn't receive anything. "Plus there are issues of corporate money spent on personal perks and sexist and homophobic language creating a hostile work environment. Is it really appropriate to use bandwidth and disk drive space to download pornography? Same for illegally downloaded songs, in violation of various copyright laws and exposing the company to a massive lawsuit by the Recording Industry of America."

All of them but Frank were now looking in the files Chloe had passed out. He didn't even bother to touch his. "You really might want to look in there," said Chloe. "It's got nothing to do with all those songs you download." Frank smiled without humor and opened the file.

As they read what was in the files, Jerry and Evan began to visibly blanch. Frank's smirk disappeared, replaced with concentration and anger. Chloe continued, "We all know that there's a lot going on here that shouldn't be. And we all know that there's some things that are better kept quiet."

Marie, who hadn't seen the materials in any of the folders, spoke up. "I think we need to wrap this meeting up. I'd like to talk with my clients and we all need a chance to cool down."

"I think your clients would like to continue this meeting right here and now," said Chloe. "Get this whole thing sorted out as quickly as possible. That way we can all get on with our quirky, secretive, sometimes perverted little lives."

The four other board members were all ashen faced. Evan just kind of nodded. Frank was on the verge of exploding in anger, but he was probably afraid that it would only make things worse for him. Jerry had stood up and was now whispering in Greg's ear. Jerry always knew when the ship was sinking, thought Paul. He was the first to give in.

"Marie," asked Greg after listening to Jerry for a minute, "could you step out for a minute?"

The lawyer was shocked. This had to be way beyond weird for her and unlike any meeting she'd ever been to. "I don't think that's a good idea, Greg. You should stop now and give me a chance to look into this. Find out some more about what's really going on here."

"Yeah," said Chloe, "Let's give everybody a chance to find out a little more about what's really going on here." She smiled cheerfully.

"Please, Marie, I can handle it from here," replied Greg, looking down at the table in front of him. He was angry, too, which surprised Paul. He'd seen Greg frustrated and annoyed, but now the first-time CEO seemed to actually seethe with rage. It was kind of scary, but also sort of funny. He was the wild card, though. Greg had enough "fuck you" money to call their bluff. He would only give in under pressure from the other three.

Marie started to protest but then seemed to realize that there was something going on in the room that she was missing. She gathered her briefcase and laptop and walked out the door. Jerry was still next to Greg and they were whispering back and forth. Once the door had closed behind Marie, Chloe started up again.

"As you guys can see, I've got the goods on all of you. There's stuff in those files you probably don't know about each other. Fuck, in your case, Jerry, there's stuff in there your wife probably doesn't even want to know, isn't there?" Jerry didn't respond. He was still whispering in Greg's ear. "So, let's get this over with, shall we? I'm here to give you a…"

"How did you get this?" snapped Frank. "You couldn't have gotten what's in this file legally. There's no way."

"It doesn't matter," said Chloe.

"It matters," insisted Frank, "Because you can't use it in court."

"Who said anything about using it in court? I have plenty of things to use in court, as I already said." Chloe sat down in her seat next to Paul for the first time, propping her feet up on the table as she leaned back in her chair. She smelled really good, thought Paul. Not perfume, but something else. Something subtle. "To be honest Greg, your file there is the least interesting. Sure you've spent some money on some questionable things like call girls and weird sex toys, but that's not really such a big deal. I can assure you though, there's stuff in those other files that makes for much, much juicier reading. Just ask Jerry there."

"This is bullshit," said Frank. He stood up and pounded on the table. "It's fucking bullshit!"

"Yeah, well, we're playing hardball now, sport," Chloe mocked. "And you're losing big time. You guys got nothin'. You already fired Paul and he's got nothing left to lose. He doesn't have families and marriages he wants to preserve like Jerry or Evan. And he doesn't have a legal skeleton in his closet like you do Frank. A skeleton that might just come with some serious jail time."

Frank started to say something, but then thought better of it and sat down. None of them knew what to do or what to say. They all snuck furtive glances at one another, trying to suss out the other guys' secrets while hiding their own.

Chloe's friends—her "crew" as she called them—had had a busy night. They'd gone through everything in the company's computers, including all the e-mail and, almost as importantly, all of the Web traffic for the four founders. They had social security numbers, bank account info, e-mail messages, porn site accounts, travel information, credit card statements, phone records and more. They'd taken it all in under an hour and then used some blackmail-grade search tool Kurt and Raff had designed to weed through the mountains of data looking for the good stuff.

At 4 o'clock that morning, Raff had come into Chloe's living room with the good news. Everyone had secrets, and Raff had found some real doozies. It helped that Paul already had his own suspicions about each of them that had allowed Chloe's crew to focus their search parameters.

Jerry's marriage was, at best, strained. Paul had always suspected Jerry was up to something—too many unexplained weekends away and mysterious phone calls to "no one important." Raff had announced that he was now about 99 percent sure that Jerry was cheating on his wife, judging by the flights, the calls, the hotel rooms and the steamy e-mails Jerry had been sending to a woman named Carla in Portland. All of which was information Jerry's wife would go ballistic about. The phone calls alone probably would have been enough for her to file divorce papers. And that would mean Jerry would lose half of everything, including his stock.

Evan's was even more interesting than that, although Paul felt more than a little bad about using such secrets against the man. But then Chloe had reminded him that it was better to fuck than be fucked, and besides, did he want the money or not? Evan had a reputation for being into the S&M scene and all that, which in this day and age wasn't so bad. But this was the surprisingly homophobic world of computer game programmers, and even though Evan might not be gay, he apparently did like to dress up in women's clothing. His wife knew all about it (she apparently helped pick out the dresses), but Evan was a very private person and he would have a hard time commanding respect from his bigoted employees if they knew the truth. Actually, they probably would tease him for a week and forget about it, but Paul knew that Evan didn't think that—he would do whatever he could to keep his secret.

Frank's was the worst of them all—although it was also the one they had the least proof about. It appeared that one of Frank's co-workers from a former job was sending rather angry e-mails accusing Frank of stealing his code. Indeed, this code apparently comprised the core for the graphics engine that made their current project possible. Of course the angry former coworker didn't have any proof. But now Chloe and Paul did, thanks to Raff. They found encrypted e-mails from Frank discussing the problem with one of the other programmers. They'd also found the original code—which was line for line what the angry coworker had said it would be. This wasn't quite proof, but if the info Raff had dug up found its way into the right person's hands, Frank could be in some serious shit.

"What do you want?" asked Greg.

Paul wanted to say something, but Chloe, sensing this, put a hand on his knee to stop him. She answered Greg. "Like I said before, we want Paul's fair share. Simple as that. You personally buy Paul's stock at $1 per share, right here, right now. Otherwise, Jerry's wife finds out he's cheating on her, everyone finds out Evan's a transvestite, and several other lawyers find out all about how Frank stole code."

Now everyone was looking down at the table except Chloe and Jerry. Chloe was staring straight up at Greg, watching Jerry whisper in his ear once more. A moment later Frank got up and started whispering in Greg's other ear, which looked almost ridiculous enough to make Paul laugh out loud. The three of them retreated to the far corner of the room to converse with a little more privacy. Chloe took out a cell phone and started dialing.

"Gentlemen," said Chloe, causing all three conspirators in the corner to turn back toward the table. "I'm not full of patience at this point, so I'm calling one of my assistants. He's going to start e-mailing the contents of those files. I think we'll start with… Evan. Company wide, with pics. Also, he'll CC all the computer gaming press." Now it was Evan's turn to get up and join in on the whispering, but Greg cut him off before he could plead his case.

"You know this means we're through, don't you Paul?" said Greg. "I've done a hell of a lot for you. Spent a lot of money on this game of yours. It didn't work out, and I'm sorry for that, but we could still be friends. Call this off now, and you and I can work something out. Maybe start a new project together, something more suited to your temperament."

Paul was tempted. Why burn bridges? Why cast aside a fifteen-year friendship? Tears started to well up in his eyes. Just as he started to say something, Chloe leaned over and put a hand on his upper thigh as she whispered in his ear. "He's playing you," she said. "I didn't want to show you last night, but Raff got some e-mails he wrote about you. If you read them you'll know how full of shit he is. Don't fall for it. We've already won."

Paul closed his eyes and wiped away an errant tear. He knew she was right. They'd already won and, quite frankly, the friendship was finished anyway. He turned to Chloe and nodded.

"Enough bullshit, kids," stated Chloe. "Game's over. Either you pay money now or you all pay in different ways later today." Chloe grinned at Greg. "Besides, Greg, if the game does as well once Paul's gone as you said it will in your e-mail, then you'll make your money back several times over. Just write the fucking check and we're gone."

"I don't have that kind of money in my checking account," said Greg.

"Yes you do," replied Chloe smugly.

"What?"

"Yes you do, Greg. You've got 1.2 million dollars in your checking account because you're buying a house for your mom and stepfather. You sent out the check yesterday but it hasn't cleared yet because the closing's not until 3 o'clock this afternoon."

"How do you…?"

"Write the fucking check, call your bank, and cancel your mom's money. Or wire more money into your account. Either way, you can write the damned check, and you can do it right now." Chloe reached into her briefcase and slid a stack of papers across the table to Greg. "Then we'll sign these papers transferring the shares over to you and wham, bam, thank you ma'am, this is all over and you can get on with your day."

Everyone in the room was now looking at Greg. Jerry, Evan, and Frank were all standing behind him. The CEO was looking down at the papers on the desk. There was a long silence as Greg thumbed through the pages, although Paul doubted that he was actually reading them. He was thinking.

Greg didn't say anything for a long time. Everyone just watched and waited, holding their breaths. Finally he gave in. "Fine. Whatever. That's all I ever do around here anyway isn't it?" said Greg. "I sign checks." Then he looked at the three men standing forlornly behind him. "But this is it. I'm in charge now. You three owe me big, and I don't want anymore questioning what I say or complaining about the rules I make. This is it. I own you."

"OK, Greg. You've got it," said Jerry. Frank and Evan just nodded. Paul knew that Frank disliked Greg almost as much as he disliked Paul and that bowing down to him like this was painful. That made the moment just a little bit sweeter than it already was.

"Stay here while I go get my checkbook."

Fifteen minutes later, it was over. Greg wrote the check and signed the papers Chloe had typed up transferring ownership of the stock. The six of them probably didn't exchange more than ten words. On their way out, Chloe and Paul passed Marie sitting in the lobby talking on her cell phone. The company's lawyer was not pleased with whatever was happening. Then they were out the door and on their way.

"I took a cab," said Chloe. "You'll have to drive us to the bank."

Paul's heart raced. He was rich. He was free. He'd just stabbed his best friend in the back and extorted almost a million dollars from him. He threw up all over the parking lot near Frank's car.

Chloe handed him a bottle of water from her briefcase. "Come on Paul, we're almost through this."

"OK… I'm OK."

"Good. Now drive to Bank of America as fast as you can, and let's cash this fucker before they change their minds and cancel the check."

Paul took a swig of water to wash his mouth out and then spit it back toward the office building.

"Absolutely," he replied.

Chapter 05

A S IT turned out, Greg would have had a hard time canceling the check, even if he'd changed his mind. Chloe's Crew had already sprung into action as soon as they left the building. The company used a computer-controlled switchboard to route phone calls, and this immediately went down, same for their Internet access. Meanwhile, a crude but effective denial of service attack was launched against their company Website. If Greg decided to use his cell phone, there wasn't much they could do, but the hope was that he'd be so tied up with all this other crap that he wouldn't have time to think of that.

Paul didn't think any of that was necessary. Greg had given in, and he wasn't going to call and cancel the check now. He'd agreed for a reason, and once Greg had a reason for making a decision, it was usually impossible to change his mind. And it didn't make sense anyway. All he would have done is buy himself a little more time. Chloe and Paul would just march right back in and start all over again—probably after sending out pics of Evan in drag to all the employees. From his point of view, there was no reason for Greg to do that.

Of course, it was still a huge risk for Chloe and Paul. If Greg just wanted a delay to get the lawyers involved, then they were in trouble. Chloe and he had broken a fist full of laws in the past twelve hours. They needed to cash that check and disappear as soon as they could.

The bank put up a bit of a fuss about the check, which was one more reason Paul hated Bank of Fucking America. They always had some rule to screw a customer. But Chloe made a bunch of noise and actually jumped up and down at one point and eventually they walked out of the bank with a cashier's check. Then it was off to another, locally owned bank where Chloe had a contact who worked as an assistant manager. She'd called ahead to let her know that they were coming in with a big check that they wanted cashed right away. All the paperwork was waiting for Paul to sign, and twenty minutes later he'd opened a new account and deposited the check. Chloe's friend made sure it went through and had already placed an order for cash, since the bank didn't have anywhere near that kind of money on hand. She'd put a rush on it and said they could pick up the money at 4:30 that afternoon. It was now 11 a.m.

Paul and Chloe went back to his apartment where they met two guys named Filo and Max who had a van. The four of them descended on Paul's home and started packing up everything he cared about. That actually didn't take very long, since Paul didn't have much in the way of furniture. His artwork, comics, computer, TV, Tivo, CDs, books, video games and clothes went into an ever-growing pile of boxes. The boxes went into the van, and when that was full they went into his car. When that was full, a bag of clothes and a box of books went into the dumpster.

"Fuck 'em," said Paul. "I'm rich now, right? I should buy a whole new wardrobe anyway." He added another box of clothes to the dumpster. Then they were off, although Paul noticed Filo's van went the opposite direction. "Where are they going with my stuff?" asked Paul.

"Storage locker on the other side of town. I know the owner and got you a deal."

"Won't I need my stuff?" asked Paul.

"I thought you were buying new stuff?"

"Well, yeah, but that doesn't mean I don't need some of that. My sketchbooks and the finished art from all my old comics are in there." Paul didn't really much care about anything else, but those originals were literally priceless to him and represented eleven years of hard work.

"Don't worry, the stuff will be there when you need it." She dug a key with a tag out of her pocket and handed it to Paul. "Here's the key. The address and number are on the tag."

"OK."

"Besides, there's not enough room for all that junk at my place."

"Your place?" asked Paul. "I thought I was going to stay with Raff."

"I thought better of it," she said. "I want to keep an eye on you. Besides, after the party we're gonna throw tonight, you won't be in any condition to leave for a week or two anyway."

Paul drove over to the rental agency that owned his apartment, and passed over his keys. He signed a couple of papers while the guy behind the counter blathered on about breaking leases and forfeiting security deposits, but Paul scarcely listened. He gave a P.O. Box address to forward his mail to and left. Next he cancelled the cell-phone service. Then he closed all his old bank accounts.

The night before, he and Chloe had had a long talk about what would happen after they pulled off their little con. She had warned him that he might want to make it hard for his ex-partners to find him and cause trouble, either legally or physically.

"You're going to make a lot of enemies in that room today," she had said.

"I think they were already my enemies."

"Nope. Before, they just didn't like you very much. Before, you probably never had a real enemy in your life. Now you're gonna have three or four of them."

"I think you should define your terms here," he had said.

"People who wouldn't hesitate to do you bodily harm if they could get away with it. People who curse your name on a daily basis and wish you no end of ill will. I'm talking people who actively want to see you dead. You know, enemies."

"You're right, I don't think I've ever had one of those," he'd said.

"Well, judging from what I've seen of these guys, and based on how totally we're going to fuck them over tomorrow morning, you're gonna have some soon."

"OK."

"Which means," she'd said, "you don't want to be anywhere where they can find you. You don't want them to have any opening to strike back. Especially in the first twenty-four hours or so, when they're still so angry it's like a physical pain in their side. That's when they'll pull the crazy shit. That's when they'll come shoot your tires out or throw bricks through your window. That's why you have to be nowhere in sight. You shouldn't go home for at least three days. Maybe a week."

Paul thought about this for a few long minutes. Why leave his crappy apartment for just a week? Why not leave it altogether? The thought of just cutting every link to his old life grabbed hold of Paul's imagination and wouldn't let go. The sheer freedom that came with such a decision offered an array of intoxicating possibilities. Paul had decided then and there to abandon his apartment completely. He'd only rented the place because it was close to the office. He had no happy memories there, no ties to the place at all. Why not just move out completely and make it impossible for Greg or anyone else to find him? Chloe seemed surprised at Paul's decision, but also pleased. She had arranged for the crew to help him evacuate as fast as possible. From there he'd planned to just sort of play it by ear.

And now, apparently, the plan was for him to stay with Chloe. All in all, that sounded like a pretty appealing plan. Paul had no idea what she wanted from him or even why she was doing this, but he was assuming/hoping that she was as attracted to him as he was to her. Hopefully he'd find out tonight at this mother-of-all-parties she was planning.

They quickly unloaded the car into Chloe's living room. "We'll get you sorted out later. Right now I'm starving, let's go get some lunch."

Lunch was at a hole in the wall Thai place not too far from Chloe's house. The owners seemed to know her and brought her and Paul Thai iced teas without asking. Chloe had Pad Thai and Paul ordered the special—something involving shrimp—and then, for the first time in hours, he had a chance to catch his breath.

"Wow," he said. "It's been quite a freaking crazy ass day."

"I'll bet," she replied. "Beats drowning your sorrows in cheap margaritas though, doesn't it?"

"Definitely, assuming we don't all go to jail."

"No one's going to jail. I ain't never been caught yet."

"Do you do this kind of thing often then?" asked Paul.

"Well, not this exact kind of thing, no. But I've been in some shit way worse than this." She reached across and put her hands over his and looked him right in the eye. "Don't worry about it, Paul. Everything's going to be fine. I promise, OK?" And he believed her. He wasn't sure why, but he believed her. "So, what're you going to do with all that money?"

"I don't know," said Paul. "Probably move back to Florida. Buy a house. Invest the rest I guess."

"What's in Florida?" she asked.

"My family, most of my friends. Greg and I are both from there originally, but he moved out here years ago to start his first company. I only came out to start the game company. Now there's no real reason to stay."

"You don't like it out here?"

"Oh, it's fine," he said. "It's actually pretty cool. But it's expensive. And I think my $850,000 will go a hell of a lot further back there than it will out here. I could buy a condo like the one I was living in for less than a hundred K back home. Here it'd cost me two or three times as much."

"Yeah," said Chloe. "I grew up here so I guess I'm used to the crazy prices and stuff. I certainly understand your wanting to go home, though."

Then the food arrived, and they dug right in. It was good. Damn good for five bucks, and Paul said so to Chloe.

"You see," she said. "Not everything out here is expensive. You just need a local guide to show you the ropes."

"Maybe you're right," said Paul. "To be honest, I've been here almost three years, and I don't really know the area very well at all. Most of my time's been either at work or at home or hanging out with people from work at somebody's house."

"Sounds like you need to get out more and see some of our local sights before you head back east."

"That's a pretty good idea." There was certainly no hurry to go anywhere, he thought. There damn sure wasn't anyone like Chloe waiting for him back home. Not even close.

Chloe and Paul each took a moment to dig into their food. It was spicy enough to make his eyes water, which was just the way Paul liked it, and he was pleased to see Chloe heaping even more chili sauce onto her own dish. On some level Paul thought anyone who didn't like spicy food was a wimp, and it was becoming more obvious with each passing hour that there was nothing at all wimpy about Chloe.

"But back to my question," she said after a few minutes. "What're you gonna do with all that money?"

"I told you," he said "Buy a house, live off the interest."

"Yeah, sure, but what are you going to actually do? How are you going to spend your time?"

"Oh, well, I'm not sure. I could start up a new comic book I suppose. Maybe something based on what's happened to me here."

"Do you miss making comics?" she asked.

"A ton. I really miss just being my own master and not having to sit through endless design meetings where I have to justify every decision to everyone in the company."

"You like being master of your own destiny," said Chloe. "I'm exactly the same way. I can't even hold down a straight job anymore. I just get too pissed off at dumb people telling me what to do."

"What do you do for a living then?" asked Paul, although as he asked the question he realized that he was a little scared to hear the answer.

"Oh you know, this and that. I just try to have fun." She paused and cocked her head to the side. "Come to think of it, I don't really know how I make money. Something always seems to come up though. Life's funny that way." Paul took this to mean that it was none of his business.

"But come on Paul, answer the question," she pressed. "What're you going to do with $850,000?"

"I'm pretty sure I answered that," said Paul.

"You only sort of answered it."

"What do you mean?"

"I mean," said Chloe, leaning back in her chair and pushing her empty plate away. "That your answer sucks, and I'm going to keep asking until you come up with a better one."

"What?" said Paul, "You want me to give some of it to you?"

She laughed. "No, you big goofball. I don't need your money. But this is a once-in-a-lifetime opportunity for you. You could do something really exciting with this money. You could do almost anything, at least for a time."

"And then I'd be out of money and back where I started," he said.

"Or maybe you'd be out of money and somewhere millions of miles away from where you started," she said. "Maybe you'd do something that would change your life forever and you'd never be able to go back. Never want to."

"Haven't I committed enough felonies for one day?" he asked, jokingly.

"Shush, you!" she chided. "There's never such a thing as too many felonies—as long as they're the right felonies."

"Speaking of which," said Paul as he looked at his watch, "I think it's about time to make a withdrawal."

"OK, pal, let's go get your booty," said Chloe as she stood up.

"Booty?" asked Paul, his mind turning toward another kind of booty as he stood up as well.

"You know! You're ill-gotten gains. Your filthy lucre." She suddenly leapt toward him, jumping into his arms. He caught her—just barely—with an audible oof. "C'mon! Don't you know your pirate slang, rich boy?"

He smiled widely even as he strained to hold her whole weight. Their faces were very close now—just inches apart. "Ohhhhh…booty!" he said. "I thought we were going to a strip club or something."

"Yeah, you wish, cowboy." Her face was very close now and they were looking straight into each other's eyes. Paul decided to go in for the kiss. She turned her head just enough so that his lips pressed against her cheek instead of her lips, but he played it cool like he'd always planned it that way. He made a loud fake kissing noise as he pulled away.

"All right then," said Chloe, disentangling herself and finding her feet again. "Let's finish this up and get you paid." She tossed a twenty-dollar bill on the table and turned toward the door. Paul watched her walk off and caught his breath. Suddenly he felt sick again. What was he doing? What had he done? Who was this person? Then she turned and looked over her shoulder at him, smiling. "Come on, pirate-boy. Your booty awaits." Paul couldn't have stopped himself from staring at her ass even if he'd wanted to.

"Right behind ya," he said and went to go get his money.

Forty-five minutes later they were fighting their way through rush-hour traffic. However, the gym bag full of money in the trunk made it easy for Paul to tolerate the crowd of cars.

Everyone at the little bank had watched them the entire time they'd been in there. It wasn't often that someone took out $850,000 in cash. Chloe had put her wig and sunglasses back on, just in case, and Paul wished he'd had a disguise of his own. As they drove away, Paul watched Chloe out of the corner of his eye as she removed the wig. She'd worn it because she didn't want to be recognized on the videotape. She didn't want to be recognized because what they'd done was probably illegal. She didn't want to be recognized because she was a thief.

Paul stopped the car, pulling into a McDonald's parking lot.

"You're hungry again?" said Chloe in surprise. "There's going to be food at the party, you know."

His throat was dry and his stomach roiling. But he had to do this; it was the only thing that made sense. "Can I meet you at your house later?" he asked. "For the party."

"What do you mean?" she said, looking at him intensely. "Paul, what's wrong?"

"Can you get a ride from here?" he asked.

"From here... I don't..."

"I just," Paul said. "I just need to be alone for a little while. Do some things. Some private things."

Chloe stared at him hard. Then she leaned forward and kissed him on the forehead and then opened her door. "OK," she said sweetly. "I understand. You're still coming to the party though, right?"

He smiled unconvincingly. "Of course," he said. "I'll bring some champagne to celebrate with."

"Great," said Chloe. "I'll see you in a few hours then?" He just nodded and she closed the door. He pulled immediately back into traffic, heading for the freeway.

He hid the money. Made sure it was safe. Even if Chloe and her friends did turn out to be heartless thieves, they wouldn't be able to steal from him. He took out $10,000, which seemed a ridiculous amount of money to carry around, and stashed the rest away in a safe place he knew.

After that, he drove around for a while, debating back and forth whether to go to the party or just disappear. Or maybe even give the money back to Greg. Or maybe… no. They'd done nothing but help him. He owed them some thanks at the very least. And he wanted to find out. To find out about Chloe and see what it was that she really wanted.

He decided to stop by the house, just for a few minutes anyway. Just to say thanks.

Chapter 06

PAUL was late for the victory party. When he finally arrived back at Chloe's house he found her driveway and neighborhood so crowded with cars that he had to park on the next street over. He was ever so slightly worried about leaving his car out of sight in this neighborhood, but really it was his nervousness about the party that tied his stomach in knots. A $120 bottle of champagne under his arm, Paul walked bravely up to the front door, which opened from within before he could touch the doorbell.

"8:17!" shouted Chloe as she flung the door wide, a wristwatch held in her hand. "Who bet closest to 8:17?" Chloe wore a green and blue sari wrapped low around her waist and a white T-shirt on which someone had used a sharpie to write "HOOK-HER" on the front.

A young, stocky Asian-American woman named Bee stepped forward. She held a little piece of paper in her hand, which she shoved playfully in front of Chloe's face. "8:15! I had 8:15!"

Behind the two women a tall, rail-thin man appeared, wearing a faded blue polo shirt with the Microsoft logo on it and a pair of khakis. Paul recognized him as Raff, whom he'd met the night before. "Just barely beat my 8 o'clock." He said. Raff was the computer guy—the lead hacker in the group who'd been responsible for sorting through the reams of electronic data they'd stolen and finding the juicy bits. He'd also masterminded the attack on the company Website and some of the other problems that had tied his former partners up in the hours after Paul had gotten the check. "I wanted to bet "never," but Chloe had already taken that one."

"Don't listen to him, Paul," said Chloe. "I just bet never because I knew everyone else would want it, and I alone had faith in your return. But the others decided to have a little betting pool about when you'd finally show up after you pulled your little disappearing act earlier." Chloe waggled her finger at him in mock scolding. "You're a naughty little boy, giving me the slip like that."

Paul had been expecting this chastisement, although he'd feared that Chloe would be much more serious about it. He had, after all, pretty much dumped her at the side of the road with nothing but cab fare. "Yeah, I'm really sorry about that. I want to explain…"

Chloe grabbed him by the arm and pulled him into the house. "Forget about it. I completely understand. You had something you needed to do alone. All that matters is that you're here now, and it's time to have some fun!"

The house was full to capacity, a feat that wasn't too hard given that there really wasn't much room for humans in the crowded house to begin with. The number of computers in the living room had tripled over the course of their little "operation," and now they served as makeshift tables for cups of beer, ashtrays and plates of food. Paul recognized most of the people from the night before, although there were plenty of new faces as well. He wondered what the protocol was in a situation like this. Did all these strangers know about his crimes and the con they'd pulled earlier that day? Should he even mention it?

"Chloe, can I ask you a question?"

"Sure, Paul. The beer's in the kitchen." She pointed toward the back of the house. "You can put your champagne in the fridge if you want. We should save it for later, I think. Just help yourself to anything that looks good."

"Actually, I had another question."

She smiled at him and put an arm around his shoulders. "Whatcha need, babe?"

"How do I…" he stammered. She felt warm and inviting and, once again, smelled so good. "What should I…What should I say to people? About what happened today I mean?"

"Whatever you want. Everyone here's in the know. Hell, almost everyone here had a hand in making it happen. So, I guess the first thing I'd say is 'thanks' and then go from there. No worries though, we're all family here. This is my crew—you can trust them."

"Oh," said Paul. "OK, that's great then." All these people? All of them knew? There had to be fifteen strangers in this house, and they'd all helped him extort a ton of cash from his best friend. He was starting to think that maybe he had made the right decision about coming late and taking care of his little errand first.

"Cool," she said. "Right now I gotta pee. Go get yourself a beer." With that, Chloe disappeared down the hall, and Paul was left to his own devices, although not for very long. It was as if Chloe's stepping away had been a sign for the others at the party to descend on him. Raff was the first, holding out his long-fingered hand in congratulations.

"That was a great score today, man," stated the tall hacker. He had to be six-foot-five at least, mostly skin and bones and brain. Raff however, didn't have the physical insecurity that Paul associated with the computer programmers he'd worked with. This hacker radiated confidence and even a certain amount of grace. More like a star basketball player than an awkward desk jockey. "We were listening to the whole thing through the mic in Chloe's briefcase. She really went to town on those guys, huh?"

"Yeah," said Paul, "She's pretty amazing. She was pretty amazing, I mean. They didn't know what hit them."

"They never do with Chloe," Raff replied. "That's why she's the man."

"Right," said Paul. "Anyway, Raff, right? I just want to say thank you for helping me out. I really appreciate it."

"No problem, man! It was a real kick. I live for this shit. Listen, can I get you a beer or something? Newcastle? Guinness?"

"A Newcastle'd be great, thanks," answered Paul. "But I'll get it— you've done plenty for me already." Paul sidled by Raff and into the kitchen, where he saw Bee and another woman already standing in front of the open door to the refrigerator.

Bee was maybe five feet tall and had a stocky build that would never be thin, even if she lost some of the extra weight she was carrying around. Chloe had said that she was a very talented electrical engineer and would have been in charge of wiring up the hidden cameras if the crew had chosen a different plan last night instead of the one they ended up going with. Bee had already pulled a bottle of Newcastle out and was handing it to Paul.

"Thanks," he said.

"There's a bottle opener on the counter there," said Bee, her attention now focused on the refrigerator's contents, which Paul saw consisted almost entirely of a brown rainbow of different beers. "Let's see. Let's see. What looks yummy for my tummy?"

"What do you care? You don't even like beer," snorted the woman standing next to her, who'd pulled out a Newcastle for herself. She then turned her attention to Paul, leaving Bee to make her choice on her own. She held out her beer to Paul, who had just finished opening his own after putting the bottle of champagne down on the counter. "Could you do me as well?"

"Sure thing," he said. Paul took her beer and opened it. Returning it to her he said, "I'm Paul, by the way."

"Of course you are," she said. "You're the only stranger here, so you'd have to be, wouldn't you?" She was an attractive young woman, with dark brown hair that fell in loose curls to her shoulders. She wore jeans and a black T-shirt with a steel-studded leather belt. She wiped her hand on her pants before extending it back toward Paul, who promptly shook it. "I'm Popper."

"Nice to meet you, Popper."

"So," she said, stepping close to Paul and leaning against the kitchen counter. "You satisfied with how things went today?"

"Yeah, definitely. I mean—wow. It's pretty impressive."

"I'll say. We haven't been part of a score like that in months."

"Four months, at least," chimed in Bee, who was still trying to pick a beer.

"I don't know what's more impressive," said Paul. "The fact that you guys helped me pull this off today or the fact that you've done something just as crazy before."

"Ha!" said Popper. "This was nothing, sweet cheeks. This was a short job for us. I mean, Chloe happened to find you in the right space at the right time and so we did it. It was a lark, you know what I mean? No real risk for us on this deal. Just a little fun yanking around the gamer geeks, which is always a blast."

"Well, thanks again. What did you—you know, do? I hope that's not rude of me to ask."

"No, no problem at all. It was your score, right? Who're you gonna rat us out to?" She took a swig of beer. "Actually, I was pretty light on this one. I culled through some e-mails from your old producer pal. There was some juicy stuff in there between him and that piece on the side he's keeping. I picked out the best bits for Chloe to use in her blackmail files. Then I did some driving and was waiting around the corner as backup in case things went sour."

"What do you mean by 'sour?'" asked Paul.

"You know, if they'd called the cops or if someone got violent or if maybe you had freaked out or something."

"What would you have done then?"

She took another drink of beer and eyed Paul for a moment, her expression saying that she wondered if he was clueless or just dim. He couldn't tell which option she decided on. "I can't say. Not exactly. It depends what went wrong, doesn't it? I'd have done what needed to be done to get Chloe clear of any trouble."

"Just Chloe?" Paul asked.

"Well, if you were the one who went sour, then hell yeah, of course just Chloe."

"Makes sense," said Paul. "To be honest, I'm still not really sure why you guys helped me in the first place. I mean, what's in it for you?" This was of course the big question he'd been asking himself over and over again for the past twenty-four hours.

She looked a little surprised and was about to say something when Bee cut her off and announced that she had decided she didn't want a beer after all. "I want champagne!" she said, "Paul? Can we open that?" Bee pointed at the warm bottle he'd brought in with him. "I like the bubbles." Paul wondered if she was changing the subject on purpose.

"There are bubbles in beer, too," Popper pointed out, having gotten the message to not answer Paul's question.

"Yeah," added Bee, "But I don't like beer, remember?"

"Sure," replied Paul as he handed the bottle to Bee. "But you should probably stick it in the freezer for a bit first. It's not cold at all."

"Nope," she said, "I've got a much quicker way." She put the bottle on the counter and started digging around in the cabinet underneath the sink. "Ah-ha!" exclaimed Bee. She had a fire extinguisher in her hands. "Paul, can you do me a favor and open the back door for me?" she said as she pulled out a large cooking pot as well.

"OK," said Paul. "Sure."

The house had a surprisingly big back yard, with trees and a hammock and a large grill on the cement patio. Three people Paul didn't recognize were hunched over the grill and cooking hot dogs while they passed a joint around. Bee placed the large pot on the patio floor and then put the champagne bottle in it.

"OK, stand back!" she said. The guys by the grill looked over and laughed. Popper grasped Paul's hand and drew him back a few steps. Bee released the safety pin and pointed the fire extinguisher down into the pot. She let it rip and a cloud of white vapor soon enveloped the pot and her legs. She kept firing bursts for the next couple minutes, until the extinguisher was empty.

After the fire retardant fog had cleared, she reached in and pulled out the frosty bottle. "All set she said," bringing it over to Paul. The bottle was ice cold.

"I didn't know that really worked," he said in amazement.

"CO2 under pressure," answered Bee. "Better than a salt-water ice bath." She took the bottle and unwrapped the top. A second later and the cork went flying through the air.

"You guys sure have an interesting way of having a good time," said Paul.

"You ain't seen nothing yet, cowboy," responded Popper. She took the bottle from Bee and drank down a swig before handing it to Paul. Then she and Bee each took him by an arm and started to lead him inside.

"Come on," said Bee. "Let's go into the living room. It's story time!"

Chapter 07

STORY time, it turned out, was just that—a time to recount to the whole group what had happened that morning. The whole crew, which numbered eighteen people, crowded into the living room, occupying every empty bit of couch and floor space. Paul somehow ended up with Bee on his lap, which, while not doing anything to relieve the heat of the crowded, smoke-filled room, had a certain pleasantness to it. She held a pot laden pipe to his lips for him to take hits off each time it passed around the circle. Paul was no connoisseur, but he'd seldom had pot go straight to his head as quickly as this did.

Chloe presided over events as the master of ceremonies, telling the story with some incredibly funny (if inaccurate) impersonations of Greg and the rest of Paul's partners. Former partners. She also played a few choice clips from the audio recording she'd secretly made with the microphone hidden in her briefcase. Bee laughed the hardest and loudest, repeatedly lamenting that she hadn't had a chance to put in the cameras so they could watch it all on video. Paul laughed as hard as anyone, and took some good-natured ribbing for his own meek part in the affair.

When she finished her performance, Chloe took a bow as the whole room applauded, whooped and hollered. She took a second, deeper bow and then popped the CD from the player she'd been using during her story. She held it up along with two other unmarked discs.

"What say you cool cats? Have we well and truly triumphed?" shouted Chloe.

"WE HAVE!!!" the whole room (except Paul) responded. Paul realized that this must be some sort of ritual they'd performed before.

"And have all records been well and truly erased beyond any hope of recovery?" she shouted again.

"THEY HAVE!!!" the room replied.

Chloe singled out Raff, who was standing against the back wall of the room, smiling drunkenly. "What say you, Mr. Raff? Are your decks and disks clear?"

"They are!" he shouted. "Clear and ready for new action!" Everyone cheered at this as well, and Raff took a deep draught of his beer in acknowledgement.

Chloe now turned to Bee, who squirmed in Paul's lap. "What say you, Ms. Bee? Are your tapes erased and your cameras clean?"

"They are!" Bee shouted. "I never even got to use the cameras. Next time." The others jeered, pelting her and Paul with popcorn as she giggled uncontrollably. They'd all heard enough about not using the cameras.

Chloe let the impromptu food fight die down before she continued. "Then I, as El Capitan du Jour, officially certify this latest sortie a success!" Everyone really cheered at this announcement, throwing more popcorn every which way, but mostly at Chloe. She then held the three CDs aloft once more. "And I do further certify that these represent the only remaining record of our adventures."

With that, she snapped the disks in two, one at a time. Paul had never seen anyone do this—it seemed dangerous to him, but no one else seemed scared of the sharp shards of plastic that went flying through the room with each break. Snap! The room cheered. Snap! More drunken revelry. Snap! The biggest cheer of all. Chloe let the silver pieces fall to her feet.

"What do we always say?" she shouted. "If they're ain't no record…"

"NO ONE KNOWS WHAT HAPPENED!" the room roared in reply.

Paul realized that something bound these people together besides technical ability and miscreant natures. They had done this before, as they freely admitted, and as best as Paul could gather, they had done it a lot. This ritual was old hat to them, as precise and maybe even as meaningful as a Catholic mass. Paul was the outsider here and, although there was a pretty girl in his lap and a beer in his hand, he suddenly felt more like a fish among sharks than a guest at a party. These were criminals. They weren't would-be Robin Hoods or merry pranksters. Maybe it wasn't always about the money, but whatever they did, it was probably very seldom within the confines of the law.

"OK," he thought, "time to make my getaway." He was glad—so very, very glad that he'd decided at the last moment to hide his money from Chloe and the rest. He wasn't sure he'd have gotten out of the house with it if he'd brought it back with him. As the ritual wound down around him, he started thinking of excuses to get up and leave. But then Chloe singled him out.

"Now," she said, coming over to stand in front of Paul and Bee. "Let's hear from the man of the hour himself. Come on Paul! Stand up and give us a toast!" Bee somehow managed to find enough room on the couch to squirm off Paul's lap and into the seat beside him so that now she pushed him from behind as Chloe pulled at his arms from the front. "Come on, big boy! It's your turn," chided Chloe.

Paul was a little embarrassed and nervous. He still wanted to get out of there, but the pot had mellowed him out enough that he wasn't too worried about it. There was plenty of time. After all, the money was safe and he'd always enjoyed public speaking. The crowd clapped as he stepped into the center of the room. Chloe took his place on the couch, this time sitting on Bee's lap.

"OK, OK," he said. "First of all, I have to say thanks. Thanks to all of you for helping me out today." He paused to let them clap and cheer for a moment—although it was certainly nothing like the applause Chloe had gotten. "Yesterday was just about the worst day of my life. I saw everything I'd worked for taken from me. Everything was turning to shit. And then this girl," he pointed to Chloe. "This girl right here came out of nowhere and, well, said the craziest shit I'd ever heard. I mean, just the absolute craziest shit I ever head." Everyone laughed and Chloe buried her face in Bee's shoulder, laughing with embarrassment that might or might not have been real.

"But anyway, I just have to say, that you guys have done more for me here than I can ever thank you for. It's really amazing. I mean, the risks you guys took for a complete stranger. It boggles the mind. Maybe it's just the really good drugs you guys have here, but wow. You guys… you guys really fucking rock! If there's anything I can ever do for you— anything at all, just ask."

"Give us shares of the money!" shouted someone from the back of the room. Everyone laughed at this. Paul tried to smile. Was this the moment? Was it time to pay the price for what he'd done? What they'd done for him.

"Well, I… uh," Paul was thinking fast. "I mean sure. You know." He was grateful to them. Well, part of him was anyway. He wouldn't have the money now if Chloe hadn't seduced him into this crazy scam. But at the same time, looking back on it, he was starting to think that maybe it had been a big mistake. Yeah, he'd cashed out. But if he'd held onto that stock it probably would be worth something someday, maybe even a lot more than what he'd extorted out of Greg. But he'd been rash—and that was their fault. In a way, they might have cost him money in the long run. Not that he was about to tell them that.

Fortunately, Chloe saved him. "He's just fucking with you, Paul. We all know this was a freebie." Everyone laughed, apparently agreeing with her. They'd enjoyed his moment of discomfort, but that was all. "You can, though, if you want, pay for the beer!" Chloe yelled.

"You got yourself a deal!" said Paul, genuinely smiling now that he'd found this out. "Beer for everyone!" They definitely cheered at that—the biggest response he'd gotten so far. He thought that would be it and so he took a step toward the kitchen, inching gingerly through the crowd. But he wasn't quite safe yet. Someone was yelling from the back of the room. Apparently they wanted one more thing from him before he could go.

Chapter 08

"PLOTS and Plans!" shouted Raff from his perch at the back of the room. Paul looked back at him. What had he said? Pots and pans? "Let's let Paul do Plots and Plans!" People started clapping and whistling. They seemed to like the idea of Paul doing the dishes. What were they talking about?

"What?" said Paul.

Chloe stood up now, thankfully coming to Paul's aid. "C'mon Raff, you know he's not a crew member. He doesn't have to do Plots and Plans."

"I'm not saying he has to," replied Raff. "I'm saying let him. It'll be fun."

"What's he talking about?" asked Paul.

"It's just a little ritual we have," she said. "Every time we take down a big score—like we did for you today—we have a little session called Plots and Plans. Basically, whoever we judge benefited the most but did the least on the last score has to come up with the next one. Now, obviously this rule doesn't apply to you, since you're not a part of our crew. But if you wanna play, that'd be cool. It is a lot of fun."

"How does it work?" Everyone was watching them now, waiting to see if Paul would play along or chicken out.

"There's not much to it, really. No rules or anything like that. You just come up with an idea of what to do next. Don't worry if none of the ideas are any good. It's really just a fun game. We hardly do half the things we come up with."

"C'mon Paul," said Popper, from the floor near Paul's feet. "It's fun! Just think of a scam. Some way to make money or have fun without, you know, really working for it."

"OK, OK, I'll play," said Paul. It did sound sort of intriguing. "Can I have a minute to think of something?"

"Sure, if you want," said Chloe. "But part of the fun of the game is just thinking off the top of your head. We're not looking for a carefully thought out scheme planned down to every last detail. It's all about coming up with ideas. You know, brainstorming."

"Um… ok. How do I start?"

"We'll help you out—that's the fun part for the rest of us." She gave him a quick peck on the cheek and then sat back down on the couch next to Bee. "Just throw out the first idea that comes to you." The first idea that came to him was grabbing Chloe and kissing her, but he didn't suppose that would go over very well.

"We could…" Paul was thinking fast. How to steal money? He searched his brain's rather comprehensive movie catalog—*Heat*, *The Sting*, *Ocean's 11*, *Hudson Hawk*. "We could rob a bank." This suggestion produced a chorus of good-natured boos.

"We're looking for something a little more original than that," said Raff.

"And a lot less dangerous," added Chloe. "Try and be more creative."

"How about counterfeiting?" Paul ventured. More boos. What the hell did they want from him? They were the criminals, not him.

"C'mon Paul," This time it was Popper chiming in. "We like 'em quick and dirty like today. Nothing too fancy or that'll take a bunch of time and equipment."

"Let me think here," said Paul. To his surprise, this was turning out to be a kind of exciting challenge, even though he wasn't very good at it. "So, something more in the line of a con right?"

"Exactly!" said Bee.

"And the best cons are the ones where the person never even knows they were conned, like in *The Sting*, right?" said Paul. "We need to come up with something that the victims never even know about."

"Well, it's not a necessity," said Chloe. "They just need to not know about it long enough for us to get away with it!" The crew laughed in appreciation.

"So not counterfeiting money," said Paul. He was on a roll now. An idea was coming to him. "But counterfeiting something that's, you know, easier to fake."

"Like what?" asked Raff, still leaning against the back wall.

"Ok, I have this friend who collects wine. He buys these real expensive bottles of Bordeaux and whatever and then he just holds onto them for years and years. It's supposed to take like ten or twenty years before some of these wines are ready to drink." Paul didn't actually have a friend like that; he'd just read about this kind of thing in an in-flight magazine once. But he thought that would've sounded lame. "So we could make fake bottles of wine. You know, buy cheap wine and use Photoshop to make expensive labels for them."

"Not bad," said Chloe. "That's a good start."

"Who would we sell them to?" said Raff. "Who's going to buy $500 bottles of wine from people they don't know?"

"I don't know," said Paul. "Don't they sell wine on eBay?"

"I didn't think you were allowed to do that," said Bee. "We'd have to check."

But Paul was still rolling. The answer was in eBay. "Not wine!" he said. "Comic books. We could sell counterfeit comics online!" They laughed. This was a crazy, silly idea, but the crew seemed to like it. "Hear me out now, hear me out. I know comics. I published my own for seven years." It was all coming together in Paul's head—a ridiculous plan to be sure, but he was certain it met all of the criteria for success in this game of theirs.

"You all know that comic-book collectors can be pretty rabid about the quality of their books and what-not, right? You know, mint, near-mint, and whatever. Well, there's this company now called the Comics Rating Group. They've basically totally taken over the comics grading business. How it works is this, you send them a comic book that you think is maybe worth some money now or might be worth more money down the line. They have these professional graders who look at the comic and then give it a score on a scale of one to ten." Paul had their attention now, although some of them looked unsure as to where he was going with all this.

"Of course, that score wouldn't do you any good unless you could assure a potential buyer that it was still in the same condition that it was when the graders looked at it. So here's the cool thing. The CRG guys then seal the comic book in a clear, stiff, plastic envelope thingy with the score sealed in there with it. Now, as long as that seal's not broken, then anyone who buys the comic is guaranteed to know that the comic inside is in the condition that they say it is. People pay like thirty bucks for this."

"You're making this up," called one of the crew, a guy named Chris, if Paul remembered correctly. "If it's sealed in plastic, then you can't even read it!"

"Exactly!" said Paul. "That's the beauty of it! As long as it's in the plastic, collectors know exactly how much it's worth. If they take it out to read it, then they've wasted their money on getting it graded and sealed in the first place. Plus, since most comic books get reprinted in book collections these days, they can read it that way. This sealing in plastic thing is only for the hard-core collectors."

"So let me get this straight," said Chloe, leaning forward in her seat. "People buy these graded comics that're sealed in fucking plastic and never open them?"

"Exactly."

"Which means that, they have no idea what's actually inside of those plastic cases," she continued.

"Exactly. Except the front and back cover, which of course they can see."

"Which means, if we can figure out a way to fake our own plastic sealing thingamajigs, we can sell 'graded' comics to folks and they'd never know the difference," said Chloe, making air quotes around graded.

"Exactly!" said Paul. "How would they ever know? They wouldn't want to check, and if we only did comics that'd been collected in another form, they wouldn't even be tempted to read them since they could read them without breaking the seal some other way."

"I have to say," said Chloe, smiling broadly. "That's not a bad little plot for a swabbie like you, Paul." Paul swelled with pride. He was having a blast, especially now that he'd earned Chloe's approval. But there was only one problem with his plan, and fool that he was, he couldn't stop himself from mentioning it.

"There's only one problem," Paul said. "I don't have any idea how they seal these things up. And they're pretty tight-lipped about the process." He hoped that this omission wouldn't sour their good impression of him.

Chloe stood up and came and stood beside Paul, slipping her arm around his waist. "Don't sweat the details right now. Plots and Plans is all about coming up with crazy ideas. You can always worry about the how-to shit later. I, for one, think you've come up with a swell idea—certainly swell enough for a first try." She kissed him on the cheek once more and then turned to the rest of the crew. "What say you?" she shouted. "Is this a Worthy Plan?"

The assembled crew cheered and most of them rose to their feet. Bee hoisted her glass of champagne and said in a loud voice, "You bet his sweet ass it is!" The rest of the crew joined in the toast.

And just like that, story time was over and the assembly spun apart into a half-dozen different cliques and conversations. Paul had passed whatever test they'd just thrown at him, a fact that pleased him much more than he'd thought it would. Chloe kissed him a third time, a quick peck on the lips, and said, "Good job, Paul."

"Thanks," he said, his heart pounding in his chest. "I have to admit, that was kind of cool."

Chloe slid her arm around Paul's waist and gave his butt a little squeeze. He jumped a little at her touch. "I told you we'd show you a good time, cowboy! We'll make a crewman out of you yet."

The rest of the night quickly melted into a blur of the senses for Paul. Several hours and many drinks later, he found himself sitting on the floor between Chloe and Bee while the three of them, along with Kurt, tried to blow each other away on a first-person shooter that was being projected onto a big white sheet they'd hung in front of the book cases. According to the rules, every time you died you either had to drink or take a hit off one of the three or four joints being passed around the room. He held his own for a while until Chloe and Bee started jostling him every time he lined up a kill in his sights.

When he was too drunk to shoot straight, he resorted to grabbing Chloe's controller from her. She jumped on top of him, smothering his face between her breasts as she tried to wrestle it back out of his hands. He enjoyed that quite a bit, at least until he couldn't breathe anymore. Then he rolled over so now he was on top of her, the lower halves of their bodies pressed together. His erection was strong enough to hurt as it strained through his pants against her hip. She smiled knowingly at him and winked, but before he could be embarrassed Bee grabbed his leg and started chortling madly as she yanked him off Chloe.

At that point, Raff and Popper stepped in with two others and claimed the game for themselves, banishing Bee, Paul and Chloe to the couch in a giggling heap. Kurt, who'd never stopped playing the game for a moment suddenly threw up his arms in victory and shouted "Yes! I win!" He couldn't quite figure out why everyone started laughing at him.

Chloe took a joint as it was passed around and announced loudly that she was claiming it for the People's Republic of the Couch. She took a long toke and passed it to Paul. He was getting really, really fucked up. Really too fucked up to even think straight, which was fine as far as he was concerned. Except maybe in so far as it might negatively impact his plan to seduce Chloe later.

Right this moment, everything was totally, absolutely fine. He sprawled across the crouch and Chloe sprawled across him as they watched the other guys play video games. He idly stroked her arm and this seemed fine, although the one time his hand brushed the tip of her breast, she shifted position to make sure it wouldn't happen again. He took the hint. For her part, Bee had curled up at the other end of the couch and fallen asleep.

He couldn't remember the last time he'd been to a party like this, a party this fun. Most of the social life he'd had revolved around friends from work. Conversation at such events inevitably focused on work as well. But these people, Chloe and her friends, they were totally free, totally in the moment. They didn't even talk about what they'd done for him earlier that day. No work talk here.

Chloe shifted atop him, snuggling her head into his shoulder. He smelled her hair, which, despite its bubblegum tint, gave off the faintest scent of fresh apples. A wave of guilt passed down through him, as he remembered how he'd kicked her out of his car earlier that day. He didn't understand why they hadn't asked for any of his money, and he knew that it didn't make sense. But these people weren't like anyone else he'd ever met before in his life. They had welcomed him into their home and helped him in his time of need. As he drifted to sleep, Chloe snoring lightly in his lap, he sighed. "This is all right," he thought. "I could learn to live like this."

But that might've just been the pot talking.

Chapter 09

PAUL heard thumping. Not the regular thumping of music. Not even the regular thumping of a hammer. This was occasional thumping. There would be nothing for a while and then a muffled thump. Something heavy being dropped onto a carpeted floor. Thump. He squeezed his eyes as if he could close them more than they already were, and then tried to bury his head in the couch to make the thumping stop. The couch. OK, he was on a couch. Chloe's couch. His head hurt. Maybe the thumping was all in his head?

No. There it was again. THUMP. This time it was close enough to where he lay that he felt the vibrations. Some damn fool was dropping heavy things on the floor. Bowling balls maybe? He didn't want to know. He heard a door open. Traffic noises from outside. People talking in whispers. Why would they whisper and yet not seem at all bothered about making those horrible thumping noises?!?! Footsteps on carpet? Or was he imagining—THUMP—no, there it was again.

He obviously wasn't going to be allowed to go back to sleep. He let himself become more aware of his situation. He was on the couch in Chloe's house. OK. He'd been here with Chloe who as far as he could tell, was gone. Yes. He remembered her leaving. A quick kiss on his forehead as he drifted off to sleep. Someone had put a blanket over him, which was good, because he just realized he wasn't wearing any pants. He still had his shirt and socks on, but damned if he knew where his pants and underwear went to. There was a dim image of being half asleep and very drunk and complaining loudly about being hot or uncomfortable. Something.

He felt around with his foot and found what he thought might be jeans, bunched up and stuffed in between the couch cushions. That's good. Assuming they're not Chloe's. No. She'd taken her clothes. She'd been wearing her clothes even. She'd been wearing her clothes, and her clothes were a skirt. They were probably his. Good. THUMP. OK, they're not done dropping bowling balls yet. Why would they need so many goddamned bowling balls?!?! Fuck! Of course, they might be something besides bowling balls. He'd have to open his eyes to know for sure. THUMP. OK, OK, he got the point.

Paul squinted against the light as he opened his eyes. His contacts felt sticky. He usually took them out before he went to sleep. He had to gingerly rub his eyes for a moment before anything would actually come into focus. He made the waking man's moan as he stretched and rubbed, letting the whole world know he was awake and not necessarily pleased about it. Someone was walking over toward him. It was Chloe.

He looked up at her and smiled sheepishly. "I must've passed out," he said. "Sorry."

"No worries. You're welcome to the couch anytime." She was wearing black cutoffs and a white tank top with a black bra. He felt a familiar stirring down below. Crap! Not what he needed right now. What he needed was his pants on.

"What's going on?" Paul asked. "What time is it?"

"It's about one in the afternoon," she said. "As for what's going on, well—it's your plan in action!" She gestured to the boxes that now littered the room. Boxes. Not bowling balls at all. That made more sense. And they weren't just any kind of boxes. They were long, rectangular boxes designed specifically to hold comic books. There were at least a dozen comics boxes stacked willy-nilly around the room.

"Are those comics?" he asked.

"Yep."

"Whose? Are those mine?"

"Nope, I guess they're mine," she said. "Or rather ours. The Crew's. We bought them today."

"What?"

"We bought them today so we could carry out your plot."

Paul sat up, clutching the blanket around his waist. Chloe was talking about the fake comic-book scheme he'd dreamed up last night. Were they crazy? "Are you crazy?" he asked. "That plan was idiotic. I should know, I came up with it."

"I guess you don't realize your own genius then. We all thought it was a pretty good plan ourselves. So we started looking into it. Then Raff and I went out and got a bunch of quarter and dime comics from some local comic shops, which is what you see here before you." Paul just looked at the assembled boxes in confusion. Were they serious?

"Come on," said Chloe. "Put your pants on and get up. I'll fix you a sandwich and fill you in on your part." Paul blushed as he realized that there hadn't been a blanket last night when he'd passed out. Someone had no doubt brought one out to cover him up and that someone was probably Chloe. Thankfully, Chloe had gone into the kitchen already, either tactful or disinterested enough to give him a moment to put his clothes on in privacy. He pulled his pants from between the cushions. He still didn't see his underwear, but he pulled the pants on without them. Then he went into the kitchen to find Chloe making peanut butter sandwiches again.

"Did you sleep OK?" she asked.

"I must have," said Paul. "I haven't slept past noon in years."

"Well, you had a busy day."

"Yeah," he said, sitting down at the kitchen table. "So, what's with all the comics?"

"I told you," she replied. "We're following up on your plan."

"But why do you need all these old, crappy comics?"

"I thought about it some, and we can probably pull off counterfeits of the covers and what not, but I didn't see why we should bother going through all the trouble of counterfeiting the whole thing. So we're going to take the covers off of these here and put our fake ones on them. We just bought up all the cheap ones we could find so we'd have plenty to choose from when it came to matching size and age and condition or whatever." This line of reasoning made a lot of sense to Paul, although he still didn't really believe they were going to go through with it.

"The first thing we need from you," she continued, "Is to have you pick out some choice candidates for counterfeiting. The way I figure it, we don't want to do anything too famous or high profile, like Superman number one or whatever. Anything really well known like that and it's going to attract a lot of unwanted attention. Instead, I'm counting on you to pick out comic books that're worth, you know, between $100 and $300 each. I bet there's a ton of those out there, right?"

"Sure," he said. "A ton. It shouldn't be that much of a problem. I just need a price guide, and I can go through and pick out however many of those you need." Already he was agreeing to help! Last night he'd wanted to leave, but now he felt guilty. He felt like he'd somehow betrayed Chloe by kicking her out of his car, which made no sense at all, since it was probably the only smart thing he'd done yesterday. Plus, Chloe seemed totally cool about it. Or maybe she was just playing it cool and inside she was really pissed or disgusted or annoyed. Paul didn't know, but he did know that, for whatever reason, he didn't want to let her down. She was counting on him. "I've got some good candidates in mind already," he assured her.

She'd finished the sandwiches and brought them over to the table along with a glass of water and two aspirin for Paul. "Thanks," he said. He swallowed the two pills with a gulp of water. He wasn't really hungry though, so he let the sandwich be for the moment. "But how are you going to fake the plastic seals the grading company uses?"

"That, my friend, is the hard part. We're still working on that angle. Raff's out doing some research on these Comics Rating Group guys. Apparently they're based out of L.A., so we might have to take a drive down there tomorrow and check them out. Have you ever had any contact with them before?"

"No," said Paul. "I was never much of a collector. I just like to read and draw them, so I never felt the need to seal anything up. Besides, I mostly read indie press comics that aren't worth much. Not to a collector, anyway."

"OK," she said. "Well, Raff'll turn up some good solid info. He always does. When he gets back, we can plan our next move from there. Hey, are you going to eat that?" She nodded toward the sandwich. He shook his head and she took half for herself. He scarcely noticed; his thoughts had already turned to choosing comics.

After lunch, Paul helped Chloe sort through the boxes of comics, just to make sure there weren't any hidden gems in there that were actually worth money already. There weren't—it was pretty rare for a store to make that kind of mistake these days. Paul suggested they might try garage sales this weekend—they don't often have comics for sale, but when they do, you can occasionally find some goodies. He pulled out some of the better-preserved issues, especially if they were from the '70s or early '80s, figuring that this would be the period where most of their counterfeits would come from. After a few hours, Paul had collected a good pile of about fifty issues ready to donate their insides to fraud.

Raff showed up around seven, and he had a bucket of fried chicken with him. "Chow time!" he said as he came through the door. Bee suddenly appeared from one of the back rooms, much to Paul's surprise. He hadn't even known she was in the house. She must have been hidden away in one of the bedrooms, no doubt engrossed in some technical project or on the computer doing something. The four of them sat down to dinner with chicken and beer. Raff tucked a paper towel into the neck of his black polo shirt, covering up the Cisco logo, and then filled them in on what he'd found.

"OK, here's the deal with the Comics Rating Group," Raff said between bites of chicken. "They're based down in San-something or another, one of those suburbs in the L.A. area. Normally they don't take submissions directly, you have to give your comics to a normal comic book store and then they send them on to CRG to be graded and sealed. But, they do make exceptions for big-time clients. If you've got a huge collection of valuable comics that you want graded, they'll let you come in person. Just like any business, the big whales get special treatment. Most people are only having one or two books graded at a time—remember it costs $30 per book. But someone comes in and says they've got 500 or 1000 rare comics they want rated and sealed, well, now we're talking real money. So I think that's got to be our in."

"Makes sense," said Chloe. "We send in a face to play the big shot. That gets us in the door and into their system."

"OK," said Paul, "But why do you want to get in the door? Can't you hack their computers from the outside?"

"Well," replied Chloe, "We want to figure out how they do the sealing process so we can fake it ourselves. And yes, we do want to get into their network, but that's a lot easier to do if we can get into the building."

"It's important that we make sure the finished product looks just like the real thing," Raff chimed in. "So ideally we'll order our supplies from the same place they do and have their every move down exactly."

"You guys are really going to do this, aren't you?" asked Paul. Raff gave him a look that was somewhere between annoyed and surprised. Having Raff and Bee around had at least partially broken the spell he'd been under when it was just him and Chloe. He liked Bee and Raff well enough, but as a group it all seemed much more sordid. The past six hours had been a fun diversion. He'd spent the afternoon in a room full of comic books and a beautiful woman—every geek's dream. But now he was starting to wake up.

"Hey Paul, listen a minute," said Chloe. "We're not asking you to do anything illegal here. We're really not. This is just what we do for fun, OK? I'd like you to help us out with some of the prep-work because, well, we don't know anything about comics. Your idea sounded good, but we don't have an expert like you. Sure, I mean, we've all read a ton of comics and stuff, but you were actually in the business. You

know that side of things. If you can help us get through this, I'd really
appreciate it."

Paul wasn't sure what to do. He did owe them. Certainly from their
perspective he owed them. He bluffed for time. "I'm just surprised is
all. I mean, is there really that much money in this? Why go to all
this effort?"

"Honestly Paul, it's just to see if we can," Chloe said. "Like yesterday,
when we helped you out. We'd never done that before. Never pulled a
score with so little prep and never played it so fast and loose. I have to
tell you, I haven't had that much fun in years! It's a real high, you know?
Sticking it to those assholes that fucked you over. I love fucking with
real bastards like that. It's kind of what we live for. Do you see what I
mean?" Raff and Bee were grinning as Chloe talked, watching her. They
seemed to feel the same way she did.

Paul nodded. He did see what she meant. In all honesty, getting even
with his "partners" was far and away the most dangerous, thrilling thing
he'd ever done in his life. And while he had some regrets now, he still
relished the shocked looks on their faces when Chloe had laid into them.
She'd been brilliant—the whole crew had been. And now he was more
than a little flattered that they actually thought his scheme worth pursu-
ing. It made him feel like one of them. Maybe it would be a bit of a lark
to do this comics scam.

"Besides," said Raff, pulling another drumstick from the bucket, "This
is practically a victimless score. I mean, like you say, no one's going to
ever open these sealed books right? So really, we're just making wealth
for people. Buying one of our fakes will be like buying the real thing.
They'll probably turn around and sell it themselves in a few years and
make a profit."

"That's something that really appealed to me personally about this
thing," said Chloe. "It's kind of the exact opposite of what we pulled off
yesterday. That was high wire, in your face, smash-and-grab stuff. This is
so subtle no one will ever know they've been taken. That's the challenge
here—do it just right, and no one ever knows."

Paul knew that this was all bullshit, of course. But somehow it was
enough. Enough for him to keep playing along, at least, and see where
things led from here. "OK, guys, no worries. I'm… like I said; I'm surprised is all. Flattered really. I'll help you out. I've already got some good
ideas for books you can fake."

"You don't have to do anything you're not comfortable with, Paul,"
said Chloe, putting her hand on his to comfort him. "But any help
is good."

"Speaking of which…" said Raff.

"Right." Chloe cut him off. "I almost forgot. Paul, do you have any comics in your collection that would be worth getting rated and sealed?"

"A couple maybe. A full run of Miracleman. Those are pretty hard to come by. Why?"

"Well, we might need some honest-to-God valuable comics to bring into the CRG offices when our face man goes in to scout the offices."

"I have those and a couple of other things, but nothing worth over a $100. If you want someone to pose as a real big time collector you'll need something more impressive."

"Well then," said Chloe. "I guess tomorrow you and I are going shopping for bait."

"They do kind of know me at most of the stores in town here," said Paul, suddenly wary about visiting any of his old familiar haunts for fear of running into one of his former co-workers. "I'd probably be recognized."

"We'll go up to San Francisco then," she said. "We'll make a day of it. Maybe buy you some new clothes, too."

The prospect of spending another day with just Chloe brightened Paul's whole outlook. "Sounds like a plan," he said. "What time should I come by?"

"What do you mean?" she asked.

"Tomorrow. What time should I come by so we can go up to the city?"

"Are you going somewhere?"

"I thought I should get a hotel room or something," said Paul. He'd assumed that was what he was going to do.

"Don't be silly. Someone could trace your credit card, and you don't need any unwanted attention right now. You should stay here, with me."

That sounded perfect to Paul. "OK, thanks. I really appreciate it." For a brief moment he wondered idly what bed he might get to sleep in.

"That couch actually does fold out into a bed," she said, crushing his dreams. "It's really pretty comfortable." She picked up her chicken, which she hadn't even started on and turned her attention to Bee. "Now, Bee baby, what're you going to need to get this all set up the way you want it?" They began to discuss the dirty details of all the prep they were going to need to do, and Paul's thoughts wandered. He hoped the fold out bed really was as comfortable as she said it was. It looked like he might be crashing there for some time.

Chapter 10

IT didn't take them long to finalize their plans. Bee and Raff had their to-do lists and Paul had thumbed through a price guide they'd picked up and chosen about fifty promising comics to make fakes of. To finish off their plan they'd need high-resolution images of the front and back covers of each of these, which is part of what he and Chloe would work on the next day. The rest of the evening was pretty laid back, which was fine with Paul since his headache had never really gone away.

He did get a full tour of Chloe's house, which consisted of three bedrooms, two baths, the kitchen, and the living room, which had a den area off of it that could be closed off with sliding doors. This den was officially known as The Server room. As far as Paul was concerned, it looked like a cave. It had its own window AC unit to keep it icebox cold and cheap folding tables covered with computers lined every wall. Heavy curtains covered the single tiny window, and he never saw them opened. Paul would come to learn that the Server room was open to all members of the crew at all hours and that people came and went as if they were visiting another building. They'd walk in the front door, go right into the Server room and never even say "hi." There was an understanding that this one room was somehow different from the rest of the house, which was definitely Chloe's domain.

Bee lived in one of the two smaller bedrooms. She proudly showed off her collection of Simpson's action figures, still in their packaging, which covered one entire wall, floor to ceiling. Other than that, the room consisted mainly of piles of clothing under which a bed hid somewhere and shelves lined with sci-fi and engineering books. Chloe was a fanatic about not leaving dishes around; otherwise, Paul guessed there would have been dirty cups and plates everywhere. Bee probably would've left little bits of electrical engineering tools and pieces all over the place, too, if she hadn't already taken over the garage.

The garage was Bee's workshop. Aside from a heavyweight punching bag and a set of rusty barbells in one corner, workbenches and electronics tools took up every bit of space in the room. Bee spent most of her time in here, taking apart and putting computers back together, fiddling with tiny cameras and hacking together her own inventions. Other members of the crew used the workshop as well, but they always made sure to ask Bee first. Unlike the server room, this space was definitely not open to all, and even though it looked like a mess, Bee claimed to know exactly where everything was.

The second small bedroom seemed to have a kind of rotating occupant. Right now it was Kurt, who was off doing something else that night, but whom the others assured Paul would be back tomorrow. Since he wasn't home, Paul's tour didn't include this room, although he snuck in later that night on his way back from the hall bathroom and was disappointed to find it pretty Spartan—just a futon, a dresser and some clothes. Kurt hadn't done much to make it his own, but maybe he hadn't been there long enough.

Chloe's room was at the end of the hall and qualified as the master suite. It was the only room in the house that felt like it had been decorated. There was a kind of sparse, Asian or maybe Scandinavian feel to it—lots of simple lines and blonde wood furniture. One wall had several different Kabuki style masks placed in careful arrangements on it, while the other had two large, painted fans tacked elegantly to the wall. Hers was the only made bed in the house. Paul glimpsed the glint of a chain, which was attached to one of the double bed's feet, most of its length hidden beneath the bed.

She was especially proud of her closet, which took up one whole wall of the room. It was the closest Chloe came to being disorganized, and one only got that impression because there was so much stuff in there that she was running out of space. It contained such a wild variety of outfits that Paul believed that maybe she really did have an outfit for any occasion. Dresses, jeans, suits, blouses, T-shirts and even uniforms hung from wooden hangars. Chloe pointed out a row of boxes along the top shelf, "Wigs," she said, "I've got like a dozen of them. This bubblegum pink hair of mine tends to attract attention." These weren't just clothes of course. They were costumes. Like the lawyer outfit she'd worn the previous day, they were tools of the trade.

Late the next morning, Paul and Chloe climbed into his car and headed north up the 101 toward San Francisco. Paul had put together a list of several comic stores in the City that they should visit before crossing the Bay Bridge over into Berkeley and the really good store over by the University. By the time they got back to San Jose, they'd have circumnavigated San Francisco Bay and hit half a dozen shops. Paul figured that would be enough to find everything they needed.

"You know," said Chloe as she thumbed through his iPod's menus, "Your selection of music is kinda limited here, sport-o."

"I'm more of a talk radio kind of guy really."

"I guessed from all the Al Franken podcasts, but you know, sometimes you need a great driving song. And sometimes that great driving song wasn't written by Madonna or the Barenaked Ladies, which seem to be the only two choices you've got in here."

"I like what I like. I have trouble picking out new bands, a fact I blame not on my own limited knowledge of music but rather on the fact that there's so much crap out there. Have you seen MTV lately?"

"Of course I haven't seen MTV lately. All the music's crap. I should say all their music's fucking crap. In the entire world of all music there's tons—literally tons—of great shit. You just need an expert guide is all."

"See, that's the problem with music," said Paul. "You need an expert guide to find the good stuff. It should just float right to the top and be self-evident."

"And I suppose video games and comics are different?" she asked.

"Hell no. Comics are even worse. Well, not worse, but certainly just as bad as music. Or movies. It's all about the hype and advertising and, well, tradition. X-Men's always going to sell, no matter if it's really good or really bad. Video games are maybe a little different. Unlike the others, you have to actually sit down and interact with the game. You can't say 'oh, everyone says this is good, and I suppose it's not actively offensive, so I'll pretend I really like it.' With a video game, you actually have to play the thing, and if it's a bad game, there's no hiding the fact that you're having a shitty time."

"Makes sense, I guess. Which do you prefer working on, comics or video games?"

"Oh, comics for sure. Definitely. I have a lot more fun just concentrating on telling a story. With a video game, you have to worry about making sure all the stuff you want to do is technically possible, plus you have to make sure it's fun, and it takes dozens of people to make it happen. I can do a comic myself, and all I have to do is tell a good story."

"Which isn't always easy."

"Nope. But at least it's something within my control. I hope so anyway."

Chloe had finally picked out a song. "Hah! Here's something with a little more bite to it. Violent Femmes! Old school '80s fun." She pressed a button, and the two of them immediately started singing along cacophonously to the brilliance that is "Blister in the Sun." Paul kept sneaking glances at her as she bobbed her head back and forth and hammered each line as she sang it. Damn she was sexy.

"What about you?" he asked, after the song was finished. "What do you like most about what you do?"

"What is it that you think I do, Paul?"

"You know, steal from people."

"Apparently that's what you do now, too," she replied with just a hint of tartness.

"No, I only steal from my former best friends."

"So far."

"I'm not planning on making a habit of it. Besides, I'm running out of friends fast."

"But you're making new ones all the time." She patted him on his shoulder. "You'd be very good at it, I think. You came up with this comics con."

"Comics con. That's funny."

"What do you mean?" she asked. "I really do think it's a good idea."

"I meant the phrase 'comics con,' as in comics convention. They call the big comic book convention down in San Diego 'Comic Con,' and that's what we're doing. A comic con."

Chloe laughed at this. "You're right, it is pretty funny. Maybe some day we can pull a score at the real thing—do an honest-to-God Comic Con comic con. You should start thinking about that."

"Yeah, you know. I'm really not all that interested in making this a full-time thing. I'm only helping out on this one because I feel like I owe you guys for all the help you gave me."

"That's cool," she said. "No pressure. We'll just see how things go."

They drove on in relative silence for a while, listening to music. Paul wondered what she was thinking. If they'd been dating, he would have just asked her. He had the habit of asking his girlfriends 'what are you thinking?' every time they got a pensive look on their face. Some of them found it pretty damn annoying and hadn't been shy about telling him that fact. He didn't think Chloe would appreciate it any more than they did. Probably less. After a while, he couldn't handle the silence.

"How much do you think you'll make with this deal?" he asked.

"I'm not sure. Raff ran some numbers and thinks we can clear fifty grand gross without too much trouble. That about makes it worth it, although I don't want to spend more than a week on it. We've got too much else going on."

"Can I ask you something?" said Paul, slightly nervous now.

"Sure."

"What the hell are you guys?"

"We're a crew."

"You mean a gang."

"Same sort of principle, I guess, except we're a crew. Not a gang. I don't really know how gangs work these days, but from what I've seen in movies they've got bosses and soldiers and everybody does what they're told. We're not like that."

"Aren't you the boss? Or is Raff?"

"Ha! He wishes. If we had an official leader, I suppose it would be me. I'd be the captain of this crew. We're actually modeled on how pirate crews used to work, although we rotate the "captain" responsibilities on each score, depending on whose idea it is and who has the best plan."

"Pirates. As in 'yo ho ho and a bottle of rum'? You don't even have a ship." Paul paused. "You don't have a ship do you? Do you have cannons? Or parrots?"

"I think Filo has a parrot, or maybe a cockatiel. I don't really know the difference. No ship or cannons though—although not for lack of trying."

"But I thought pirates had captains who ran the ship. Like Blackbeard or Captain Hook."

"Sure, they did, and some of them were certainly pretty fucking authoritarian, but not all of them. In fact, lots of pirate crews were about the most democratic institutions you were likely to find anywhere in the world back then. In a lot of ways, they worked like kind of floating communes. They voted about where to go and what kind of prizes to take. And when they took down some booty, everyone got a pretty much equal share. The captain got maybe like a share and a half or something. It was really quite egalitarian, which only made sense, since they were all in it together—outlaws with no one to count on but each other."

"Is that how you guys see yourselves? A band of outsiders?"

"I suppose so. But without the scurvy."

"How did you find all these guys anyway? Did you pick all of them up in Mexican restaurants on the day they were fired?"

"You might be surprised how often that works," she said with a smile. "But no, most of them have a little more criminal experience than you."

"So did you, like, go to the local thief's market and start recruiting? Or is there a chat room or something where you all hang out and sharpen your digital knives?"

"I think you're great and all, Paul. Don't get me wrong. But if the others heard you asking too many questions like this, they might take it the wrong way. You're still an unknown quantity to them and they—well, me too, I guess—we're all kind of guarded about our own history."

"Oh, man," said Paul. "I'm sorry. I should've realized. It's just, well, this is all so weird for me."

"Chill. It's cool. I'm not mad or anything. I'm just giving you a little advice by way of preface for what I'm about to tell you. And just to let you know, I'm not going to tell you anything about any of the others. About how they got into the crew or where they came from. But I'll give you the abridged version of my story. Keep in mind though that the names have been changed to protect the innocent and that I'm probably making the whole thing up."

"OK. I like a good story, fact or fiction."

"Good, because mine's got a little bit of both."

Chloe's Tale

"LIKE all great stories, mine begins at the tender age of 14, which is the first time I ever saw a live theater production that involved real actors and sets instead of middle-school kids in homemade costumes. It was a school trip to see a touring production of "Macbeth," and man was it cool. I mean, the actors and stuff were probably fine, I don't really remember, but it was the costumes and the sets that blew me away. Their set designer was a miracle worker. They'd gone all out for realism—not something you see much anymore with these wacky modern-dress Shakespeare productions—and they'd turned that stage into a fucking castle. It was brilliant. I just assumed it was real stone they'd used, it looked so good. But afterwards we got a backstage tour 'cause our teacher knew the stage manager or something. Anyway, I saw those stone walls up close, and they were Styrofoam. It blew my little teenage mind.

"That's when I decided theater was my new obsession. I've always been an obsession-prone kinda girl. Not so much about guys or bands or any of that bullshit, but more about hobbies. Before theater it had been rock climbing, and before that it had been rollerblading, and before that it had been gymnastics. Always something. And I wouldn't just do whatever it was; I'd also learn everything there was to know about it. I'd read every book the library and the local bookstores had about mountain climbing. I'd planned out all these elaborate trips I was going to take some summer—all this even though I'd never climbed a rock outside of a climbing wall in a gym.

"But the theater thing was different. My high school had something approaching a decent drama club, and I joined the day after we got back from the play. There weren't a ton of us in the club, so everyone got to do a little bit of everything. I acted some, made costumes, learned to run the lame-ass lighting system we had. And by lighting system I mean a couple spots and not much else. But mostly I was all about working on the sets. I read everything I could find and talked my way backstage and into the prop shops of every major and minor theater company here in the Bay Area. Our little school plays got to lookin' pretty damn cool by the end of my run in high school.

"In college I was still all about the theater. I thought maybe I'd get into making sets for movies or something like that, so I stuck with it. I never did finish that degree—I ended up getting distracted. This was back in the early '90s you know? And the Internet was just coming on strong. BBS's and newsgroups were the shit back then, and there were even a couple devoted to theater and prop making and stuff like that. I was so hungry for any little piece of knowledge, I was posting on all of these all the time. I became addicted.

"Then came that fateful day. Some guy posted a thing on a theater BBS about trying to duplicate a fancy corporate office. He said it was for a movie or a documentary or something like that that he was making and that he needed it to be exactly like the real thing, but he only had a limited budget—like maybe a thousand bucks. The real tough part was that he wanted to recreate the view out the window of this office, which was twenty stories high and in Manhattan somewhere. I had some ideas on the problem, and we got to going back and forth online and through e-mail about it.

"He was real cagey about who he was and what this movie was about, but he seemed pretty smart. We even talked on the phone a couple of times. Finally he invited me to come on down to L.A. (it turned out he was in L.A., not New York at all, as he'd said in his posts) and help him build the thing. I was a 19-year-old college girl whose parents paid for her gas. Of course I went.

"Without going into details that, while I'm sure you'd love to hear them, I'm not ready to tell you, the whole thing was a con. Luckily, I wasn't the one being conned. But I could also tell fairly quickly that these clowns weren't making any movie or anything like that. They were actually working out of a rundown warehouse that they were squatting in. I only ever met them there. Each night they disappeared to wherever their homes were, and I sure as hell wasn't invited to come along. I ended up sleeping in my car. But they never would've pulled it off without my help, I can guarantee you that. They had pictures from a magazine and from some shitty videotape that they'd shot in the office (which turned out to be in L.A., too, not New York). They'd scored some professional grade lighting and shit, but the hardest part was getting that backdrop to look real. We finally figured it out, though.

"One of them went away for a day and then came back. He had us make a bunch of different small changes to the office set up we'd built. We changed the calendar on the desk and added a new set of pens that he'd bought somewhere. Small shit like that. They were going to cut me loose then and promised to send me my money in a week (they'd promised me a couple hundred bucks). I was like, 'Fuck the money, I wanna help on the shoot.' This didn't go over real well at first, but I held my ground. I hinted that I knew they were up to something hinky here and I wanted to be in on it. That went over even less well.

"Now Paul, here's a little tip for you. What I did back then was wicked fucking stupid. I mean, just dumb, dumb, dumb. First of all, the golden rule—never let 'em know what you know. Second, I didn't know these guys. In retrospect they were pretty right but kinda taking a risk bringing me in on the set-up. A good risk, as odds are I was gonna be some ditsy theater chick. Turned out they were wrong. If they'd been a different, harder core crew, they probably would've disappeared me right then and there. I could tell one of them was maybe thinking that very thought. But I was lucky. They let me stay and help with the shoot before sending me on my merry way. They even let me do the make-up. Although, for the record, I never did get my money, the fuckers.

"This other guy came in. Someone I'd never met before. He didn't seem at all curious to see me—treated me like a flunky on a film set. To this day I'm pretty sure he was some wannabe actor that they'd conned into thinking he was playing a part in an indie movie. Hell, they might've even paid him. I did his make-up for him, and then we lit the set and put him to work. He was wearing some kind of little domino mask and a suit. He looked like the Green Hornet or the Spirit or one of those old pulp heroes. It was kind of silly, I thought.

"They shot the thing on SVHS and had a boom mic on the guy to pick up every word. He gave this weird speech about how he'd obviously compromised their state-of-the-art security system and could do so at any time. Then he said that whoever was going to see this tape should give in to his demands or face serious, serious consequences. Next time they wouldn't be shooting a videotape. Next time they'd be planting a bomb. The actor guy actually sold it pretty well. I felt chills going up my spine. I knew then for sure that I'd been right, and that these fuckers were up to no good.

"We did a few takes and then let the guy go. We broke down the whole set in less than an hour, piling everything into a couple of vans and combing the warehouse for any last piece of evidence that we'd ever been there. I was scared shitless by this point. I thought about making a run for it, but I realized that one of the vans had blocked my car in. I'd never get away from them. As it turned out, once we'd finished cleaning up, they piled into their vehicles and took off. They said they'd call me in a week. I never heard from them again.

"I had to know what the fuck these guys had been up to. In fact—that became my new hobby-obsession. I needed to find out what I'd been a part of. I knew a few things—that the office was in L.A. and even generally what part of town it was in (based on the backdrop we'd created.) It could still be one of a dozen different buildings at least, and then any of hundreds of different offices. I also knew it had been photographed professionally for some magazine since they had cut out pictures to use as a model. I blew off school and spent the next week at the public library in L.A., going through every damned home and garden and local magazine they had on file and poring over the daily papers for any signs of some kind of story related to any of the businesses in any of the buildings I'd identified as possibles.

"Eventually, I did find the office. It had been featured in some local magazine like three years earlier. It was the offices of a pretty well known lawyer who specialized in medical malpractice cases. I looked him up, and he actually had a pretty darn good record on such things—not the kind of guy who makes lots of baseless lawsuits or whatever. I couldn't find anything about him in the news. I even went down to the Clerk of Court and read the files on all his recent cases, but I didn't see any names I recognized or make any connections to any of the people I'd worked with. I eventually came back up here and somehow managed to pull offt barely passing grades despite the three and a half weeks of school I'd missed. I used the old dead-grandmother routine.

"I kept tabs on the lawyer as best I could, and I learned that about six months later he retired early at the tender age of 42. Said he wanted to get back in touch with his roots and that he was moving to Portugal of all places. I gotta think that had something to do with whatever con those guys were pulling, but of course I have no idea. They didn't leave a single trace that I could find.

"And so, just like that, conning people became my new obsession. Well, not just like that. I had a little guidance from an old friend, but that's another story," concluded Chloe.

Paul had listened with rapt attention as she spun this tale. It hadn't been what he expected.

"Is that really true?" he asked.

"Yep," she said. Then she winked at him. "As far as you know, anyway."

"And how long ago was this? The early '90s right? How old are you anyway?"

"A lady never tells. Let's just say I look good for my age."

"I think you look good for any age."

"You charmer, you. I'm still not telling you how old I am." She started rooting through the camera bag she'd brought with her and pulled out a very expensive looking digital camera. "Do you know how to use one of these?"

"Sure," said Paul. "I mean, I've never used one that nice before, but yeah, I know the gist of it. Why?"

"That's your job for the day—you're the photographer."

"And what are you?"

"I'm the reporter, silly! What else?" She pulled out a business card identifying her as Rachel Moore, a lifestyle reporter for the San Francisco Chronicle. "We're on assignment."

The plan went delightfully well. Chloe and Paul went into every comic book store in the Bay Area over the next eight hours. She posed as a reporter doing a story about collecting comics. The new Spider-Man movie was due out next month and so the Chronicle was allegedly preparing to do a companion piece about comics. In return for promising to mention the stores in the article, the owners were more than happy to let Paul snap away.

With the camera set at a resolution approaching that of 35mm film, Paul took careful pictures of every valuable comic he could find. Whenever possible, he tried to convince the owners to let him take the books out of their plastic sleeves. This was impossible to do with those that had been graded and sealed, but he got some good shots of those as well. They'd all need some fairly substantial touching up in Photoshop before they'd be ready for "press," but the high-quality camera gave him a solid base from which to build their fakes.

Paul was constantly impressed by what a charmer Chloe could be. She had the owners eating out of her hand—and not just because she was an attractive blonde (thanks to a wig)—but because she knew how to engage them on their level, whatever it was. For the guys who were real fans of the genre and comics in general, she talked to them about their favorite characters and storylines. For the ones who were all about the bottom line, she emphasized how the article could help bring in new business for them. And for those who just didn't care, she knew when to leave them alone.

By the day's end, Paul had collected good shots of about a hundred likely suspects, both front and back covers. He was already going over in his head what he'd have to do in Photoshop to make them picture perfect for their scam. It was going to be pretty simple, he thought, but he'd have to do some test runs to make sure it came out looking convincing enough. As long as they figured out how to fake the hard plastic case for the sealed and graded comics, he thought they had a pretty good chance of pulling this con off.

When they got back to Chloe's house, they found it crowded with about a half dozen crew members. They'd set up the big bed sheet screen again and were all ready to run a little first-person shooter tournament. Paul had played in plenty of such events while at the Fear and Loading, and in many ways coming home to something like this made it all seem a little more normal. Besides, he was eager to show off his skills while he wasn't drunk and high. He took a seat and dove right in, blasting away at his new friends for the next four or five hours until finally the Red Bull wore off and he crashed on the couch once again.

Chapter 11

THE next few days flew by for Paul. He enjoyed the hell out of his time in the house. It was not unlike being back in college—everyone around him was smart and ready to do something fun at a moment's notice. There was always plenty to drink and good pot to smoke if you wanted it. They all worked hard, Paul himself working more than he ever had at his own company, but computer game marathons and spontaneous parties frequently punctuated the work. Chloe was particularly fond of old school Street Fighter-style fighting games, and she routinely challenged all comers to bouts on the Playstation. Paul took her on again and again but never came close to beating her.

He spent most of the time in the Server room, working in Photoshop on one of the computers. Kurt had finally shown up again, and he'd brought a professional quality color laser printer with him. Apparently he had a friend who had a friend in the printing business, or something like that. Kurt stayed only a single night, most of which he spent doing laundry and eating noodles in his room. Then he was gone again the next morning, leaving the printer still in its box for Paul to try and figure out how to set it up. Bee offered to help.

"What's the deal with Kurt?" asked Paul as the two of them finagled the bulky printer from the Styrofoam padding.

"What do you mean?" she replied.

"He's not around much, huh?"

"No, not lately. Sometimes. It just depends."

"Depends on what?"

"What he's doing," said Bee. "This comic con isn't the only thing going on right now. Kurt's in charge of another whole deal that some of the guys are working on."

"I had no idea," said Paul. Except for the night of the first party he'd never seen the whole group together in one place. He'd just assumed they were off living their own lives or holding down jobs or something. There'd been no hint of another con going on.

"Well, why would you?" asked Bee with surprise. "You're not really involved in it. Well, come to think of it, actually you are a little bit."

"Huh?" asked Paul, confused.

"Well not really involved, but you know, you saw the opening move," Bee said.

"When was this?"

"The day you met Chloe. In that Mexican restaurant where she was arranging for the little mariachi salt shakers to be put on the tables."

"Oh yeah," Paul said. He'd forgotten about Chloe's original excuse for being in the restaurant. She'd claimed to be doing market research, but in retrospect that had to have been a lie. "What were those things anyway?"

"They were bugs," Bee said. "The target eats there all the time or something, and Kurt wanted to listen in on his table talk. So we had to figure a way to bug every table. I made them myself."

"Wow," said Paul, seeing new depths to this crew and the lengths to which they'd go. "Did you make the mariachi men, too?"

Bee laughed, "No, Kurt found those. He's actually pretty amazing that way. It's kind of what he does."

"What do you mean?"

"Kurt's a scrounger, you know? His whole deal is he knows how to find stuff. But he keeps his methods to himself. It's always a friend of a friend or something like that, but we never know for certain. Personally, I wouldn't be surprised if he's just stealing the stuff."

"Really?"

"It could be. I don't have any reason to believe it, but come on. A guy that quiet? He can't have THAT many friends! He can almost always find any piece of equipment we need, and he rarely takes more than a few days to get it."

"Huh. Interesting." They started uncoiling wires and digging around behind one of the computers, trying to find the right port. "I'm surprised you didn't have a high-quality printer like this before. Seems like it would come in handy."

"Not as much as you'd think," said Bee. "We don't do much that's on paper, you know? The more digital it is the better, as far as we're concerned. It's much easier to cover your tracks that way, assuming you know what you're doing. Paper can theoretically be traced, or you might leave a fingerprint on it or whatever."

"Fingerprints. I hadn't even thought of that. We should probably wear gloves whenever we're handling these fake comics, huh?"

"That's a good point," agreed Bee. "I'm sure Chloe thought of that—she always thinks of everything, which is part of why she rocks. But make sure you mention it to her. At the very least it'll make you look smart." She gave him a reassuring pat on the shoulder. "Chloe always falls for the smart guys."

"Thanks," said Paul, surprised but pleased with this piece of romantic advice. "I will."

After they spent a few hours trying to find the right drivers to install on the machine, they hooked the printer up and it worked like a dream. Paul made a few test runs, and they came out great. It occurred to him then that they should have a burn bag for everything they didn't use or that was left over—shredded papers could still be reassembled. Not so much with ashes. He'd mention that to Chloe as well. He wanted to show her he could hold his own. After all, this whole thing was his idea.

All the crew members working on this job met the next day, even the elusive Kurt, who was pulling double duty. Paul had his samples with him. They crammed into Chloe's living room once again, and she presided over the assembly wearing a tight-fitting Supergirl T-shirt in honor of the occasion.

"OK, kids, the game's afoot. We're about to spring into action here and I want to make sure everyone knows what's what." She turned her attention to Paul for a moment. "Just so you know, Paul, we always try and keep everyone in the crew in the loop as much as possible. While everyone might not have much of a role in this one, they're all part of the team, so they all have a right to know." This insight drove home the fact for Paul that he wasn't really a part of the group, otherwise they'd have told him what Kurt was up to. At least for the moment, he was still an outsider.

"We're about ready to go green on this comic-counterfeiting thing," Chloe continued. "But there are a few things we've got to decide. It's a little more complicated than I thought at first, but that's OK. Still nothing we can't handle.

"We've got three main teams working this. I'll give the bad news first. Most of you guys are going to be e-slaves for this one." There was a chorus of groans from the group. Chloe had already explained this term to Paul. "E-slaves" were the ones who would spend hours and hours selling all the forged comics on eBay. It was a thankless but definitely necessary job, and since they wanted to pull their plan off quickly, they'd need as many people focused on selling as possible. "I know, I know, it sucks. But you get the same share as everyone else.

"Team two is going to be net-heads. There is, it turns out, a computer security aspect to this caper. I've been poking around on the Comics Rating Group's Website, and they have a database up there that lists every single comic book they've ever graded. So, every time they grade Punisher #1 or whatever, they add it to the database. That way, collectors know how many of every issue there are out there. It's a way to discourage, you know, people like us." This got a laugh.

"We're going to need to get into that database and be able to make some changes at will. Getting into it shouldn't be much problem. I know you guys could probably hack it clean right now if you wanted to, but we're going to get inside the door, so you might as well wait until that's set up. Once we're up and running in their system, Paul will let you know what books we're forging, and you can eke up the database numbers gradually, so as not to tip anybody off. We're also going to need you to fiddle with some numbers in their inventory system as well, but I'll get to that later.

"And that leaves our main team. We get to go on a road trip. The company's offices are down in L.A., and we need to get a good look around at how they do things. We've taken apart a bunch of these sealed and graded books, and it's a fairly specialized process. It'd cost more than it's worth for us to set up our own facility to seal these things up the right way, so I think we're going to have to use the machines in the actual company, which should be fun."

"The road team will be me, Raff, Bee and Filo. Paul will be coming along as well. We're heading out tomorrow—as soon as these fakes get printed." She took Paul's samples from him and passed them out to the crowd. "Everyone take a look at these and see if you can find any faults or flaws. The more eyes on this, the better. They look great to me, but what the fuck do I know?" The group looked at the fake covers, most of them pretty carefully, some of them only cursorily.

"As of now, we're full sail ahead, so everyone needs to act accordingly. No leaks. No chit-chat with outsiders. Everyone focus on your jobs, and we can make a nice little score. Capisce?" Everyone nodded. "OK, kiddies, break up into groups. Kurt, pick yourself four hackers. After we get inside their offices and plant the Trojan Horse, you need to start poking around anything and everything related to this CRG—but keep a low profile! Popper, babe, you get the e-slaves. Sorry girl, you had all the fun on that hotel job last month. Take everyone who's left, pour a round of shots, and start setting up those false fronts for the eBay accounts, mail forwarders, too, OK?

"And Paul? Put your latex gloves on and get ready to have some fun. You and me are making sweet, sweet counterfeit comics for the rest of the night." She grabbed him by the hands and yanked him up off the couch and into her arms. "Come on, big boy, Bee's gonna give us a hand."

They spent the rest of the evening and most of the next day making their fakes, as promised. Paul had gotten the process down to a science while making his test runs, so the work went pretty fast. The resulting fake covers then got cut down to size and stapled onto the comics insides that Paul had selected from the boxes and boxes the crew had brought him. They had particular fun mixing classic X-Men covers with worthless Archie interiors and plastering Batman's visage over Richie Rich. "They're both spoiled trust fund babies," Chloe had pointed out.

Paul had gone to the trouble of washing out the covers on some of them in Photoshop, making them appear faded by the sun and time. Not so much that it would seriously compromise the value, but enough to make them more believable. Bee spent her time with some small tools and a cup of tea. She was adding other signs of aging to the "older" comics—staining some with the tea. Using the tools, she made small stress fractures and folds. Bee loved detail work like this, and Chloe had to keep pushing her to make just a few changes and then keep going.

They put the new fakes into plastic sleeves for safe keeping, and over the course of the next sixteen hours or so, they filled out three long boxes of comics, each holding over a hundred forgeries. An hour later, Raff and Filo pulled up with an extended cab van they'd gotten from somewhere. They loaded the comics up, along with some electronics gear, sleeping bags and a cooler full of food. Then they were on the road, Raff and Filo up front, driving them south to L.A. while Chloe, Paul, and Bee crashed in the back. "One thing's for sure," thought Paul, "Chloe and her friends seldom wasted much time."

That night they set up shop in a pair of motel rooms located about a mile from the Comics Rating Group's headquarters. They were all in one room going over the plan for the next day. An arsenal of electronics lay spread out on the bedspread as Raff and Bee explained how each piece worked. But Paul wasn't really listening. He was thinking about his role in the plan and the fact that it wasn't as significant as he wanted. To be honest, he wasn't even sure why they'd brought him along. This was his plan, after all, and he wanted a more central part.

"Can I make a suggestion?" asked Paul, interrupting Raff, who shot him a surprised look. "Why is Raff going inside posing as the collector? No offense man, but you don't know anything about comics."

"That's why you're here, Paul, to help me out."

"Why don't I just go in instead?" said Paul, his stomach suddenly swirling. Is this what he wanted? Apparently so.

"You want to go in?" asked Chloe. "Why?"

"Well, I just think it makes more sense. I speak their language, you know what I mean? Besides, from what you've said, there's not much to it. I basically go in and be myself, they show me around and stuff. I just think there's less of a chance of me rousing suspicions or whatever."

"You've never done anything like this, have you Paul?" asked Raff. "It's great that you're helping us and all, but what if you get nervous? What if you suddenly realize that you're about to commit fraud and you chicken out? We're not going to have a second shot at this—not without REALLY arousing some suspicions."

"I hear what you're saying, but I'm telling you guys, I can do this." Paul turned his attention to Chloe. "I can do this. I'm the best man for this job."

Chloe laughed and reached over and tousled his hair. "OK, champ, you got it. We'll let you go in. That means we gotta get your ass checked out on some of this equipment here. Raff, this is cool with you, right?"

"As long as he doesn't fuck up, it's cool with me, yeah," said Raff, smiling as well. "If it means I don't have to spend an hour babbling with some comics geek, that's great."

"OK, then," said Chloe. "Let's start again from the top. This time we've got Paul as the face."

"You mean like on the A-Team?" said Paul, remembering the character of "Face" from the old '80s action/adventure show. "I loved that show."

"Yep," said Chloe. "Except we're not blowing anything up. At least not this time."

Chapter 12

THE Comics Rating Group's offices sat in the front corner of the Redfield Industrial Park, just one of many identical buildings in the area. The door had an electronic lock that employees put their pass cards up against to gain access. Since he didn't have such a card (yet), Paul had to tap lightly on the glass in order to catch the receptionist's attention. She politely buzzed him in from her desk. He had an appointment to meet with the head grader, who would be out in just a minute.

The man's name was Kevin Carrey, a well-fed fellow in a blue polo shirt with the company logo on it and khaki pants. He shook Paul's hand warmly while Paul glanced briefly at the security card hanging from his belt.

"Welcome to CRG, Mr. Feldman. I'm Kevin Carrey, vice president of customer relations."

"Pete Feldman. It's nice to meet you," said Paul. "I appreciate you letting me stop by in person. I know that's a little unusual."

"We try to be as accommodating as we can, especially for new clients. Would you like the grand tour?"

"That'd be great."

The main grading rooms were divided into three different sections. The largest contained five graders who worked on comics published since the 1980s, the lion's share of the company's business. The two smaller sections dealt with silver age ('60s and '70s) and golden age ('30s to '50's) comics respectively. Carrey also pointed out a restoration room where damaged comics could be brought back to their former glory. The office had an informal feel, with music blaring from stereos and walls covered with comics-related posters. Probably a fun place to work if you like comics, thought Paul.

But the tour's highlight—indeed one of his main goals in coming inside in the first place—was the sealing room. Here they took the graded comics and sealed them in two layers of plastic. First a flexible plastic sleeve that fit snuggly around the comic. Then a hard plastic outer case that included a hologram and the comic's title with the grade printed directly onto the plastic. They used heat to melt the plastic and make the seals, so there was no way to open the final product without breaking the seal and thus eliminating the veracity of the grade.

Paul took a long, good look all around this room, including up at the security cameras mounted high on the wall. The digital video camera hidden inside the thick, black glasses he wore transmitted everything he saw to the rest of the crew, who were in a van around the corner. Paul insisted on watching the entire sealing process from beginning to end twice, which his guide found a little boring, but he accommodated Paul's request.

"Very cool," said Paul. "You've got a pretty neat set-up here. How many of these do you do a day?"

"We average around a thousand a day. We're actually still a little understaffed—we get more books in per day than we grade out, but we can push favored customers to the front of the line, especially if they do a lot of business with us."

"Speaking of which, shall we talk about my little collection?"

"Certainly. Come on back to my office, and we can talk there."

Paul suddenly put his hand on his pants pocket where there was the unmistakable bulge of a cell phone. "Oh shoot, I've got a call. Do you mind?"

"No, please, go ahead."

Paul pulled the phone out and turned it on, pretending to talk to someone about a real estate deal as he turned his back on Carrey. In fact, the phone wasn't a phone at all. It was a little device that Bee had cooked up and then put inside a cell phone shell. Paul made a good show of wandering about the room, talking angrily with his realtor. Mr. Carrey stood by silently, pretending not to eavesdrop.

"Listen. I'm in a meeting," said Paul. "I have to go. I'll call you back. Just get it done, OK? Just. Get. It. Done."

Paul hit the button to end the call, in fact activating Bee's device. He strode over to Carrey, the phone in his hand still.

"I'm sorry about that. Let's get going." As Paul stepped close to Carrey he let his arm carrying the cell phone swing forward until it almost touched the security card hanging from the vice president's belt.

The fake cell phone worked very much like the electronic security card scanner on the company's front door. Like the door scanners, all it needed was to be within an inch or two of a security card to read the signal of the card's microchip. Bee's invention recorded this signal automatically and would allow them to make a duplicate card later. Paul looked down at the phone's digital display as he followed Carrey back toward his office. It said "Call Complete," signifying that the card capture had worked. Two jobs down, one to go.

They sat down in Carrey's spacious office. It lacked the color and character of the rest of the facility but had five very valuable, scaled and graded comics hanging tastefully on the wall. Paul wasn't acting when he whistled appreciatively at the copy of Amazing Fantasy 15, which was the first appearance of Spider-Man and worth several hundred thousand dollars.

"Wow. How cool is that?" said Paul, pointing to the image of the Web-slinger on the wall.

"Yeah, isn't that great? That's the first thing I bought once the company was up and moving. It's only graded a 5.4, but it's still awesome to have, you know?"

"Definitely. I don't have that in my collection, but I've got some keepers, that's for sure." Paul contorted himself awkwardly in his chair in order to remove a CD in a paper sleeve from his other pocket. He pointed at the computer on Carrey's desk. "Does that thing have Excel on it?"

"Of course," said Carrey, taking the disk and putting it in his computer. "You have your whole collection on this?"

"Yep, I actually don't know much about computers, but I hired some college kids to inventory my whole collection and record it all in a big database thingy. It took them all summer. They also weighed my comics—turns out I have a literal ton of comics. Over 2,000 pounds."

"That's pretty impressive. I've culled my own collection down in the past few years, just a couple thousand that I really want to hang on to."

"I'm planning on doing the same thing, but first I wanted to get four or five hundred of them graded and sealed by you guys -- just the most valuable ones, you understand." At $30 a pop for grading and sealing comics, Paul had just offered the man $15,000 worth of business. It wouldn't make him their largest customer, but it was enough to command some respect. "That disk is just a list of the books I think would be the most likely candidates for grading. If you could look it over and get back to me with your suggestions, I'd really appreciate it."

In fact, the list was just a fiction Paul had whipped up over the course of a few hours. He'd been careful to make sure that only a handful of the books actually overlapped with the ones they'd counterfeited. No sense leaving a list of their forgeries around, even if no one would ever be the wiser, assuming the scam went off as planned. The disk had no doubt already accomplished its true purpose. When Carrey had opened the database, he'd also released a Trojan Horse into the company's network. The small program was now hidden away in the system and would leave it wide open to the hacker team. Goal three accomplished. Time to get a move on.

"I'd love to go over that list with you myself," said Paul. "But I really have to get going. My real estate agent seems bound and determined to screw this deal up, and I need to make sure it goes as planned." He pulled out his wallet and handed Mr. Carrey a fake business card. "Just give me a call or drop me an e-mail when you've had a chance to go over that."

"Sure thing Mr. Feldman. We're happy to help you out with your collection. Just glancing at it, it sure looks like you've got some impressive books here."

"Thanks," said Paul, turning to leave. "Oh, just one more thing, actually. Can you just save that file to your computer and give me the disk back? I don't have a copy on my laptop back at the hotel and I'd like to look it over myself a little more."

"Of course. Just hold on a second." Carrey saved off the file and popped the CD back out, handing it to Paul. "There you go, you're all set."

"Cool," replied Paul. "All right, I gotta run. Thanks again."

"Let me show you out," said Carrey.

Two minutes later, Paul was climbing back into the van. As soon as he closed the door behind him he whooped with glee. "Whoo hooooo!" he shouted. "That was awesome."

He'd been calm during his whole visit, but as soon as he'd walked out the door his heart had started racing. It was an exhilarating feeling, tricking someone so thoroughly like that. Pretending to do one thing but secretly doing something much sneakier.

Chloe gave him a big hug and a quick kiss on the lips, which was all he thought about for the next few moments as he slapped hands and exchanged congratulations with the other crew members.

"Great job, Paul," stated Chloe. "You played him like a pro."

"I almost forgot to get the disk back," he said, handing both it and the cell phone/card scanner over to Bee.

Raff was already driving the van back toward the motel. "You covered well, though."

"Thanks," said Paul.

"Hell, I didn't even realize you'd forgotten it," said Chloe. "I thought you were playing it real cool in there. Pulling a Columbo on him. 'Just one more thing, sir.'"

"I don't think he suspected a thing," replied Paul, almost panting with excitement and pride.

"Why would he? Who the fuck would do something this silly but us?"

Back at the motel, they planned for the actual dangerous part. Or, if not dangerous, then at least the part where getting caught was hardest to explain. Bee made a duplicate security card that would get them in the front door. Meanwhile, the hacker team back in San Jose tore through the CRG system, looking for anything and everything that might be helpful. With the Trojan Horse in place, they had free rein over the company's internal network and its Website. They began to inch up the database figures for the comics they planned to forge. A search through employee e-mails turned up a current alarm code that someone had foolishly sent to another employee. They also had everyone's schedules. It was Friday night, and no one was expected to come in on Saturday, so they should be safe, but they wanted to be out before dawn just in case.

This next part of the operation belonged to Filo. He was a pretty cool guy, Paul had decided. He hadn't spent much time with him before the trip down to LA, but he'd grown to like the tattooed, shaven-headed crew member. Filo's main skill set was in sculpture and metal fabrication. He was also a gear head, fixing (and maybe stealing) cars in his spare time. He'd spent a good chunk of time examining how the plastic cases went together and watching the video Paul had taken inside the facility and seemed confident that he could duplicate the process pretty easily.

They went back at 11 p.m., a half hour after the maid service's scheduled clean-up was finished. Everything looked clear, so they pulled the van around behind the building and unloaded the boxes of fake comics. Then Chloe came around front and used Bee's new security card to open the door. The alarm code worked, and they were in. She opened the loading door out back and Raff and Filo started carrying boxes back toward the sealing room.

Paul had wanted to go with them into the building to help put the fakes together, but both Chloe and Raff had vetoed this plan. He'd done well earlier, definitely, but this was precision breaking and entering work they were doing now. They couldn't afford any screw-ups. Besides, they needed a lookout, and that meant Paul. He drove the van to the other side of the street where he could see anyone approaching and begrudgingly stood watch.

In his head he imagined what was going on inside. They'd have made their way into the sealing room by now. The room had no windows that faced the street, so he couldn't tell if they were set up and running or not. The CRG guy had told him that they locked up the valuable comics in safes each night, so there wasn't much chance that they'd be tempted to steal anything. Not that he thought they would. This whole plan centered on the idea that no one would ever realize that a crime had been committed. The hacker team had already gone in and changed the inventory numbers in CRG's computer to account for the missing plastic cases and sleeves. They'd even accounted for the ink the crew would be using to print their forged rating inserts and the holograms that marked them as official CRG graded books.

Paul had Chloe's cell phone on speed dial, ready to make the call as soon as anything happened that looked like it might blow their cover. He had a moment of panic three hours into the operation when an old-school Camaro he'd seen on his earlier visit pulled into the parking lot. He was about to make the call when he saw the driver go into the office next door. He called Chloe anyway, just to let her know.

"Go," she said as she answered the call.

"You don't need to get out or anything, but I thought you should know that there's somebody at work in the office next door. I don't know what he's doing in there, but make sure you keep quiet or whatever."

"Thanks. Make sure you let me know if he's still there when we're ready to leave."

"How's everything going in there?"

"Good. Gotta go." And she hung up. Definitely all business when it came to pulling these jobs.

Paul waited for several uneventful hours, sitting in the van and trying to stay awake. He must have drifted off to sleep at least once because he woke with a start to the sound of the Camaro's throaty engine firing to life around 2:30 in the morning. The excitement of the entire venture had begun to wear off by this point, and he was just feeling totally exhausted. He was tired of sleeping on couches and in the backs of vans. He'd never tried a waterbed before and wondered for a sleepy while what that might be like.

In order to stay awake he turned on the map light and started thumbing idly through a copy of *Wizard Magazine* he'd brought along. Devoted to comics news and collecting, the magazine also contained a price guide in the back of every issue. He flipped to the section on indie publishers and found the entry for the comic book that had defined his career—*Metropolis 2.0*. Issue 1 in top condition was going for $12. Up a few dollars since the videogame had been announced. Paul sighed and turned off the light, realizing that with it on, he could be seen from the street.

He'd been working as a freelance artist in the comic book industry for just shy of three years when he had the idea for *Metropolis 2.0*. Inspired by the Fritz Lang movie rather than *Superman*'s fictional home, the comic told the story of alienated robotic workers fighting against a tyrannical utopian system in their quest to gain equal rights. This quest involved a great number of epic, robot vs. cyborg battles, elaborate twists and turns, and as much dark humor as Paul could reasonably cram into each 22-page issue. But since he could only work on it in his spare time, he was having trouble just finishing that first issue.

Paul had built up his portfolio working for various second and third-tier publishing companies. He'd drawn a lot of comics based on movies and TV shows and even some video-game tie-in work. After thus establishing himself, both of the big comic book companies, Marvel and DC, expressed an interest in hiring him, a break that was almost every penciler's dream. But Paul had become obsessed with seeing *Metropolis 2.0* in print and so he pitched the book to the two comics companies. Both publishers turned him down, and in the process, he managed to lose his chance to work for them as well. They wanted eager young artists whose sole ambition was drawing *X-Men* or *Batman*, not a headstrong would-be auteur who just wanted to work on his own projects.

Frustrated, Paul did the only thing he could to get the damn comic printed—he applied for as many credit cards as he could, dropped his other freelance gigs and threw everything he had into publishing his comic book on his own. After a year of eating ramen noodles and oatmeal every day, no one was more surprised than Paul when his comic became a hit. It never did *X-Men* numbers, of course, but he got a lot of good buzz as he went out on the convention circuit to pimp his comic. He was soon selling close to 15,000 copies a month—a huge number for an independent book. He'd become the new golden boy of underground comics and had never been happier in his life.

After sixteen months, the monthly grind started to wear him down. Writing and illustrating twenty-two pages is a huge amount of effort, and the grueling labor took its toll. While the comic was doing better than ever, Paul just wanted a break. At the same time, he didn't want to hire on another artist because he didn't trust anyone with his baby. And that's when he and Greg had had their fateful conversation. They both agreed that *Metropolis 2.0* would make the perfect setting for an online computer game. Together with the other partners, they formed *Fear and Loading*. Greg invested the money, and Paul invested his ideas, turning over ownership of the *Metropolis* intellectual property and copyrights to the new company. Obviously that hadn't worked out as planned, and now he didn't even own his own creation. But at least he'd made them pay dearly for taking it away from him.

The phone buzzed on the dashboard, startling him out of his half-conscious reverie. It was Chloe. He concentrated hard so he didn't sound as sleepy as he really was.

"Go," he said, mimicking Chloe's response from earlier.

"We're ready. Is it all clear?"

"Yeah, Camaro-guy's gone." It was now pushing 5 a.m. "Should I pull the van around?"

"Yep. Come on back." She clicked off.

They loaded the boxes into the van. Paul got out to help and noticed that there were more boxes coming into the van than they'd taken out originally. "What's with the extra boxes?"

"It's always the little things that get ya," said Chloe. "We didn't calculate right on how bulky these things would be once we'd sealed them in these hard plastic sleeves. We couldn't fit them all into the boxes we brought, so we had to snag a few from their warehouse here."

Paul was surprised at how anxious this made him feel. Everything had gone so perfectly; even this small mistake suddenly filled him with nervousness. "What if someone notices?"

"Hopefully they won't—it's just boxes after all. Not much we can do about it now." She and Raff loaded the last box into the van. "I'll reactivate the alarm and then meet you out front. Call the hacker team, and have them do what they can about resetting the entrance and exit logs for the door and the security system. No one ever checks those things, but I want it done before they open up again, just in case."

A minute later and they were on the road, headed back north toward San Jose. They were all too tired for much celebrating, and the van was now overflowing with boxes and technical equipment. Within twenty minutes of hitting the highway, the whole crew had passed out, leaving Paul to fight off sleep as he drove up the I-10. He was kind of exhilarated and relieved that it was over. Soon the excitement faded, and he was starting to yawn. Soon he felt more like a delivery driver than a thief.

By the time they got back to San Jose, everyone in the van had perked up quite a bit. They stopped for coffee just outside of town and called to let the rest of the crew know that they were on their way back in. Even in his sleep-deprived state, Paul found the excitement in the van contagious. Like the rest of them, he was in the mood to brag and crow a bit and, thanks to his role as the face-man, he figured the group might start accepting him as one of their own.

Once they'd loaded the boxes into the house they started unpacking them. A few of the hackers and the e-Slaves were already in the Server room, so the triumphant road team had a ready-made audience for their stories. Things got especially fun when Chloe pulled out a comic book price guide and started verbally calculating their potential profits.

"Here we have Ultimate Spider-Man, graded a 9.6—a little generous I think. I'd give it a 9.2 myself, but you guys should be able to sell it for $180.00 at least. Don't accept a penny less." She tossed the sealed comic across the room to one of the waiting e-Slaves and pulled another from the box.

"Ooooh, here's a rare but very cool book, one of my personal favorites, Tales to Astonish 46. Currently going for somewhere in the neighborhood of what? What would you say, Paul?"

"Oh, about $150.00, at least."

Chloe tossed it to another e-Slave team member. "There you go. $150.00. Paul and I will go through the price guide and eBay and put post-its on all of these. Then it's up to you guys. Remember, don't flood the market all at once, but don't take too long either. Raff's got another play in the works, so we should try and wrap this up within a week, maybe two."

"Sure thing," said Popper, leader of the e-Slaves team. "We've got the accounts set up and ready to go. I've scouted out the most popular comic-book forums and message boards, too, and we've all established multiple IDs on those, so we can talk up our offering there some. A little free advertising."

"Great thinking," said Chloe. "This is right up our alley now, kids. No different than when we sold 'vintage' clothes or rare Magic cards, so no excuses."

"What's the count looking to be?" asked Popper. This was obviously a question on everyone's mind, as the whole room turned its undivided attention to Chloe.

"Well, the way I see it, we're looking at something in the neighborhood of $40,000 to $65,000. Maybe 85K if you work the auctions right. You think you guys can hit that? Can you make $85,000 out of $50 worth of crappy old comics?" She was practically shouting by the end, riling up excitement amongst the e-Slaves.

"$85,000?" said Popper. "Hell, girl, we can do that in our sleep. We'll do 100K by the time we're done. You just wait and see!" The other e-Slaves greeted this with enthusiastic support and a chorus of "Fuck yeahs."

"OK, OK, we'll see. That'll be great if you can pull it off. If anyone can, you can. Just remember, this is a carry-over con. We're not looking for the hugest score in the world, not if it attracts attention we don't want."

"Right, right, we know the drill. Don't sweat it, Chloe, we've got this covered. You guys should get some rest."

"Thanks, Pops. This is in your hands now. Paul and I'll price these books and then get out of your hair."

Paul and Chloe sat down on the couch with a price guide and started sticking post-its on the forgeries with suggested starting bids.

"Man," said Paul, as he stuck a "$110" post-it note on one of the plastic cases. "I need a vacation. This con-man shit is real work."

"Oh, come on, you know you love it," Chloe replied.

"Yeah, maybe I do. But that doesn't mean I don't want a vacation. We should go somewhere."

"We just got back from L.A."

"I meant somewhere fun."

Chloe smiled at him. "Maybe you're right. But first things first, let's finish pricing these puppies."

"Yes ma'am, captain ma'am," he said, but he only remembered getting through about twenty more of them before passing out from sheer exhaustion, his head in Chloe's lap. She carefully pulled away the price guide from his hands and went into the kitchen to finish up, leaving Paul snoring blissfully away in the living room.

Chapter 13

"YOU were right, Paul. Let's go on a trip," said Chloe, standing over him as he lay on the couch, rubbing the sleep out of his eyes. She wore another in a never-ending series of tight fitting T-shirts, this one with a picture of a gorilla dressed in army fatigues throwing a Molotov cocktail.

"What?" he asked, blearily.

"Let's go on that vacation you wanted. The operation's in the hands of the e-Slaves now. They sure as fuck don't need us here. Let's go to the beach."

"Great! But it's your turn to drive."

"Of course. Pack a bag—three or four days clothes, and I'll try and find a sleeping bag around here for you. We'll take off as soon as you're up and ready to go."

"Sleeping bag? What beach are we going to?" Paul's clothes were still stuffed in the suitcases he'd thrown them into when he abandoned his apartment. Packing should be easy.

"Up the coast a bit. Some friends are letting me use their beach house." She started yanking on his arm, pulling him off the couch. "Come on, lazy bones! There's coffee in the kitchen and a sexy con artist wants to go on a road trip with you! What more can you ask from life?"

"Not much, I guess." Paul rose to his feet, cracking his neck and back. A sleeping bag probably wouldn't be any worse than this old couch.

An hour later and they were on the road, this time with Chloe driving a car Paul had never seen before: a red Saturn SUV that looked brand new. She said it was a friend's car, which Paul was starting to figure out was Crew-code for "don't ask where it came from, just be happy it's here."

It was a Sunday morning, and the usually jam-packed 880 was relatively car-free, allowing them to make good time through Oakland and Berkeley before veering off into wine country. Paul, wanting to catch up on the news he'd missed in his five-day forgery fugue, tried to convince Chloe to turn on Air America, but she refused to put up with something as boring as politics on such a beautiful day. She set her iPod to shuffle and they listened in comfortable quiet to a succession of punk and Ska bands Paul had never heard of. They made their way past wineries big and small, headed toward a small beach community near where they'd filmed Alfred Hitchcock's movie The Birds.

"You know, I've never been up here," said Paul.

"Really? I thought you liked wine."

"I do, but I never made it up here. Never had anyone who wanted to go with me. It was so easy to get wrapped up in work, I hardly ever made it out of San Jose."

"Which is a shame," said Chloe, "Because San Jose is a hole."

"It's kind of like one big strip mall, gone bad," agreed Paul. "But if you hate it too, why're you here? Couldn't you guys do your stuff, whatever it is, pretty much anywhere?"

"Yeah, we could. But this is where the action is. We're a tech-heavy group of geeks for the most part. I'm more the exception than the rule. I know the face-to-face cons, but most of my crew are tech-heads to the core. And there's no better place for that than here."

"I would've thought most of your hacking and what have you could be done from anywhere. Isn't that the point?"

"Sure, that's one way of doing things. It's even one of the ways we do things, but it's not the only way. You can sometimes hack a system from the outside and get access and maybe even make some money using that access, but not always. Like the play we just made with the comic-book stuff. We couldn't have done all that digitally—or at least it wouldn't have been so cheap and quick.

"Being in Silicon Valley lets me use my skills and those of people like Filo and Bee much more effectively. It gives us a lot more options. If we left it to just Raff and Kurt and the other hacker kids, we'd have a limited number of moves in any situation. And variety isn't just the spice of life; it also keeps you out of jail. Since we can play things so many different directions, we don't have any easily discernible patterns. And no pattern means it's hard for the police to home in on us. Plus, it's a hell of a lot more fun to play dress up and con people than it is to just sit in front of a computer and rob them with ones and zeroes.

"There are hackers out there who break into systems and fuck with them just for the fun of it. Just to be a pain in the ass or to prove to themselves that they can. That's not what we're about."

"You're about the money," said Paul, uncomfortable with the fact that he was getting used to the idea of falling for a thief.

"Yes. Fuck yes, we're about the money, but not because we want to get rich. Selling fake comics isn't going to make us rich, but it is going to pay the bills and put food on the table and no one ever has to be the wiser about where that money came from. And by no one, I mean the IRS, the government and anyone else who wants to stick their noses in my business. We're living totally off the information grid, which is what we're REALLY all about."

"So you don't pay taxes or anything?" asked Paul. "I mean, I figured that you didn't report stolen income, but how do you stay completely 'off the grid' as you say? How do you rent a house or get a driver's license or credit cards?" Paul found the concept incredibly compelling. He'd long dreamed of disappearing from public and government scrutiny. In fact, that dream had been one of the driving themes in his comic-book *Metropolis 2.0*.

Chloe, keeping one hand on the wheel, dug her wallet out of her pocket and pulled out her driver's license, handing it to Paul. "Take a look at that," she said. The license showed a picture of a smiling Chloe, with her name but a different address on it. It looked perfectly legitimate to Paul.

"What, is it fake or something? Why the wrong address?"

"It's not fake. But it's not real either. The address is obviously wrong, but I never carry around anything that has my real address on it. That's easy—it's not like they check up on you at the DMV when you move. And that is a real, official California driver's license. But it's not my real name. And it's not the only one I have. Same for the social security card in there. They're not fake, but they're not me."

"Identity theft?"

"Sort of. Sometimes. Typically it's dead people—use an old birth certificate right, and no one's the wiser. So yeah, that license there is for Chloe Carmichael. And I file a tax return every year for Chloe, too. She makes minimum wage as a freelance house cleaner and just barely gets by, which means she ain't paying much in the way of taxes. But it's a clean cover if I ever need it."

"That's all pretty much what I figured," bluffed Paul, handing the license back to her. In fact, the thought hadn't even crossed his mind. Who was she, anyway? "But now something new's bugging me. What the hell's your real name?"

"Chloe."

"Just not Chloe Carmichael, right?"

"For the world, for my friends, for you, I'm Chloe. That's my real name. What does it matter what name I was born with? Who the fuck cares? Whatever it was, I didn't choose it. My parents did. I chose Chloe, and that's all you need to know." She said this matter-of-factly, although Paul detected a hint of annoyance beneath her words and decided to drop the subject.

"Cool," he said, although he wasn't at all sure if it really was.

They rode along in silence for a few minutes, before Chloe spoke again. "Speaking of parents, have you talked to yours?"

"Yeah, a couple of times. They want me to come home to Florida and see them. They feel really sorry for me. All they know is that I got fired—they don't know about the money or, you know, anything else I've been up to."

"You should. You should go see them." She paused to fish an Altoid from the tin below the ashtray. "I've never been to Florida." She let this hang there. Was it a request to come along or just a stray comment?

"I will. At some point, I will. There's a Pirate festival in Key West in November. I thought I might go back for that. Stop by Sarasota and see them at the same time."

"A pirate festival? Now you're talking my language! I could bring the whole crew—we'd go wild on that shit. Have you ever been?"

"Nope, but it's supposed to be a lot of fun. I've been to Fantasy Fest—which is kind of Key West's version of Mardi Gras, except it's around Halloween—and that's awesome. If you're into drunken debauchery and public nudity."

"Which I most definitely am," said Chloe.

"I imagine the pirate festival's the same, except, you know, with pirates."

"Sounds like a party. We'll definitely have to pull that one. I'll look into it, see if there are any angles we can play to make a few bucks while we're there."

"You're always looking for the angles aren't you?"

"I never seem to find any angels, so angles are all that's left."

Although it was late afternoon and early summer, when they crested the hill and came into the "town" of Killian Beach, there was already a fog rolling in off the Pacific Ocean. Nevertheless, Paul had to admit that it was a beautiful sight. The town was little more than a single convenience store/gas station/restaurant and about fifty expensive beach houses spread out along the cliffs overlooking the beach below. For Paul, a native of Florida's west coast, these northern California beaches always seemed surreal to him. Instead of the flat expanses of white sand and warm water that he'd grown up with, these beaches were often just bits of sand at the foot of towering walls of rock and the water was inevitably too cold for him to swim in. Nevertheless, it sure did look pretty.

Chloe drove them to one of the fancy beach houses that sat further up the cliff side, a good three hundred or so yards from the actual beach. It still had a great view, looking down on the other houses and the water below. Inside, the two-story vacation home was fully furnished and tastefully decorated. It felt like something between a lived in hotel and a model home. There was a spacious, bright living room/dining room area with floor to ceiling windows looking out on the water. Three bedrooms, two baths, a rec room with a pool table and big screen TV, and a well-appointed kitchen finished off the interior. But the best part was the large wooden deck that wrapped around two sides of the structure and supported that most classic and important of California accoutrements: the hot tub.

"Very nice," said Paul.

"Yes indeed. The only drawback is that they only have dial-up for Internet access, but other than that, we're set." She dropped her backpack in the center of the living room and started to unpack her laptop. "Take any of the bedrooms you want, and make yourself at home."

Separate bedrooms of course, as he'd assumed but secretly hoped wouldn't be the case. Paul, out of spite, took the master bedroom for himself and unpacked his clothes into the empty chest of drawers. There was a king sized bed and as he flopped down on it he was in heaven, so much more comfortable than the couch. He was already starting to nod off when Chloe knocked on his open door.

"You wanna take a walk with me down to the beach? I need to stretch my legs after being cooped up in that car for hours."

"Sure," he said. "Let's go."

They walked at an ambling pace down the winding road toward the beach access, Chloe passed the time with tales of her wild high school years which had apparently involved a lot of camping out on beaches much like this one. She had her messenger bag with her in case they wanted to do some shopping at the convenience store. They wandered up and down the beach, shivering slightly in the brisk breeze blowing in off the water. The fog was truly settling in now, and they couldn't even see all the way back up to their house anymore.

The convenience store had a little bit of everything, including some wine and frozen pizzas, which they bought for dinner, and a small general delivery post office where Chloe dropped off a letter.

"Who's that for?" asked Paul.

"Just getting in touch with an old friend. Something I forgot to mail before we left, and I found it sitting in my bag."

"Oh, OK. Are you about ready to head back? I'm starving."

"I know how cranky you get when you haven't eaten, Paul, so let's get a move on. That hill we walked down isn't going to be nearly as much fun going the other way."

They huffed and puffed their way back up to the top of the cliff and set about preparing dinner. Paul volunteered for the arduous task of preheating the oven, opening the wine and sticking the frozen pizza into the oven. Chloe started the hot tub warming up and then checked her e-mail at the dining room table.

"How're things going with the comics con?" Paul asked as he set a glass of wine down next to Chloe and sipped on his own. A little tart for his tastes, but it was certainly drinkable.

"Seems good. They've got about two dozen of them up on eBay already, and they're getting some interest. It'll be a five or six days before we really know how it's going." She drank deeply from her glass. "Well that's a mediocre vintage to be sure. You'd think they'd do better, being so close to Napa and all."

"Cheap wine is cheap wine the world over," said Paul.

"I hate cheapness. Inexpensive is good. It's fucking great sometimes. But that doesn't mean it has to be cheap. There's great wine to be had in these parts for what we paid for this bottle, but all we got is this cheap stuff."

"Yep, but on the bright side, there are three bottles of it in there, so there's more than enough to get us too drunk to notice how cheap it is."

"Fucking right," said Chloe with a smile, draining her glass. "I'll pour us another round."

They ate and finished off another bottle of wine in the living room, chatting away about wine and beer and food, subjects about which Paul knew quite a bit. One of his many un-pursued hobbies was fine dining and cooking, and Chloe seemed impressed with his expertise.

As they drank the last of the second bottle, Chloe got up to get the third, but when she came out of the kitchen she continued walking right on out to the deck. "Come on," she said.

Paul forced himself up off the comfy couch, his head spinning from the wine, and followed her outside. There was a crisp, cold bite to the air. Chloe had peeled off the cover on the hot tub and was testing the waters. "Still not as near-boiling as I like it, but it's plenty hot. You wanna join me?"

"Sure, why not? Let me go get my bathing suit."

She laughed. "You're kidding, right?"

"I guess I am," he said, although he hadn't been.

"This is California. A hot tub in California. The dress code is strictly au natural." And then, as if to make her point, she stripped her T-shirt off over her head with one quick motion, revealing a black bra that could have been a modest bikini top. "Come on, don't be shy."

Paul took off his own shirt self-consciously. He wasn't in the best shape of his life, but he wasn't looking too bad either. He showed the earliest signs of love handles and was a bit soft around the middle. Chloe now stepped out of her shorts, and to Paul's surprise, he saw that she wasn't wearing any panties. She revealed a thick, black bush of pubic hair, above which was a tattoo that said something he couldn't quite make out in the dim light. She turned her back to him as she unhooked her bra, and he couldn't help but take a good, lingering look at her full, round ass. He felt a stirring in his pants, which he was already in the process of unbuckling. She tossed her bra to the deck and climbed up into the hot tub, sinking down fast into the hot water.

Paul stripped off his shorts and underwear and now stood naked in the crisp night air. His slight embarrassment and the chill worked against his growing arousal, which was fine with him. He followed Chloe into the tub, but as soon as his toe touched the water, he pulled it back. "Damn that's hot!" he said.

She laughed. "Don't be such a wimp. Just plunge on in, you'll get used to it in a second." She reached over to the side where she had set the wine next to the controls. She spun a knob, setting the water jets in motion with a roar and then poured them both glasses of wine. Paul eased himself below the water; glad for the cover the frothing bubble afforded him. He watched Chloe pour, her wet breasts and pink nipples the sole focus of his attention until she turned toward him to hand him a glass.

"So this is genuine California hot-tubbing, huh?" he asked, which sounded much lamer when he said it out loud than when he'd thought of it a moment before. She smiled and sat back in the tub so only her head and shoulders were above the water, making it easier for Paul to look right at her without ogling at her breasts.

"A prime example. Usually the view's not nearly this nice, but the wine's better. I take it you've never done this before?"

"Not really, no. Not like this."

"See, I'm good for you Paul. I get you involved in all kinds of interesting new activities."

"Sure. Forgery, fraud, breaking and entering, and hot-tubbing."

"Now be fair, the forgery was your idea, not mine."

"You do have a point. I'll cop to that one."

"And you're the one who said you needed a lawyer. I just offered to represent you is all. And since I'm not a real lawyer, I had to make up for my lack of legal knowledge with pure zealousness for my client."

Paul raised his glass toward her in a salute, "Which I greatly appreciate! Thanks again for that."

"My pleasure," she said. "It was an easy gig to be honest. I wish they were all that simple."

"So what's next?" asked Paul. "Where do we go from here?"

"You mean while we're on our little vacation or what's my crew up to next?"

"Both I guess."

"Well, hopefully we'll get a chance to see a friend of mine while we're up here. I'll have to take the car tomorrow and poke around a bit, so you'll be here by yourself most of the day, if that's OK."

"I could come with if you want."

"No, no, that's OK. I've got some stuff I need to get done. We'll take a drive around the day after, though. Tour on up the Pacific Coast Highway a bit, which is just gorgeous."

"Sounds good." Paul knew she'd be up to something tomorrow, but there was no sense in pressing her on it. She'd deflect any inquiries he made. "I'll just hang around the house and do some drawing, I guess. Maybe start working up some ideas I had for a new comic."

"You're thinking about starting a new series? That's great! You know, when we were gathering all those comics for the comic con, I dug up a few old issues of your stuff. I especially loved that six-issue series you did five or six years ago. 'End Dead' I think it was called."

"Thanks. That's one of my favorites, too. I love drawing zombies and that kind of stuff. It didn't sell real well, but the critics liked it."

Chloe poured them both some more wine, flashing wet boobs again as she did. "Zombies are fucking cool," she said. "The original *Dawn of the Dead* is one of my favorite movies ever. I just got the four-DVD set that came out a while ago. It's amazing."

"What's your fascination with zombies? Aside from that fact that they're so cool."

"That's about it, really. I've loved monster movies since I was kid. When I was 14, I even got my tattoo inspired by monster movies, sort of."

"What tattoo?"

"You didn't notice it a bit ago?"

"I saw something, but I couldn't make out what it said."

"Here, have another look." She stood up on her seat, so the water only came up to her knees. Her pubic hair was matted down and dripping, which was all Paul was looking at for the first moment. Then his vision expanded to include the pleasing form of her hips. Like a cello he thought. It was only third of all that he concentrated on, the Gothic-script lettering just above the line of her hair. "MANEATER" it said.

"Maneater? Is that a warning or should I not take it personally?"

Chloe laughed as she plopped back down into her seat, splashing Paul as she did so. "The funniest part is that I didn't even get the whole joke of it at the time. I was 14, and my best friend convinced me it was a good idea. There might have been some acid involved, I don't remember for sure. I just thought it was funny—you know, a man-eater, like Jaws or a zombie or something."

"You missed the whole vagina dentate angle?"

"I didn't even have sex until I was 16! That was the last thing I was thinking about. I just wanted to have that tattoo somewhere my parents wouldn't see it. I wore one piece bathing suits for years as a result."

"Did you ever think about getting it changed or removed?"

"Are you kidding? Of course not! Unlike when I was 14, now it's actually true," she said with a smiling bite at the air. "Rrrowr."

"OK," Paul laughed, "Now you've got me really scared. I definitely need some more wine."

"What about your ink there, sport?" Chloe pointed to Paul's right shoulder, where he had the logo for his former company, Fear and Loading Games, tattooed in bright red. "You gonna cover that baby up now that you've, shall we say, severed all ties?"

Paul craned his neck and looked down at the tattoo—a logo he'd designed. It featured a very Ralph Steadman-like gamer reeling back from his laptop, different-sized eyes goggling in what might be fear or, more likely, narcotic frenzy. Below, in a harried, graffiti script it said Fear and Loading Games. He'd grown so used to it he scarcely remembered it was there sometimes. "I don't know. Sometimes it's good to have a reminder of your mistakes. Besides, it's my design. At least that's one thing they can't take away from me."

Chloe reached across the tub and topped off Paul's wineglass. "That's the spirit," she said. "Now drink up, sailor and tell me more about where you got the ideas for *End Dead*."

They finished the final bottle over the next hour and stayed up chatting about zombies and comics and tattoos and everything else that came into their heads until their skin wrinkled from the water. Yawning, Chloe finally called it a night and headed for bed. Paul watched her nude body as she went inside to get them some towels, leaving watery footprints across the carpet. Was she coming on to him? Nothing in her body language—aside from the naked thing—suggested this. But then there was the naked thing. Hot tubs were well out of Paul's area of expertise, and he didn't know what the etiquette was on something like this. Luckily, he was drunk enough not to put too much thought into it.

She returned with a big beach towel wrapped around her body and tossed one to him. "I might be gone by the time you get up tomorrow, but I'll be back by late afternoon. Good night."

"OK. G'night," he said, clambering out of the water and wrapping himself in the towel. It was only then that he dimly remembered that she never had answered his second question. His attention had quickly wandered to other subjects, especially that tattoo. What was the crew planning to do next? And did whatever it was include him? He'd have to ask again tomorrow.

Chapter 14

CHLOE was indeed gone by the time Paul stumbled out of bed late the next morning. He felt a little awkward in the strange, empty house, so he decided to do a little exploring. He puttered around, poking through drawers and looking for signs of who owned the place. There wasn't anything that led him to believe that anyone actually lived here. The kitchen was fully stocked with three different kinds of silverware and a ton of cheap, mismatched ceramic plates. There were two blenders. Everything was immaculately clean and recently dusted. It all looked to him not like someone's beach house, but rather like a vacation rental. He knew this area teemed with such places, which went for hundreds of dollars a night. Was Chloe just renting the place for the week, or did she really know the owners?

After a bagel and cream cheese breakfast/lunch, he sat down at the dining room table with his sketchbook. Chloe had taken her laptop with her on whatever her mysterious errands were and the TV reception turned out to be nonexistent. He doodled away for a while, trying to figure out some way of getting back into the comics business again. Not that he really needed to. He had $840,000 hidden in a storage locker back in San Jose, a fact that he didn't really think about as often as he might have. The money didn't even seem real to him. If he played his cards right, he'd never have to work again in his life. Buy a little house somewhere. Invest the rest. He didn't need much more than $20,000 a year to be happy. As a comics artist, he'd lived for four or five years on less than that.

If he wasn't going to make comics for money, then what was he going to make them for? Flipping through the sketchbook, he looked over the elaborate revenge-inspired sketches he'd been working on in the bar when he first met Chloe. There was a thought. He could do a comic about what he'd experienced since then. It was, so far, the most interesting thing that'd ever happened to him. Of course he'd have to change it so as not to implicate himself in the crimes he'd committed. But that was easily done. Change the setting maybe, make it a sci-fi story. Or maybe horror. Maybe a sequel to the "End Dead" comic that Chloe had liked so much. It was a starting place anyway, which was all Paul needed to begin drawing.

But Paul found it hard to concentrate on images of revenge. His first attempt at a zombie was a buxom, undead cheerleader using severed arms as pom-poms. He liked the joke, but the sketch turned out to be surprisingly sexy and, most disturbing of all, the creature had Chloe's lips and eyes. Well, almost Chloe's eyes. He flipped the page and started again, trying to capture her face on paper. Then he moved on to full-body portraits, recreating her luscious form as he remembered it from the night before. As the day went on, the drawings became more and more erotic and then explicit and finally, just plain pornographic.

It was nearly 4 p.m. before he heard the car in the driveway. He slammed the sketchbook shut and tucked it away in his backpack, pulling out a paperback novel. The last thing he wanted was for Chloe to see what he'd been drawing. At least not until after he'd had a chance to act some of those images out in real life. He heard voices in the entrance hall. Had Chloe brought a friend?

"Hello?" he said. "I'm in the dining room."

Silence. Then a thick Spanish accent. "Hello? Is someone here?"

Who was that? He got up from the table and went through the living room to the front door. There stood two middle aged Hispanic women with a vacuum cleaner and a basket of cleaning supplies. That explained why the place was so clean. They seemed startled to see him.

"Oh… um, hi," he said.

"There's no one s'posed to be here now," said the maid with the vacuum. "Who're you?"

"I'm a friend of… my friend Chloe. She's friends with the owners. We're visiting."

"My list said no one's s'posed to be in this house until one more week," she said, pulling a folded piece of paper from her pocket.

"I don't really know anything about that. Like I said, I'm just a guest here. Maybe you should come back or…" He was about to suggest that she call the owners but suddenly realized that that might not be the smartest move. "Yeah, could you just come back tomorrow?"

The maid was looking down with supreme concentration at the piece of paper from her pocket. Paul didn't think she'd even been listening to him. "No, no. No one's supposed to be here all week. This is from this morning." She waved the paper at him.

"Listen," said Paul, "I don't know anything about that, OK? I mean, I'm just here as a guest." What would Chloe do? She'd spin a story. He could do that. He thought about yelling at them, blustering and shouting his way through the situation, but he realized that would backfire. It might even make them call the cops and certainly the owners. No, he needed sympathy.

"I've had a just…" He stammered. "It's been a bad week, a bad month, OK? I found out that… I found out… let's just say I found out something about my health? Something not good." He tried to make it sound like he was choking back tears. The two maids looked at each other, not sure what to do. Were they buying this?

"I don't have a lot of time left, OK? Months the doctor said. My girl-friend and I wanted to have a vacation… one last trip before I… before it gets too bad." They looked sympathetic or at the very least embarrassed. "She called up her friend and arranged for this last minute. Maybe it's off the books or it's a favor or whatever. I don't know. I'm sorry." He put his hands to his face, as if hiding tears, although in fact it was because he couldn't make himself cry on cue and didn't want them to notice that.

"We'll come back," said the lead maid. "We're sorry you're not feeling well. We'll come back."

"Thank you. Sorry to have inconvenienced you or thrown off your schedule or whatever." He sniffled.

"It's no problem. Really. We'll come back." She and her companion backed out the door, shutting it behind them. He heard them talking in low voices as they left, but he couldn't make out what they were saying.

"Damn! What the fuck!" he said to no one in particular. And then, not for the first time in the last five minutes, he wondered where the hell Chloe was.

She finally showed up around 6:30. When he heard the SUV in the driveway, he went to a window, fearing the maids or even the owner had returned. But no, it was Chloe, thank God. The SUV was a little dirtier than he'd last seen it and she'd obviously driven through mud somewhere, since the wheel wells were coated in it. He met her at the door, opening it before she put her hand on the knob.

"And where have you been, young lady?" he asked in mock (or maybe not so mock) disapproval. "Your mother and I have been worried sick!" She smiled and handed him one of the two bags of groceries she'd brought in from the vehicle.

"Oh you know, Dad, skipping school and doing drugs with my friends, the usual stuff."

He followed her into the kitchen. "How was your day? When did you finally wake up?" she asked.

"Around 11:30."

"I was going to let you come along, but you looked so peaceful there, snoring away in your bed, I couldn't bear to wake you."

"Yeah, right. How was your secret mission?"

"Oh swell. Stole the secret plans, blew up the enemy airbase, and rescued the girl. Plus I picked up some decent wine and a couple of steaks for dinner," she said as she unloaded the groceries.

"Sounds good. I actually had an interesting day as well. We had visitors."

She stopped dead in her tracks for a moment, then turned around to look right at him. She was smiling, but Paul detected surprise, maybe concern. "Really? The neighbors come by looking for a cup of sugar?"

"Nope, it was the maids. They wanted to clean the house. They were more than a little surprised to find me here. Apparently, your friend didn't tell them we were coming."

"Yeah, imaginary friends are really bad about that kind of thing. They never talk to anyone but me."

"So I'm guessing this isn't really your friend's house."

"Um, no. Not really. Which is to say, not at all."

"What does that mean?" he asked.

"It means we should go. Right the fuck now." She started to put the groceries back in the shopping bags. "What did you tell them?"

"That I was dying of cancer and that this was my last hurrah with my girlfriend before I died."

"No, really, what'd you say?"

"Just that. I said I was dying and that the owner was a family friend who hooked me up at the last minute. I think they even believed me, but I'm not sure."

She looked over her shoulder and eyed him for a moment, scanning him up and down with a quick glance. "Not bad there, sport. You might have bought us 'til morning. But we can't risk it."

"So we go back to San Jose? You know, if we find a hotel or other rental around here, I wouldn't mind springing for it."

"No need for that," she interrupted. "There's a kind of party we were invited to later tonight anyway. It's a camp-out kind of thing. We'll go there."

"I guess that sleeping bag you had me bring will come in handy after all."

"Of course. You should know by now that I always think of everything."

"Except the maids."

"OK, except the maids." She smiled. "Now come on, let's pack up and get out of here."

They were packed and in the car ten minutes later, ready to head out. Chloe went back inside to do one last sweep of the place, using a damp towel to wipe down everything she remembered touching, or at least all the obvious places. When they were done, there wasn't a sign that they'd ever been there. She got in the driver's seat and they took off, heading out of "town" and back north, toward the Pacific Coast Highway. Or at least Paul thought it was north—the roads all twisted and turned so much that he'd lost track of which way was up.

Chloe seemed to know where she was going, even in the gathering fog and darkness. She hummed tunelessly to herself, as if she didn't have a care in the world.

"You're enjoying this, aren't you?" he asked. "You're really grooving on the fact that we have to run."

She thought for a moment before answering. "I guess I am. It's exciting, right? Almost getting caught doing something you're not supposed to be doing? That's part of the fun of this whole life-of-crime deal."

"So what crime exactly were we committing back there? I thought the house belonged to a friend of yours?"

She laughed. "Oh come on, you never really believed that, did you?"

"No, not really. I think I've figured out that particular code of yours. Unnamed friend equals 'I stole it.'"

"Not always—I'm not that predictable—but in this case, you're right. A while back we pulled a scam that tangentially involved using some vacation rental properties as safe houses and cover locations. We broke into the offices of one of those big property management companies that takes care of a couple hundred of these vacation places and, well, we copied all their keys. Plus we got hooked up on their computer system. Anyway, it lets me know when a place is being rented and when it isn't and so on. So whenever I need a break, I just check their reservation computer and see what's available that day. The perfect plan."

"Except for the maids," Paul added.

She slapped him on the leg playfully. "Will you shut up about the fucking maids? They usually come right before and after someone rents the place, and no one was scheduled in this place for two more weeks. They must either be behind schedule or maybe they were going to be doing some uninvited goofing off, just like us. Either way, we're out of there, and no one's any the wiser."

"Don't you think the owners or property managers or whoever will get suspicious when they hear the maids' story?"

"Maybe. But what are the odds they're going to suspect what actually happened; that I have the master keys to all their properties? Who'd be crazy enough to dream up something like that?"

"Someone pretty damn crazy, I'll give you that."

"That's me, guilty as charged."

She concentrated on the road for a while, as they came into a particularly twisted section that led up onto the highway. As it turned out, the Pacific Coast Highway wasn't much of a highway at all, but rather a two lane paved road that wound dangerously along the aforementioned Pacific coast. Paul had a slight wave of vertigo as he looked off to the left and saw nothing but fifty feet of sheer rock plunging down into the fog (and presumably the water below). He imagined it would be a beautiful sight in the daylight, but now, in the darkness and mist, it looked like the end of the world.

Chloe turned on her iPod and played one of her many Ska bands—Paul couldn't tell them apart—and they drove on through the dips and curves of the road. They passed several other small beach towns like the one they'd just left, along with lone homes and clusters of houses. Paul thought about what an odd life it must be to live in such a place. Sure you've got a great view, but you're not near anything convenient, like a grocery store. And at the same time, you're right on top of one of the most famous highways and tourist attractions in the state, so it's not like you have a ton of privacy and peace and quiet either. Not the life for him.

Not that it was an option—he bet even the smallest of those houses would've cost every cent of the $850,000 he'd gotten off his old partners. If he bought a place like that, he'd have to get a real job to put food on the table, and he had no intention of doing that anytime soon. He needed a break. Of course, there was the Chloe option. She and her crew certainly didn't have straight jobs, and they seemed to be having a blast. The past week that he'd spent with them had, truth be told, been about the happiest time he'd had since moving to California.

And now here he was, driving along a famously romantic stretch of road with a beautiful, vivacious con woman and $850,000 stashed away.

All he needed now was a way to figure out if Chloe was really interested in him or not.

"We're almost there," she said, all of a sudden.

"Almost where? The party?"

"Yep."

"How can you tell?"

"Because I know where I'm going, you goofball. How do you think?"

Paul looked out into the fog beyond. "How can you even see where you're going in this stuff?"

"You just have to listen for the signs."

A few minutes later Chloe abruptly slammed on the brakes and pulled her SUV over to the other side of the road, across the (thankfully empty) oncoming lane of traffic. They came to a sudden stop in a patch of gravel along the side of the road, which had enough room for maybe ten cars to park. Right now there were two others besides theirs: a rusting white conversion van and a late-90s Honda sedan. Nothing you'd ever look twice at.

"We're here."

"Great! Where's here?"

"The party, of course; can't you hear the music?" She turned off the car and the stereo with it. With the music off Paul could now hear the beating of drums coming from somewhere below.

Chloe got out of the SUV and went around back to get her gear. She slung her messenger bag across her shoulders and then pulled on a small backpack with a sleeping bag lashed to it. She fished a flashlight out of her pocket and pointed it in Paul's face. "You're going to want to figure out a way to tie that sleeping bag to your duffle bag or back or something. You'll probably want both hands free for the descent."

"Isn't there a path?"

"Nope, not really. Sort of. You'll see."

Paul decided to see first before making any decisions. The cliff on which they were parked was maybe forty or fifty feet high. It wasn't quite a sheer drop, and shrubs and brush covered the cliff side. Chloe's light revealed a thin trail of sand that cut down through the undergrowth at a severe angle. It wasn't quite a path, but it would almost serve as one. Below was a beach, a stretch of sand maybe fifty feet wide that followed the curve of the cliff and disappeared around a corner. Paul could hear the drums much more clearly now, although he still couldn't tell where they were coming from. Looking back at the trail, he decided Chloe was right. He would need both hands free to safely climb down. Even then, he felt the odds were good that he'd slip or fall.

After messing around with the bulky sleeping bag for a few minutes, trying to figure out a way to attach it to his back, he gave up. He carried the mass of cushioned nylon to the cliff's edge. Chloe whooped with appreciation as he took a three step running start and hurled it into the night. She followed its arc with her flashlight as it sailed through the fog and landed in the brush about five feet from the beach.

"Not too shabby," said Paul, stepping down onto the precipitous path behind Chloe.

"You have a future in the Olympic sleeping-bag toss."

"I think it's going to be an exhibition sport in the X-Games next year."

Chapter 15

THE way down was even trickier than Paul had anticipated, and several times he fell on his ass when he lost his balance—better than falling face-first down the cliff though. Chloe seemed to have less trouble, although she was the one holding the flashlight. After he'd retrieved his sleeping bag from where it had landed, they set off down the beach toward the sound of the drums. It was downright cold this close to the water, and a fine mist of condensation from the fog already covered his entire body. He wished he'd put on a sweatshirt before they left the car.

They followed the thumping, swirling drumbeat through the mists. As they rounded the corner of the cliff, Paul saw a large bonfire about a hundred yards up the beach, surrounded by a circle of several dozen people. As they drew closer, Paul could see that most of the figures were sitting astride or beside various kinds of African drums, while in the center, four or five figures danced with wild abandon around the fire, grooving to the tribal-inspired beat.

"Wow," said Paul.

"Yeah, isn't it great?" said Chloe, "I love these guys."

As they approached, a figure stepped out of the shadows near the cliff and intercepted them. Paul wasn't sure if he'd been standing guard or had just wandered away from the circle to take a piss or something.

"Hey, Chloe, glad you could make it," he said as he hugged Chloe.

"I wouldn't miss it." She released him from the hug and motioned to Paul. "Keith, this is Paul. Paul, Keith"

The man embraced Paul in a friendly hug that smelled of patchouli and sweat. "Good to meet you, brother."

"Hey," said Paul, who had no problem with friendly hugs but really didn't like the sickly sweet herbal stench of patchouli. "Nice to meet you."

Keith led the way toward the drum circle, chatting with Chloe enthusiastically about who was there and what kinds of drums they were using and who had the best pot. Paul followed along a pace behind them; his attention focused on the dazzling spectacle of fire and beat just ahead.

The fire pit was big, at least six feet across and piled high with fresh logs on top of older, red-hot coals. There were five people dancing in the space between the drummers and the fire, two men and three women. They were so close to the fire they wore little in the way of clothes, despite the chill in the air. Two of the women had on flowing skirts and tank tops, while the third danced in sweat pants and no top at all. The two men were also shirtless, one of them young and extremely fit, the other a middle-aged man with a frizzy white beard and a drum-like round belly. This last dancer seemed the most lost in the beat, twirling and jigging madly. To Paul's utter surprise, he even took a running leap through/over the fire, eliciting cheers and whoops from the assembled group.

Paul counted fourteen drummers in the circle, along with three others who clapped their hands or drummed their knees as they swayed with the music. Most had African-style drums that looked hand made, each around two to three feet tall and played with bare hands. Others had larger, bass drums that they played with soft tipped sticks. A few had conga drums and other store bought pieces. Most kept a steady, simple but fast rhythm, which the more skilled players then embellished upon with even faster and more intricate beats. No music expert, Paul couldn't fathom the complexity of the group's sound, but he knew it sounded good.

Chloe took him by the hand and led him to the circle. They dropped their camping gear in the sand and squeezed into the group, a drummer and a hand clapper each grinning and welcoming them to the party. Chloe pulled a thin blanket from her bag and laid it down in the sand amongst the various rugs, towels, and other blankets that the circle had already put in place. Paul sat down slightly behind Chloe, and she leaned back against him as they relaxed and beheld the spectacle.

The older man soon emerged as the leader in the circle. The other dancers played off his movements as he leaped and cavorted around the circle. Occasionally he would stop in front of a drummer and squat down to bang away on their instrument in a frenzied rhythm. He'd been so lost in this wild, freeform celebration that he hadn't noticed Chloe and Paul's arrival. It was only after twenty minutes or so that he recognized her, and his face lit up with delight.

"Ha HAAAAA! Chloe!" He shouted, grabbing her by the hands and pulling her to her feet. She squealed as he drew her inside the circle (although when Paul later implied that she'd squealed, she denied it). Immediately they were dancing hand in hand and the circle picked up its beat. Then they spun apart as the older man's own movements caught him up in a twisting movement that no partner could follow. Chloe, fully in concert with the drummers now, danced off in her own direction, gracefully moving near and through and back near the other four dancers, all of whom momentarily matched their movements to hers by way of welcome.

Paul would never have imagined that the normally self-controlled Chloe would dance with such abandon, and the sight entranced him. She moved with a certain grace to be sure, but it was her vivaciousness and energy that he found most attractive. Her legs pumped up and down, her arms pressing in and out in time with two of the women dancers. Rising and crouching, the older man circled around them like a pot-bellied scarecrow, not in a lascivious way, but as if he was somehow honoring their contribution to the dance.

The man next to Paul—the clapper, not the drummer—offered him a hit off of his pipe. Paul thanked him, drawing a deep lung full of pot smoke and holding his breath as long as he could before passing the pipe back. He watched Chloe dance for many more minutes as the euphoria of the hit (and the three he took after that) washed over him. Two other members had joined the dance now, and once they'd finished the bowl, the clapper suggested they both join in as well. Paul used to love to go out to clubs when he was in college, but he'd scarcely done any dancing since and none at all after he'd moved to California. Why not? He thought, if I can't drum, I might as well dance!

Paul stood up and swayed in place to the music for a moment, trying to get a handle on the beat. Then Chloe spotted him and swished over, grabbing him around the waist, pulling him close. He moved his body with and against hers, learning the rhythm from her hips, an altogether enjoyable process. Once he was going Chloe, stepped back for a moment and shouted, "Isn't this great!"

"Yeah!"

"It's so hot by the fire!"

"Sure!" he said, as he watched her pull her long-sleeved shirt up and over her head, tossing it onto her blanket. Now wearing just jeans and a bra, she pulled him back close to her again. "Come on! Let's dance!"

And they did. For hours they circled the bonfire, moving to the beat. The circle shifted and morphed along with the changing beats as individual drummers dropped out and came back in when they got tired or decided to join the dancers for a while or just needed a quick smoke. By the time the circle began to wind down, Paul had taken off his own shirt. Some of the time he and Chloe danced close, their bare skin touching. Other times they cavorted separately around the circle, briefly intertwining with the other dancers. And always there was the old man, seemingly everywhere at once, leading the bacchanalian assembly through pure enthusiasm for the dance.

When the dancers and drummers finally collapsed from exhaustion, Paul and Chloe fell back into their blankets, covered in sweat and panting for air. The others produced bottles of water and wine, which they passed around the circle. Paul leaned close to Chloe, whispering in her ear.

"Who are these people?"

She took hold of his head and guided his ear to her mouth, whispering into it, "This is a real crew. They're the real deal."

Before Paul could ask what the hell that meant, the potbellied scarecrow man started addressing the whole circle.

"That was wonderful—just wonderful. I thank you all, from the bottom of my heart, for once again sharing your bodies and souls with me in the dance. This special communion never fails to move me. On a night like this, I realize that we really do have all we ever need as long as we have our freedom and each other." He smiled broadly and then shouted, "Freedom and company!"

"Freedom and company!" the group yelled in response. Paul thought back to the call-and-response session Chloe had led her crew in after they'd helped him. Were these people high tech criminals as well? They didn't look the part.

The man continued. "Tomorrow, once again we begin. We'll rise up from the underground like the first blossoms of spring and bring a little bit of our own version of life into the cold hard world around us. And in return we'll take what we need to keep going, to keep teaching the world that there's another path, a way to live in true freedom. Our actions will resonate through the universe, like ripples in a pond. What we start, others will someday finish. The Revolution will come."

"The Revolution will come," intoned the circle, like a congregation at prayer.

"Let it be so." The man looked around the group in silence for over a minute, waiting to see if anyone wanted to add anything, but the only sounds were the crackle of the fire and the susurrations of the surf. Then he grinned an infectious, toothy smile.

"Ok, we'll deal with the details tomorrow brothers and sisters. Tonight we have guests and there's still fun to be had. Drink, toke, and be merry! For tomorrow you might fly!" The group laughed and then broke down into a dozen different small conversations. Two of the drummers stood up to confer with the old man, passing him a joint as they did so.

Paul had to know what was going on. "So they're a crew like you and your friends?" he asked Chloe.

"Yes and no. They're much more old school than we are. And they're much more of a community. Really more like a commune."

"So they're communists?" Paul joked.

"Some of them probably are. Communists and Anarchists and whatever else lies between those two."

Paul vaguely knew that such people were out there, but he'd never really considered that anyone could seriously still be a Communist. In his mind that whole thing was a distant memory from the '80s, like Ronald Reagan and New Kids on the Block—nothing he'd ever want to go back to.

"Huh," was all he could think of to say.

"These guys really have it figured out," continued Chloe. "They're a tight knit crew—much tighter than me and mine. They love and support one another. For them, the next score's never what it's about, it's just a way to get from here to there in peace and prosperity."

"If that's the case, couldn't they just, you know, get jobs? Start an organic farm or something?"

"They could. Sometimes they do, at least for a while." Chloe was becoming more animated now. She plainly admired this group a great deal. "But they live totally off the grid. They leave no footprint in the industrial/information complex. No social security numbers. No taxes. No driver's licenses. They're a real deal crew, like the classic pirate crews of the 17th and 18th centuries."

"I prefer to think of us as hunter-gatherers myself," said a soft, deep voice. It was the old man, towering over where they were seated. Chloe and Paul both started to stand up, but he motioned them to stay as he sat down in the sand next to them, his back to the fire. "I've never been fond of the pirate metaphor, but I know some of us truly groove on that idea. As I see it, we're just a tribe of hunter-gatherers."

"That's because you're an old damn hippie," joked Chloe.

"True, true." He held out his hand to Paul. "My name's Winston. Welcome to our circle."

"Thanks," said Paul as he shook the rough, strong hand. "It's great. I'm having an awesome time. My name's Paul."

"I'm happy to have you both here. I enjoyed your dancing a great deal. Chloe's never introduced me to a member of her crew before. You must be very special."

This surprised Paul and his face must've shown it. "I… uh…"

"Paul's not really part of my crew," asserted Chloe. "He's more of a former client turned friend. I brought him along because I thought he might enjoy the circle and we were… in the neighborhood together."

"Ahhh, I see," he replied. "Well, it's wonderful to meet you in any event, and you're welcome to stay with us here as long as you like. Of course, we won't be here come tomorrow morning, but that doesn't mean you have to leave. It's a pretty little stretch of beach. I suggest you really take it easy and make the most of your time. It's a rare gift you've been given, this life of yours."

"Thanks," said Paul. What an odd thing to say, he thought. The whole situation was odd, of course, but there was something in particular about Winston that he couldn't quite put his finger on. The way he talked, it was like he was always saying two things at once, maybe more, and Paul wasn't quite getting the full meaning of any of them.

"Winston, will you take a walk with me?" asked Chloe as she stood up.

"Of course, sweetie. It would be a pleasure." He nodded to Paul. "It was nice meeting you, Paul. Enjoy the circle. Make it your home for the night."

"We'll be back in a bit," Chloe told him. "Will you be OK here?"

"Sure," said Paul, "I'll be fine."

Winston put his arm around Chloe's bare shoulder and they walked off into the fog. As they did, the older man leaned over and whispered something in her ear and then kissed her on the cheek, eliciting what Paul jealously thought of as a girlish giggle from her. But odds were that they were discussing some sort of crew-related business. Maybe she was pitching him an idea for a score or something like that. Still, he couldn't help but feel a twinge of envy, both for the secrets they were sharing and their obvious closeness.

As he watched the two of them disappear into the fog, several of the drummers came over and sat beside him, complimenting him on his dancing. They passed joints and bottles of homemade beer and unlabeled wine around the fire and talked about different kinds of drums, different styles of dance, music, movies, and even comic books for a while. None of them ever asked him his name or anything about his background. Even when he brought up topics relating to his past, they politely but pointedly shied away from them. They didn't want to know anything substantive about his real identity and they certainly weren't sharing any intimate details with him. If, as Chloe said, they all lived "off the grid," then they would naturally be very protective of any details that might pin them down. He could certainly accept that. Actually, he kind of envied it, this idea of dropping out entirely and never looking back, never having to deal with all the bullshit of the modern world.

Without a watch, Paul wasn't sure how long Chloe and Winston had been gone. One of the drummers was teaching him the basics of keeping a beat when suddenly he noticed her across the circle, taking a hit off someone's pipe. She caught him looking at her and winked before turning back to her conversation. Paul concentrated on his drumming; trying to master the basic strokes and keep in rhythm with the woman teaching him. After about ten more minutes he thanked her for the lesson and then returned to his blanket. He'd long ago put his shirt back on, and someone had loaned him a rugged but clean sweater to further protect him from the cold night air. The fire was starting to die down now, and although they kept it going with fresh logs from time to time, it wasn't the roaring blaze it had been when Paul first arrived.

Paul felt good, really good. In a way he even felt powerful. Thinking back on how well the comic con had gone he recalled a very different, much more controlled fire that he'd sat beside three years earlier. It was in McGarry's, a bar in downtown San Jose. Next to the bar sat a gas fireplace that more than compensated for the mild chill in the air outside. He'd been in California for a month, working with Greg to get Fear and Loading off the ground. They had the money and the idea, but they lacked a technical staff to make it reality. They needed a smart, talented lead programmer but were having trouble finding viable candidates. Frank was their final lead, and Paul knew that if he couldn't convince him to join their fledgling company, the project might never get off the ground. A skilled, experienced computer game programmer, Frank had a cushy coding job at Electronic Arts. He was at the top of his game and bored out of his mind. He wanted to strike out on his own, but had his doubts about Paul and Greg's plan.

"No offense," Frank had said, "But neither of you has ever made a computer game before. And, Paul, you've never even worked in a technology job. I think you're both underestimating how hard this is going to be."

"Well," Paul had replied, "That's why we're talking to you. You've got the experience and the technical expertise. We've got the money and the concept."

"I know Greg's got the money, and that's really the only reason I'm meeting with you. As for the idea, I have to say I'm just not sold. I don't see what makes it better than a dozen other games that are in the works right now."

At that moment Paul had thought to himself that Frank was kind of a dick. But he had kept his cool and risen to the occasion. "I think the thing you have to remember, Frank, is that *Metropolis 2.0* is a proven idea. It's one of the best selling indie comics of recent years. I've received two Eisner nominations for it. Unlike a lot of the derivative tripe that other companies are working on, this will be a game with a built in audience, based on stories and art that have already proven themselves in the marketplace."

"But that's just comic books. That's a tiny industry."

"Yes," agreed Paul, cutting Frank off, "But comics are where many of the best-selling ideas come from. It's the ultimate test lab for the imagination, because there are no limits on the form. You can tell any kind of story with comics. Anything you can dream up. And all that determines your success is how good a storyteller you are and how original your ideas are." Paul was simplifying things greatly here—in reality big names like X-Men or Superman mattered a lot more than original stories when it came to producing actual sales, but Frank didn't know that and Paul wasn't going to tell him. "The fact is, my ideas have proved themselves time and again. They were a hit there and they'll be a hit as a computer game, too. Why? Because nothing succeeds like success."

Paul had kept on in this vein for an hour, touting his own achievements and appealing to Frank's own sense of superiority as a software engineer. Paul had sensed that the programmer wanted to help found their new company more than he was letting on, but that Frank was a cautious, conservative man and he needed all his fears allayed before making such a drastic, life-changing decision. He put up a skeptical front and made it clear he needed convincing. Over the course of the evening Paul did just that. He showed the veteran programmer a cockiness and self-assurance that were compelling and even contagious—qualities that he saw reflected in Frank's own demeanor. Scribbling sketches on bar napkins and speaking with true passion, he had described in detail the world he'd created in his comics and how it would perfectly evolve into an online gaming experience. Finally he broke Frank's defenses down, and when the programmer started making his own simple suggestions about storylines or how to best implement the comic world in digital form, Paul knew that he'd won him over.

Coming away from the first fireside chat, Paul had felt a kind of high, like he could convince anyone of anything if he put his mind to it. The same feeling he'd had as he left the CRG offices a few days earlier. Greg had congratulated and complimented him and the two had laughed like children with happiness for their success. Looking back now, Paul wondered if he'd ever actually convinced Frank that he was truly capable of the great things he'd said they would accomplish. In retrospect, maybe not. But after what he and the crew had done to Frank and Greg and the others, Paul was sure he'd finally gotten the prickly programmer's attention and respect. He'd shown him just how capable and convincing he could really be. Now, the memory of the look on Frank's face in the boardroom when he and Chloe had sprung their trap warmed Paul more than the dying fire.

Eventually Chloe found her way back to him from the other side of the circle. She was still wearing just a bra and jeans and was now shivering. "Fuck, it's cold," she said.

"You'll catch your death, young lady, running around with your breasts hanging out like that," said Paul, in his best faux concerned grandmother voice. He handed her sweatshirt over to her and she quickly pulled it on.

"Oh, you know you love it," she quipped.

She sat down between his outstretched legs and he wrapped his arms around her shivering body. "Fuck, that was stupid," she said.

"What?"

"Wandering off into that fog with no shirt on. I got so riled up during the dancing I was sweating my ass off. The cold air felt good for about five minutes."

He held her tighter against him, relishing the feeling of having her in his arms. "Why didn't you come back and get some clothes?"

"Oh, I dunno. I guess I wanted to look tough for Winston. He didn't have a shirt on, either."

"Yeah, but, and I'm just guessing here, isn't he kind of crazy?"

"Hmmm, that's a good point."

"If she'd thought of it my momma would've always said, 'No one ever got anywhere trying to impress a crazy person.'"

"Your mom sounds like she would be giving good advice if she'd thought of that."

"Yes indeed. She'd be cool like that."

Across the fire, one of the drummers had materialized a guitar from somewhere out in the fog. Did they have a car out there somewhere? Where did that come from?

"Oh!" exclaimed Chloe, "Andre's going to play! He's really great, we should listen." She was still shivering from the cold.

"You're still cold," said Paul. "Maybe you should get inside your sleeping bag or something." In the background Andre started tuning his guitar.

"Good idea. Give me a hand and we can zip the two together—I don't want to give up the warming power of your body heat."

Paul liked this idea a lot. It took them a few minutes to unpack the two sleeping bags and lay them out together. Andre started playing some classical guitar tune. He was very good, thought Paul. He had an ease and smoothness to his playing that spoke of profound expertise, even over the most complicated chord changes. The pair of them wormed their way into their dual sleeping bag arrangement, Paul lying toward the outside of the circle, and Chloe snuggled up against him, closer to the fire. They lay there like spoons in a drawer, listening to Andre play and drifting slowly off to sleep.

Paul woke-up again a few hours later. There were unconscious forms in sleeping bags and under blankets all around the dying fire. Somewhere someone was snoring very loudly, and it had woken Paul up. He was cursed with being a light sleeper. Chloe was sound asleep, his arms still around her. That was great and all, except his left arm had gone numb under the weight of her head. He'd managed to develop a rather uncomfortable erection during his sleep as well, which he found vaguely embarrassing given that his lower body was currently pressed fast against Chloe's.

He tried to maneuver his arm out from under her head without waking her up, but no such luck. She stirred as he lowered her head to the sleeping bag. "Whassup?" she whispered hoarsely.

"Shhh, it's nothing," he replied. "Go back to sleep."

"Issat you snoring ?" she asked sleepily.

"No, I'm awake. That's someone else."

She laid there for a few moments while he rubbed his pained arm, trying to find a feeling that wasn't pins and needles. Then she spoke again. "Whoever it is, he's really fucking loud."

"Yep."

They laid there for a while, their bodies still pressed together. Trying to get comfortable, Chloe squirmed around a bit, moving even closer and rubbing her rear against his front. Paul felt rising embarrassment, knowing she must feel his hard on. That didn't seem to stop her moving though. If anything, her back and forth motions seemed to go on longer than was necessary to get comfortable. "What're you doing?" she asked.

"What do you mean?"

"With your arm? Is something wrong?"

"It fell asleep."

She rolled away from him briefly and turned so they were now face to face. "Let me see," she said. He held his arm toward her and she began rubbing it vigorously for a minute or so until normal sensation returned. "Does that help?"

"Definitely."

Her hands moved on up his arm to the sides of his shoulders, squeezing them. In the dim light he could barely make out her features, even from only a few inches away. Her touch wasn't doing anything to lessen his excitement. He reached over and returned the favor, gently stroking her arm and shoulder and then moving his hand down along her side to her hip and then back up.

"I like that," she said. "I like being petted."

"Me too," he replied, as her own hand motions mimicked his, mirroring every movement on him that he made on her. She shifted her bare foot forward so that it rubbed against his.

He slipped his hand under her shirt at the back, rubbing her bare skin. She did the same. He pulled her closer now, his hand roaming up and down her back beneath the sweatshirt, up past the bra strap and then back down. She closed her eyes, enjoying his touch even as her own hands broke their pattern and moved down to squeeze his ass, pulling them even closer together.

Paul took that as an unmistakable sign and the dam burst on their restraint. He kissed her gently on the lips and she responded, which was all the added impetus he needed to go for it, kissing her full force, tongue springing into action. His hand moved from back to front, grasping at one of her breasts and maneuvering it out from its bra cup. She moaned ever so quietly and then rolled over on him, straddling him beneath her and throwing off the sleeping bag. She pulled her shirt off over her head and he leaned forward greedily to suck on her one bare nipple, flicking at it with his tongue, which seemed to be just the right thing to do, given her enthusiastic moan. He fumbled with her bra clasp, and she had to help him undo it before she started pulling up his shirt as well.

They kissed with gusto as they fumbled out of the rest of their clothes, rolling back and forth on the bunched up sleeping bags and trying not to wake the others in the circle. Paul was in a near frenzy, moving up and down Chloe's body with his mouth, nipping playfully at her in between licks and kisses. He paused only once, when they were both fully nude, to wonder at his good fortune. She looked at him quizzically, wondering why he'd stopped, which was all he needed to start again. He rubbed the length of his body against her, one hand exploring fervently between her legs, the other cupping a breast as he suckled on it. Then she uttered those five, fatal words.

"Do you have a condom?"

Of course he didn't have a condom! Why would he have a condom? Who knew they'd be having sex? He hadn't bought condoms in months and months, not since he'd broken up with Jenny!

"Um, no," he said, pausing once more. "Do you?"

"No," she said. "So we have to play nice." She wrapped one hand around his penis and stroked it a few times. "But we can still have fun." She climbed atop him, her head toward his feet and slowly took him into her mouth. She moved up and down for a few moments of pure bliss before she stopped and turned back to Paul. "Hey there, buddy, can I get a little help back there? 69 takes two digits, if you take my meaning."

Looking at the opportunity that was now literally right at the tip of his nose he said, "I definitely do." And he showed her just how much he knew.

Afterward, both felt very satisfied, but also suddenly very cold. They untwisted the blankets and sleeping bags from the knots they'd worked them into and crawled back inside the covers. Paul fell asleep almost at once, a feat made simpler by the fact that the snoring had stopped. Had they woken the snorer up? Who cares, he thought, as he held Chloe's naked body against him. Nothing else out there matters right now.

Chapter 16

THEY slept through the dawn, and Paul even managed to sleep through the rest of the circle waking up and packing up their things. When he finally did open his eyes, Chloe was stirring next to him, squinting against the white light that was bouncing off the fog from every direction. Was it 8 a.m. or noon? Paul couldn't tell. He heard movement around him, people walking through the sand and talking quietly to one another. Then, out of nowhere, there stood Winston, beaming down at them.

He wore a blue windbreaker and jeans now, and had his long hair tied back in a ponytail. He was holding a thermos of coffee and two ceramic mugs.

"You cats want a cup of joe before we go?" he asked.

"Um, sure," said Paul.

"Whossat?" murmured Chloe. "Win, is that you, you old hippie fuck?" She sat up and Paul noticed that at some time during the night she'd put her sweatshirt back on. As she let cold air into their sleeping cocoon, he wished he'd done the same.

"Do you kiss your mother with that mouth?" asked Winston as he poured coffee into the mugs and handed them over.

"Nope, but your mom seems to like it."

"Always with the mom jokes," the old man said. "What is it with you? Is it some kind of Elektra Complex? Some repressed antipathy toward your own parents or a profane manifestation of your own inner need to reproduce?"

"Yeah, any one of those works. Plus you know, they're funny."

"Some would say so." He screwed the lid back on the thermos. "It's a conversation we're going to have to finish some other time. My little family here has to get a move on. Stay in one place too long and nothing good can come of it. Even a place like this."

"Well, thanks for having us, Winston. It's always great to see you. And you'll remember that thing we talked about last night?"

Winston patted the pocket of his windbreaker, where Paul saw the corner of an envelope sticking out. "All taken care of, my sweet."

Chloe stood up to give him a hug, even though she hadn't got around to putting on any pants yet. "Thanks again old man. I really appreciate it. As always."

He released her from his embrace and smiled down at her one last time. "My pleasure. As always." He turned and headed down toward the water, although Paul couldn't actually see the surf through the thick fog. "You kids have a safe drive back."

"Where's he going?" asked Paul.

"It's none of our business," she said as she started hunting through the bedding for her pants. "Fuck, it's cold."

"I mean, like, right now. Why's he walking toward the ocean?" The sudden roar of a diesel engine answered the question for him. They had a boat out there in the fog, which explained a lot.

"Didn't I tell you they were a pirate crew?" said Chloe. "They're going to their ship, silly."

"They have a ship? Does it have cannons and a jolly roger?"

"Well, by ship I mean motorboat. But you get the idea. That's how they do most of their moving around, in a little flotilla of small boats that travel up and down the West coast."

"Huh, wild."

"Speaking of which," she said, "We need to get going. Which means you should probably get dressed." Paul was enjoying watching her pull on her jeans.

"What's the rush? Can't we just sort of lie around here a bit longer, have a little fun?"

"Sorry there, kiddo, but this is a private beach and we're not, you know, the owners. We don't wanna get caught out here with our pants literally down. Trust me, I've been there." She plucked his jeans from the pile and tossed them at his head. "So cover up and move out soldier. We're on the march."

"Yes sir," he said. "Where're we going then, General?" He played along, but he was disappointed. He'd hoped that last night hadn't been just a one time drunken/sleepy thing between them, and if she'd been amorous this morning that would've been a very positive sign. Instead he was getting signals that were, at best, mixed.

"We're going home. There's work to be done."

They joked back and forth as they packed up their gear and hiked back up the cliff side to the car. Anytime Paul even approached a topic dealing with sex or what had happened last night, Chloe deftly twisted the conversation in another direction. He caught the hint fast enough and stopped trying, which seemed to put them both much more at ease. As they packed up the SUV and headed back onto the road, they fell into a relatively comfortable silence, listening to yet more ska.

"Why're we going home early?" asked Paul, a little astonished that he already sort of thought of Chloe's house as his home.

"Well, we lost our place, and I got done what I needed to get done with Winston. Plus, Bee mentioned in my e-mail yesterday morning that Raff's been up to something, and I want to be there to make sure he doesn't fuck things up."

"Don't you trust Raff? I thought he was, like, your second in command."

"Oh, I do, as much as I trust anybody. But we don't really have a 'command structure' in the crew. It's not like I'm actually the captain or anything like that. We're all equal. Raff and I tend to take the lead in things because that's what we're best at. The problem with Raff is that he doesn't always have the best judgment."

"Is that why you've never brought him to meet Winston?"

She was silent for a beat. Not long enough that anyone who didn't know her would notice, but Paul picked up on it. "What do you mean?"

"Winston, when he thought I was part of your crew last night, he said that you'd never brought anyone from your crew to meet him. I was wondering why you brought me."

"I don't really know to be honest." She didn't take her eyes of the winding highway, but she put a hand on his knee. "I guess I must trust you more than -- more than I usually trust people. Winston's special to me. He's my little secret, and the others don't know about him. I'd like it to stay that way. Can I trust you not to talk to them about this part of the trip? Not any part of the trip."

"Is this some kind of 'what happens in Vegas stays in Vegas' kind of thing?"

"Something like that." She obviously hoped it would end there, but he just kept looking at her, waiting for her to continue. Finally, she did.

"There are things about this trip that the others wouldn't really understand. I've let you in on a lot. Let you into my life a lot in general. People will already be wondering about our trip. If they knew about Winston and, you know, everything else, there'd be some jealousy. Maybe a lot of jealousy. So I need you not to mention any of this to anyone. Does that make sense?"

"None of this makes much sense at all. What do you mean you let me in on a lot? I don't know anything."

"You know more than you think you do. Or at least you've seen more." A note of frustration started to creep into her voice. "Can you just do this for me, please? Can you just keep our private affairs private? Is that so fucking much to ask?"

"No, no, of course not. It's fine. I won't tell anyone. Not that I was going to anyway. I mean, who would I tell? You're the only one in the whole group I'm close to." He struggled to find the words. "It's just… It's frustrating."

She massaged his thigh and then gave him a comforting squeeze. "I know. I know. But are you having fun?"

"Yeah, for the most part."

"Well, just concentrate on that for now. It's a fun life if you let it be that way. Look at Winston. Have you ever seen anyone who loves life more?"

"He did seem pretty happy."

"He's amazing. He's my inspiration."

"So, what's his deal then? I'm assuming he didn't get started making scenery."

"It's a secret. He doesn't like to talk about it." They drove on in silence for a minute.

"But you know, don't you? He told you."

She let out a surprised snort. "Yeah, sort of. Actually I kind of figured it out by accident. But he copped to it."

More silence, Paul just stared at her. But she wasn't going to fall for it this time. "Well come on then, tell me the story."

"I can't. You think I'd do that?"

"Yep."

She paused for just a moment. "You're right. I'll tell you. But there's only one reason—because Winston said I could. I'd never betray a secret from a friend. Never."

"He told you that you could tell me? Why me?"

"Not you specifically. When I found out, he said I could tell whomever I wanted. That it didn't matter. His old life's so far behind him now, there's no worry. No one cares about his old secrets anymore. I think that's actually as sad as I've ever seen him, when he said that to me. He said, 'Chloe, when you live this life, eventually everything you fought so hard to keep hidden becomes irrelevant. After a while, no one really cares anymore.' I still remember that like it was yesterday."

Paul didn't quite understand why that was a cause for sadness, but he wanted to hear the story. "OK, so spill. Who's Winston?"

Chloe reached over and turned the stereo off. If she was going to reveal Winston's story then she wanted undivided attention. "Of course first of all, his name's not really Winston."

"Go figure. Named himself after Churchill or something?"

"Close, Winston Smith from George Orwell's *1984*."

"Interesting choice. Do you know his real name?"

"Fuck, I barely remember my real name. And no, I don't know it. But I saw a picture of him once, from when he was young. I recognized him. That nose and those ears maybe, I don't know what it was, but I knew it was him as soon as I saw the pic."

"Where was this?"

"It was in a book I was reading, about radical groups from the '60s and '70s."

"You were looking for inspiration, I'll bet."

"Yes, as a matter of fact I was, now are you going to let me tell this story or not?"

"Sorry," he said, "Go on."

"Well, he was in the book. There were a bunch of black and whites in the center, you know how they do that—put the glossy pages in the center. This section was on the Weather Underground, and there he was, standing on the streets of Chicago in 1968 with a baseball bat in his hand, watching someone throw a brick through a window. The caption said simply, 'Two Unnamed Weathermen During the Days of Rage.' This was right before they went underground, you know."

"Kind of. The Weathermen were, like, '60s peace activists or something right? What was their deal?"

"They were a breakaway group from one of the big protest organizations in the late-'60s, the Students for a Democratic Society, or SDS. They had an argument with SDS about how to do things and so they split and started doing their own thing. Around 1970 they decided their own thing included blowing shit up. That's when they went from being the Weathermen to the Weathermen Underground. Or Weather Underground. Same difference."

This was starting to ring bells for Paul. He'd seen something on TV about them once a few years ago. "OK, I think I've heard of them. Didn't they bomb all kinds of places? They were basically terrorists right?"

"If you asked Winston, he'd say it depends on your perspective. The Weathermen never killed or even hurt anyone, even though they set off scores of bombs over a whole decade. They attacked government centers, banks and other conservative institutions. But it was all just property damage. They always gave plenty of warning. The only people ever killed were some of their own when a bomb they were working on accidentally went off in their apartment."

"But still," insisted Paul, "They set off bombs and terrorized people. They were terrorists."

"But it didn't mean the same thing then as it does now. This was way before 9/11. This was Vietnam, when the biggest terrorists in the world were us. We were the ones bombing the fuck out of civilians in Cambodia and Laos. The Weathermen felt the only way to fight back was with violence of their own—just not deadly violence."

"I can tell it worked out real well for them, huh?"

"No, of course not. I think it probably did more bad than good for their cause. But still, you have to admire their devotion and their commitment and their bravery. Many of them lived underground for years— over a decade in many cases."

"Or four decades in Winston's case," said Paul. "He was one of these guys you said?"

"He was, although he says he didn't become really involved with them until the mid-'70s. In that picture from '68 he was only 16. He'd been living in Chicago with an aunt and heard about the student rally that night and so he showed up. He eventually became a Weatherman, but he wasn't actually part of the group when that pic was taken, which is kinda weird if you think about it.

"So anyway, I don't really know anything about what he did while he was with them. I just know that he lived a life on the run, always using false names and moving from place to place. He was probably part of a cell and he probably helped in some bombings, but he would never admit to me for sure, one way or the other. All I know is, that's where he learned how to live the life, and he's never looked back once. Most of the others turned themselves in around 1980. They lucked out actually, because the FBI had broken so many laws trying to catch them that none of the cases against the Weathermen could really hold up in court. Most of those cats are out on the street today, living normal lives."

"But not Winston," said Paul. "Why does he like this crazy-ass life so much?"

"What did I ask you earlier? Are you having fun? For him, the answer to that question is always yes. He's always having fun. And he hasn't given up on his idealism either. Unlike my crew, he and his group pull scores that have a point, and I admire that. I sometimes wish we were more like them. They hit the capitalists and the polluters and the fascists where they live. Nothing flashy, nothing public, but they get their licks in and live the good life while they do it."

"What do you mean get their licks in? Do they still bomb things? What kinds of things?"

She smiled wryly. "That would be telling. And Winston didn't give me permission to spill those secrets. Not that I really know any details anyway. But no, they don't bomb things, nothing violent anymore. No blowing things up either. But as to specifics, I don't know. Just like Winston doesn't know anything about us helping you settle your score with your old boss or you helping us counterfeit comics. No good can come of telling people shit they don't need to know."

"You mentioned that you wished your crew was more like Winston's. More socially active or whatever. Why aren't you? Why not do cons with a political point instead of just stealing from people?"

"Like I said, I'd like to. I'd probably love it if I tried it. But that's just not our vibe."

"That's right, you're all about the money."

"Sort of, yeah, of course. We're about the money because the money is what keeps the crew together and happy. And the crew's my family. My peeps. I want them to be happy."

"Huh," said Paul, mulling her words over. There was something to what she was saying, but he couldn't put his finger on it, something about the difference in the vibe between Chloe's crew and Winston's. Chloe's crew felt like a fraternity or a club—people who were very close and supported one another, but who all had their own agendas. Winston's crew on the other hand, felt like a family. Like the most important thing in the world was supporting each other. That was the sense he'd gotten anyway, but he'd only spent one night with them. "So how did you meet Winston anyway?" he asked. "How did you two become so close?"

"There's a whole network of groups like ours out there, each crew operating totally independently from one another. But we do keep in touch. Winston, in fact, is the one who originally set up the network, at least here on the West Coast. Not that many people know that anymore. But we all communicate with one another through coded message boards and secret drop sites. It's good to have other contacts in the game in case you need something from an area of expertise you can't cover. We're pretty well rounded, because that's the way I like my crew to run. But others specialize. There's hacker specialists or surveillance specialists or even breaking and entering specialists, all kinds of different crews out there. More than the government would care to imagine I'm sure. When our crew was first getting started, Winston somehow found out about me and introduced my little group into the network. He's my mentor in the life."

Paul sat in silence and thought about this idea for a moment. Chloe started to say something else, but he interrupted her. "I never know when to believe you and when not to."

"Why's that?"

"Well, you're an admitted con-woman for one."

"Sure, but why do you doubt me now?"

"Because it's crazy, that's why! You're telling me you're part of some vast underground conspiracy or something. That there's this whole network of you out there living off the books and pulling scams on us normal folk."

"What's crazy is that you consider yourself normal folk," said Chloe. "Beyond that, why's the rest of it so crazy? We're a community, not a conspiracy. Like Dead Heads or the mob or biker gangs or any other specialized group in this country. It's not crazy—in fact, it's so commonplace I'm surprised you're surprised."

Paul didn't know what to say to this and so said nothing. After a moment Chloe turned the music back up and concentrated on the drive. Her story seemed to fit everything he'd seen with his own two eyes over the past couple of weeks, but it didn't fit at all into the world-view he'd developed over the past thirty years or so. He still had a lot of questions but decided it was better not to press the issue now. He rode on in silence for a few more minutes before launching a new conversational gambit aimed at lightening the mood.

"Who is this band we're listening to anyway?" he asked. "The woman singing sounds familiar but I don't know the song."

"It's me, you goofball, of course you recognize it," she said. "Me and my band. The Flying Crutchmen."

"You were in a band?"

"You've obviously never heard me sing—of course I was in a band." She looked wistfully out the window, as if remembering her glory days on the stage. "Man, I could tell you some stories about those days."

"Go ahead," said Paul, "It's a long drive."

It was over an hour later, when she couldn't stop herself from laughing during her description of the band's tour of Albania, that Paul finally realized she was bullshitting him once again. But her stories made the ride pass in fun, and they both laughed when he called her on it. And Paul definitely preferred her when she laughed.

Chapter 17

WHEN they got back to Chloe's house, there wasn't a parking space to be found—the place looked like it was full to the rafters with crew members, but there wasn't any party going on. Paul and Chloe opened the door and stepped into chaos. Bee was there in the living room, networking together several computers, connected by a thick cord to the server room. "Hey, Chloe, Paul," was all she took time to say before bending back to her work.

"Looks like I got back just in time," said Chloe, to no one in particular. She handed Paul her backpack and said to him, "Paul, could you put this away in my bedroom. Might as well unpack your own stuff in there as well; the crew seems to have co-opted your couch."

"Sure," said Paul, bristling a little at being told what to do, but happy to be making the jump up from couch to Chloe's bedroom. "What's going on?"

"Raff's little score, isn't looking too little anymore." She said to herself as much as to Paul, and stalked into the kitchen shouting, "Where's Raff?"

"He's in the garage," said Bee. Chloe swept back through the living room toward the back of the house. Paul followed her as far as the garage door, but she opened it and closed it behind her before he could get in a word or a glimpse. He went back to Chloe's room and dropped their bags. They'd tell him what was going on eventually, and right now he felt sticky and cold, and decided he should probably shower before he even sat down on Chloe's crisp, white sheets. She had her own bathroom, which was a nice luxury in this crowded house.

He stripped down and took a shower, hoping that Chloe just might decide to join him.

As it turned out, Paul didn't see Chloe again that day. By the time he came back out, she'd gone somewhere, although none of the dozen or so crew members in the house seemed to know where (or, more likely, were unwilling to tell him). Bee intercepted him as he tried to go into the garage, saying that he wasn't allowed in there right now, same for the Sever Room. He had the run of the rest of the house, but no one had time to talk to him. He made himself a turkey sandwich and watched the hustle and bustle whirl around him. From his vantage he could only see the operation's periphery and couldn't even begin to guess what it was they were doing.

Bee made a little time to sit with him while she shoveled Ramen noodles into her mouth, "How was your trip?" she asked.

"Good. It was fun for sure."

"Great."

"What's going on here?" he asked.

"Not much," she replied. "What'd you do on your trip?"

"Not much really," was all he could think to say. He got the message though. Everyone here had secrets and you had to respect those boundaries and not ask questions you know people don't want to answer. They finished their meals in silence.

"You should see a movie or something," said Bee as she rinsed out her bowl at the sink. "It's not going to be very exciting or fun around here tonight."

"Maybe," said Paul. "Do you know when Chloe's getting back?"

"Nope."

"OK, thanks" He watched her as she jumped back into the fray. She'd spotted something that one of the other crew members was doing wrong and corrected him on it, immediately becoming lost in her work once more.

Paul decided against the movie. He wasn't interested in anything that was playing. The truth was, there wasn't any movie out there that was more interesting than his own life had become since he met Chloe. He ended up lying on her bed and reading a pile of the old comics left over from the comic con. He fell asleep around 1a.m. with the lights on.

He saw Chloe the next morning, as she came into her room to grab a quick shower and change out of the clothes she was still wearing from the day before. Paul took the fact that she brought her clean jeans and shirt into the bathroom with her and locked the door as a sign that whatever had happened at the beach might not become a habit between them. He pretended to be asleep as she quietly gathered her clothes and then he slipped out into the living room while she showered.

Not much had changed in the rest of the house. With the shades drawn tight and the crowd of hackers hunched in front of their computers, Paul noticed little difference between now and eight hours ago. He scrounged up some cereal but had to settle for soymilk. A few minutes later Chloe came into the kitchen, still damp from the shower.

"Hey," she said. "Any coffee in here?"

"Not that I can see," said Paul into his cereal.

Chloe pulled a bag of coffee beans from the freezer and started measuring them out into the grinder. "You sleep OK?"

"Yeah. Did you manage to sleep at all?"

"Sadly, no. I'm running on fumes here. Well, fumes and a little pharmaceutical help. It was a busy night."

"What's going on?" asked Paul, still looking down into his bowl of soy soaked corn flakes. The high-pitched buzz of the coffee grinder filled the room in place of Chloe's refusal to answer his question.

As she waited for the coffee to brew, Chloe cleaned dishes and straightened up the kitchen, her back kept studiously to Paul as he finished his breakfast. He had known she wouldn't tell him what was going on, but that didn't mean he was happy about it. Let her deal with the awkwardness of the situation. No reason to make it easy for her. And so he waited for her answer in silence.

Chloe finally gave in and sat down next to Paul at the table with a fresh cup of coffee.

"Listen Paul, you know how this works right?" She sipped from her mug. "We're obviously up to something and only those, you know, 'in the know' get to, well, know."

"And I can't be in the know?"

"You're not a member of the crew, Paul. You haven't paid your dues. This is some serious shit, and no one really trusts you yet. Nor should they."

"What about the comic-book thing? Didn't that prove my loyalty or whatever?"

"Sort of, sure." She leaned forward and gently brushed his cheek with the back of her hand. He raised his head and looked her in the eye. "I trust you Paul. You know that. I've told you shit no one else in the Crew knows, and I trust you to keep my secrets. Our secrets. And now you have to trust me. Trust me on this one thing. You absolutely do not want any part of this bullshit we're perpetrating right now. This is a serious score, and there's no room for mistakes. It's not phony funny books. It's not the right time. After we're free and clear on this one, then, maybe, we can talk about you joining up for real." She paused to take another sip of coffee. "If that's what you really still want to do."

"Why wouldn't I?" asked Paul, his voice taking on an edge of defensiveness.

"Why would you?" she replied. It was a fair question. Why would he? Why get involved with people like this? Chloe was thinking along the same lines. "You've just made a shit load of money Paul, if you play it right and invest it well, you probably won't have to work again, or at least not for a few decades. It's a single score that any one of us would envy. Fuck, all of us already do envy it. Why fuck around with lowlifes like us?"

"I don't know," said Paul. "Maybe because this is the most fun I've ever had. Because I've got nothing else to do. Because I like you."

"I think you should take a break," said Chloe. "Spend some of that money. Have a night out on the town. Get a fancy hotel room in SF and hire a bunch of hookers. Live it up a little, my friend."

"That sounds great," he said. "Why don't you come with me? We'll live it up together."

"I can't Paul, not right now. I don't have time for you."

"I'll wait."

She took an extra long sip of coffee and was silent for a moment. "I know you will, Paul. But you can't make life decisions based on... based on that."

"Based on what?"

"Based on waiting for me."

"Oh," he said. "Yeah, you're probably right." Paul knew what she was trying to tell him. And she was right—he'd made this kind of mistake before. By any reasonable logic she was right. But of course he didn't give a fuck about logic. However, he'd learned enough in his thirty-two years not to push her away even more by pressing the issue.

Chloe seemed thankful that Paul had gotten her message without her having to resort to blunter language. She softened the blow a little with a pat on his knee. "We will have that night on the town though, Paul. Just not right now. When we've made the score. Until then, why don't you take some time for yourself? Get out and just relax a little. I'm not going to have much time for anything but work and breathing between now and then."

"Ok," he said. "Sounds like a good idea. Maybe I'll go down to Santa Cruz or something. Learn to surf."

Chloe stood up and smiled down at him. "That's a great idea! Then you can teach me." She quickly downed the rest of her coffee. "I gotta run. Have fun. And hey, there's a cell phone for you that I left by the side of the bed. Use it all you want; it's clean and paid for."

"Thanks," he said. "I appreciate it."

"No prob," she said as she walked back toward the living room. "And have some fun!"

Over the next few days, Paul tried to do just that, although it was a little harder than he'd thought it would be. The only time someone talked to him for more than a minute was when Popper gave him five to pay him his share of the comic con. The crew had finally sold the last of the counterfeit comics on eBay and had brought in over $80,000 in bids. Paul's share came to almost five grand. Coupled with the money he already he had, he could do whatever he wanted. It was the figuring out what he wanted part that he was finding so difficult.

He didn't want to go to any of his usual haunts where he might run into someone from work. He had no friends in San Jose outside of his former partners and coworkers, so that didn't leave him with a lot of social options. The comic-book store and game store were no good either—he was friendly with the staff of both and knew they'd mention him to one of the guys he'd so recently extorted money from. Better to just leave all that shit behind and start fresh.

He did spend some time on the phone with his parents, who were understandably worried about him. They'd heard from his former partner and CEO Greg about what happened—apparently Greg had been trying to get in touch with him and the only number he had left that worked was Paul's folks' place back in Florida. Paul shortened the tale considerably, saying only that he'd sold his stock to Greg and now he wanted some time alone to think about what to do next. Although they pushed him for more details, Paul's stonewalling made them give up soon enough. They were used to him not telling them much about his personal life.

Mostly he just drove around the Bay Area. He got his comics up in Berkeley and wandered around San Francisco for a few afternoons. He'd never taken the time to actually do the tourist thing—he'd been working since the day he'd moved out here. Well, working or resting. Either way, he'd only been up to the city a handful of times, even though it was less than an hour away. Like all big cities, San Francisco both fascinated and overwhelmed Paul. He loved the fact that there was so much going on, so many interesting people, but without a local to show him the ropes, he had a hard time choosing one thing to do. Although he never actually encountered any crime in SF, for some reason a fear of being mugged nested in the back of his brain and refused to leave until his car was back on the highway. It was only as he headed south on the 101 that he realized this newfound paranoia's root cause. It was perfectly natural, he thought, for someone that now lived with a bunch of criminals.

He liked Santa Cruz more—a small beach town like his own home turf, but it didn't feel quite right either. An inexplicable mix of hippies and incredibly high housing costs made the small beach/university town less than appealing as a permanent place of residence, but a fun place to visit, even if the Pacific Ocean was too cold to even think about swimming in, much less surfing without a wet suit. With freshly stolen money in his pocket and nothing else to do, he decided to follow through on his threat and get a motel room by the beach. It was certainly less frustrating than staying around Chloe's house.

He went by the Crew's HQ just long enough to get his suitcase. The operation had taken over almost the entire house. The living room had become a staging area and a storage place for spare parts and malfunctioning computers, without even an outlet left to plug the TV into. The kitchen overflowed with dirty dishes and pizza boxes—a sure sign that Chloe wasn't spending much time there. He never saw Chloe at all, and Bee seemed to be the one in charge of running the house-based portion of the operation. The only place where there was any peace and quiet was Chloe's bedroom, and he didn't feel comfortable there.

He had spent the first few nights after his talk with Chloe trying to figure out just what the hell they were up to. He didn't have much luck. The crew was very security conscious and most of the really "sensitive" stuff happened in the garage or the server room, neither of which Paul was allowed even a glimpse of. Still, they were all perfectly nice to him, if a bit closed mouthed.

Despite their best efforts however, he overhead and saw enough small details to piece together some vague notion of what they were up to. From the constant whispered references to "him" and "the guy" and "he," Paul surmised that they had one specific person as their target. Furthermore, from what he gathered, they seemed to know an awful lot about this man, whoever he was. That meant they were probably spying on him and not just looking at his credit card records and what not.

One thing that did confuse him was that sometimes it seemed that they were spying on this person and other times it sounded like they were actually working with or at least talking to him. Or maybe there were two "hims." Paul couldn't tell for sure. But there was no way of telling without some serious snooping, and he knew the crew was watching him too closely for that. Getting out of the house and down to the beach was the only option he had left before his curiosity and imagination got him into trouble.

After a few days by the chilly beach and a few nights spent in bars filled with college kids, Paul started to get restless again. He'd hit the local comics store and loaded up on comics. He'd even bought a new X-Box just so he could play games in the motel room. But once he'd watched all the movies playing at the local theaters and had drunk more bourbon than he should while listening to local bands, he was bored once more. He called the house to see what was going on and if it was safe to come home. He talked to Kurt, whom he hadn't seen since the comic-book gig. Paul asked him to tell Chloe that he called, and Kurt promised he would, as soon as he saw her again.

Two days later, just as he was thinking of driving down to Monterey for a few days (another Northern California thing he'd never done), his bag started playing the theme song from *The Greatest American Hero*.

"Believe it or not, I'm walking on air.

"I never thought I could feel so free-ee-ee.

Flying away on a wing and a prayer,

Who could it be…"

It was the cell phone Chloe had given him. He'd never used it and never heard it ring, although he kept it on and charged just in case she called. He fished the singing phone from his bag and looked at the caller ID. CALLER UNKNOWN it said. Paul pushed the talk button and put it to his ear.

"Hello?"

"Paul. How's it going?" It wasn't Chloe. It was Raff.

"I'm good, Raff. What're you up to?"

"Too much to even think about, man. Listen, can you do me a huge favor?"

"Um, sure, I guess." Paul assumed Raff was going to ask him to pick up some take-out or batteries or toilet paper, all of which he'd fetched for them before he checked into his beachfront vacation. "What do you need?"

"I need you to pick up something for me."

"I'm down in Santa Cruz right now. I can't really just swing by the house or anything."

"This is important Paul." Raff actually sounded a little anxious.

"What is it? What happened?"

Raff was silent for a long moment. "We've run into a bit of a snag. With the score." He paused again, "We really need your help or, well, we're kinda fucked. I was ready to scrap the whole thing, but Chloe said I should call you."

"Is she there? Maybe I should talk to her."

"She's busy man. All tied up in this thing. Deep in it, if you know what I mean."

"Not really. I mean, I don't really know what you mean."

Exasperated, Raff started to lose his patience. "Listen, can you help us out or not Paul?"

"Yeah, yeah, sure. Of course." Of course he'd help them—what else was he going to do? "Just tell me what you need."

"Great. Do you have a pen and paper? You're going to want to write this down so you get it exactly right." The line was silent for another moment. "There's no room for error here, Paul. No room at all."

"OK," Paul said as he pulled a pad of paper from the bedside table drawer. "I'm in."

An hour later, Paul stood in Gillespie Park, near downtown San Jose, waiting. Raff had told him to look for the man in the red tie and simply take the briefcase from him. Sounded simple enough, especially since there didn't seem to be anyone within five blocks wearing a tie, much less in the park. There were a few homeless; a few parents watching their kids play in the grass. Not a lot of business types in view. No red ties in sight.

Paul sat on a bench, staring blankly at the paper and listening to his heart thump. There was nothing to this simple job. Certainly nothing compared to the comic con job. All he was doing was picking up a briefcase. He didn't even have to talk to anyone. Raff had actually been rather insistent that he not talk to the man except to give the code phrase. Still, whatever this con was, it was big. That much was obvious from how everyone in the crew had been behaving the last few weeks.

A car pulled up beside the park, stopping in a no parking zone and disgorging a pair of middle aged men. Bingo. One of them had both a red tie and a briefcase, an oversized case, twice as thick as the typical lawyer's accessory and finished in dull steel. The men peered brazenly around the park, challenging anyone who met their gaze. Even Paul looked away when Red Tie fixed his glare on him. But he stood up and concentrated very hard on folding his paper as he moved toward the men.

Red Tie's companion, a gaunt, white-haired man in a gray suit, noticed Paul's approach and the pair stopped in their tracks, staring with open menace at him as he approached. Red Tie looked to be in his late 50s, pudgy and angry, with thinning brown hair and a wrinkled blue suit. He didn't look like he'd been getting much sleep lately.

As soon as Paul came within earshot the gaunt man called out in a deep voice. "You him?" Paul stopped walking.

"I'm here for the package. Christmas comes early this year," said Paul, wincing inside as he uttered the code phrase Raff had given him.

"Very fucking funny," replied Red Tie.

They just stared at each other, the two men waiting for Paul to say or do something else. For his part, Paul decided to just wait them out.

"Well?" asked the gaunt man. "Are we going to do this?"

"Yep," said Paul. "Give me the package. Christmas is early this year."

The two men just looked at each other. "So you said, asshole," growled Red Tie. "Now don't you have a phone number for us?"

Paul of course didn't have a phone number. What was he talking about? Thinking back to his encounter with the maids at the beach house, Paul said "Sure. You better have a good memory though. I'm only saying it once. Now give me the case, and I'll give you the number." He held out his hand expectantly. After a moment's intense thought, Red Tie stepped forward and handed him the case. "408-349-1969." It was his old work number, the first thing that came into his mind.

"A local number?" asked the gaunt guy. "You're kidding right."

Paul's heart raced. He took complete custody of the case and started to walk away. "Nope. Call it, you'll see." But the gaunt guy was way ahead of him, already pulling his cell phone out and dialing. Paul tried to hurry without looking like he was scared. His car was all the way across the park.

It wasn't thirty seconds before they started shouting and came running at him. Paul broke into a sprint, racing for his car. The gaunt man was surprisingly quick for his age and Paul wasn't. As red tie huffed and puffed along, the other guy was gaining on Paul fast.

Then a white conversion van Paul had noticed earlier roared to life in its parking place on the street. It jumped the curb and came careening onto the grass, headed right for Paul. Startled beyond comprehension he froze, holding the briefcase to his chest for either protection or comfort. His pursuer turned out to be more fight than flight oriented and a moment later he smashed into Paul's back, sending him hard to the ground right on top of the heavy case.

Before his attacker could follow up his tackle, the van's driver slammed on his breaks right in front of them, tearing up grass and dirt. The side door swung open and three men with pink bandanas wrapped around their faces jumped out and rushed the prone duo. One of them came running forward and swung his leg up like a football player making a punt. The foot connected with the gaunt man's shoulder, sending him spinning away from Paul. The kicker went down in a heap as well, having lost anything resembling balance as he executed the kick.

The other two grabbed Paul, who still gasped for the breath that had been knocked out of him when he'd been tackled. He struggled for a moment against the two of them before the taller of the masked intruders whispered harshly in his ear. "C'mon Paul! Make it look good, but don't fight too hard. Play along!" It was Raff.

Paul screamed and kicked in mock futility, even as relief flooded through him. Thank God they'd come for him. Red Tie was still running their way, shouting unintelligibly. The gaunt man may have been quick, but he hadn't planned on getting kicked, and all the fight had gone out of him. He just sat there, glowering at the three masked men and Paul as they piled into the van and raced off through the park. Paul wondered if the man could hear Raff laughing like a maniac as soon as they closed the door.

"That was just great," Paul said.

"You're right, that WAS just great," Raff agreed.

"I was, you know, being facetious," said Paul, as he awkwardly twisted in his seat in an attempt to catch a glimpse of the huge bruise he was sure the gaunt man had left on his back when he slammed him to the ground. "What the hell happened?"

"What's the problem, Paul? You were great. Awesome even. We didn't have to resort to plan B or anything."

"So this was plan A? You might have told me."

"Told you what?" asked Raff, although he'd turned most of his attention to the briefcase's combination lock.

"That they were going to ask for a phone number. I had to pull that out of my ass."

"And you did a great job!" Raff tried the lock but the combination he'd spun didn't work. He began again. "To be honest, that was their mistake, not ours. They must've misunderstood. We told them we'd call with the number after they handed over the case. They must've gotten cold feet."

"Yeah, but what about the stupid 'Christmas comes early' shit you had me say. I thought it was a code word, but they didn't have a fucking clue as to what I was talking about."

"I thought it would make you sound cool." Another attempted combination failed.

"You were wrong. I sounded like an idiot."

"Maybe it was in the delivery. If you'd put a little more Clint Eastwood into it you could've sold the line."

"I'm gonna have to say it's the writer's fault this time Raff. You gave me shit to work with, no matter how much Clint I put into it."

"OK, OK, you're the writer. You can come up with your own lines next time." The lock popped open this time. "Ha!" exclaimed Raff. "If it's not 666 or 911 it's always 321. People are so predictable it would make me sad if I weren't stealing from them!" Raff didn't open the case. Figuring out the code seemed to have satisfied him for now, and he placed it by his side.

"What? You're not going to open it?" asked Paul.

"Why? I know what's inside, and there's nothing I can do with it right now."

"What is in there anyway?"

"That would be telling," said Raff with a smile.

"What is this, the fucking *Prisoner*?" asked Paul. "I'm a partner in this now. I figure getting my face driven into the turf entitles me to at least know what I risked my neck for."

"That was unexpected wasn't it? I didn't think he would bring anyone with him, and even when I saw the second geezer, I never would've figured he'd chase you down like that. He was pretty spry for an old guy, huh?"

"So that wasn't part of Plan A either then? Sounds like you're flawless strategy almost crapped out on you completely."

"No battle plan survives contact with the enemy, Paul. That's something you've got to learn in this game. But hey, you brassed it out and made it work."

"And I've netted you one briefcase containing what exactly? Or does only Marcellus Wallace get to know what's inside the case?" said Paul, referencing the Ving Rhames character in *Pulp Fiction*.

"So does that make me Samuel L. Jackson or John Travolta?" asked Raff.

"You can be Travolta, Raff. You've got the hair for it."

"You sure about that Paul? If Chloe's Mia in our little *Pulp Fiction* drama, then that means I get the big dance number, not you."

"But on the plus side, you're the one that gets gunned down by Bruce Willis," replied Paul. "I like to play the long game."

Raff laughed and picked up the case, handing it over to Paul. "Go ahead, sport, take a look. No glowing orange light I'm afraid."

Paul took the case and balanced it on his lap. He popped that latches and was disappointed to see nothing inside but what looked like four smoke detectors and a Ziploc bag full of portable hard drives. He shut the case.

"Not very sexy, huh?" said Raff. "I told you there wasn't anything I could do with them right now."

"Well, what's on the damn drives then?"

"That really would be telling Paul, and we don't have time to go into it. Suffice it to say that your friend in the red tie has just fucked over his employers big time, and the stunt we pulled on your former friends pales in comparison."

"And that's all you're going to tell me?"

"That's all getting tackled earns you. At least for the moment."

They rode on in silence. Paul was angry but still excited. Raff's teasing was intended to be good-natured, and Paul really did appreciate being allowed to help on the score. He hoped that his part in today's snatch and run excitement might be his ticket back into the group. At the very least it would give Chloe something to think about next time they discussed him joining up.

Fifteen minutes later they pulled into a parking garage in Cupertino and quickly unloaded everything in the van into two rental cars. They split into two groups and headed back to Chloe's house. Mission accomplished and time to debrief.

Chapter 18

THE whole crew came together again at Chloe's house, which looked the same as when Paul had last seen it. Computers still crowded every flat surface and serpentine cables crisscrossed the floor on their way into the server room. None of the crew trusted wireless networks; they had too much experience hacking them. The crew members moved with purpose, wrapping up the final phases of the operation by wiping hard drives and otherwise covering over any digital tracks they might have left.

Raff had come in the other car, which arrived behind Paul's group. As had become the norm, no one paid much attention to him as he stepped through the door. It took the lanky leader's arrival a few minutes later to spark some excitement in the group. Raff bounded into the room, ducking through the doorway, and held the briefcase aloft with both hands, like an athlete showing off a championship trophy.

"We got it! We got the fucking bastard by the balls now!" shouted Raff. Crew members turned in astonishment and started to cheer. As they ran up to hug and congratulate Raff, Paul managed to squeeze past them toward the kitchen and thus avoid being trampled. They buzzed with questions for Raff, who seemed bound and determined to try and answer all of them at once. Apparently he'd found time to check the contents of the hard drives while he was in his own car, out of Paul's view. More members came out from other rooms to see what all the fuss was about. Paul watched from the kitchen entrance, rubbing his bruised back in discomfort.

When Chloe walked in from the back of the house she made a beeline for the crowd that had Raff at its center. As if they sensed her presence, the crew members stepped aside so she could embrace her partner in crime. Her hair was still wet, and she wore just a loose fitting tank-top and men's boxer shorts. She must have been in the shower when she'd heard Raff come in. Paul straightened up and started to move back into the room but found forward progress impossible as the throng of crew members pressed back toward him. He retreated into the kitchen and decided to wait out this burst of piratical camaraderie.

They went through much the same kind of ritual as they had after they'd helped him get his revenge on his former partners. Paul sat at the kitchen table and drank a beer he'd found in an overflowing cooler beside the refrigerator. They'd planned for a celebration tonight. He listened to Chloe as she took the group through the self-congratulatory debriefing. This time though, Raff did almost as much talking as she did, and he certainly got all the biggest laughs. The whole operation had been his idea from its inception, and Chloe was a strong enough leader to stand aside and give him his moment in the limelight. Paul thought that she sounded like a proud and indulgent mother.

Paul drank three beers in the time it took them to retell their tale of victory. The whole crew had helped out on this job, which was unusual. However, only a few of them had been intimately involved in every detail of the plan, so Chloe and Raff went through the whole thing from the beginning.

The target had been a man named Jackson Gondry, the CEO of a software development company in nearby Cupertino. A year ago, Gondry had started his own company, Advantriq, after a feud with his former partners at Bendix Software got him fired. It took Gondry less than a month to gather start-up money and hire a staff for Advantriq, leaving many industry observers speculating that he'd secretly planned to start his own firm all along. From day one, Gondry openly boasted that his new company would put Bendix out of business in less than two years. By all accounts, Gondry was well on his way to fulfilling the boast. Bendix's new software line was late shipping, while Advantriq had gotten a competing product onto the market in less than ten months—a pace unheard of in the software industry.

Everyone assumed that Gondry must have taken some of his work from Bendix and brought it with him, but there was no way of proving it. Even once the Advantriq software hit the shelves, the Bendrix analysts couldn't find any proof positive that Gondry had illegally used software code he'd developed while working for them. To hear Raff tell it, Bendix had all but given up. If their already delayed next release didn't sell well, they were going to have to lay off half their work force, maybe worse.

In all this Silicon Valley turmoil, Raff saw an opportunity. It was no secret that the new CEO of Bendix, a businessman named Oliver Fruch, hated Gondry beyond all reason. He'd famously thrown a drink in Gondry's face during an industry conference just a few months ago. Even as the rest of the crew had been working on the comics con, Raff and a select few had been digging into Fruch's life and history in every way they could. It didn't take much digging to get a read on him. Like most Silicon Valley CEO's, he lived at the office, putting in sixteen hour days as a matter of course. He had a wife and son but scarcely ever saw them except on Sundays. His only other recreation was his weekly volleyball game at a local 24 Hour Fitness. Raff decided to track him down there.

Raff had also researched Gondry of course, which was easy since the fiery programmer was never shy about talking to the media. He even maintained his own daily blog that served as his favorite forum for criticizing everyone in the world who wasn't him or one of the three or four other people in the universe he respected. Not surprisingly, Fruch came under frequent fire on the blog. Raff bragged that this fact made it almost too easy to approach Fruch one evening at the gym.

Raff explained: "I just walked up to him and said, 'Hey, you're Oliver Fruch right? You and I should talk, man.' He just kinda looked at me like, 'Who the fuck are you.' I said, 'I'm Larry Carlson, and I used to be Gondry's college roommate.' As soon as he heard that, he offered to buy me a drink right then and there. So that's what we did."

As it turned out, one of Gondry's favorite targets on his blog was his former college roommate, someone whom his readers knew only as Larry. Gondry never gave a last name, but he used the name "Larry" as a synonym for the most moronic person imaginable. He constantly wrote stories that referenced idiotic things this former roomie had done in school and even had a regular "Larry of the Week" prize that he awarded to someone in the news who's done something he judged particularly inane. Raff immediately saw potential in the roommate's infamy. He made a diligent search, trying to uncover 'Larry's' true identity but found nothing that pointed to Larry's last name or gave any indication of who he really was.

"I figured Gondry probably just made this Larry guy up," explained Raff. "He loves to lord it over people stupider than him, but hates it when he's proven wrong by one of them. What better whipping boy than someone you just make up, right? Since there was no sign of the real Larry, I stepped in and took the role for myself. I knew that Fruch had to be reading Gondry's blog. By all accounts he'd become obsessed with the man. And since the only person who Gondry gave more shit to than Fruch was this Larry guy, I figured he had to know who I was. Or who I said I was."

"Larry" and Fruch hit it off immediately. Raff had read through the whole archive of Gondry's blog and knew every Larry story backward and forward. More importantly, he had an alternate version of most of those stories wherein it was Gondry who played the fool, not Larry. Fruch ate this up, excitedly interjecting his own stories of how Gondry had mercilessly slandered him time and again. They ended their conversation hours later, with "Larry" prompting Fruch into expressing his fervent desire to wreak some sort of vengeance on the bastard who'd tormented them both. Unfortunately, they both agreed that, right now anyway, Gondry seemed untouchable. They exchanged business cards before they parted ways for the evening. The seeds had been planted.

It was while Chloe and Paul were at the beach house that Raff made the follow-up call. He waited until Gondry inevitably made yet another scorching critique of Fruch, just to make sure his new "friend" was primed and ready.

"I told him that an opportunity had presented itself to me and that if he was interested, we might actually have a chance to get that vengeance we'd been dreaming about. He perked right up at that. I said I had an old college buddy who was now working with Gondry. We'd all supposedly known each other back in college. It didn't take much to convince Fruch that my fictional friend was willing to sell Gondry out after the villain of our piece had screwed him over one too many times. Fruch couldn't wait for me to tell him more, but I refused to do so over the phone. I said I was scared and hinted I might already be having second thoughts."

As Paul listened, he recalled some of what Chloe had told him about Raff's particular style. He liked to take risks, particularly risks in the name of verisimilitude. The more nervous and hesitant and even bumbling he came off when dealing with a mark, the more they got sucked into the false reality he was pitching them. Occasionally this backfired of course—Raff would convince the target he was so nervous and bumbling that the mark lost confidence in the whole situation and pulled out. But the gamble paid off more often than not, and Chloe couldn't fault his style, even if it wasn't really her cup of tea.

When Fruch and "Larry" finally met up at a Jack in the Box near the fitness club, Raff managed to maneuver the CEO into actively convincing him to reveal his plan for retribution. They agreed on a very simple plan. Raff's mole inside Gondry's company was willing to turn over all sorts of confidential files to him, for the right price. That price was $200,000. Larry said he would put up almost half, if Fruch could come up with the rest. The crew had already analyzed Fruch's financial situation and experience, and analysis told them that Fruch could easily put his hands on a little over 100K without stretching himself too thin.

"It turned out to be the perfect amount," Raff explained. "He pretended to think about it for a minute, but as soon as I told him we wouldn't have to pay until we received the goods, he was sold. He came in for $112,000 and even promised me some stock in his company if the purloined data turned out to be as valuable as he thought it would be. I told him I'd make the call and we parted ways with smiles on our faces, although mine was supposed to be a nervous smile."

This whole scheme also followed another of the crew's rules that Chloe had explained to Paul. Never steal something that you don't already know how to sell. Raff set up the payday first and then the crew started the hard part—delivering on the goods. They'd just begun this part of the process when Chloe and Paul got back from the beach house and now Chloe took over telling the story.

"As you know," she said, "I took the news of Raff's little plan pretty well." Everyone laughed at this, which Paul figured meant that she hadn't been pleased at all. "After a little… discussion…" (followed by more laughter) "we started the hard part—actually getting the fucking data out of Gondry's company."

Chloe was the self-proclaimed bitch queen of organization. She got everyone into gear, building on the research Raff and his sub-crew had already done. She quickly decided that a frontal hack assault on Gondry's network from outside wasn't feasible. "The guy might be a prick, but he's smart and his security is top notch." The odds of them getting in and out with the data they needed without being noticed were practically nil, if indeed they could get in at all. "Besides," said Chloe with a smile in her voice, "you know me; I prefer the human touch."

And so they started working the employees for weak links. It didn't take them long to find one. Gondry liked to run his company mean and lean and put all his resources into software engineers and equipment rather than those he referred to as "useless idiots." Thus there was very little non-programming-oriented management, such as personnel directors or the like. "Just one part-time office manager who paid the bills and, joy of joys, a part time chief financial officer," explained Chloe. Gondry uses a service called CFO On The Go, which provides very competent and experienced CFOs to smaller companies that don't need a full-time financial expert. Since Gondry made most of the important decisions about money himself, the On The Go CFO only had to make sure they did all their tax and financial stuff according to the law.

"This was our guy," interjected Raff. "As soon as I saw the file on him, I knew he was our guy. Fifty-six years old. Divorced with two kids in college, just a few grand in the bank account and an underperforming IRA. Like most of these Silicon Valley money guys, he'd been burned badly in the 2000 bubble burst and he was still trying to make up the losses. We just had to find the right lever, and I knew we could tip him."

Paul listened as Chloe briefly went through the details of how they dug through every inch of the CFO's personal and financial life. Credit-card statements from the trash told them where he liked to eat and shop. Records from the video store's computer clued them into the kinds of movies he watched, and his phone records told them about everyone he talked to. They even knew his golf handicap.

"He's a pretty normal guy, all things considered. But like most of us he could use a little extra cash. But he's also a decent sort, not at all the type who's likely to steal from work just to make things easier on himself. No way this good citizen would buy into the typical win/win set-up where we both make money on the deal. Sad but true, we had to go win big/lose big for the CFO du jour."

Paul didn't know for sure what "win big/lose big" meant, but he guessed that it wasn't pleasant. He assumed that the man with the red tie he'd met earlier that day had been the CFO, and he certainly hadn't seemed happy with how things had turned out.

As Raff explained things—with helpful interjections from the other crew members who'd been involved in specific aspects of the shake-down—while Gondry had great security, the CFO did not. And he often took his work home with him and left his files wide open on his home computer. And while he didn't have anything particularly useful on his machine about Gondry, he did have more than enough private info about his clients to put his job in jeopardy if those files ever became public. And going public was exactly what Raff and company threatened him with.

From there it had been pretty straightforward. They contacted him anonymously and proved to him that they knew more about his computer's files than he did. If he played ball, the information remained private. If he didn't, he'd lose his job and maybe his whole career. All he had to do in return was copy some files from Gondry's network. The mark resisted at first, but eventually broke down. Now only one problem remained—he didn't actually have access to the parts of the network they wanted data from. Like Chloe had said, Gondry's security was tip-top.

"Which is where my team comes in," said Bee. It was the diminutive engineer's time to shine, and she sounded like a proud school kid describing her prize-winning science-fair project.

Their mole was, at best, uncooperative and unwilling to take much in the way of risks on the crew's behalf, even with his career on the line. Chloe had explained that an unwilling co-conspirator was always dangerous. You had to know just how far to push him. Too far, and the whole con is blown. They needed him to do something that didn't seem too dangerous.

"We wanted a modified camera array covering four different departments," Bee explained. "Gondry's security was tight enough that any kind of unauthorized software or key registries we put in place might be detected. However, the human security was pretty laughable. The employees are really driven, hard-working types, like me. And since they're like me, you know just what that means—they're totally oblivious to the world around them while they're working. Certainly too oblivious to notice something as boring as a new carbon monoxide detector installed above their desk."

Chloe and Bee had decided to make the CFO's job simple. All he had to do was tell Gondry that they needed new detectors for their insurance and then schedule the appointment. Then Kurt and Filo went in and installed four hidden cameras in the right offices. Each detector had a small camera inside it along with a connection to the phone lines that provided both power and a conduit for the video feed. Installation took place over the lunch hour when all but one of the offices were empty (the large group lunch being a Silicon Valley tradition that's almost as reliable as sunrise and sunset). They also picked a day they knew Gondry would be out of town, just to be safe.

"The number three camera never really gave us much," said Bee. "We placed it at the wrong angle and when the programmer sat down he was taller than expected and blocked the view. But the others worked great! We got them typing their passwords and saw how they navigated their networks and file systems, everything we needed to access the system at will."

From there it should have been pretty straightforward. The CFO had everything he needed to get whatever data they wanted. Now all they had to do was wait until he went into the office again. This was actually a risky time. Everything was in place, but nothing could be done. The CFO only went in once, maybe twice a week, and while they waited for his scheduled day, he had plenty of time to get cold feet, which, of course, he did.

They'd given him a number (a disposable cell phone) that he could call and leave messages for them at. Two nights before the big day, they left an envelope in his mailbox containing the passwords and file directories they wanted copied, along with instructions to buy a couple dozen flash drives to download the information onto. They'd followed him from a distance to make sure he bought the gear, and monitored his calls and e-mails to make sure he didn't contact the police or, worse, Gondry. He had dinner with a friend, but other than that everything seemed to go as planned.

"And we all know what happened next," said Chloe, taking the meeting over again. There was a communal groan from the crew. Paul perked up in his shadowy perch in the kitchen and opened up another beer. Maybe this would explain why Raff had suddenly called him in at the last moment.

Chloe described how the CFO had called and left a message saying the deal was off—that there was no way he was going through with this, damn the consequences. Raff and Chloe had half expected this was coming, and they were ready. They had to use the only other leverage that they had over their asset: his kids. More specifically, his oldest daughter who, judging from the man's phone calls, was a bit of a wild thing and a constant source of irritation.

Two days earlier, Raff had called the daughter in her dorm on campus at San Jose State. He told her that she'd won a contest through her cell-phone provider, which included a new free phone and a three-night trip to Hollywood. Like most college kids, she wasn't one to pass up a good time, especially if it was free, and the daughter squealed with delight. Raff Fed-Ex'ed her the phone (which already had her new number programmed in it) and the tickets—which were for that day. She and her boyfriend barely made it to the airport on time and certainly never bothered to call and tell her parents where she was going.

When the CFO tried to call things off, Raff called him back and explained that they had kidnapped his daughter and that she'd only be returned safely once he'd done as he was told. He hit the ceiling—started yelling and screaming and threatening to call the police. Raff calmly told him to call his daughter and see for himself how serious they were. When he called, instead of his daughter's usual outgoing message he heard a strange voice (disguised by a gadget Bee whipped up) warning him that she was in safe hands for now, and that she would be returned to him when his job was done. A couple more quick calls revealed that no one else seemed to know where his daughter was either, including his ex-wife. Fortunately he didn't tell her or anyone else that she was missing for fear of panicking them. He called back and said he'd play along.

Hearing Raff relate this particular bit of nastiness made Paul sit up in his chair. He'd known that they were up to something hard-core, but threatening an innocent man's daughter, even if she wasn't in any real danger, made Paul realize just how nasty they could be. A part of him wanted to just sneak out the back door and never look back. But the desire to find out how the story ended and why they'd involved him made Paul stay put and listen to Raff as he continued the tale.

The next morning, the CFO woke to a message taped to his front door—instructions on where and when to drop off the flash drives and fake carbon monoxide detectors. That only left him a few hours to copy the files and go. After he made the drop off he'd receive a telephone number to call and find out where his daughter was.

"And it looks like everything worked as planned," said Chloe. "Raff, how did your meeting with the target go? I heard he tried to pull some shit. You look OK, though. Must not have actually tried anything, otherwise I know he would've beat your skinny ass." Everyone laughed at that, including Raff. He still hadn't heard anything about why Raff had called him in. Apparently even Chloe thought Raff was supposed to make the pickup.

"Actually," said Raff, "I was afraid the guy would make me. I wanted a fresh face for the pickup. So I brought in a stringer."

"What the fuck?" said Chloe, "Why in fuck's name wasn't I told about this?"

"I'm sorry Chloe, but I didn't have time. I got a little spooked and…"

"Whatever, Raff," she interrupted, pissed off. "So who'd you get? It wasn't Leo again was it, because that fucker…"

"It was Paul."

"Paul who?"

"You know, Paul, Paul. Your Paul."

There was a long of silence, which Paul took as his cue. He wondered if Raff had planned it this way—or was it just happy circumstance that he'd waited out of sight in the kitchen for the whole debriefing? It didn't really matter now—he knew a dramatic moment to enter when he heard it. He walked into the living room and saw Chloe standing on the far side of the room, the much taller Raff right beside her. Like everyone else, she was staring right at him. He enjoyed being the center of attention again. It was a nice change from the past couple weeks, when everyone had ignored him so studiously. He especially liked the fact that he was so obviously catching Chloe totally by surprise. That was a rare treat.

"I thought I heard someone call my name," said Paul. "What's going on?" Several of the crew chuckled at that.

Chloe tore her gaze from Paul and fixed Raff in his chair, where he sat a few feet to her left. "What the fuck, Raff? What. The. Fuck?"

"I don't have…" Raff started to reply.

"You know what, Raff, just forget it for now. We'll have this conversation later. You can bet for sure that you and I will have fucking words." She glared at Raff for a long moment, her whole body tense with anger, but she was trying to act normal and keep it under control. She then turned to Paul and smiled as best she could, beckoning him over to her side. "Paul, come up here. Why don't you finish the story? Let's see here, you don't look too worse for wear." He made his way through the crowd to the front of the room. She pulled up his shirt to reveal the black and blue bruise creeping up his lower back. "Shit, that old guy hit you pretty good. What happened?"

Paul told his own tale as it had happened, starting with the phone call and ending with piling into the van with Raff and the others. He added a few little embellishments and jokes in there to lighten the mood, which the rest of the crew seemed to appreciate. Raff himself laughed the hardest at most of these. Chloe just stood next to him with her arm comfortably slung around his waist. Her touch fueled his storytelling and he dragged his brief tale out as long as he could.

When he'd finished, Chloe led the others in giving him a brief round of applause in appreciation for his good work. Then she spoke to Raff again.

"So, who the hell was this other clown who tackled Paul here? How come we didn't know about this guy?" she asked, anger creeping back into her voice.

"I don't know," said Raff, still calm and genial. "He looked familiar but I couldn't place him."

"I think I know," said Bee, raising her hand like an overachiever in school. "Is this him?" She held up her laptop with the screen pointed out so Chloe, Paul and Raff could see it. There was a pic of the man who'd tackled Paul a few hours earlier. It had been taken at night, apparently in a parking lot.

"That's him," Paul said. "Who is he?"

"He's someone the CFO had dinner with several nights ago. It's one of the few conversations he's had that we couldn't overhear. My guess is that he took the opportunity to bring him in the loop on what was going on. If I had to bet, I'd say he's some sort of private investigator or security consultant."

"Fuck," said Raff. "I'm sorry, Paul. If I'd known, I never would've called you in."

"Which is exactly why we don't fucking call people in for no goddamned reason," said Chloe, almost shouting.

"It's OK, Chloe," interjected Paul. "I'm glad I helped. It was good to finally get in on what the rest of you were doing. You know, get in on the fun."

Chloe fixed Paul with an intense look and started to say something that Paul suspected would've been quite vicious. Instead, she closed her eyes and took a deep breath, aware that the entire room was watching them. "We'll talk about this shit later. Right now let's finish things up."

Paul sat down on the floor near Chloe's feet (about the only free space left in the crowded living room) while she presided over the ritual that the crew performed every time they completed a job. Everyone handed over disks and files to Chloe and Raff and gave their word that there was no record of anything they'd done left on any computer anywhere. Bee collected any surveillance gear and other technical gewgaws that had been used during the extensive surveillance. They officially cut all ties with the CFO, and everyone swore to never have any contact with him again.

With the ritual complete, the celebration began. Raff had already been in contact with Fruch, and he'd agreed to make the payment tomorrow afternoon. Hopefully they'd double or triple their profits if Fruch agreed to pay an extra finder's fee in exchange for the very high quality data they'd managed to secure. But no one seemed too worried about that right now. They were too busy digging through the coolers for beer, breaking out bongs and popping pills.

Chloe helped Paul to his feet, saying, "Thanks, Paul. I'm really sorry Raff did that to you. It shouldn't have ever happened like that."

"Chloe, listen, it's OK…" he started to say.

"No. No it's not. We've got rules and Raff broke them." Her eyes darted across the room to where Raff stood with Kurt and Filo, laughing. "I can't have this kind of shit going on. This is the way people end up in jail."

"I wanted to help, Chloe. Don't you get that? I wanted to…"

Again she cut him off. "Not right now, OK?" she said, her voice pleading with him to just let it be for the moment. "Could you do me a favor and get us something to drink?"

Paul looked into her eyes. She was not in the mood for him right now. Maybe a drink would do her some good. Even with three beers in him already, he knew it would help him. "Sure, absolutely." He gave her a quick kiss on the lips. "I'll be right back."

He wove through the crowd back into the kitchen to get beer. As he leaned over the cooler, someone came up behind him and gave him a bear hug from behind, "Hey there, killer!" said Bee in a tone hyper even for her. "Nice work."

"Nothing to it," said Paul, as he turned around to face her. She drew back from him and revealed a small white pill in her hand. "This is for you. Take it while Chloe has a word or four with Raff. It should kick in after about half an hour"

Paul paused for a beat before taking the pill from her and popping it in his mouth. He assumed it was ecstasy, which he'd only tried a couple of other times. But he trusted Bee, and if he'd found out anything, it was that the crew always had access to high quality narcotics. Bee watched him swallow the pill and then produced one for herself. She flashed him a goofy grin and downed it. Then she skipped off into the crowd, handing out pills to everyone she came in contact with.

By the time he came back into the living room, Chloe and Raff were nowhere to be seen. He talked with Popper for a while and drank both his and Chloe's beers. Then he finished Popper's as well. As the X started to kick in and euphoria washed over him, he searched the house in vain for Chloe. He heard shouting coming from inside the garage, but the door was locked. Were she and Raff having it out in there? "Better let them be," he thought. No reason to get involved in some heavy shit like that.

Grabbing another beer from the cooler and another pill from Bee, Paul decided to wait for Chloe in her bedroom. As he lay down he thought he could still hear them shouting. But it might've been the music. It was hard to tell. And then he was asleep.

Chapter 19

WHEN he woke up the next morning, Paul's mouth tasted like he'd swallowed a pound of raw cotton. He was in a bed. Chloe's bed. He tried to recall how he'd gotten there and couldn't quite put all the pieces together. It took another moment to realize that he was still wearing all his clothes, sans shoes. That meant it was unlikely anything had happened between him and Chloe last night, which was probably for the best, since if something had happened, he would want to remember it. He heard the unmistakable sound of someone peeing from behind the bathroom door, followed by a flush and then the shower being turned on. He assumed that was Chloe.

Paul wondered once again just what the hell he was doing here. Things with Chloe weren't proceeding the way he wanted. At least not at the speed he wanted. Although, as he remembered the pills he'd taken last night, Paul realized that there was a good chance that this most recent romantic setback might have had more to do with his inability to handle his drugs rather than any lack of interest on her part. Still, he needed to take some initiative here—push things forward or get out of Dodge.

A few minutes later the shower stopped and Chloe stepped out into the bedroom. An oversized green towel was wrapped around her torso and she rubbed her short hair vigorously with a smaller white towel that had once belonged to a Holiday Inn. She noticed Paul looking at her.

"Hey there, sport. Finally awake, huh?"

"Yeah," Paul croaked, his mouth still dry. "I was really out of it, huh?"

"Fucking right, you were. Anyone ever tell you that you snore like a motherfucker?"

"I do have that reputation."

"Fortunately you respond well to a sharp elbow and the occasional shove, so I didn't lose too much sleep." She sat down on the bed next to him, tossing the small hotel towel to the floor.

"What'd Bee give me that knocked me out like that?" Paul asked as he levered himself up into a sitting position, rubbing the sleep out of his eyes and blinking to moisten his contacts.

"It was just some X. The same thing everyone else took. I dunno why it knocked you on your ass like that, although I'm guessing it was all the beer, not the drugs." She felt his forehead briefly. "You feeling OK?"

"Yeah, yeah, I'm fine. Just thirsty." He swallowed a few times, trying to work up a coating of saliva in his dry throat.

"Lemme get you a glass of water," said Chloe. She hopped up and went back into the bathroom to fill a glass from the sink. "Listen, Paul, again, I'm sorry Raff pulled you into that job like that. I chewed him a new asshole, last night, I tell you."

"I keep trying to tell you, it's OK, Chloe, really it is." The cool glass of water brought instant relief, and he sounded much more awake now. "I actually enjoyed it."

"You enjoyed getting beat down by an old guy? I knew you were a kinky little fuck."

"Well no, not that part. And to be honest I'm kinda weirded out by the whole kidnapping thing, even if it was fake. It seemed sort of needlessly cruel. But I liked playing a role. I..."

"Still," said Chloe, interrupting him. "If he wanted to get you involved, that wasn't the way. He used you, Paul. I know he thinks he was doing you a favor, and I know you're happy now because everything came out OK, but that's not the way I do things. That's not the way we run this crew. We don't use people without fully briefing them."

"What do you mean?" asked Paul. "You use people all the time. I heard that whole debriefing last night you know. You used and abused that CFO. I mean, he obviously..."

"Stop right there, Paul. I know where you're going with that. Yes, we 'used' him. Sure we fucking used him, he was a goddamned mark. Screwing around with guys like him is what we do. But you're a friend, Paul. You're my friend and I care about you, and we don't fuck with people we care about."

"I appreciate that. I really do. But I don't want to be coddled or protected anymore. I want in. I want to be part of the crew."

Chloe looked at Paul hard for a long moment then turned away in disgust. She dropped he towel to the floor, exposing her naked backside to Paul. He stared openly as she bent down and pulled on a pair of shorts that were on the floor and put on a T-shirt before turning around and facing him.

"Why, Paul? Why would you want to do this? You've already gotten your payday. A bigger payday than any individual one of us is likely to see anytime soon. Why the fuck would you want to risk all that?"

"Because I need to do something. And I've never imagined anything like you people. Anyone like you, Chloe. You're like some sort of…"

"We're not Peter Pan and the fucking Lost Boys, Paul. We're just not." She was almost yelling now. "This isn't for you. You should be drawing. You should be writing. You should be working on your next great game."

"But I thought that…"

"The answer is 'No,' Paul. I love having you here. You've become a good friend, and I'm happy that I could help you make your score. But this life, it's not for you. It's a huge, life-changing commitment to join a crew, Paul. And frankly, you're not ready to make that decision. And you're sure as hell not making it for the right reasons. So just fucking drop it, OK?" She slammed the door open as she finished and strode out toward the front of the house.

"Well, fuck," said Paul, to no one in particular.

Fifteen minutes later, Paul stepped out of the bathroom after his own quick shower and was surprised to find Raff lying on Chloe's bed, reading one of Paul's comic books. He was too tall for the bed, and his legs hung off one end. As always, he wore khakis and a polo shirt from a tech company he'd never worked for. In this case, it was Sun Systems.

"Hey, Paul," he said, "Wanna go to Hobee's, get some breakfast?"

"Um…"

"Chloe left about five minutes ago. She looked pretty pissed."

Paul thought for a moment before answering. What the hell? He needed a break from this place anyway. "Sure. Lemme just get dressed."

"Great," said Raff as he went back to reading the comic. He showed no signs of letting Paul have any privacy. Like Chloe, Paul dropped his towel after fishing some clean clothes out of his suitcase. Casual nudity seldom seemed to matter much with this crowd.

They rode to the restaurant without talking much, listening to two local politicians on KQED discuss a new bond issue that would be appearing on the ballot that fall. Neither of them gave a damn about it, but it gave Paul an excuse to try and collect his thoughts. He hadn't spent much time with Raff and wasn't sure how to act around him. Maybe this breakfast was his way of apologizing.

As they waited for the waiter, Paul finally broke the comfortable silence. "So it sounded like Chloe really laid into you last night."

"Oh yeah," said Raff. "She tore my head off, that's for sure. And she was right. Bringing you in was against the rules, but hell, we're freaking pirates, right? We're supposed to break the rules."

"So what's going to happen to you?"

"Oh, nothing. I agreed to give up some of my share as punishment, and I have to clean the bathrooms in Chloe's house for a week."

"Is that how it works when someone breaks the rules?"

"If I'd wanted, I could've had a hearing before the whole crew, and then they'd have decided together, but that would've been a real downer. I'd already kind of figured on facing some sort of punishment, so I suggested this one."

"And Chloe was cool with that?" asked Paul, intrigued to learn more about how the crew worked.

"Sure, of course. I mean, she was still mad as hell at me, but she knows a fair punishment when she hears one, and she didn't want a big group hearing anymore than I did."

"Why not?"

Raff smiled and shook his head. "They're just total buzz-killers. Everyone gets all serious and depressed and then people start yelling at each other. We've only done it twice and, well, no one wants to repeat that unless we have to."

The waiter arrived and took their orders. Paul had the breakfast scramble with home fries, as always. Raff went for pancakes. It wasn't until after they'd ordered their food that Raff revealed his true purpose. "I got into this for the money," Raff said. "I'm actually kind of unique in that way. I mean, I'm here because I wanted to make money and not have to work for anyone else."

"Aren't all of you in it for the money? That's what Chloe said."

"Sure, sure," he said, sipping his coffee. "We all want to make money from these jobs we pull, but for most of them that's only because without the money we couldn't afford all the stuff we need to pull more jobs. They do it so they can keep doing it, because it's fun. But me, I started scamming folks because it was the only way I had to make a buck when I didn't have two nickels to rub together."

"I think I got this lecture from Chloe already."

"Just hear me out for a second, OK? I got into it for the money but, you know, to be honest the money isn't all that great. Take this last job you helped us pull. I think I can work our guy for another 50K, maybe more. Let's say we bring in $160,000 total. We spent about seven grand on equipment and other expenses—and that's with having a certified mechanical genius like Bee recycle as much as possible. So that's 153K. Now, all told, the entire crew played a role in this scam. There was a lot of surveillance work, which takes a lot of man-hours. You following me so far?"

"Sure," he said. The intricacies of the financing was a topic Chloe had avoided with him, so he was surprised that Raff was talking so openly about it.

"And we always divide up every con equally between everyone in the crew. And since I brought you in at the end, you get a share, too."

"I don't need the money, don't worry about that."

"That's not the way it works. Everyone gets an equal share. Always. So in this case each person's share works out to about eight thousand, five hundred bucks."

"That's not bad."

"No, it's not bad at all, but measured against the higher costs of living under the radar and the risk of getting caught and going to jail, it's not a whole lot either."

"Why not go for more then? Why stop at $160,000?"

"Because $160,000 is a lot of money. But not so much that our banker will balk at paying it. But that's not the point. Where I come from, $8,500 tax-free is a lot of money, too. Certainly more than enough to live for three or four months."

"I guess," said Paul. "But you guys—like Bee or you hard-core hacker guys—they could be making ten times that in the private sector."

"Hell, I could sell used cars and make more money. This is my point entirely. It's the same reason you want to join our band of merry mischief makers."

Paul understood. "It's not the money. It's the life."

"Exactly," said Raff. "It's The Life. Even I stay in it for the life. All I ever wanted was an easy buck, and now it's the crew itself that keeps me coming back for more."

"I think I know what you mean. It's hard to find a…I don't know the word. Fellowship? It's hard to find this kind of camaraderie outside of a family."

"It's impossible to find. I suppose in the Army maybe, but they don't have the kind of fun we have and nowhere near the kind of freedom.

Nowhere near." Raff paused as the waiter delivered their food. "The freedom is really the key. We can do whatever we want and there's no one—no one, looking over our shoulders."

"Except the police of course."

"Yeah, yeah, and the IRS if you want to look at it that way. The FBI too, probably. But I don't think about that."

"How do you not think about something like that?"

"It's easier than you think. I haven't seen hide nor hair of a law enforcement official since I was a punk-ass skateboarder in my teens."

"From how serious Chloe handles security, it sounds like you all think about it a lot."

"Yeah, but for us it's this distant thing, like getting old or getting a heart disease or some shit like that. Sure, we take a ton of precautions, just like you'd exercise and eat right to avoid getting fat and sick. We do it because doing it lets us not worry about the future. Because we're so safe, we're effectively invisible."

"How can you be invisible and do the things you do? That guy who tackled me saw me pretty clearly."

"But did he go and call the cops afterwards? I can tell you he didn't because we still had taps on his phone and had someone following him. When we do our job right—when we take all the right precautions, the authorities never know that anything happened. We never pop up on their radar."

"And I assume the same thing is true for taxes and that kind of shit," said Paul. "You don't have jobs on the books. You don't own property under your real names. The IRS can't audit you if they don't know about you."

"Exactly," said Raff as he shoveled food into his mouth. "Now, there's two ways to live off the grid—you can move to bumfuck Montana, build a little shack in the woods and grow or kill all your own food. Or, you can get a group together and live a civilized life with all the trimmings like we have. Personally I'd rather have fast food, comic books and video games and forgo the homegrown potatoes."

"Plus the company's good," said Paul. "The people, I mean."

"Yep," said Raff with his mouth full. "You can't buy that."

"Don't I know it," agreed Paul.

"Which is why you want to be a part of the crew, but Chloe's never going to let you join. Not really. She thinks it would be a mistake for you. And if it were just about money, she'd be right. You've got all you need now, right?"

"Not everything, no."

"No," said Raff. "Not everything."

"Like you said, there's some things money can't buy."

They ate in silence for a while. Paul knew that Raff had put his finger exactly on the how he was feeling. There'd never been a moment when he'd felt entirely welcome at the very company he'd helped start. His lack of previous game experience had always argued against him with some of his partners, and he'd never really gelled with them as a team. As they hired more and more employees it had only gotten harder to maintain that group *esprit de corps*. By the time everything started to fall apart, he was scarcely on speaking terms with some of his co-workers. And prior to his "dream job" he'd worked most of his professional life in private—an artist at his drawing board working from scripts or writing his own material. What he'd felt while working with Chloe and the crew had no comparison in his life. Moreover, he'd never felt as strongly about anyone as he felt about Chloe.

"It's weird, you know?" said Paul after he'd finished his breakfast platter. "Chloe says she wants me around. Says she cares about me. But she doesn't want me in the group. She doesn't realize how hard that is. I mean, while you guys were busy on this last thing I felt like a ghost walking around the house."

"I know exactly what you mean. I saw what you were going through, but there wasn't much I could do." Raff paused and looked down at his plate. He looked as if there was more he wanted to say. Paul took a guess at what it was.

"That's why you called me in, isn't it?" he said. "You didn't need me to make the pickup—but you wanted to include me in the job."

Raff didn't say anything for a long time. Paul pressed him. "Why do me a favor like that? Doesn't that go against the code of the crew or whatever? Why cross Chloe like that?"

"Listen, Paul, I think you'd be good at this. You've got a great imagination. A great imagination. And that's a vital commodity in this business. The comic-book thing you thought up was brilliant, mostly because it was so off-the-wall. Who would imagine counterfeiting comic books—especially without actually bothering to make real counterfeits! We've got great, great technical skills in the group. And I've only met one person in the world better than me at the fast-talking and that's Chloe. But we're getting stale; all our cons are kind of the same. Steal something from a computer. Blackmail someone into doing something for us. Lather, rinse, repeat. I think we need you for the very thing I've been talking about—to make this more fun."

"But Chloe doesn't agree."

"Chloe's not the captain of our pirate band, Paul. She's just the best at making us get our shit together. We don't have a leader. No gods, no masters, as the saying goes. If the rest of us want you in the crew, she'll let you in. The trick is convincing them when Chloe so obviously doesn't want it. She might not be their master, but we all respect the hell out of her opinion."

"So what're my options then? Keeping in mind that I don't want to piss Chloe off or undermine her position or anything like that. I don't want to push her away."

"It's tricky. You have to prove to the rest that you're committed. That you really want to give up everything and join this group. Not only join this group, but join this life."

"What's the distinction?"

"Well, like we talked about earlier, in order to make this lifestyle work, you have to pass without leaving any traces behind. No taxes, no credit cards or bank accounts in your own name. Nothing like that. You'll never lack for anything you need, and more often than not you'll get everything you want, because we share what we take and take whatever we need. You need to prove that you're that generous."

"I huh," said Paul, "That's a tough one."

He had just realized where Raff was going with all this. The money. Raff wanted Paul to share the money they'd extorted from his old partners. If he offered everyone a split of that big payoff, then he would be welcomed into the fold. Or would he? Would just paying the others off really buy him any respect? Would it buy Chloe's? He didn't think so. Giving up his money didn't sit well with Paul, but he decided to let Raff believe he was really considering it.

"I hear what you're saying," Paul continued. "It's something to ponder."

"Well, take your time and think about it some," said Raff. "But I wouldn't push Chloe anymore until you have an idea of how you want to proceed. Take it from someone who's known her a long time. She doesn't like the hard sell, and she's stubborn as hell. She won't change her mind once it's made up unless there's some new dynamic that wasn't there before."

"Thanks, Raff. I really will think about it. I appreciate you laying everything out for me like this; it really helps me understand how everything works with you guys."

"No problem, man, glad to help. If you're finished, we can get out of here. Maybe if you're lucky, Chloe will have calmed down by the time we get home, and you two can kiss and make up."

Chapter 20

PAUL didn't go back into the house when he and Raff returned from breakfast. Instead he went and found his own car (which one of the crew had brought back from the park for him). It was parked three streets over from the house, so Paul just had Raff drop him off there, explaining that he needed to run a few errands and think some things through. He said that he'd be back around dinnertime and that he'd talk to him then. Raff seemed very understanding and, like any member of the crew, knew better than to pry too deeply into a friend's private affairs.

He got on the highway and then made his way to 17 South, heading back toward Santa Cruz. He'd left his things in the motel room there and hadn't actually bothered to check out yet, so he figured he'd better do that before they charged him for another night's stay. He didn't want to run up unnecessary charges on the credit card Chloe had given him. It also gave him some time to think about what the fuck he was going to do next.

On the one hand, he wanted to stay with the group and with Chloe. But he knew that unless they welcomed him into their inner circle fully, staying with them wasn't a tenable option. Either he'd get too frustrated with his position or they'd become so annoyed with him that he wouldn't be welcome anymore. He could get his own place of course and try to just date Chloe like a normal person, but that didn't sound very plausible either. Chloe didn't lead the kind of lifestyle that lent itself to casual dating.

The only option left was to try and find a way to force/convince Chloe into letting him into the crew without alienating her in the process. He could take Raff's thinly veiled suggestion and try to buy his way in, but that money was his security blanket and right now it was about all he had going for him. He had no intention of splitting it up with fifteen other people, no matter how much he envied their renegade lifestyle. Besides, he doubted Chloe would respect him if he did pay the others off. Nope. Buying his way in was out of the question.

He much preferred the other option: coming up with a scam of his own that would be so brilliant that the rest of the crew couldn't resist it. Then, as Raff had explained, Chloe would have to come along. His problem was that he hadn't really liked much of what he'd heard about the last job they'd pulled. Sure, this programmer guy, Gondry, sounded like a real asshole and maybe even deserved to have his stuff stolen. But what really disturbed him was the way they'd treated the red-tie guy, the CFO. Paul understood why they chose him as their entry into the company, but the business with pretending to kidnap his daughter left a really bad taste in his mouth. The poor old guy hadn't done anything wrong, and they'd put him through a week of hell for it.

He blamed Raff for this streak of cruelty in the job. Although as a leader Chloe had claimed joint responsibility for everything that went down, he got the feeling that she never would have gone along with it if she'd been involved in the planning from day one. In a way, her cooperation in the con bolstered Paul's faith in his own strategy for getting into the crew. If she had bowed to the group will on something as potentially cruel as blackmailing the CFO, then she'd surely go along with his brilliant plan. As soon as he figured out what that plan was.

Paul thought back to Chloe's deep admiration for Winston and his crew. She'd really connected with the way the aged hippie and his cohorts pulled off jobs that had some sort of larger political meaning. He also recalled that she'd wished that her crew had more of a social conscience with its cons. Maybe if he could think of something along those lines he'd have a better chance of coming up with something he could live with but that would still impress everyone. He'd certainly have a better chance of sleeping at night if he could tell himself he was stealing for the greater good. Like Robin Hood or something. If he could come up with a target worth taking down, and maybe even divert some of the money to a worthy cause, then he would have the perfect plan. And he was pretty sure Chloe would think it was the perfect plan, too.

The motel management had never noticed Paul's absence, and he found all his stuff where he'd left it in his room. Apparently, maid service was running behind today, as it was already well after noon. He'd missed checkout by an hour and a half, but they were cool about it and didn't charge him for the extra day. This was Santa Cruz after all—hippie central—and the locally-owned businesses tended to be pretty easy going about stuff like that. After checking out, he drove downtown to Pacific Avenue to look in the shops and bookstores and hopefully find some inspiration for this grand scheme he kept telling himself he had hidden away in his brain somewhere. Not even the comic shop had anything for him (which didn't stop him from loading up with the past week's new comics). Becoming a criminal master-mind wasn't turning out to be as easy as he'd thought it would be.

He found a seat in a coffee shop called Latitude 23.5 and plopped his sketchbook down on the table. Maybe his pen would provide some inspiration, since his brain seemed to be failing him just now. He started sketching the panoply of interesting people that walked by on the side-walk. Everyone from homeless hippies to dotcom millionaires wandered up and down Pacific Avenue. Across the street, a man in a clown suit set up shop with a cart full of balloons. Paul sketched him as he started making inflated animals for passing children.

The kids seemed happy with the clown's creations, and the parents dutifully paid the man for his work. In the pages of his sketchbook how-ever, the clown was a terrifying creature, his teeth ragged and broken, with tusks like a wild boar. His wild wig had insects crawling in and out of it, and his ragged costume had ominous stains on it. He had a barrel of toxic waste at his side, which he used to fill the balloons before twist-ing them into demonic forms and hurling them at terrified children. After an hour or so, Paul looked back at his dozen or so toxic clown sketches and shut the sketchbook in anger. They were good, very good even. But they weren't a plan, and they wouldn't get him in the crew. He decided to head back to Chloe's.

Back on Highway 17, Paul tried putting his iPod on shuffle. Maybe when he heard the right piece of music, inspiration would finally strike. Highway17 is a four-lane highway that winds up and over the Santa Cruz Mountains and back down into Silicon Valley. It can be treacher-ous in fog or rain, but on a sunny day like today, between rush hours, it was kind of fun to drive. Hints of vertigo overtook him on some of the tighter turns; especially when the road dropped off precipitously to his right. A flatland Florida boy by birth, he still wasn't quite used to all this three-dimensional road stuff.

Near the halfway point, at the highway's summit, there's a brief run of nearly flat road before it starts its descent toward Los Gatos and points north. A large, late-model Ford Taurus that Paul had been oblivious to chose that moment to stop following Paul and instead run him off the road.

As always on this road, Paul was in the right-hand lane. The sedan sped up suddenly and then whipped around Paul's left before pulling back into the right-hand lane and slamming on the breaks. Paul had just enough time to notice the faded pro-Rush Limbaugh sticker (RUSH is RIGHT) on the car's bumper before he slammed on his own breaks and involuntarily spun his wheel to the right then back to the left. Both cars skidded and screeched to a halt; Paul's own vehicle showering sparks as it ground against the guardrail.

When Paul finally stopped screaming, he realized that he wasn't careening off the cliff side and therefore was going to be OK. He rethought that assessment a moment later when he saw the driver of the offending Taurus fling open his car door and come running back toward him. It was the older, gaunt man who'd tackled him yesterday.

"Oh shit!" he said. The car had stalled out, and Paul quickly restarted it. But before he could throw it in reverse, the man was at the car door that, he only now realized, was not locked. With his left arm the attacker swung the door open. With his right he grabbed Paul by the hair and yanked him out of the car.

Two years of Tae Kwon Do in college had taught Paul one thing— he didn't know how to fight worth a shit. He flailed at the surprisingly strong man, who still wore the same suit and shirt Paul had last seen him in. There were even grass stains on the left side. Somewhere in his mind Paul suspected that the man probably hadn't slept nearly as well as he had last night. But most of his brain was working right along with his mouth and screaming "FUUUUUCK!" as he got slammed hard into the side of his own car.

"Where is she, you little shitbrain? Where is she?" He didn't give Paul a chance to answer before he slammed him into the car once more. "Where's Erica?" That would have to be the CFO's daughter, he assumed.

"She's fine!" Paul tried to shout, although he found shouting difficult between the man's hand on his throat and the fact that he'd had the wind knocked out of him. "They never really kidnapped her! She's in Hollywood! On vacation!"

"What?" said the attacker, his voice a mixture of anger and confusion. "Say that again."

"They never kidnapped her!" croaked Paul. "They just sent her on a free vacation and gave her a new cell phone!"

The attacker looked, at best, confused. Still angry of course, but also confused. "Where? Where can we reach her?"

"I don't know! I was just the pickup guy."

Not happy with this answer, the attacker slammed Paul back against the car and ever so slightly tightened his grip on Paul's throat. He really was in great shape for his age, and he had to be pushing 60. For the first time in his life, Paul thought that maybe he should've stuck with that whole martial-arts thing. If he got out of this, he'd look into taking lessons. Assuming he got out of this.

"Excuse me, guys. Can you give me a hand here?" asked a female voice from far, far away. Paul thought he recognized it, but the lack of oxygen in his brain was starting to make everything seem kind of dim. "I'm so glad I found someone stopped here!" the voice continued, getting closer. "My car broke down, and I can't get any reception on my cell up here. Can you guys give me a lift?"

Didn't she see that they'd had an accident and that this guy was choking him? The attacker seemed to be asking himself the same question as he began to loosen his grip on Paul's throat. At last! He could breathe again! On the downside, the slackened grip also released a fierce coughing bout that made his throat ache even more, only this time from the inside out.

When he looked up, the woman was just a few yards away. More importantly, the woman was a black-haired, bespectacled clone of Chloe wearing an oversized green sweater. As more oxygen finally made its way to his brain, Paul realized that this was probably not a clone at all, but the actual Chloe in a wig.

"What was that," said the old man. "I didn't hear you." He was stalling for time. Suspicious.

"I need help with my car," she said, pointing to a car Paul had never seen before that was pulled over to the side of the road about fifty yards ahead. "Can you give me a lift to the next exit?" She continued walking toward them and was now just a foot away.

"Ma'am, I'm sorry, but we just had a little fender bender of our own," the man said. "We need to exchange some insurance information and what not."

"Oh my!" said Chloe. "Is everyone OK? I'm a nurse. Maybe I should check you two out to make sure there's no neck injuries or anything." She took another step forward, almost inserting herself between the man and Paul.

"No, no, we're both fine," he insisted. "Just a little shook up is all."

"Wow, he looks really hurt," she said, peering closely at the red marks around Paul's neck. She gingerly touched the side of his face with her left hand and applied just enough pressure to turn his head to one side. "Look at this here," she said as she leaned close. "That's really something."

The old man hesitated a moment and then, just to be polite, leaned forward to look. It was all Chloe needed. Unseen by either of the two men, a stun gun slipped down the sleeve of her sweater and into her right hand. In one smooth motion she activated it and jammed the two prods into the back of the old man's exposed neck, dropping him to his knees in an instant.

She grabbed Paul's wrist and pulled him behind her, racing for her car. They were in and on their way before the man could even lift his head to watch them escape. Paul looked back through the rearview mirror and saw the attacker struggle to his feet and curse as they drove out of sight.

"So," said Chloe as she maneuvered the car down the winding road toward home, "what've you been up to today?"

As his heart ever so gradually began to slow down, Paul thought back to the last sight he'd seen before the fucker had run him off the road. The goddamned "RUSH is RIGHT" sticker. Of course the bastard was a right-wing talk radio fan. He always knew the Republicans were out to get him.

"I've been looking for inspiration," Paul said. "What about you?"

"Just following you around."

"Thanks, I guess."

"No problem, sport," She said, turning up the stereo. "You know I've always got my eye on your backside."

Chapter 21

"HE must've staked out Paul's car at the park," said Chloe. "It's the only thing that makes sense."

"I guess that has to be it," agreed Raff. "Chloe, I'm really sorry I let this happen. I mean…"

"It's Paul you should be fucking apologizing to. And me. And the whole crew. What if he'd found us here, huh? What if he'd shown up at the house—we'd be well and truly fucked then wouldn't we? It would be fucking Fremont all over again."

"I know. I know! I feel just super shitty about the whole thing."

"Let's just move on to the damage control. I need you to take care of Paul's car. It's stuck on the side of 17 and has to have attracted police by now. If we're lucky it hasn't been towed yet, but I wouldn't count on it staying that way very long. Paul left his keys in the ignition, so you might have to hotwire it if our mysterious new friend took them."

From the hallway where he stood eavesdropping, Paul heard Raff open the front door. "I'm on my way."

"Fuck me," sighed Chloe after the door closed. "What a clusterfuck."

Paul moved from his hiding place and into the living room. "Am I ever going to see that car again?"

She looked up at him with a wan smile. "Sorry, but probably not. We'll turn it into some cash for you, though. And we might be able to get into the DMV records and muss things up with the registration, but if this guy was a real P.I., he probably already knows who you are."

"That can't be good."

"No, not really. On the plus side, by running you off the road and choking you he's now broken more laws than we have, so he's not likely to go to the cops. Plus Bee heard on the phone taps that the daughter has called in to her dad, so their main motivation for coming after you is gone."

"Huh," snorted Paul. "Cold comfort." He plopped down on the couch next to Chloe, who swung her legs up so that they rested on his lap. He started to idly rub her bare feet. "So here's a question for you, Chloe."

"Why was I following you?"

"It had crossed my mind."

"I was feeling bad about yelling at you this morning and I got worried that you might do something stupid."

"Stupid like what?"

"Stupid like leave."

"You were afraid I was going to just run off without saying goodbye?"

"Wouldn't be the first time. People I meet through this... this lifestyle have a habit of vanishing into the wind. Myself included."

"So maybe I'm the one who should be following you."

She chuckled. "You could try."

"Well, I met a nice private eye earlier today. Maybe he could help me out."

"You should ask him next time you two run into each other."

"Assuming he doesn't have his hand around my throat, I'll do just that."

They were both silent for an awkward moment before Chloe said, "I am really sorry about that. I jumped all over Raff for making such a blunder."

"As a wise woman once suggested, let's move on to damage control."

She smiled. "OK, well, Raff's taking care of the car and I've got some of the guys trying to track down just who the hell this fucker is. I got his license plate number before I zapped him."

"You're pretty handy with that thing by the way. He never saw it coming."

"They never do."

"But that's not the kind of damage control I'm talking about. I think we need to revisit our conversation from this morning."

"Do we have to? Every time we have this talk you run off and get beat up by some complete stranger."

"I'm serious, Chloe. If anything, this proves that I'm in this now.

Right, square in the middle of this. He knows who I am. I need you guys to help hide me."

"We'll do that, Paul. I'll take good care of you, I promise, but…"

"No, Chloe. I don't want to be your protectee, if that's even a word. I want to participate in my own defense. I want to pay my own way."

"Do you know what you're saying, Paul? It's going to take something big to win the crew over."

"I think you're the only one I'm having trouble winning over, Chloe. The rest of them seem pretty willing to accept me."

"I wouldn't be so sure about that Paul. And please, don't do anything you'll regret later."

"I've got it all figured out, Chloe," Paul said. In fact he only had the basic outline of an idea, but he'd figure it out by the time of the meeting. After all, he was a game designer and an artist. Big, cool ideas were his stock and trade. "I'd like to tell everyone at once. Can you call everybody together tonight?"

"Why?"

"You'll see."

"I don't like surprises, Paul. It's bad for business."

"You'll like this one. Trust me."

He'd thought he would be nervous, but he wasn't. The idea had gelled in his head, and the more he thought about it, the more he loved it. Paul had no problem addressing crowds, and he'd given dozens of presentations more complicated than this when they were looking for a publisher or more funding for the game. Unlike corporate money men, these people theoretically already liked him. Nothing to worry about. Just lay it out there for them and they would go for it.

Earlier, as he'd been working out the details of his grand scheme, he made a list of everything he didn't like about the plans he'd seen the crew execute. First of all, they lacked panache. There was no drama to them, no theater. And while that probably made for better crime, it didn't work for the kind of lasting impression Paul wanted to make. Like with his comics and his games, he wanted to create something new and exciting and that people would be talking about for years to come.

Second, he didn't want to do anything that hurt people—especially innocent people, like the CFO in Raff's con. There wasn't anything fun about scaring an old man and threatening his daughter, even if the threat wasn't ever real. He needed to pick choice targets, the kind of people he imagined Winston might choose if he were coming up with the plan. Annoying, hypocritical, greedy and, most importantly, gullible people who could use a little comeuppance. The bumper sticker had given him the spark of inspiration, and he'd fanned the creative flames from there. His plan was a little more baroque and involved than anything he'd seen the crew do before, but he thought they'd appreciate it once he laid it out for them.

The room wasn't quite as full as it had been the night before. Chloe had warned him that not everyone would show up just to hear him talk. Raff had finally returned from doing whatever it was he'd done with Paul's old car. He'd given Paul a thumbs up as he walked through the door and then took his customary place leaning against the wall at the back of the room.

"It looks like we've got as big a crowd as we're going to get, so let's get started," said Paul. There were ten of them there, including everyone who'd worked with him on the comic con. At least he'd earned a few fans with his first crazy scheme.

"I don't know who knows what about my situation here, but it's probably been pretty hard to miss me loitering around for the past few weeks. I've had a blast working with and hanging out with you all and, well, I'd like try to and make this a more permanent relationship." No one seemed surprised at this announcement, so he pressed on.

"I realize that this is usually an invitation-only club and, well, no one's officially invited me or anything like that. I imagine that probably has a lot to do with the fact that I don't have any actual skills or background that could be, you know, helpful." He got several polite snickers of agreement at that. "I'm certainly no hacker or anything like that."

"However, I do have something going for me, something I owe all of you for and something I think I can share with you." Several leaned forward expectantly at this. Paul wondered how many of them were hoping he was going to give them his money. "You've made me realize that I can use my imagination for more than just drawing comics and making video games. I think I've got creativity and an affinity for the unexpected that I can harness for the benefit of us all. And so I've come up with a plan I'd like to pitch you. A plan that I think can make us a lot of money."

"Here's my proposal. I pitch this nefarious scheme of mine. If you guys are up for it, and if all goes well, you let me in as an official member of your merry band." He looked out across the assembled faces and realized they expected something more from him. Without thinking he added, "And if it all goes balls up, well, I'll make up the difference out of the money you guys helped me get from my old company."

He'd almost lost them until he threw out that last line. He hadn't planned on making that offer, but he could tell that he wasn't wowing them with his little speech. The words had just kind of slipped out of his mouth. Chloe was shaking her head sadly, but at least he had everyone's undivided attention now.

"Let's hear the plan," said Raff from the back, giving Paul a conspiratorial wink of support. At least one person thought this was a good idea.

"Well, I was driving around earlier today looking for inspiration and then it literally hit me. Who are the most credulous, illogical people out there? Who'll believe any damn fool thing, no matter how ridiculous, as long as it's said with authority? Who deserves to have their money separated from their bank accounts on general principal, just for being so obnoxious?" He paused to milk the moment. "The answer's obvious—right-wing talk-radio listeners."

Chapter 22

TWO weeks later, the Annual Los Gatos Street Fair sprawled across the length and breadth of the wealthy community's largest downtown park. Located just a few miles south of San Jose, Los Gatos is just another in the sprawl of towns that carpets Silicon Valley. Unlike places like Cupertino, Milpitas, Santa Clara and Campbell, which are entirely indistinguishable from San Jose proper, Los Gatos has just enough physical and socio-economic distance to make it distinctive. Paul had once heard the town described as "Yuppie Heaven," and he'd never found any reason to disagree.

On a normal Sunday afternoon, the park would be full of people walking their pedigree dogs, sipping their designer frozen coffee drinks and ushering their spoiled toddlers about in high-tech strollers. Today was no different, except that they had the added distraction of knick-knack-filled arts and crafts tents to navigate through. At one end of the park sat a good-sized stage where a band was set up and waiting for the mayor to say something official and nice about the afternoon. The backdrop prominently featured the logos for the fair's two main corporate sponsors—Starbucks and BP. Paul wondered if the mayor would change her speech in light of what they were about to do.

The clock hit 1:45 and, as he had hoped, a sizable crowd of a hundred or so people had gathered in the general vicinity of the stage. A flunky tapped the microphone three times to make sure the sound system worked and nodded to the mayor offstage that everything was ready when she was. Standing in the crowd, Bee noticed all of this and sent the signal.

Inside the large white conversion van parked less than a block away, the signal reached Chloe. "All right troopers. On the bounce." The van's rear doors swung wide and out came five sad-faced clowns wearing bright yellow knee-high rubber boots and neon green jumpsuits with biohazard symbols sewn onto their backs. Chloe led the way, wearing a clown mask and an astonishingly large purple afro-style wig. She brandished a bullhorn in one hand and a sign proclaiming "FREE TRADE = BLOOD TRADE" in the other.

Behind her came Paul and Popper, who were wrestling with a six-foot tall papier-mâché Starbucks coffee cup that had a bent straw poking out of the top of it. The final two clowns, Filo and Kurt, unfurled a long canvas banner strung between two wooden dowels that they used as handles. As soon as they cleared the van, they lofted the banner above their heads and revealed its entire ten-foot-long message: "BEANS BREWED IN BLOOD—OIL DRILLED FROM FLESH." Paul had been very insistent that the slogans have a very visceral tone.

Chloe put the bullhorn to her mouth as she led her squad of protestors straight for the gap between the crowd and the front of the stage. Four blocks away, two other crew members were staging a boisterous "domestic dispute" that had already drawn the full attention of the nearest police officers.

"Ladies and Gentlemen!" shouted Chloe, "Boys and Girls, Children of All Ages! Welcome to the Bourgeois Festival of the Exploited!" Everyone from the mayor on down turned toward the bizarre troupe. Expressions ranged from startled puzzlement to startled anger, with little in the way of friendly smiles except from some of the kids.

"We are the Harlequins of Hegemony! The Clowns of Corporatocracy! The Jesters of Justice! We're here to bring you all the news that's fit to spew! Everything you were afraid to ask about the startling link between the black bile you pour down your throats and the black bile you pour into your gas tanks!"

The mayor, being a take-charge kind of woman, stepped up to the microphone and said, "Excuse me, you need a permit to…" Which was all anyone heard once Bee hit the switch that remotely shorted the stage's sound system. Without electronic assistance, the mayor couldn't compete with Chloe's magnified verbal screed. That's OK, thought Paul, it would all be over soon enough.

Under the cover of Chloe's shouted ravings, the team had reached the front of the crowd, all of whom were more than eager to make way for them. Fear of the unexpected intimidates large crowds of yuppies with ease. Plus, five of the crowd members were part of the crew, planted there right up front to help direct the assembled yuppie mob in the right direction.

Chloe continued, "You fuel your bodies with the fruits of wage-slave labor! You drive your SUV's with liquid drawn from the body of Mother Earth without any concern for her or even your own well-being!"

Paul and Popper raised the coffee-cup contraption onto their shoulders, the bent straw pointed directly at the crowd. Paul reached under the cup's bottom with one hand and found the pump switch.

"This festival of the damned you've all come to! This desperately contrived, false, feel-good affair is sponsored by two of the world's most despicable and hateful criminal cabals!" She gestured with her sign toward the corporate logos on the stage backdrop. The mayor was yelling for security, but no one could hear her. "This is a festival of death, oppression and, most of all, BLOOD!"

Paul hit the switch and Bee's ingenious pump mechanism sprang flawlessly into action. The straw atop the coffee cup concealed a nozzle that shot forth a jet of blood-red liquid that arced out over the crowd. Paul and Popper swiveled the coffee cup back and forth, spraying as much of the suddenly screaming and retreating yuppies as possible. Urged on by the crew members in their midst, the crowd began to retreat back toward the craft tents.

After thirty seconds, the blood reservoir was empty. Chloe was just shouting wordlessly into the bullhorn now, ululating madly to further rile up the crowd. When she saw the blood run empty, she paused for the briefest moment to turn toward her comrades. "OK, ditch and run. Now." She then started screaming again as she turned toward the van and took off at a full run.

They heaved the coffee cup forward toward the retreating crowd. With the reservoir empty, it was pretty light. No one had ever touched any piece of the contraption without wearing latex gloves, and none of the common parts used in its construction could ever be traced back to them. Even the tools used to put the pump together had been disposed of, lest some ambitious policeman someday try to compare tool marks. The long banner fell to the ground as well, and the four clowns raced off after their leader.

Behind them, the police had finally arrived on the scene, but there was too much going on for them to even make sense of what had happened here. The mayor was screeching at them from up on the stage, so naturally their first instinct was to make sure she was OK. As the two cops fought through the crowd toward the stage, Chloe and company were already piling into their van.

Across the park, perched on the porch of a nearby restaurant, a lanky diner watched the whole scene unfold through the viewfinder of his camcorder. He didn't manage to catch the van's license plate as it sped off toward the highway entrance, but that was by design. As order once again exerted itself in the park, Raff shut the camcorder off and put down $20 to cover his lunch. He wanted to make sure he got on the road before this crowd decided they'd had enough excitement for one day and headed home. He had at least one TV station to visit before the evening news.

Chapter 23

"Fuck Yeah!" hooted Paul in the back of the van as he clawed the clown wig from his head. "Whoooo!" The rest of the crew couldn't help themselves from laughing at Paul's enthusiasm. "That was awesome! I can't believe that actually worked! The blood! Did you see their reaction?"

"And let's not forget the all-important getaway," Chloe chimed in. She was watching out the van's tinted back window, alert for any sign of police pursuit. They'd gotten off the highway just a few miles down from where they got on and were now driving at a sensible, circuitous pace through the streets of Campbell, working their way toward San Jose proper, where they could ditch the van and transfer to separate vehicles.

"Right!" said Paul. "The getaway! Very important to the whole plan. Fuck! I still can't believe we pulled that off, can you? They're going to be talking about that for YEARS!"

"So, what's next, Paul?" asked Chloe. "This is your show."

"Well, first we see how good Raff's videotaping skills are," said Paul, his mind racing forward through the next steps of the plan. "I checked out the Website this morning and that all looked great. So as soon as we get Bee's pics, we can upload those to the site along with our communiqué."

"Sounds like you've got a handle on everything."

"I think so. You'll let me know if I'm screwing up too badly, I'm sure."

"No, I won't let you screw up at all." Chloe turned back and smiled at him. "You're doing great. Just keep your head, and everything will come together for you."

"Thanks. I hope so."

"It will, but first you've gotta get that fucking clown makeup off."

Paul laughed. He had forgotten all about the white face paint. Chloe had worn a mask so she could change back to normal quickly and do the driving. The other four had gone for the full-on make-up. "Really? Just when I was starting to like my new look."

"Your choice hotshot," she said as she tossed him a damp towel. "But I'll tell you one thing—no way I'm kissing that face."

Paul started to wipe his face clean, "Well, the clown look is so last season. Perhaps I should reconsider."

"Good choice," said Chloe.

Three of the four local TV stations led their early evening newscasts with the Los Gatos protest story. Raff had managed to quickly cut up his video into different bite-sized chunks so that each station could have its own "exclusive." Even with the video, it might have been a minor human-interest story or even gone unnoticed. Instead, it had been catapulted to the lead by the mass e-mail that Paul sent out to every media outlet in the Bay Area.

The anchorwoman on Channel 4 said, "Shock and dismay today in Los Gatos as radical anarchist protestors calling themselves the Global Freedom Army disrupted a community event with a grisly display. As this exclusive video shows, although they were dressed as clowns, these protestors were anything but funny."

This particular clip showed a wide shot of the five clowns standing before the crowd and then cut to a closer in shot of the giant coffee cup spraying blood over the surprised onlookers.

"Channel 4 has just received a message from the group claiming responsibility for the disruption in which they claim that they sprayed Mad Cow infected blood on the unsuspecting fair goers. Channel 4 has not been able to confirm this with local health authorities but we are urging everyone exposed to take appropriate precautions."

"Perfect!" exclaimed Paul from the couch in Chloe's living room. "They'll have the story right in a couple of hours when they find out it's just food coloring and water, but that Mad Cow meme is going to make it around the Internet and back before the real story gets out. We've got our first impression!"

"And we all know how important those are," said Raff from the easy chair. "Great job, Paul. I can't believe they bought it."

"It's local TV news. They'll show anything as long as it sounds exciting. What's the saying? If it bleeds, it leads."

They flipped to the other news channels and saw similar stories.

Everyone was leading with the Mad Cow angle, and Raff's videos were the stars of the show.

"How's our Web coverage going?" Paul called out.

From the Server room, Chloe shouted back, "Ready to go now. We're hitting all the big-time right-wing blogs as soon as the news finishes their coverage."

Paul, a longtime blog reader, had created a dozen or so personas for the crew to use as they posted on the message boards and comments sections of some of the most popular conservative Websites. They'd been using these false identities for two weeks in order to establish some bona fides with the other people who regularly visited the sites. Each persona had a different but decidedly right-wing point of view, ranging from the radically religious to the ultra-free market conservative. The crew members would post a wide range of comments that Paul had prepared about the "horrible happenings" in Los Gatos, stirring up the pot of outrage with as many different spoons as possible.

As the last of the newscasts finished its coverage, the crew sprang into action and posted the first comment. Over the next two hours, they spread the word to every conservative corner of the Web. Paul himself logged on to post one of his favorite concoctions:

So-called "radicals" (read, left-wing whackos) are at it again. They sprayed Diseased Blood over families and CHILDREN in a park in California. Diseased like their own blood but supposedly from a cow with Mad Cow sickness. Can you believe these traitors?!?!? They don't deserve to breath air in the USA much less have rights and vote (not that they're ever smart enough to do that probably). We need to do something to help stop these people and help the good people they sprayed diseased blood on.

Paul thought the awkward writing and grammatical errors more than captured the hurried phrasing of an incensed right-winger. He'd written a couple hundred of these things, including complete dialogues between different on-screen identities. Thus armed, the crew could control the direction of conversation and steer things their way.

They stayed away from chat rooms, where the dynamic flow of conversation was harder to monitor and shape. Besides, all the best debate (and flame wars) took place in the comments sections of political blogs and on a few select message boards. Within just a few hours, several of the sites had whole comment threads devoted exclusively to the outrage in Los Gatos. The crew was actually having a hard time keeping ahead of the conversation—although they'd hacked some of the sites so they could control the discourse with even more precision.

The six o'clock news repeated the same story as an hour before, although they'd inserted an extra bit affirming that authorities denied that anyone had been exposed to Mad Cow Disease and that the blood was fake. Nevertheless, in the service of sensationalism, the newscasts left enough qualifiers and doubts in their news copy that a panicky viewer might still suspect that something truly awful had happened. It would be another five hours before the local news would come out with a more forceful (and truthful) view of what had actually happened. By that time, the Internet version of the story would become an almost unstoppable force.

At 7 p.m., Paul gave the signal for the Global Freedom Army's Website to go live. Hosted out of the country and through a series of blinds that made tracing it back to them impossible, the site featured video clips taken by Bee's hidden camera along with the full text of the group's anti-corporate, anti-free-trade manifesto. The front page featured a large pic of a man in a polo shirt and Dockers getting drenched in "blood" as he stood in Los Gatos park earlier that day. Above it was the headline: "THIS IS ONLY THE BEGINNING," while below it said "WE WILL STRIKE AGAIN FOR FREEDOM!"

As soon as the site went live, the crew started linking to it on all the blogs they'd spent the last few hours prepping for this very moment. Even without their further intervention, the right-wing readers would have exploded into outrage at the site, but with Paul and company leading the way, the self-righteous calls for action reached a fevered pitch.

By 9 p.m. both Instapundit and the Drudge Report were linking to the story, as were a number of left-wing blogs like Atrios, Talking Points Memo and Daily Kos. Paul felt a twang of liberal guilt at this last development, but he knew he couldn't let his own political leanings get in the way of the greater con. Besides, ultimately it was the radical right-wingers who'd feel the pain on this one, not the Dems. So they launched the left-wing phase of the misinformation campaign. In the past two weeks, they'd also established a handful of liberal screen names for the express purpose of adding fuel to the fire. While most of the liberal commentators decried the protest as either juvenile or dangerous (or both), a few people posting offered their full support for the Global Freedom Army's action. They even got support from screen names they hadn't created themselves.

And of course, the right-wing false identities quickly noticed what the left-wing false identities were saying and posted links and quotes to them on the conservative sites. Every political junkie and sad-sack Internet monkey who didn't have anything better to do on a Sunday night was getting involved in the debate, and before too long there was more chatter than the crew could control.

At 10:45, Chloe shouted from the Server room, "We're on MSNBC!"

Paul quickly clicked on the bookmark in his browser for MSNBC. com. And there it was. A single headline link along the right hand side of the screen: "California Pranksters Cause Mad Cow Scare." Perfect. It was Sunday, a slow news night, which they were counting on to get them more attention than they deserved. He knew that lots of the Internet reporters who managed the big-time network news Websites also kept at least one eye on the political blogs. Something this outrageous and politically charged was likely to end up on the Fox News site, too, especially since Drudge had picked it up.

It was now past midnight, meaning after 3 a.m. on the East coast, and things were finally starting to die down. Paul suggested they wind things down and get some sleep. Tomorrow they'd release the full video that Bee had shot on her hidden camera (disguised as a pair of glasses), along with a threat to disrupt another public event in the next two weeks. Paul was ready for bed anyway, and besides, tomorrow he needed to be ready for what might prove their most difficult challenge—talk radio.

Chapter 24

WHEN Paul had first taken a stab at being a professional comic-book artist, he'd also worked as a pizza delivery driver for Papa John's. Since he was at his most creative at night—especially late at night, Paul had taken the lunch shift. His beat-up old '86 Volvo's stereo system ate tapes and that left him with nothing but the radio. It was during these long hot afternoons zipping around Tampa that he'd learned to appreciate the horror and spectacle that is Rush Limbaugh. He hated just about everything that came out of Rush's mouth, and the only things worse were the dittohead callers and their inane blathering. But for whatever reason, he couldn't turn it off. He couldn't stop listening. Know thine enemy, as the saying goes, or at least that's what he told himself. In truth, what really fascinated him was how easily lying and distortion came to Rush and how quick his listeners were to lick up every word of it.

As the right-wing radio revolution blossomed throughout the '90s and into the Bush II era, Paul listened right along with it. Now, thankfully, he had the left-wing Air America network to satisfy his politico-talk cravings, although their callers sometimes seemed just as high-strung and over the top as Rush's. Having logged untold hours listening to both sides, Paul considered himself a true expert on the ins and outs of conservative talk-radio. With Monday morning here, it was time to put that knowledge to the test.

He'd slept poorly the night before, tossing and turning so much that Chloe had kicked him out of the bed because he was keeping her awake.

Although they'd shared a bed ever since he returned, there hadn't been anything sexual between them since the beach. Paul got the impression that she was waiting to see how he handled himself as a leader. He felt sure that if he pulled this scam off as he'd planned, she would finally see him as an equal partner and, he hoped, lover.

Although almost everyone in the tech-savvy crew had been conversant with blogs and Internet bulletin boards, none of them had ever listened to much talk radio. They were definitely more a music kind of crowd, so Paul had to brief them pretty extensively about how your typical caller behaves. He'd created a simple persona for each of them to play and written just a couple basic script sheets for them to work off of. He wasn't too worried about them sounding the same on two different shows, because the odds were they wouldn't get on in any case—at least not on any of the national shows.

The big boys who had national syndication like Rush and Hannity and even O'Reilly had thousands of callers every hour. Getting on any of those shows would be pure luck. Unlike every other aspect of the con, this was something Paul couldn't plan for or control. While getting on the air wasn't necessary, it would be a nice boost to the overall plan. As soon as the national phone lines opened, the crew members started calling. He'd warned them to expect to be on hold for an hour or more.

Meanwhile, Paul, Chloe and Raff decided to focus in on the local call-in shows, where they figured they'd have a better chance of getting air-time—especially since they'd be posing as eye-witnesses to the actual event. Well, not really posing, since they were definitely there when it happened, but rather posing as mere innocent bystanders full of outrage at what had happened to them.

Each caller had their own Walkman and headphones tuned to their assigned station and a phone that Bee had especially prepared for the occasion. Some of the bigger shows kept logs of incoming calls, and all of them had caller ID. Simply blocking the ID signal might raise some suspicions, so instead Bee had whipped up a little device that gave a fake name and number. Each black box had the fake ID's name and number printed on it so the crew member using it wouldn't forget who he or she was supposed to be.

Chloe was the first to get through, in her case to a local call-in show called *The Sam Evers Show*. The host, a 50-something former Top 40 DJ who suddenly became conservative when he started to lose touch with the youth demographic, ran a show that the *San Jose Mercury News* had called "The right-wing equivalent of shock-jock radio." He delighted in making crude parody songs about gays in San Francisco, California's two Democratic Senators and, of course, Hillary Clinton. He rose to prominence during the California recall election as one of Arnold's biggest boosters, appearing at dozens of rallies around the Bay Area.

In many ways, Paul had Evers in mind when he'd conceived of Los Gatos as the site for his prank. He knew Evers lived in the mountains just north of the town and had hoped he might even be present. No such luck, but they did catch a break in one respect—the prank turned out to be the lead item on Evers' show. He railed against the "Unwashed Berkeley Punks" who'd "Waged War against everything good and decent in the Bay Area" with their "Godless, communist, terrorist tactics."

Chloe having gotten past the call screener, was the third caller he took.

"Jody in Campbell, you're on the air with Sam Evers," he said.

"Uh, hi Sam. Love your show," said Chloe. "Long time, first time."

"Great to have you with us, caller. I understand you witnessed this terrorist attack firsthand? Is that right?"

"It's absolutely right Sam. I was there and… and I have to tell you Sam, it was the most outrageous thing I've ever seen."

"Tell us what happened, Jody. What did these patchouli-soaked nimrods do?"

"I have to tell you Sam, I live a good, decent, Christian life. There's not a lot left for families like mine to do these days. Not many places that are safe for a family with real values. So my husband and I were really looking forward to taking our little daughter to this arts festival."

"How old's your daughter?"

"She's five, Sam. And she's just a darling, sweet girl. She's never been exposed to anything like this and, I have to tell you, last night she had nightmares like you wouldn't believe. We were up all night with her, the poor little thing."

"An innocent child, scarred, possibly for life," said Sam, his voice as serious as a funeral. "If these degenerates really cared about poor, supposedly exploited workers so much, then maybe they'd be bothered by the fact that they scared this poor little girl half to death with their evil, self-indulgent BS."

"That's right Sam. And I just wanted to call and say that, you know, someone should do something. I mean, the police say they're looking into it but I'll bet that even if they catch these guys, they won't do anything about it. I bet the ACLU will be out here with their stupid garbage and they'd be defending these people."

"These terrorists," interjected Sam.

"Right. Exactly. These terrorists. And the ACLU and the liberal judges would just let them go. Someone else needs to do something. The decent folk around here need to get together and send them a message that this kind of thing isn't OK." Chloe's voice started to become choked with false tears. "Not here, not in our America."

Knowing that it wouldn't get any better than the tear-soaked line that Chloe had just thrown him, Sam took over from there. "Thanks for your call Jody, and give your daughter a big hug from all of us here at the Sam Evers Show." Chloe was now disconnected, which was a relief, because she immediately started laughing.

Paul and Raff had both tuned into the Evers show once Chloe got on the air, and they started laughing as well.

"God, that was perfect," said Paul, taking off his headphones and giving Chloe an encouraging slap on the knee. "Pitch perfect. I could picture Jody exactly. And her poor daughter!"

Raff still had his headphones on one ear, "God this annoying fuck is still going on about the daughter," he informed them. "That was a great angle, Paul."

"The right-wingers always buy into the 'protect our children' line," explained Paul. "It's their own excuse for everything they do, so they'll take any opportunity to jump on that tired old bandwagon."

"So," said Chloe, turning to Paul. "When do we go live with the second site?"

"I'm not sure," he replied. "What do you think?"

"We've got two different factors to consider. It's the choice you have to make with almost any con. Right now the topic is hot. If anything we're getting more exposure than we figured on. So the sooner we move on to the next step, the more people we'll suck in."

"But," said Paul, "Does it strain credulity to think that someone could get a Website like that up so quickly? Will people start to suspect that something's up?"

"Exactly. That's the question. And I think, in something like this, you have to go with the momentum. I know we weren't planning to go with the site until tomorrow, but our target audience is talking about it right now. It's not going to get any bigger than this unless we push it there."

"I don't know," said Paul. "Don't you think it will come across as really convenient? This only works if people believe it's real."

"But you're on the inside, Paul. To you, all the deceptions seem too convenient and too obvious because you know they're deceptions. But no one else is looking that hard. These talking heads and Internet goons, all they want is a great story to run with. And you came up with a great story. They're going to go with it because they're going to want to believe it. They're not looking for holes in the story; they want something to get mad about. You can't over-think it. Once the game starts, you have to make decisions in the moment and not be paralyzed with over-analysis. Remember, as we always say around here, no battle plan survives contact with the enemy, so you can't over-think when real life gets ahead of your plan."

"Ahhh," said Paul. "Gotcha. OK, let's do it. Put the site up. But maybe dumb it down little—take off some of the features like the streaming video. Just the basics."

"Including the part where you donate money," Chloe reminded him.

"Of course. That's why we're here, right?"

Chapter 25

"**I**T'S a good sign when complete strangers are doing your work for you," said Chloe.

It was evening now, and they were waiting on hold for yet another local call-in show. Only three other crew members had gotten through during the day—one of them on the G. Gordan Liddy Show and one on a local NPR show out of San Francisco, while Popper actually got on the Sam Evers Show as well, saying the same kinds of things that Chloe had. Liddy had already picked up the prank story, as had Rush and Hannity. They didn't make any of the major network news broadcasts that night, or CNN. However, O'Reilly mentioned them on his Fox News show, which was quite a coup.

They'd put up the Concerned Citizens for A Moral America site shortly before noon. Over the next few hours, they'd painted the right-winger sites with links and had managed to scare up well over ten thousand hits by dinnertime. Now, as they listened on hold, another local talking head, Dr. Nancy Keller, was taking a call from someone totally unrelated to the crew. This unknown caller could've been reading from one of Paul's scripts; he hit all the right marks. Like Chloe had said, it's great when others do your work for you. The caller even gave the address for the Concerned Citizens site and the host promised to link to it from her own Website. Perfect.

Concerned Citizens for a Moral America was, of course, a total crew fabrication. The group's Website claimed that the CCMA formed itself in the wake of the "Outrageous and Immoral Assault" committed in

Lost Gatos on Sunday. Although the site had firsthand accounts and pictures from the incident, the main attraction was the reward. The site promised a cash bounty to anyone providing information that led to the unmasking and arrest of those responsible for the Mad Cow scare. It even had a form tipsters could use to e-mail their accusations directly to the Concerned Citizens volunteers, who would then supposedly pass them on to the authorities.

Most important of all, the site had a section for other concerned citizens to make donations. For every dollar donated to the reward fund, the group's founders would donate two of their own. The site started with a $10,000 initial bounty, and had already risen to $37,000, over $10,000 of which were real life generous gifts from actual concerned citizens that had been matched by phantom Crew dollars. So far, so good.

"All right, I think we've done enough for one day," said Chloe as she disconnected her phone. "We need to save something for the rest of the week."

"I'm going to stay at it a little while longer," said Paul, "At least to monitor the late-night shows. You sure you won't join me?" He was so buzzed with excitement from the con, sleep was the last thing on his mind.

She yawned and stretched. "Nah, I'm fucking beat. I have newfound respect for telemarketers though, I'll tell you that. Sitting with a phone to your ear all day sucks ass."

"Next time we do this we should get headsets," said Paul.

"Next time we should hire a call center in India."

"Great, now we're outsourcing our nation's fraud work, too? You know there are American con men here at home who need to put food on the table."

"Don't go believing your own rhetoric there, tough guy; it's the surest way to become disillusioned in this biz."

"I'll remember that. I wouldn't want to end up a bitter and crusty cynic, now would I?"

"Who're you calling crusty?"

"I'm sorry. Bitter and beautiful cynic."

"That's better," said Chloe, giving him a quick peck on the cheek. "G'night. And don't tell anyone but, you're doing a great job. Keep your chin up."

Paul paused long enough to really assess their progress today, but it seemed like everything really was coming together. He thought briefly about going back to the bedroom with Chloe now, but she was obviously tired and he was still wired on adrenaline and coffee. He'd want something more than sleep from her right now.

They'd shared nothing more intimate than a casual kiss or hug since the night on the beach. Things always seemed to work out that they were going to bed at different times or one or the other of them was passing out on the couch. Always something, and he was getting tired of it. But the high he was getting from seeing his plan come to life more than compensated for the lack of sex. Well, almost compensated. Besides, he couldn't afford the distraction right now. Everyone was both depending on him and watching him closely. Watching for any indication that he'd tripped up or let the pressure get to him. "Focus on the game," he told himself. The rest will come when it comes. No pun intended.

He turned his radio back up and dialed the phone again. Maybe he'd get through this time.

Over the next three days, the Concerned Citizens for a Moral America Website got more and more hits as news of their crusade to unmask the Mad Cow Terrorists (as the site referred to them) spread. A few times a day, Paul would compose updates with false leads and revelations about who the mysterious vandals might actually be. They encouraged the wildest speculation, inventing ties to the Green Party, the French Arts Council and, of course, right-wing punching bag Hillary Clinton.

On the flip side, the Global Freedom Army kept up its own pace and was garnering its own support from the radical left. They issued daily communiqués, promising future action and decrying corporate hegemony and "Big Coffee." Both sites hosted furious, flame-filled debates between the two sides. At first, these were purely staged events carried out by the crew, but soon the feud took on a life of its own, and the left vs. right throw-down became entirely self-sustaining.

The bounty rose to $75,000, representing just over $30,000 in real money brought in through the Website. Profits were good, and the groundwork was laid for stage three. The crew had assembled in the living room again, and this time there was a lot of interest in what Paul had to say. The buzz in the house had been good ever since the park prank, especially since the money started coming in. As always, Chloe opened the meeting.

"OK, kids, we're doing great here, as I'm sure you all know. We're still ahead of schedule and it looks like we're going to stay that way. We're moving up the big party to next week if we can swing it." This generated a hum of excitement in the room. "I'll turn things over to the Paulster and he'll give you your assignments."

"I know this is the part that worries some of you the most," said Paul. "We need to interact face to face with a large number of people here, including some government official types, so Chloe's ready to set us up with disguises and what not. But still, I don't want to ask anyone to do anything they're not confident in. I'm going to take the lead with the party planners and caterers and so forth. Raff's going to handle getting the permits. Chloe's going to head out and glad hand the local politicians and radio people. So we've got all the real big risk jobs covered."

"What's left then?" asked Kurt, always one to cut to the chase.

Paul glanced nervously at Chloe. "We talked about it and, well, we decided not to go with hired help for the catering. So…"

"You want waiters!" said Popper. "You know, most of us got into this job so we wouldn't have to wait tables." Everyone laughed at that.

"I know, I know," said Paul. "It's suck work to be sure. All I can say is, think how big the tip is going to be at the end of the night."

"We're hoping to take down a big score," Chloe said. "And things will go a lot better if we don't have a bunch of stoned college kids in penguin suits serving canapés and memorizing our faces. Guests don't pay much attention to caterers, but caterers pay a lot of attention to the people paying the bills. Plus, we need to be able to make sure we cover our withdrawal once the deed is done."

"So," said Paul. "Any volunteers?"

Everyone raised their hands, a show of support that Paul took to mean that they all believed the con was going as well as he did. "Cool," was all he said as he swelled with pride.

Chloe stepped in. "Great, you're all hired. Now, Popper honey, since you've got the waitressing experience, can you run these cats through a quick training session or two to get them up to speed. And everyone see Bee to get fitted for radio ear pieces, OK?"

"Thanks guys," said Paul. "Let's throw one hell of a party, OK?"

Chapter 26

A T FIRST Paul had wanted to get a permit to use the very same
park where they'd pulled their prank nine days earlier. But permits
turned out to be harder to get than he'd thought, and so they'd had to
use an alternate venue—The Woodbine Restaurant, which happened to
be the very place Raff had been eating when he videotaped the prank for
TV. As Paul watched the rabid-right radio and techno-conservatives of
Silicon Valley mill about the two open bars and munch on sushi and crab
cakes snatched from trays carried by roving crew members, he realized
this was a much, much better choice. For one thing they didn't have to
worry about a tent or any expensive equipment when it came time to
make their getaway. For another, it was raining outside.

The Concerned Citizens for a Moral America's inaugural fundraiser
showed every sign of being a successful event. There were already almost
a hundred and twenty people here, with more coming through the doors
all the time. They'd rented out the entire restaurant for the night and
paid for the food and the bar. The Woodbine was your typical oversized,
upscale California fusion cuisine eatery. In the days of the tech boom,
it had been full of venture capitalists and nouveau riche engineers every
night. Now they were more than happy to rent themselves out on what
would've been an otherwise slow Tuesday night. Still, they'd charged
$20,000, and it'd taken a sizable chunk out of the "reward" money they'd
raised online.

Chloe and Paul stood in the kitchen, watching through a crack in the
door as the marks listened attentively to none other than local talk-show

host Sam Evers as he harangued them with horror stories about the Los Gatos park prank. The crowd was eating up every word of it, which was no surprise since he'd been instrumental in getting many of them here tonight. The crowd was rich and credulous, just as they'd planned.

Raff stood a few feet behind them, his phone pressed to one ear, a finger jammed in the other to block out the noisy kitchen. Like Chloe, he was dressed in the black pants and vest of a caterer. Paul, wearing a brand new suit, was the face of the operation, and so far he was the only one with any public connection to organizing the fundraiser.

With his hair dyed blonde, a fake moustache glued to his upper lip, and glasses, he hoped his face wouldn't be easily recognizable. Under his suit he wore padding that added another four waist sizes and made him look forty pounds heavier than he actually was. Bee had sewn the costume herself, and he was surprised at how comfortable it was to wear. He was having a little more trouble with the shoes, which lifted his height but made his walk a little wobbly if he didn't concentrate.

Raff got off the phone and came over to them. "That was the Congressman's chief of staff. He's on his way. Should be here in twenty minutes. Maybe thirty with the rain." Getting the congressman to appear had been their greatest coup. A notoriously rightwing representative from the central valley, Representative Andy Felson was a darling of the talk radio circuit and a famously successful fundraiser. His agreeing to speak lent an air of credibility they really needed to pull this scam off, although it had cost them a $10,000 campaign donation.

Evers was finishing up on stage, ranting about liberal terrorists and the threat they posed to everything decent and good in America. He finished with his famous tag line—"Not here! Not in my America!" and the crowd went wild for him.

"OK, time to give my spiel," said Paul, straightening his tie for the umpteenth time.

"Just keep it short and sweet, and you'll do fine," said Chloe.

"Yeah, just remind them the drinks are free and they'll love you forever," Raff added.

"Right. Ok. I'm on."

Paul strode confidently out of the kitchen and toward the small stage they'd set up at the far end of the dining room where Evers was shaking hands with his fans. As he wove his way through the crowd, he passed by the silent auction tables that lined one wall. The tables had bright, glossy pictures of cruise ships, spas and the dining rooms of some of the best restaurants in San Francisco and Napa Valley. There were also photos of jewelry, watches and even a display promising personalized helicopter tours of Muir Woods. Attached to each display was a small digital screen and a credit-card reader that showed the current high bid on each of the items.

As Paul scanned the current bids, he saw that every package had at least one bid on it. And it was little wonder. Compared to the extravagant trips and gifts on display, the minimum bids were all quite reasonable. $500 for a dinner for six at the French Laundry? A steal at thrice the price! A weekend with Robert Mondavi touring his wineries? If you could put a price on such an experience, it would surely be much more than the $3,000 minimum bid. Of course the only things real about any of these packages were the signs describing them—and the credit-card machines the marks were using to make their bids.

Paul had also insisted that they set up a number of tables where people could donate directly to specially chosen charities. These were all relatively obscure, small international aid groups and labor-rights advocates that none of the guests had ever heard of. Paul correctly assumed that the party-goers would blindly give to the charities since they had the seal of approval from the right-wing group that was hosting the event. They'd never know that their cash was going to buy condoms and birth control in Africa or to support trade unions in South America. Paul himself planned to donate his share of the con to these groups—after all, he didn't need the money. This charity angle was the one area where he'd met the most resistance from some crew members, but Chloe and Raff had both backed him on it and so he'd gotten his way. She'd seemed impressed with his generosity.

Behind the tables stood Kurt and Popper, two of the more respectable looking crew members. They were carefully and patiently explaining to the attendees how to use the credit-card donation system. Chloe and Raff had both worried that people wouldn't accept this new innovation in silent auctioneering. Would people blithely swipe their cards into a strange machine? Paul was gratified to see that the answer was apparently yes. After all, this was Silicon Valley. Everyone here loves a new gadget.

Paul slowed down to listen to Popper as she gave her spiel to a would-be bidder.

"Good evening, ma'am," Popper said to a middle-age woman wearing incredibly large pearls and enough perfume for any five women in the room.

"Now I've never seen anything like this before," said the woman, as she looked the table over with a curious eye. "How does it work?"

"It's very simple, ma'am," Popper replied with a smile. "These are credit-card machines just like you see in any department or grocery store. As you can see, each one is labeled with the name of a different auction item. You just swipe your credit or debit card and then type in the amount of your bid. You then get a printed receipt showing your bid. Only the highest bid gets charged of course. All proceeds go directly to finding the liberal terrorists responsible for drawing America down into a cesspool of communism." Paul thought this last bit was kind of over the top, but the bidder seemed to like it.

"Well, how clever is that?" chimed the woman. "Isn't technology just amazing?"

"It is indeed, ma'am."

"And how much did you say these machines take?"

"You can bid whatever you want," Popper repeated, admirably hiding her frustration at having to deal with the same question for what was probably the hundredth time that night. "Just check the screen to see what the current bid is."

"Well, let's see here," the woman said, pulling her wallet from her purse and thumbing through the dozen or so credit cards inside. "Do you take AmEx?"

"Of course," Popper said. Paul moved on, happy to see that the targets were buying into this new innovation.

Paul moved on to the front of the room, where he took the stage for the third time that evening. Standing next to Evers onstage, he shook the radio personality's hand and thanked him for all his help. The talk-show host had fallen harder for their con than anyone and was more than happy to have the extra exposure appearing at the event gave him. His speech finished, he thanked Paul and made his way back to his table where his wife was waiting for him with a fresh drink.

Paul wiped the sweat from Evers' hands on his pants and then tapped on the microphone. "Um, hello again, everyone," said Paul. He tried to pitch his voice higher than normal, with the nasal tone Chloe had described as bureaucratic officiousness. The idea was to sound like someone no one wants to talk to. That way, they'll pay less attention to details about you because they'll be looking away in embarrassment or distaste. It seemed to be working, as only about a third of the guests bothered to turn toward him. "I just wanted to remind everyone that there's only an hour left before the silent auctions close. We've got some really coo... really wonderful packages for you to bid on, and I encourage everyone to check again on items they've already bid on because it's getting fierce out there." He let out a nervous laugh. A few people chuckled out of pure politeness.

"Also, Congressman Felson is on his way and should be taking the stage soon. So let's be sure to give him a warm, patriotic welcome when he arrives, OK?" Paul started clapping and the crowd showed some cursory enthusiasm by clapping along with him before returning to their drinks and bids. Paul was no Sam Evers, for which he was grateful.

As Paul turned off the microphone he looked out and saw what must've now been over two hundred people. The place was packed to capacity. If every fake item they'd put out there got just the minimum bid, they'd make $296,000, but from the looks of things, it was going to be much higher than that. Maybe two or three times that much.

He stepped off the stage and picked his way through the crowd, headed back toward the kitchen and its relative safety. The brief anxiety of being on stage had passed now and exhilaration came flooding in to replace it. He looked around the room and thought about the simple fact that everyone in the room was there because he had engineered it. He'd spun the greatest tale of his career as a storyteller, and these people were paying thousands of dollars to participate in it. It was like seeing his first comic book in print, only a hundred times more gratifying. They were all playing the rolls he'd written, and playing them perfectly.

Someone grabbed him by the back of his arm and said, "Paul, is that you?"

Startled at the sound of own name, he yanked his arm away and spun around to see a very familiar and very unwelcome face. It was Frank—lead programmer for his former company and one of the four people in the world who probably hated Paul more than everyone else he'd ever pissed off combined.

"Fuck," said Paul.

"Whatcha doing, Paul?" Frank asked.

Paul didn't have an answer.

Chapter 27

PAUL and Frank had had a complicated working relationship. In any other setting the two would not have been friendly. Actually, Paul had trouble imagining any other setting where their paths might have crossed. Frank lived for three things—writing great code, listening to really loud music and racing sailboats. Paul didn't like any of those things.

Frank was, without a doubt, a very, very smart man and an excellent programmer. He had both the eye for detail and the imagination needed to make him a real software innovator. At the same time, Frank's world view was all practical and all about getting the job done as quickly and efficiently as possible, which kept him from getting mired down in minutiae. Paul on the other hand had been the official dreamer of big dreams at the company, and the two of them often came into conflict whenever his pie-in-the-sky dreams collided with Frank's pragmatism. Both men had a habit of slowly but surely raising their voices during a discussion, and design meetings often resulted in them yelling at each other, although neither of them were really all that mad.

Up until the day Frank had proposed firing him, Paul had always thought they had a kind of mutual respect. As it turned out, while Paul respected Frank's abilities, the lead programmer had always viewed him as a flighty, unprofessional slacker. Once he had the other partners on board, he'd jumped at the chance he'd been waiting for to show Paul the door.

And now, here they were again, facing one another, and Paul realized that he had forgotten one thing about Frank. The fourth thing about Frank, besides the code, the music and the sailboats. Frank was a Republican.

"Fuck," said Paul once more, because he honestly didn't know what else to say. He was flashing back to the boardroom. To how angry Frank had been. Fuck, he thought, what was he going to do?

"Nice moustache," said Frank. "You buy that yourself?"

Paul just stared as he backed up a step toward the kitchen door.

"What's going on, man?" Frank persisted, his mouth twisted into his trademark smirk that managed to convey massive disdain with just the slightest twitch of the upper lip. "Don't you have anything to say to your old business partner?"

In fact, Paul didn't have anything to say. Somewhere in his mind he thought that maybe he could still play this off as a case of mistaken identity. Somehow convince Frank that he wasn't Paul at all. But the sheer ridiculousness of this idea kept him silent, prevented him from forming any kind of speech. His back pressed up against the kitchen door and he flinched in surprise.

"I always thought you were a liberal, Paul," said Frank. "I remember all those talks about worker's rights for our employees and what things we can and can't say in the office without offending women or gays. That doesn't sound like the kind of guy who'd be in charge of something like this." He waved a casual arm toward the room behind them. "What gives?"

Frozen. Mind blank except for visions of everything going down in flames. He retreated through the door. Frank, always one to press the advantage in an argument, followed him right in without thinking about it twice.

"What's up, Paul?" said Raff, who was looking down at the PDA in his hand, monitoring the bids. "That was great. I think…" and then he stopped and looked up as Frank walked into the kitchen. "Who's this?"

Chloe, who had been overseeing the crew members working as caterers whipped around at the sudden change in Raff's tone. As Paul shrank back toward Raff for support, he opened up a clear line of sight between Frank and Chloe, who locked eyes. Frank's gaze narrowed and recognition dawned immediately. Even with a different wig and glasses on, he recognized her.

"Well, this is some party," said Frank. "You even brought your lawyer."

Raff stepped forward and extended his hand toward Frank with a friendly smile. "Hi there. Randy Mitchell, Coalition for the American

Family. Nice to meet you. Are you enjoying the party?" Paul hoped that Frank wouldn't notice that he was dressed like a caterer.

"Sure, sure," said Frank as he smiled in return, his eyes full of mischief. "Me and Paul here go way back. Way back."

"That's great," said Raff. "We're certainly glad you could make it tonight."

"When I got the invitation in the mail, I didn't think I was going to come. This sort of thing isn't really all that interesting to me, but now I'm very glad I did."

"Well, again, thanks for coming down," said Raff. In the background Chloe was moving up toward the front where the three men stood talking. Paul, feeling slightly more confident with his friends at his side, was actually coming close to the point where he could speak again. Raff continued to try and sweet talk Frank. "Now, we've got a bunch of details we need to sort out right this moment, so if you could just give us ten minutes then I'm sure you and your old friend here can catch up later."

Ignoring Raff, Frank turned to Chloe. "I know all about you now."

"Excuse me?" said Chloe. "Have we met?"

"You're no more a lawyer than Paul here is a conservative fund raiser."

"I'm afraid you have me confused with someone else," said Chloe. "You're right, I'm not a lawyer, but I've never said I was."

"Gretchen is from the Republican National Committee," said Raff. "She flew in from Washington to help organize this event. Now please, if you'll…"

"The hair's different. The glasses," said Frank. "But it's you. I won't be forgetting you any time soon." He nodded toward Paul. "How could I forget either of you?"

Raff turned his gaze on Chloe and Paul and feigned confusion. "Gretchen, Paul, what is this gentleman talking about?"

"I have no idea," said Chloe. "I've never seen him before." She put a hand on Paul's shoulder to steady him. "You don't know him, do you Paul?"

"Yes, I…" Paul took a deep breath. "Yes."

"Of course he knows me," said Frank. "We worked together night and day for years. Well, day anyway. Paul wasn't around much at night." He laughed and then pointed an accusing finger directly at Chloe. "And you're the bitch of a lawyer. I'm sorry, fake lawyer, who helped him out the day we fired him."

"I've told you before…" Chloe started to say.

"You think I'm that stupid? You think I don't recognize you because you've got a different wig on? Jesus Christ, lady, who else could you be, standing next to him like that."

Chloe, instead of getting mad, took a bemused air. "Listen sir, I don't know what your problem is, but it's got nothing to do with me."

Before Frank could reply, Raff stepped between him and Chloe and snaked a hand up onto Frank's shoulder. A good six inches taller than Frank, Raff was looking straight down at the programmer from less than a foot away. He lowered his voice to an almost conspiratorial whisper. "Sir, I appreciate that you've got some issues to resolve with Paul here, and I'd be more than happy to let you sort them out later. But right now we've got a lot of work to do and not a lot of time to do it. This is an important event for us and, since you came out here tonight to support it, I assume it's important to you as well. I promise you, you can speak with Paul and Gretchen in just a little while, but please give us some space to finish our work, Ok?"

Frank looked up at Raff for a long moment, as if deciding whether or not to trust him. Finally he shrugged off the hand on his shoulder and took a step backward. "OK, OK, I'll leave you guys to it. You've got to get things ready for the congressman, right?"

"Exactly," said Raff. "And afterwards we can all get together and get to the bottom of this."

"Fine," said Frank. "Heck, maybe that's even better. Maybe the congressman himself would be interested to know the kind of criminals and con women he's got fundraising for him. I'm sure Sam Evers will have a lot of fun with it on the radio when he finds out." He turned and started back toward the dining room.

"Wait," said Chloe. "Come here."

Startled, Frank turned around and looked at Chloe.

"Let's settle this right now," said Chloe. "Come here."

"Why?" asked Frank, his voice less confrontational than before in the face of Chloe's commanding tone.

"So we can settle this nonsense right now. Come. Here."

Frank took a few tentative steps toward Chloe. Not knowing what to expect next, Paul backed well out of the way. He noticed Chloe's eyes dart toward Raff, who was now behind Frank. He made the slightest nod of acknowledgement.

"What?" asked Frank, "Are you going to take off your wig for me or something?"

"I'm going to settle this," Chloe was reaching into the small purse she had slung over one shoulder. "I'm going to show you my driver's license."

"OK, let's see it." Frank was now less than three feet from Chloe, whose attention was still squarely focused on digging through her purse for something.

"Here." She said as she started to pull something out of her bag. Then her eyes flicked up to Raff, and she shouted, "Now!"

Raff grabbed Frank from behind, one long arm wrapping around the unsuspecting programmer's torso, the other clamping down over his mouth. Chloe's hand whipped out of the bag with her stun gun. It crackled with electricity as she thumbed the power on and jabbed it into Frank's chest.

Frank convulsed and strained and then fell to the floor, twitching and stunned but not unconscious.

Chloe and Raff both immediately knelt beside Frank and started securing him. Raff whipped off Frank's belt and used it to bind his hands. Chloe took a kitchen rag and stuffed it in his mouth. "Come on," she hissed to the crew members still dressed as waiters. "Help us move him quick, before someone from outside comes in."

Paul watched as they secured Frank in a pantry. He was agog. His mind raced, trying to conceive of some scenario where this could possibly turn out well. He leaned against a countertop, breathing hard.

Popper came through the kitchen door. "The congressman's here," she said and then looked at Paul. "Fuck, are you OK? You're pale as a sheet."

"I'm OK," gasped Paul. "Just need a sec here."

"You need to get out there and introduce him," she said. "Like, right now."

"I'll do it," said a voice from behind him. It was Chloe.

"No, I'll be fine," protested Paul.

"Not right now you won't be," she said, walking right past him and out the door. "I'll do it."

Paul stood there and watched her go. Thirty seconds later he heard her give the speech he had written for himself, welcoming Congressman Felson and praising him for his ultra-conservative track record. He was still breathing too hard and too fast. The crowd cheered as Felson took the stage.

Raff leaned on the counter beside him and handed him a glass of water. "Here, have a drink."

Paul sipped at the water. "Thanks." They both sat there in silence for a moment, listening to the muffled sounds of the congressman's speech. He had opened up with an attack on those responsible for the prank in the park, just as they'd hoped. "Is he OK?"

"Your friend? He'll be fine. The cleaning staff will find him tied up and gagged in the closet once we're gone."

"Are we totally fucked?" asked Paul.

"Depends. Did you see if he came in with anyone? Is someone waiting for him?"

"I don't know."

"If there is, well, that'd be a problem."

"But if there's not?"

"Then we might be OK in the short term. Of course he's going to call the cops as soon as they find him."

"Fuck!" said Paul. "Fuck! Jesus Raff, I really screwed up, didn't I?"

"It's not your fault, man," said Raff. "No way you could've expected that he'd show up. No way." He patted Paul's back. "This was a great little scam you put together, man, A great plan. And you ran it well. Shit like this just happens sometimes is all. You gotta learn to roll with the punches."

"I just froze up. When I saw him. When I saw him I just froze up and didn't know what to say. I shouldn't have brought him into the kitchen. I should've taken care of it out there."

"Don't fret that shit now, Paul. Just get yourself together. We need to see this through the next hour or so and then we're home free."

"Will we get the money?"

"I don't know," said Raff. "With the cops involved. And the congressman. I don't know. We'll have to see how it all pans out."

"But honestly, Raff. We're totally fucked aren't we?"

Raff looked at him and then sighed in resignation. "Yeah. Probably."

Out in the dining room, the congressman was finishing up his speech by encouraging everyone to bid on the silent auction items and to vote for him next election. The room erupted in enthusiastic clapping. Paul and Raff sat in silence and listened as the hum of conversation rose. As agreed, the congressman would meet and greet for only five minutes before heading off to his next engagement. It ended up taking seven and a half minutes, but they heard Chloe on the mic again, thanking the congressman and announcing his departure.

Thirty-eight seconds later she came bursting through the kitchen door and grabbed Paul by the arm, hauling him toward the rear exit. "We need to leave," she snapped. Paul couldn't have agreed more.

"Where are you going?" said Raff in surprise as Paul followed Chloe toward the rear exit.

"I'm getting him out of here. Have Popper do the wrap-up. And don't forget to make sure Frank can breathe in that closet. The only thing that would make this worse is somebody dying on us. I'll call you from the road."

"Hey!" shouted Raff to their fleeing backs, "What about…"

But it was too late. They were out the door and gone.

Chapter 28

"WE'RE not going back to the house?" Paul asked as Chloe turned the car south onto the 17, heading up into the hills instead of back down into the valley. She maneuvered her way into traffic, staring straight ahead for a few long moments before answering him.

"Nope."

Paul stared at her, hoping to get some sort of reaction besides stoic calm in the face of crisis. "I'm really sorry I fucked up back there."

"It's OK," she said. "Just a bad break is all. If stealing was easy, everyone would be doing it. As the bumper stickers say, 'Shit Happens.'"

"OK."

Silence. Paul had assumed they were going to Santa Cruz and points south, but only a few miles down the road she got off the highway and headed up a winding road that climbed into the mountains. "Where are we going?"

"Boulder Creek."

"Where the hell is that?" Paul, even though he'd lived in the valley for several years now, still had a very limited geographical grasp on all the little towns and communities in the area. Generally speaking, if he couldn't get to it via a freeway exit, he didn't know where it was.

"This way," she said.

"Oh."

Not wanting to talk right at that moment, Paul shut up and just watched as they made their way up the increasingly twisted and steep road. Although he seldom got car sick, his stomach began to churn with the endless series of curves and bends. Chloe seemed to know the road well though, as she was driving at speeds Paul wouldn't have dared on these dangerous mountain roads. There was little in the way of street signs. Mostly just dirt driveways and side roads leading off toward lights in the dense trees that he assumed marked houses.

He tried closing his eyes, but that only made things worse. He felt bile as it tried to creep up his throat, and he swallowed it down. He took a deep breath. Then another. "Fuck," he sighed softly. Breathe in. Breathe out. His discomfort became obvious enough that Chloe finally had to take notice.

"You OK?" she asked.

"Feeling a little car sick is all," he replied. "We almost there?"

"Almost. Ten minutes, maybe. There's a bottle of water in the glove compartment, I think."

"Thanks." He found the water and took a few small sips. It seemed to help.

Finally they arrived, although Paul would never have been able to find his way back here on his own. It was a small A-frame house tucked away amongst the trees. It was dark, but an outdoor light came on as they pulled into the steep dirt driveway. Chloe parked and got out and said, "Wait here." She disappeared behind the back of the house.

Paul levered himself out of the car and onto shaky legs. He bent over and successfully fought the urge to vomit. The air up here was markedly colder than it had been even in Los Gatos, but at least the rain had stopped. He'd sweated pretty heavily in the car, and now the damp spots on his shirt were turning uncomfortably cold. At least he had the padded suit jacket on.

The house in front of him lit up from within and a few moments later Chloe stepped out the door.

"Jesus," she said. "You look like shit." She opened her arms and enveloped him in a hug. "Come inside and let's get you a fucking drink."

The house consisted of a great room that included kitchen, dining and living areas and a single bathroom and bedroom in the back. The furniture was a mishmash of styles and states of repair, a dumping ground for hand-me-downs and trash picks. Chloe and Paul sat on a low, blanket-covered couch that had lost its spring a long time ago. He gripped a glass of Jim Beam in his hands and sipped at it. Chloe had just hung up her cell phone after her third failed attempt to get a connection.

"Once in a while you can get a signal up here, especially at night. But not today, apparently," she said. "I'll have to get online to check in."

"Where are we?"

"The Santa Cruz Mountains," she teased.

"Yeah, yeah, I know that. I mean, what's with this house? We're not going to have to be fighting off maids tomorrow morning, are we?"

She laughed. "Do you honestly think someone could get away with charging rent for this place?"

He looked around at the frayed curtains and water stained ceiling. "No, probably not. So what is it then?"

"It's a safe house. One of the places we rent around the area. I kind of hate it because it's so far away from everything, but it is pretty peaceful. At night the deer come right up to the house. They ate the flowers Bee planted."

"Huh," said Paul, mostly because he didn't know what else to say.

"Your stomach feeling any better?" she asked, as she gave his midsection a playful pat.

"Yeah, it's mostly better. Those mountain roads are a bitch."

"You get used to them, I guess."

"If you say so," he took another sip of whiskey. He thought for a moment. No reason not to ask the big question again. "Um, why are we here again?"

"Well, Frank's going to call the police, and I didn't want you to be anywhere where they could find you."

"What makes you think they would've been able to find me at your place?"

"Nothing for sure. But I know they won't be able to find you here. And we needed a place to talk in total security."

"And that's here?"

"That's here."

Paul thought about the last couple hours. How did things manage to go so bad so fast? "OK, well, let's talk."

"Great," she said and grabbed a pen and pad of paper from the coffee table. "Let's get started."

Paul sighed. He just wanted to lie down and close his eyes and wish the whole night away, but more than that he wanted to figure out what to do next. "What are we talking about exactly?"

"Morbidity and Mortality."

"What?" asked Paul, not understanding the reference.

"It's what hospitals do when something goes wrong. In their case, when someone dies on the operating table or gets fucked up. We're going to go over the details of tonight, now, while they're still fresh, so we can figure out what went wrong."

"To find out where we screwed up, you mean."

"If we screwed up, then yeah. But there might've been something else that fucked us, or someone else. So we gotta go over it."

"OK, I'm game."

Chloe straightened her back and put on all the airs of a prim and proper psychiatrist talking with a patient. "Tell me about the procedure, Doctor. When did you first start to notice a complication with your patient?"

Over the next half hour they went over the day's events in detail. Everything had gone almost exactly as planned. The restaurant staff had been a little resistant to turning the kitchen over to them, but Chloe had handled that with a skillful combination of intimidation and bribery (her favorite one-two punch). They'd had a little trouble getting the wireless credit card network up, but that'd been fixed before the guests arrived. Otherwise, everything had gone smooth as silk until Frank had confronted Paul.

"Let's talk about Frank," said Chloe. "Tell me more about him. About him and you."

"We never really got along all that well. We fought or yelled at each other from time to time, but we'd actually sometimes get into interesting debates—especially about stuff not related to the game. Whenever we talked politics or philosophy or movies the conversation was pretty interesting. He's a smart guy, more libertarian than Republican, really. Fundamentally he's a realist. He makes a lot of money and he wants to give as little of that money to the government as he can. With the Republicans he gets what he wants. And he doesn't much care about the social issues."

"So he probably wouldn't have cared about our little prank in the park then?" asked Chloe.

"No. If anything I would've thought he would find it kind of funny."

"Do you know if he was generally politically active? Did he give money to the Republican Party or volunteer in campaigns?"

"I never even saw him put a bumper sticker on his car. We didn't talk specifics about that kind of thing, but I never got the impression that he cared much about politics at all. And like I said, he's pretty tight with his money."

"So, taking everything into account, him showing up there tonight didn't seem like much of a possibility?"

"Just my dumb fucking luck," said Paul. "Of all the times. Although who knows, maybe he does this shit all the time and just never mentioned it to me."

"But you would've bet not?"

"Yeah, I would've bet no way in a million years."

Chloe sat, tapping her pad of paper with her pen, looking over her notes. "Hmmmm," she said.

"What?"

"I've had this nagging feeling at the back of my head since Frank said something in the kitchen. Now it's starting to really worry me. And piss me off."

"What is it? I assume you mean something besides threatening to go to the Congressman."

"Yeah, besides that. He said something about how when he got the invitation in the mail, he wasn't going to go, but then he changed his mind."

"And you're wondering why he changed his mind?"

"No, I'm wondering why the fuck he got an invitation in the mail in the first place," said Chloe. "If we're the ones who sent him one, that's a pretty big screw up."

"Oh shit," said Paul. "That would be fucked up."

"It doesn't seem likely though, does it?" said Chloe. "I mean, we got the invitee list from the RNC database. They were all big time donors, people who give tens of thousands of dollars to the party every year. Even if Frank did do this kind of thing on occasion, it doesn't sound very likely that he was that generous with his money, does it?"

"No. I mean he made a good living, but not that good. I'd be really fucking surprised if he was giving away tens of thousands every year."

"Something's fucked here. Rotten-in-the-State-of-Denmark style fucked. I need to see our list."

"What do you think happened?" asked Paul.

"I don't know. I need to check into it first," she got up from the couch and headed for the kitchen counter where her laptop was plugged into the phone line.

"But you have an idea, right?"

"Yeah," she said as she clicked on the connect icon and the modem started dialing. "Fucking dial-up," she said under her breath.

"Well, what is it then? What do you think happened?"

"I think someone sold us out," she said. "I think there's a fucking traitor in our midst."

Chapter 29

CHLOE stayed online for the next few hours. It took her all of three minutes to get fed up with Paul looking over her shoulder, so he decided to retreat to the bedroom and change out of his costume. He stripped off the fat suit and took what he'd hoped would be a long, hot shower. Unfortunately the mildew stained bathroom seemed to have only a few gallons of hot water at its beck and call, and Paul had to rinse with cold water instead of hot. Shivering, he quickly toweled himself dry (towel courtesy of some Hampton Inn somewhere in the world) and started to get dressed. His sweat-stained suit lay crumpled on the floor, cold and clammy and stinking of fear. A little poking around the bedroom's sole chest of drawers yielded a pair of UC Santa Cruz sweat pants and a faded Batman t-shirt. They smelled a little musty, but not too bad, so he decided to go with them.

In the great room, Chloe hadn't moved. She still stood hunched over the computer and was now typing away with furious intent. Paul thought about asking if there'd been any progress, but from the look on her face, she had no interest in answering questions right now.

"Would it bother you if I turned on the TV?" he asked. "Maybe there's some news or something." No reply. "Chloe? TV?"

"Sure, knock yourself out," she said, without looking up.

The TV looked to be one of the newer, or at least less used pieces of equipment in the room. He found the remote and switched it on, filling the room with annoying static. He quickly muted it and started flipping channels. Nothing. No reception. No satellite. No cable.

"Crud," said Paul. "No reception."

"Hmm," said Chloe.

"How 'bout you? Any news?" he asked. Her only reply was to keep typing. "Chloe? Any news?"

"Why don't you play a game? Put it on channel 3. There's cartridges in that basket over there."

Paul got up and went over toward the table the TV was sitting on. "Cartridges?" he asked.

"Mm, hmm," she replied.

Paul couldn't believe his eyes. There, in a large basket next to the TV, was an Atari 2600, the original home video-game system from the early '80's. In elementary school, he'd spent hours upon hours playing these groundbreaking games. Digging through the haphazard pile of video-game cartridges, he saw all his old favorites. It was third grade all over again—Space Invaders, Pac Man, Adventure, Missile Command, Wizard of Wor. And there it was, his all time favorite: Combat.

"Sweet," he said. It took him a few minutes to hook the ancient game system to the relatively modern TV, but everything he needed was right there. The short cord on the simple joystick controller forced him to pull a ratty beanbag out from the corner in order to have somewhere to sit. He plopped down and started blowing the shit out of things old-school. Today, these games would look primitive if you played them on a three-year-old cell phone, but the fundamentals were all there. Of course, the games all kind of sucked, but it didn't matter. Right now, the third grade seemed like a much better time to be than the present.

After about an hour, Paul heard Chloe shut down the laptop. As he maneuvered Pitfall Harry over yet another in an endless series of croco-diles, he heard her grunt and moan as she stretched her back out. She twisted and cracked her spine with a series of snaps he heard from across the room.

She pulled another beanbag from the corner and tossed it down next to Paul. Plopping down, she proclaimed, "I got next."

"Are you even old enough to remember these games?" asked Paul.

"Of course I am," said Chloe. "I just played them six months ago."

"You know what I meant." Jump, grab the vine, swing over the croco-dile. Repeat. "Did you have this when you were a kid?"

"Nope. But we never had any video games growing up. Or TV for that matter."

Paul knew from experience he'd get no more out of her on this subject.

He concentrated on the game at hand, but somehow managed to miss the next crucial jump—probably because Chloe had rammed him in the side with her shoulder.

"Ooops!" she said. "My turn!"

"No way, I've still got two lives left."

"We'll see how long those last," she said with mock menace.

"Or we could play Combat."

"Oooh, you challenging me, little boy? You challenging the master?"

"You bet your sweet ass I am," he said.

"We'll get to my sweet ass later," she said as she got up to change out Pitfall for Combat. "Tanks or biplanes?" she asked.

"Ladies choice."

"Tanks it is!"

Combat offered a half dozen or so different tank duel variations, and they decided to play each of them in turn, best three out of five for each game. Chloe really must've been playing six months ago, because her tank commander skills far outstripped Paul's own in the first three rounds. By the end, he was out of the competition and just playing for pride.

"You're mine, boy. Bow to my armor-clad might!" shouted Chloe.

"We'll see." He moved his tank into an exposed position, taking a risk. As Chloe went to fire, he shoved his shoulder to the side, jostling her and causing her to miss the shot. He'd pushed harder than he intended, tipping Chloe over the side of her beanbag and sending her laughing onto the floor. He took the opportunity to fire a winning shot before turning to taunt her.

"Turnabout is fair…" he said, and then she was on top of him, wrestling him out of his own seat.

"Sore loser!" she cried with a grin as she pinned his shoulders to the ground.

"You started it," he said. She straddled his torso now, her hands pressed down against his chest. He slipped his hands up along her legs until they lightly gripped her sides.

"That doesn't make you less of a sore loser." She bent so her face was inches from his and he slid his hands up along her back. "S-O-R-E-" she slowly spelled out, but when she was done, she didn't withdraw from the closeness.

He slid his hands down past her belt and started to caress her ass. She just looked at him, smiling. Her smile said, "Go ahead," and Paul did, craning his neck up just far enough to lock lips. She kissed him back, hard, forcing his head back down to the floor. He grabbed onto her ass just as hard, and she pressed herself against the length of his body. His instant erection pressed back through the thin material of the sweat pants.

"I told you we'd get back to my sweet ass," whispered Chloe as she broke the kiss and sat up, pulling off her blouse and exposing her breasts to Paul's hands, which found them instantly. She ground her crotch against his erection. "Now come with me, tank commander. You've got a new mission."

They ended up in the bedroom. To his inestimable relief, Chloe revealed that this mountain safe house was indeed equipped for any emergency, including a box of condoms in the bedside table.

Afterward, as they lay sprawled across the bed, Paul watched with utter joy as Chloe idly played with his momentarily flaccid penis. He casually caressed one of her breasts in response.

"Is he going to be up for another round here?" she said as she stroked him.

"You keep doing that, I'm sure he and I will be."

"Penises are so weird," she said, staring at his.

"If you say so."

"I do."

They lay there for a long while after that. Paul stared up the ceiling and looked around the dingy room. The house wasn't so bad really—quite charming in fact. All it needed was a little elbow grease and an airing out. He could be happy here. If he were here for other reasons. And then the inevitable happened. The events of earlier that evening came crashing back on him in a flash. They were here because they'd fucked up. Or been betrayed.

"Hey, what happened?" said Chloe, holding his suddenly limp prick. "I thought I was getting somewhere."

"What's happening, Chloe?"

"I was hoping to have sex again in a few minutes. This time I get to be on top."

"No, I mean with the crew. With the job."

"Oh, that." She sighed and gave up on arousing him for the moment. She sat up in the bed and looked down at him sympathetically. "Nothing right now. I chatted on IRC with Bee and she filled me in on what happened after we left."

"Well, what happened?"

"Everything else went pretty much according to the plan. Popper ran the rest of the auction and tied things off. They took in a total of $465,300 in bids."

"And Frank?"

"They cleared out and left him in the closet. If we're lucky no one will find him until morning, but I doubt we'll be that lucky. The cleaning crew was already bucking to get in there as our team was leaving."

"Which means trouble."

"A shit load."

"Still," said Paul thoughtfully. "$465,000 isn't bad at all. I'm pretty sure I could've talked that up another 100k though. Still, it's pretty good."

"Well, it would be pretty good if we were going to get to keep it."

"What?" said Paul. Now it was his turn to sit up in bed, confused and angry. "Why wouldn't we keep it?"

"Well, Kurt, Bee and Raff are working on trying to clear as much money through as possible, but that usually takes 24 hours. We were counting on moving the money to untraceable accounts before any of the bidders realized they'd been had. But right now those charges are, for the most part, still sitting with the credit card companies. If Frank goes to the police and the police inform all the bidders about what happened and they call the banks, well, we might not get anything. Actually, we probably won't get anything."

"Fuck!" said Paul. "Fuck, fuck, fuck. Fucking Frank."

"Yep," replied Chloe. "I couldn't have said it better myself."

"So we get nothing?"

"Well, we used seven different bank accounts and a few other tricks, so we might get something out of it. Depends on what happens with Frank. Luckily no one but us actually has the full list of everyone who was there, so it's not like there's any easy way for the cops to figure out who got hit. They'll have to go to the papers and the local news to really get the word out, so that might buy us some time. And the direct deposits to the charities you set up will probably stand—we weren't lying about those—so that might stand. Maybe."

"Fuck," said Paul. He thought for a while more before saying, "Fuck me."

"Yep."

"So do you still think there's a traitor in our midst?" asked Paul, looking for someone to blame for this miserable turn of events.

"I'm working on that. I asked Bee to e-mail me the guest list, but it's on one of the secure servers at home so it'll be a few hours. After she's done helping everyone save as much cash as they can. We have to see if Frank was really on the list or not."

"And if he wasn't on it," said Paul. "Then we know someone went out of their way to invite him."

"Which means someone was sabotaging this whole event," concluded Chloe.

"But why?"

"I assume for the money."

"I thought we weren't going to make any money."

"Well, according to your stupid fucking promise, we'll all be fine. You're the only one who's out of pocket here." She patted him on the knee. "Assuming you keep your stupid fucking promise."

"Christ," said Paul, flopping down on his back and covering his eyes with an arm. He'd forgotten about his promise to pay the crew off if they didn't make good money on the con. That was it then, his whole nest egg, gone as easily as it had come. "Easy come, easy go."

"I've always hated that expression. Besides, you're not gonna 'easy-go' anywhere with that money until we figure out what happened here." She lay back down beside him.

"It still doesn't make sense."

"No, it doesn't."

"We should've made six or seven hundred grand tonight if everything went right. Why fuck it all up and risk bringing the cops into it for just $100,000 more? That's what," Paul paused for a few seconds to do the math in his head. "Another six thousand dollars for the person who invited Frank. Doesn't seem worth the risk.

"No, it doesn't."

"So what gives then? Someone who didn't want me in the crew? Does someone have it out for me personally?" Paul asked.

"It's about the money. It's always about the money," said Chloe.

"But risk the cops and everything else for just six grand? Does someone have a really bad gambling debt or something?"

"If they did, they'd know the crew would cover it for them. Especially for a small amount like that." Now it was Chloe's turn to think in silence. They lay there for a long while, naked in bed. Under any other circumstances it would be a dream come true for Paul. But these circumstances? Not so dream-like.

Finally Chloe broke the quiet. "Paul, I wouldn't ask you this unless I had to. But I need you to trust me."

"I do," said Paul, and he did, without a second thought.

"I need to know where your money is."

This was the one big secret between them. Or rather, it was his one big secret from her. He didn't even know for sure if Chloe was her real name, much less where she kept her money or where she came from or even what she wanted from life. But still, he trusted her. Besides, it looked like he was going to have to give up the cash soon anyway if he wanted to stay in the crew. And now, more than ever, with Chloe naked beside him, that's exactly what he wanted.

"It's in a storage locker in Milpitas," he said. "It's under my cousin's name. Actually it's her storage locker. She used to live out here, but when she got transferred to Sydney, she put most of her stuff in storage. She gave me the key and password so I could look after it for her and use it if I needed to."

"So there's no electronic trail to lead back to you?"

"Nope. She's not even really my cousin. I mean, she's my aunt's niece. My aunt married my mom's brother. So there's no blood relation. No last name's the same or anything." He stopped for a moment, considering whether to tell her every last detail. Oh, what the hell, why not admit it? "I didn't really trust you that first couple of days, you know? And after I saw what you did to my old partners, with the hacking and all, well I thought better safe than sorry. I even did a bunch of evasive driving to make sure I wasn't being followed. Just being paranoid, I guess."

"You weren't," said Chloe. "Being followed I mean, or paranoid for that matter. You did the smart thing. You did what I would've done." Now Chloe stopped mid-thought, seeming to mull over a confession of her own. "Of course, all the evasive driving wouldn't have helped if there was a tracking device on your car."

"Was there?"

"No." Another long moment. "We didn't have any working at the time. It all happened too fast, and Bee had taken them apart to upgrade them."

"If they had been working, would you have bugged my car?"

"I don't know. It didn't come up because we didn't have the capability." Paul didn't need to ask why they would want to track him—they would have been after the cash. Chloe continued, "But right now the important thing is that the money's safe where it is for the time being. Have you ever been back to the storage locker since then?"

"No," said Paul. "I kept ten grand in cash with me, and I haven't really needed much money since I hooked up with you."

"Good, good. That gives us some maneuvering room."

"OK, but what does this matter right now? I'm going to have to turn it over to the crew anyway if I'm going to stay with you. With you guys I mean."

"When you said earlier that fucking us over for a measly six grand didn't make any sense, you were absolutely right. If someone did sell us out, then they're after a much bigger prize."

"What, me in jail?"

"That might be a nice bonus for them, but no. They want it all."

"Fuck," said Paul with sudden realization. "They're going after the whole $850,000 for themselves."

"Yep."

"Fuck!"

"Yep."

Chapter 30

PAUL had never been on TV before.

They used a picture of him that had, once upon a time, been on his old company Website. They'd cropped out the Spider Jerusalem action figure that was on his desk in the original photo, showing just his smiling face in the upper left-hand corner of the screen. Right next to the serious looking anchorwoman.

"Authorities are seeking this man, Paul Reynolds, in connection to a con game that took place in Los Gatos last night. According to witnesses, Reynolds and several accomplices staged a fake fundraiser, exploiting community outrage over the controversial protest that took place last month." Now Paul's face was replaced with footage Raff had shot of their prank. "Police now suspect that Reynolds and his accomplices may have had a hand in organizing the protest itself, shown here, where local families were sprayed with fake blood that briefly caused a mad cow panic in the area."

Now Paul's face was back, taking up the whole screen this time. "Police ask that anyone who attended last night's fundraiser or who knows the whereabouts of this man, contact them immediately." At last the image left the screen. "In other news…" The clip abruptly ended here. Paul and Chloe both looked up from the laptop's screen and sighed.

"I always wanted to be famous," said Paul.

"I think the word is 'infamous'," she said, shutting the media-player window. Bee had e-mailed her the clip from this morning's local news. "At least it hasn't gone national yet."

"Jesus." He didn't want to think about what his parents would do when they saw it. "Do you think it'll hit that big?"

"It could," she said. "You know better than most how quickly the right-wing talk radio and bloggers pick up on shit like this. Now that they've got the name of a semi-famous comic book artist and former computer game designer to attach to the park prank story, they're going to run with it."

All of a sudden Paul couldn't breathe. He sucked and sucked but no air seemed to be making it to his lungs. His heart raced. "Fuuuuuu…" He managed to say.

Chloe grabbed his shoulders and shook him, "It's OK. It's OK. Just breathe." But he couldn't. Heart attack? All that pizza and pork rinds finally catching up? "It's OK!" Chloe shouted. "You're just panicking!" She put her hands on his back and pressed firmly but gently. "Just relax!"

"Uuuhh." said Paul. Chloe bent him forward, his head between his knees and started massaging his shoulders.

"It's OK, baby, it's OK," she said. "Just try and breathe, ok? We'll figure it out." She rubbed the back of his neck.

His heart began to slow. His breathing reached deeper into his lungs. He calmed down slowly but surely, bent over with Chloe caressing his back. "It's OK, baby," she said. "It's OK. Just relax. I'll take care of everything. Just relax." And he did relax, at least enough to keep from passing out then and there.

Paul lay on the couch, sipping water, while Chloe tapped away on the laptop behind him. Along with the news clip, Bee had also sent the list they'd used to invite potential marks to the fundraiser. They'd compiled it from various conservative donor lists that they'd either stolen or paid for. Bee had sent those original lists along too, so Chloe could check them for Frank's name. If Frank was on any of the lists then maybe, just maybe, this was all a coincidence. If Frank's name was on their invitee list but not on any of the source lists, then something fishy was going on. Same if he wasn't on any of the lists at all.

"Of course," said Paul, "If Bee's the traitor, then we're totally screwed."

"Bee's not the traitor," replied Chloe. "No way. I trust her totally."

"I thought you trusted everyone in the crew."

"I do. Or I did."

"Then what makes Bee so reliable."

"She's not like the rest of us," said Chloe. "She's like you."

"Like me how?"

"She's not in it for the money. She's in it because it's fun, because she enjoys the engineering challenges. She enjoys the life. For her it's the only real, caring family she's ever known. She had a... she had a tough upbringing."

"How's that make her so different from the rest of you?"

"The rest of us are fucking thieves."

"I keep forgetting that," said Paul, and to a certain extent he did. It didn't always seem like thievery to him. It was a game, a revolution. A new way of living. It was easy to forget what was really going on.

"You shouldn't," she replied. "Especially not now." She studied the screen in front of her for a couple of long minutes before saying, "OK, come take a look at this." Paul got up and came over to the kitchen counter. The screen showed an Excel spreadsheet listing names, addresses, and donations given over the past five years. "This is the master list we complied from all the different databases we could get our hands on."

She hit Ctrl-F and typed in Frank's name as the search parameter. The program jumped to his entry immediately. "There he is," said Paul. "And look at that, no donations in the past five years."

"Well, at least we know how he got the invitation," she said. "We sent it to him. Let me check the source lists and we'll see if he shows up there.

"Hold on a second," said Paul. "I want to check something first. See if this list has Greg Driscol in it." Greg had not only been the CEO of Paul's old company, but a childhood friend. Paul knew him very well and had never known him to be politically active. And there he was, on the list of potential donors. "Fuck me," said Paul.

"Indeed," said Chloe.

"Check the rest of them," Paul said. They were all there, every single one of his former partners, including Evan.

"I know that's bullshit," he said. "No way Evan was ever on any goddamned Republican donors list. He's old-school left wing. Union family, lifelong Democrat. Gives money to the DNC and the ACLU and the Green Party just for good measure. We used to call each other 'comrade' around the office sometimes because we were the most liberal guys in the building."

"Well, that answers that then," said Chloe. "I'll check the source lists to be sure, but I have to say this pretty much seals the deal. Somebody wanted you to get recognized, and so they invited every one of the people who hate you most in the world. Only Frank took the bait, but whoever it was only needed one."

"Fucking A! Who could have done this? Who had access to this list?"

"Well theoretically," said Chloe, thinking out loud, "Only Bee, Kurt, Raff, Me, and you. But I mean, fuck, it's a house full of hackers and there are people going in and out of that server room all the time. Anyone who was in there in the past two weeks could've added the names."

"But they had to know we were going to be suspicious. That we'd check the list."

"Which points to someone with more restricted access," she interjected. "Otherwise they would've taken off the names as soon as the invites went out."

"No," Paul said. "They'd have to wait. They invited all four but didn't know who would show up. They'd want to see who made an appearance and then leave their names on the list while deleting everyone else. We'd be even more suspicious if one of them had shown up without being on the list. So they'd have to wait until afterwards in order to make the list match what actually happened."

"OK, that makes sense," she opened up an IRC window and started pinging Bee again. "So whoever did this shit is going to want to get into the database ASAP and take Greg and the others off. They have to assume we haven't seen it yet since we haven't been home and therefore can't have accessed the secure server."

"Why didn't they change it last night?" asked Paul. "Before Bee could e-mail it to us?"

"Things were chaos over there last night. It was all hands on deck trying to save as much money as possible before the cops and the banks shut everything down. Bee or maybe Kurt was probably sitting on that machine all night. It's got all the bank routing info on it too."

"Which means it probably wasn't Kurt," said Paul.

"Probably not," she agreed.

The computer chimed. Bee was online. The words "WHAT'S UP?" appeared on the screen.

"Need your help," typed Chloe.

"OK," came the response. SHOOT

"Covert monitor the secure server and let me know everyone that uses it. Then send me fresh copies of those files again every hour."

WHY?

"Too complicated. I'll tell later."

OK. WILL DO.

Thx, Chloe finished typing and turned to Paul. "That'll give us a record of everyone who logs onto the server, and we'll get hourly updates of the list to see when the names have been deleted."

"And then we've got him."

"Or her," said Chloe.

"Then what?" asked Paul. "What do you guys do to traitors anyway?"

"Make them walk the fucking plank," she said with a humorless grin. "I don't know. It's never come up before. We did get fucked over once by an associate—someone we were working with from another crew. We kicked his ass and ruined his credit."

"A punishment spanning two centuries of jurisprudence," he said.

"We like to mix it up."

"How do you think the others will react when they find out?"

"They'll be pissed. I'll bet…"Just then the computer chimed again. There was another message from Bee on the IRC window.

WHEN ARE YOU COMING HOME? She asked.

I dunno. Soon. Why?

RAFF'S HERE. HE WANTS TO MEET WITH YOU RIGHT AWAY.

He's right there?

There was a longer than normal pause, then, HI CHLOE. IT'S RAFF. I NEED TO TALK TO YOU AND PAUL RIGHT NOW. 911.

Paul looked at the IRC window, which showed everything that Chloe and Bee had typed to each other. "Do you think he read all that," he asked.

"I hope not, but yeah, probably." She started typing again. OK. Where?

DER GROSSE MALL. YOU KNOW WHERE.

Yep. Gimme two hours.

OK. CYA.

"Fuck me." Chloe said under her breath as she concentrated very hard on the screen in front of her, rereading the exchange.

Chloe clicked the window shut. "What's Der Grosse Mall?" Paul asked.

"You know, the Great Mall. In Milpitas. He wants to meet by the fountain in front of the movie theater."

"Why there? Why not back at the house?"

"He wants somewhere public. Somewhere that's perceived as neutral ground. Somewhere where there are too many people for us to easily pick out a tail, but out of sight from the rest of the crew."

"What do you think he wants?" asked Paul, although he was pretty sure he already knew the answer.

"What do you think?" she said. "He wants your fucking money."

"He's our guy?"

"Oh yeah," said Chloe. "Dollars to fucking donuts he's our guy. I don't want to believe it but it's the only thing that makes sense. Fuck…"

Fury welled up in Paul's breast. His heart was racing but this wasn't another panic attack. This was adrenaline and anger. He'd liked Raff. Raff had reached out to him when no one else in the crew would. Fucking Raff. He'd been playing Paul all along.

"What's the plan?" he asked, ready to do whatever it took.

"I don't know yet, but whatever we come up with, it better be absolutely fucking brilliant."

Chapter 31

THE Great Mall used to be a car factory and is the biggest attraction in Milpitas, which abuts San Jose just to the north. Unlike most malls, it doesn't do a very good job of hiding its massive nature from those who approach, because, of course, they used to manufacture cars there. They've since spent a fair amount of cash on paint and décor, but the sheer monolithic nature of the place refuses to be hidden. And so, they'd embraced their bulkiness and run with it, self-appointing themselves The Great Mall. This name naturally led to oft-repeated variations by local wits to the effect of "It's not really all that great a mall." And Paul agreed; it really wasn't that great.

However, great or not, for a Wednesday afternoon, it was very crowded. The twenty-screen movie theater had been a later addition—a separate building adjacent to the main structure and connected via a sprawling concrete courtyard with a fountain in its center. Hundreds of people of every size, age and ethnicity imaginable milled about. Silicon Valley really was the proverbial melting pot, and Milpitas in particular was home to a large population of Asian and Latino immigrants. One of the things Paul liked most about the area was the diversity of cultures and the fact that you were as likely to hear Chinese, Hindi, or Spanish, as you were English.

One of the things that Paul liked least about Silicon Valley was now standing twenty feet away from him. There was Raff, his thin, lanky body hunched over the fountain, idly flipping pennies into the water jets and watching them fly up into the air and plop back down in the fountain. Showing off his past success, Raff's trademark polo shirt bore the Bendix Software logo. He appeared not to have noticed them yet, but Paul was certain this was just a planned pose of nonchalance on his part. Chloe and Paul both glanced around as surreptitiously as possible, searching for other crew members who might be watching them. Chloe had told him to assume that Raff was working with at least one partner maybe two. Maybe more. Maybe he'd turned the whole crew against them.

As they closed to within ten feet, Raff finally looked up and smiled at them. One of Raff's many gifts was his infectious grin, and Paul felt his own mouth turning upwards in response. He went with it and smiled back, holding out his hand to shake Raff's.

"Hey there," said Raff. "How're you doing? You guys settled in ok up in the mountains?" This was Raff's way of letting them know that he knew where they'd been, but they'd already expected that he'd figured out at least that much.

"We're good," said Paul. "As good as can be expected anyway."

"You saw the news then," Raff said, his look turning serious. "That's a tough break, man. I'm really sorry."

Chloe interjected at this point. "The question of the hour is; what are we going to fucking do about it?"

"You're right, that is the question. I've been up all night with the rest of the crew trying to save what we could from this scheme of Paul's, but…" He turned and looked directly into Paul's eyes. "I'm afraid it's a bust, man. We managed to move out 16K before the banks cracked down."

"Sixteen thousand?" exclaimed Paul. "That's all?"

"Yeah, I'm sorry dude, but that's all we could get safely. There's a ton of heat on this thing. A freaking ton of heat. With the congressman having been there and all, the feds are coming in on it, too. Treasury, FBI, I don't know who else. We couldn't pull down any more without exposing our asses."

"Ok, it's a total cock-up," said Chloe. "That sucks, but now it's damage control time. We need to figure out a way to deflect this off Paul. Set him up with an alibi for last night. Something."

"That's a good idea," said Raff agreeably. "Maybe find a hotel down in L.A. and hack their security tape. We should look into that, totally. But right now there's kind of a more immediate problem."

"Oh yeah?" said Chloe. "What's that?"

"It's the crew. The rest of the crew, I mean."

"What about them?"

"They're pretty pissed off. We all are. But more than that, they're scared."

"Scared of what?" asked Paul. "It's not their picture all over the TV!"

"But as far as they're concerned, it might as well be," Raff replied. His voice was calm and sympathetic. "This is much more public than anything we've ever done. It's new territory for most of them, and they're not comfortable there."

"It's like we talked about, Paul," said Chloe. "If something happens to you, it can come back on all of us. If you get caught or whatever, they'll follow the trail back to the rest of the crew and then, well, it'd be bad."

"Exactly," agreed Raff, pleased to have Chloe on his side.

"Yeah, yeah, I fucking get that, OK?" Paul growled. "But so what? I'm scared. They're scared. OK. What do we fucking do about it now that we're all in this shit together?"

Raff bent forward and put an arm around Paul's shoulder, looking around conspiratorially as if he was making sure no one was listening in on them. "That's the thing, Paul. As far as some of them are concerned, we're not all in this together."

"What do you mean?"

"I mean, some people—not me you understand—but some crew members are saying that this whole public thing was your plan, and you're on the hook for it. That you're not really a member, see?"

"What the hell?" Paul shouted.

"Shhh!" hissed Chloe. "Be quiet, Paul. Let him finish."

"I'm right there with you, man," Raff crooned in soothing tones. "It's bullshit. But when people get scared they start to freak out. Their sense of right and wrong goes out the window and they start looking after their own skins first. You start hearing things like FBI and Treasury Department and you got folks pissing their pants."

"It's perfectly understandable, Paul," Chloe added, taking his hand in hers and squeezing it. "Remember how freaked out you were when you saw your picture on TV this morning? They feel the same way."

"Except it wasn't their fucking picture!"

"No, no it wasn't, but that doesn't change what's going on. It's something we have to deal with," she continued. "We need their help if we're going to get you out of this jam. The three of us can't do it on our own, can we Raff?"

"No, we can't. You're between a big fucking rock and a huge fucking hard place, Paul. No one knows that better than you. You need all the friends you can get right now."

"I thought I had friends. I thought I was part of this goddamned crew of yours. Don't you protect your own?"

"Of course we do," Raff assured him. "Of course. But they have to know that you're one of them. They have to trust that you'd do the same for them. Loyalty is earned, not given. Plus there's another problem."

"Of course there is," said Paul. "What now?"

"It just came in on the news about half an hour ago. Remember that guy who was with the CFO when you made that pickup for us?"

"The guy who tackled me you mean? The private eye who forced me off the road? Yeah, I think I remember him."

"Right. So anyway, apparently he recognized you from the TV, and he's gone to the cops and the papers. He says you're a known extortionist."

"Oh fuck," said Chloe. Paul could tell she was honestly surprised at this. For his own part, he was speechless.

"Yeah," continued Raff. "And since we know he must've tracked down Paul to within a few blocks of the house… well, it's probably not a good idea if you come back there anytime soon."

"All my fucking stuff's there," said Paul.

"I can get that for you, no problem," Raff assured him. "But first we have to figure out what to do about appeasing the rest of the crew."

Paul fumed silently for a moment, glaring back and forth between Chloe and Raff. Finally he said, "Well, what the fuck do they want then?"

"Like you said when you were pitching your plan," Raff said. "The money we helped you get from your old partners. You said you'd pay us all with that if the deal went south. Well, it's pretty obviously gone south."

"And so you won't help me unless I pay you eight hundred grand. Loyalty isn't bought, Raff, it's earned. If I'm a part of this team, then I shouldn't have to pay you guys to help me." He snatched his hand away from Chloe's grasp and shrugged off Raff's comforting arm from his shoulder. "This sounds a fucking lot like extortion to me."

"I agree, Paul. I really do, but…"

"Well then why don't the two of you tell them to get in line and help out, huh? You're supposed to be the leaders here."

"You know it doesn't work that way, Paul," said Chloe. "We're not an army or a dictatorship. Everyone's free. Everyone gets a vote. Everyone's opinion matters."

"I'm afraid Chloe's right, Paul," Raff added. "As much as I sometimes wish it was otherwise, that's the way this crew operates. The long and the short of it is, you need to pay them that 850k or they're going to hang you out to dry, and there's nothing Chloe or I can do about it."

Paul looked deflated. Totally beaten down. "Can I think about it for a couple hours? It'd take me that long to get the money anyway," he asked in a soft voice.

Sensing victory, Raff backed off. "Of course, of course."

"How about tomorrow?" said Chloe. "Can you tell us your decision by tomorrow?"

This apparently didn't suit Raff's plans and he said so, "I'm afraid that might be too long. Some of them are ready to bolt now."

"OK, how about tonight?" Chloe suggested. "If he decides to do it, he'll bring the money tonight. Does that work, Paul?"

"Sure," Paul said and started walking back toward the parking lot. "Whatever."

"I know it sucks, man," Raff called after him. "But we'll get you out of this thing. I swear."

Paul didn't answer. He just stood there, waiting for Chloe to finish with Raff.

Raff turned to Chloe. "How're you guys fixed for cash?" Raff asked. "I've got about a hundred on me if you need it." He pulled out his wallet and opened it. "Would that help?"

"Thanks," Chloe said without actually answering Raff's question. She reached into the open billfold and pulled the money out in one swift motion.

"We'll be in touch," she called back over her shoulder as she and Paul headed for the parking lot.

Just before they disappeared around the corner of the movie theater Paul glanced back, he saw Raff pull out his cell phone and start dialing.

Chapter 32

A S THEY climbed back into her car, Chloe leaned across and gave Paul a kiss on the cheek. She lingered long enough to whisper, "Remember, they probably bugged the car." Paul nodded that he understood.

"I'm really sorry about this," she said at normal conversational volume.

"I'm sure you are," Paul said, his voice dripping venom. "You know what? This is all bullshit."

Chloe pulled out of the parking space and started to navigate back toward the highway. "I don't see that we have a lot of options here."

"I could take the money and fucking run. I could leave all you crazy bastards behind and go away somewhere. Eight hundred and fifty thousand will last me a good long time in Costa Rica."

"Do you even have your passport, Paul? Do you have any idea how to make yourself disappear? The police, the FBI, they'll be monitoring your parents' house. We need the crew if we're going to get you out of this."

"So everyone keeps telling me."

They drove on in silence for a while; Paul irritably scanning the radio stations looking for some news about himself. Eventually, Chloe grabbed his hand and pulled it away from the controls and shut the radio off.

"Listen to me, Paul," she said in a stern voice. "It's fucking decision time. If you're going to let us help you then fine, let us. If not, then tell me where to drop you off and you can run if you want to. Just fucking decide, OK?"

Paul sighed in resignation. As he did it, he thought maybe he was overplaying it a bit, acting too dramatic. But Chloe had told him that the sound quality on whatever bug Raff's accomplices might have planted in the car would be poor, so they had to ham it up a bit. "Fine!" he practically shouted. "I've trusted you guys this far. In for a penny, in for a fucking pound."

Chloe patted him on the knee. "You've made the right decision, Paul. You really have." She paused for just a beat of dramatic tension. "Now tell me, where did you hide the money?"

"It's in a storage locker, under my cousin's name. I'll take you there, but can we get something to eat first? I'm starving."

"Of course we can," said Chloe. "How 'bout this place over here?"

Ten minutes later and they were sitting in a booth at a Don Pablo's, munching idly on warm chips and weak salsa. Surprisingly, they were giggling like school kids.

"I don't know why I'm laughing. This isn't funny," chuckled Paul.

"It's just the stress," smiled Chloe. "You did great, by the way. You played the pissed off victim very well—Raff bought it, I'm sure."

"It wasn't hard. I just thought back to that time when my whole life got flushed down the toilet. You remember it, right? I think it was this morning." He munched another chip and couldn't help but smile. "Still, it did go pretty well, didn't it? He acted exactly like you said he would."

"Yeah, he's trying to keep us close, make us think he's our friend."

"Surely he's got to suspect something though," said Paul. "If he saw what you and Bee were typing, then he's got to be curious."

"Yeah, but I think I threw him a curveball there by pressing you to hand over the money. I think he bought into the idea that I'm still trying to get your cash for the crew as a whole. If we're lucky, he's betting that we haven't figured out that he's the traitor here."

"And you're now one hundred percent sure that he's the bad guy?"

"I am," Chloe said with dead certainty. "Absolutely."

"What convinced you? It still could've been someone else who snuck into the secure server."

"He asked how we were doing for money," said Chloe. "He even gave me a hundred bucks."

"What does that prove?"

"It's just not like him. He and I never talk money. Never ask each other about it. But he asked because he wanted to know how strapped we were for cash. He wanted to know what kind of resources we had at our disposal." Their waiter passed by at that moment, and she flagged him down. "Excuse me, can we get our order to go instead? And bring the check when you get a chance." The waiter nodded no problem.

"We're not eating here?" said Paul.

"I want to test a theory."

"What's that?"

"That Raff's cancelled all our credit cards."

Paul looked shocked. "What? How…?" Chloe gave him a look that said "Come on, remember who you're dealing with."

"OK, but why?"

"He wants us desperate. He wants to press us full court and make sure we don't have any moves we can make."

"If we had credit," Paul said, as he understood what was happening, "We could run and wait for things to calm down a little. But without any credit cards, we can't even put gas in the car, which means the only way to run is for us to go get the money."

"And lead Raff right to it."

The waiter returned with two Styrofoam boxes and the check. Chloe nodded to Paul and he gave the server his debit card. A few minutes later he returned and said that the card had been declined. Chloe gave him one of her cards instead. It came back declined as well, so they ended up paying with Raff's cash.

"Fuck," said Chloe. "He's a sneaky bastard."

"What?"

"That card I used, I didn't think he even knew about it. It's from one of my hidden accounts."

"Jesus… how much does he know?"

"Apparently he knows as much about me as I know about him," said Chloe. "I could empty or freeze a dozen of his accounts if I needed to, but I don't think that'll help us right now. He's probably got the whole crew behind him on this, and I can't beat all of them together."

"So we proceed with Plan A then," said Paul.

"Yep," she said as she stood up to go. "Let's hope Raff doesn't know all of my secrets, or we really are fucked."

Chapter 33

THE U-Store-Right facility allowed its customers 24-hour a day access to their storage lockers. Every customer had a unique code that gave them access through the front gate as well as another code and a key that were both required to open the actual locker. Ten years ago, the lot had state-of-the-art security cameras and three roving guards at all times. These days the staff was down to one man in a security booth who watched a video monitor that only received signals from the thirty percent of the cameras that still worked and only worked days. Spread out over an acre that consisted of row after row of metal-doored mini-garages, the whole place looked shabby and rundown during the day. At night it was downright menacing.

It was after 9 p.m. when Paul and Chloe pulled up to the front gate and reached out the window and typed the entrance code into the battered metal keypad. A motor kicked into life and the chain-link gate shakily opened in front of them. They crept forward into the facility, heading toward a row of storage lockers near the back of the lot. They both peered out into the darkness in search of signs that anyone else was lurking around. Every locker had a light over its doorway. Together they would have provided plenty of illumination down each row, but more than half of them were burned out or broken, leaving puddles of darkness large enough to hide a car. No way of knowing if they were alone or not.

Chloe pulled to a stop in front of the door marked G13. It was one of the units with a busted light, so she left the car lights focused on the door as they got out and made their way to the locker entrance. Paul keyed in a code on the pad next to the door, and the LED above the lock switched from red to green. He then produced a key from his pocket. It stuck in the lock at first, but he worked it carefully for a few seconds and finally the tumblers fell into place. The lock clicked and Paul said, "OK, here we go."

"You're making the right decision, Paul."

"Yeah, yeah. That's what you keep saying," still speaking as if Raff were secretly listening, which he probably was. He leaned down and pulled up on the bottom of the garage door entrance. With a loud clatter it rolled up toward the ceiling, revealing a 10-by-20 foot room packed to the ceiling with boxes. Paul flicked a light switch on the inside wall but nothing happened. He angrily flipped it up and down several more times, but still nothing happened. "Of course," he sighed. "The fucking light's out. Hold on a sec, and I'll go get the bag."

As Paul rummaged around inside the storage locker, two figures stepped out from around the corner. One of them, the smaller figure, remained hidden in the shadows, but the tall, lanky man stepped confidently forward. It was Raff. Chloe looked at him in surprise.

"What're you doing here?" she hissed, loud enough for Paul to hear. "What the fuck, Raff?"

He silently jogged up next to her. "It's OK," he said. "I'm just making sure everything goes down smooth."

"How the fuck did you find this place?" she asked in a low, angry voice. "I told you we'd meet up with you tonight."

"Just calm down, Chloe, everything's fine."

There was the low rumble of an engine from behind them, toward the entrance to the lot. A car turned into view, running with its lights off. It was a big old '78 Cadillac.

"Who's this?" she asked Raff, her voice louder than it should have been if she was trying to keep quiet, but loud enough for Paul to hear her inside the locker. "How many people did you bring with you?"

"Shhh," said Raff. "It's OK. We just want to make sure nobody gets hurt." He stepped in close to put an arm around her shoulder but she danced away from him and toward the open entrance to the storage locker.

"Hurt?" she practically shouted. "Why the fuck would anyone get hurt, Raff?"

The car stopped right behind Chloe's vehicle, blocking her in. Two more people got out of the car, and even in the dim light they were recognizable as Kurt and Filo, both of whom Raff had originally recruited into the group. They wore long coats and had their hands stuffed in their pockets.

"What the fuck is going on here, Raff? Why're Kurt and Filo here?" Chloe shouted. "I told you I'd handle everything."

"I know," said Raff. "But we had a little talk," he gestured to the Kurt and Filo, "And we decided to switch things up a bit. You know, keep it interesting."

"We were getting you the money," she said. "That's why we're fucking here. To bring the goddamned money back." She paused and looked up into his smiling face. "Or is that not what you wanted, Raff? Did you have something else in mind?" She pointed toward the figure that still lingered in the shadows at the corner. With Raff in front of her, Kurt and Filo to her left and the stranger to her right, she had nowhere to run. "Who's your friend there? Are you cutting him in too?"

"It's OK, Chloe," said Paul, emerging from the storage locker with a blue vinyl duffle bag in his hands. "I've got the money right here."

"Hey Paul," said Raff. "Good to see you."

"Uh-huh," Paul replied, noncommittally as he stepped forward past Chloe. "Here," he offered Raff the bag.

"What's that?" Raff asked.

"The goddamned money," Paul snapped.

"Really? That's great Paul. I know it sucks, but this is for the best."

"You didn't trust me to come back with it, huh?"

"Well, you did leave pretty angry this afternoon. I'm just here to make sure you make the right decision."

"Uh-huh," Paul repeated as he stepped forward and dropped the bag at Raff's feet with a heavy thump. He then retreated back to Chloe's side. Raff continued to stand there, still smiling. Filo stepped forward and picked up the bag.

"You gonna count that here?" Paul asked.

"Count what?" asked Raff, mock confusion in his voice.

"The damn money!" Paul shouted.

"Oh… yeah. Hey Filo, why don't you take that back to the trunk and count it real quick? We'll wait here."

Paul had a hard time hiding his anxiety as he watched Filo gingerly take the duffle bag to the car. He popped the trunk open and set the bag inside, but with the large trunk door open, Paul couldn't see exactly what he was doing.

"Giving up that money sure must hurt, huh Paul?" Raff said, ignoring Filo.

"What's up, Raff?" Chloe interjected. "What's with all the screwing around?"

"Fine," said Raff. His whole countenance changed in an instant, the friendly smile and open posture morphing into a menacing grin and an aggressive forward lean. "Cards on the table time, Chloe?"

Chloe responded in kind, puffing out her chest and taking a step toward Raff. "Absolutely. Let's lay it all out there."

"You knew we were following you," Raff stated.

"Of course we did."

"And you knew we were listening."

"Obviously."

"And yet you played along as if you didn't know. You led us here."

"So it would seem."

"Then you tell me, Chloe, knowing you as I do, and knowing all that, why on Earth would I believe that the bag Filo's examining so carefully actually contains the money?"

"Only one way to find out." She turned toward the car and shouted "Hey Filo, you find the money yet?"

"Shut up, Chloe," Filo called back.

"Just open it, for God's sake!" she shouted.

"Shut up, Chloe!" he returned, louder than before.

"Shush now," said Raff softly. "He needs to concentrate." He called over to Filo, "You take your time. We'll wait." Filo grunted in reply and Raff turned back to Chloe. "So tell me, Chloe, when did you turn against the rest of the us?"

"I could ask you the same question," said Chloe. "In fact I will. When did you turn, Raff? Was it when I took Paul with me to the beach instead of you? Were you jealous?"

"You're projecting your own drama onto me." Raff smiled "What is it about this guy anyway?" He gestured to Paul. "I mean, he's a fine fellow and all, but why the special treatment? How did he go so quickly from mark to best buddy? How did you decide to let him keep his money? And why, pray tell why, weren't the rest of us consulted?"

"We've had this conversation."

"Yes," Raff said thoughtfully. "Yes we have. Fine then, let's move on to new business." He turned again toward Filo. "How's it coming?" he shouted. Another grunt from Filo.

"Almost there," said Raff as his gaze turned back on Chloe. "Let's talk about Paul for a minute."

"Do we have to," Paul said with a sigh. "That seems to be all anyone wants to talk about these days. Me and my money."

"You and your stolen money," Raff corrected.

"Whatever," said Paul.

"What about Paul?" asked Chloe "Do you want to know if his cock is bigger than yours? It would have to be, wouldn't it?"

Raff laughed. "Leave it to Chloe to bring things down into the gutter. No, I was actually going to sing his praises for a moment."

"This should be good," said Paul.

"You're pretty good at this whole thing, Paul," Raff continued. "Your plans are clever, if a tad over-complicated. You've got the fire for the life and, judging from your performance this afternoon with me and in the car as we listened in, you can play the face-to-face con, too."

"Thanks," said Paul, although he didn't mean it.

"You've even got the secret of successfully lying to people—always include a little bit of truth. You said your money was in a storage locker and, lo and behold, here we are at a storage locker. You even explained why it wouldn't be under your name; that your cousin had rented it. Of course we didn't have time to look into the paperwork on every locker here since we didn't know which storage facility until we followed you here, so we couldn't check on that."

"Where's this going, Raff?" Chloe asked. Paul didn't like the fact that Raff was giving away so much information about what he did and didn't know. Chloe had told Paul time and again that you never reveal what you know unless you have to. Paul was wondering if their brilliant plan was really all that brilliant.

"I'm getting there," said Raff. "Patience. As I was saying, we couldn't check up on who rented out this storage facility. But we could check up on your family." Paul's heart started to thump heavily in his chest. "And it took some doing, but we found the cousin who's not really a cousin. Francesca Kohl, right?"

Paul stared at him dumbly, kicking himself for mentioning his cousin in the first place. But he knew enough not to nod or acknowledge Raff's statement. Deny, deny, deny. "Doesn't ring any bells," said Paul, keeping most of the anxiety out of his voice.

Raff kept on as if he hadn't heard Paul. "And lo and behold, the credit-card records for Ms. Kohl do indeed show a monthly rental charge for a storage locker facility in the Bay Area. Just not this one." He paused to let this sink in and then turned to Chloe. "See babe, this is what you get when you work with talented amateurs. Moments of brilliance intertwined with dumb fucking mistakes." He looked again toward Filo. "How's it coming over there?"

"Ready when you are!" Filo shouted back.

Paul glanced at Chloe. She caught his eye and ever so slightly nodded to her right. Paul looked over at the fourth figure hiding in the shadows. He wondered who the hell that was, but decided it didn't make much difference at this point.

"Go ahead!" Raff called to Filo.

Silence for a moment. Paul held his breath in anticipation. Chloe tensed her muscles. Raff watched with a serene smile, like some malevolent, skinny Buddha.

A loud, sharp pop came from the open car trunk, followed by a powerful hissing noise. "Fuck!" Filo shouted, and they all looked over to see a billowing cloud of green smoke pouring out of the car trunk. Filo came stumbling around to the front of the car, his face concealed by a gas mask. He had a tire iron in his hand.

"How 'bout that!" shouted Raff, whooping in delight. "I was right. I told you it would be gas, not a flash bomb!"

Filo regained his footing as he came to a stop next to Kurt, who'd stood motionless throughout the entire proceedings, watching everything unfold with a curious, intense look. Filo tore the gas mask from his head and said, "Yeah, yeah, you were right."

Paul and Chloe looked surprised and scared. When the gas bomb went off he'd grabbed her hand and he still hadn't let go. Together they took a step backward toward the storage locker's dark opening.

Raff followed them forward, his hand digging into his coat pocket for something. "OK kids, play time's over. We've had the fireworks show. Now let's get down to business."

"OK," said Chloe between clenched teeth. "What do you want?"

In one smooth motion Raff pulled his hand from his coat and whipped it up and then down. With a metallic snap the collapsible metal baton telescoped to its full length. He pointed it menacingly at Paul. "His fucking money!"

"No," said Paul, his voice much calmer than his heart. "Not gonna happen."

"Oh, it's gonna happen," said Raff. Behind him Filo stepped forward, his tire iron *en garde* and ready for action. Kurt also came toward them, although his hands remained in his pockets. The shadowy figure to their right remained where he was.

"One way or another. You can take us there now, which is your best option. Or you can wait for us to beat it out of you, which would suck for you. Or you can let us beat you to a fucking pulp and we'll just find the locker and get in on our own. We're pretty experienced at that kind of thing, in case you hadn't heard."

Paul held his hands up in a gesture of surrender. "OK, OK. You've made your point. I know what's best for me."

Raff didn't stop moving toward him, but he did say, "Great, just let me tie you up and we'll go to the locker."

"No, no, you misunderstood. I've decided to go with option number three. Come and get me, Fuckwad!" Paul shouted angrily.

He yanked on Chloe's arm and the two of them turned and ran into the dark storage locker, dodging behind a stack of boxes and out of sight.

Chapter 34

PEERING out from inside the dark locker, Paul watched as Raff turned to Kurt. "Now do you believe me?" he asked. Kurt looked troubled by what he'd seen. Finally he nodded in agreement and pulled his hand out of his pocket. He held an extendable baton that was a twin to the one Raff wielded. He snapped it to its fighting length and joined Raff and Filo as they advanced toward the dark opening.

"Whatcha doing, Chloe?" Raff called from a few feet outside the locker entrance. "I'm sure you figured out that that's a dead end."

There was no reply, except a shuffling of feet and boxes toward the storage locker's rear. Raff motioned with his head to his two companions and then glanced to his left at the shadow draped figure that he'd come with. Then the three of them stepped into the darkness, weapons ready.

From inside the locker, two pairs of dark arms swung baseball bats out from the shadowy corners to either side of the doorway, arcing out from the darkness and slamming into the intruders. Filo took a blow straight to his forehead that knocked him back off his feet. Raff managed to twist away at the last moment, the bat glancing off his shoulder. Before he could react further, two more black-clad figures exploded from the pile of boxes in front of him, wooden bats raised and ready for action.

"What the fuck!" shouted Raff, tumbling backward out of the doorway and into the alleyway. Kurt turned and ran as well, the mystery attackers hot on his heels.

As the fight poured out into the slightly brighter exterior, Raff must have been surprised when he realized that none of the attackers were Chloe or Paul. One of the four was clearly a woman, but she was much stockier and a little taller than Chloe. All four bat-wielding ambushers wore dark pants and dark sweatshirts in various shades of navy and black. All had dark bandannas around their faces that covered everything below the eyes and dark ski-caps that covered everything above them. They looked not so much like uniformed soldiers as a quartet of people who'd been told to dress alike for the occasion.

Raff had only a moment to take this in as the group charged forward. Kurt, who was always quick, was sprinting for the car. One pursuer stopped and set his feet before expertly throwing his bat at Kurt's retreating back. The spinning wooden shaft tangled up in Kurt's pumping legs, bringing him down hard on the asphalt. The masked man raced forward and jumped on Kurt's back before he could get up.

The other three ignored Filo, who was out cold, and fanned out to surround Raff. He held his baton up in a defensive pose, trying to keep all three of them to his front. It was a losing proposition. The attackers knew each other well and fought with frightening coordination. Once they had him flanked, some unseen and unheard signal passed between them. They all charged at once, bats swinging.

Raff jumped back and then dodged wildly to his left, moving inside his attacker's swing before the bat could connect. He dropped his own weapon and grabbed his attacker by the shoulders. He twisted hard with his hips, and the two of them went down to the ground in a heap. Raff landed on top, and his attacker hit the ground hard, his head snapping back and impacting the blacktop with an audible crunch.

Raff screamed in pain. One of the other bats had finally connected, hitting his left arm hard. He rolled off the man he'd thrown and onto his back, covering his face just in time to receive another bludgeoning blow on his forearm.

The two standing attackers loomed over him now, bats raised. Paul, emerging from his hiding place, gave Raff three, maybe four seconds before he was bloody pulp on the asphalt. Raff managed to deflect a second blow with his already damaged forearm. Now it was broken for sure. He cried out mindlessly in utter agony.

Out of the darkness came three rapid roars, a gun being fired from nearby. One of the attackers crumpled to his knees. The other dove forward and out of the line of fire. She acted as if she'd encountered gunfire before and knew to get clear as fast as possible.

Raff seemed only dimly aware of the sudden change in his fortune as he writhed on the ground in pain. Then the shooter was at his side, helping Raff to his feet.

Chapter 35

PAUL and Chloe peered out from the storage locker as the fight unfolded before them. A malicious grin covered Paul's face as he watched Raff and his thugs yelp in horror as Winston's heavies ambushed them.

After they received Raff's summons over IRC, they'd needed to act fast. It had been Paul's idea to call in Winston. He knew they needed help. In fact, they needed muscle, and Paul figured that since Winston was a former Weatherman, he must know how to swing a bat. Chloe had resisted, arguing that he'd never help and that it wasn't that easy to contact him, and furthermore, they could handle this themselves. Paul knew the truth though—she didn't want to appear weak in front of her mentor. She didn't want him to know she'd lost control of her crew.

Eventually logic prevailed over pride, and she'd made the call. They had to assume Raff had the safe-house phone covered, along with their cell phones, so they waited for their next-door neighbor in the mountains leave. Chloe broke into his house and used his phone to contact Winston. As Paul had suspected, Winston was eager to help his favorite apprentice.

She and Winston had worked out the basics of a very simple plan—Winston already had a storage locker they could use where he and his crew could set up the booby-trapped bag and the ambush. The key would be taped to the door, out of sight; all Paul had to do was palm it when he entered the code and then pretend to take it out of his pocket. Chloe and Paul would lead Raff and whomever he was working with into the trap. Then, voilà, they'd ambush him and take care of the whole problem.

And so far, everything seemed to be working out just as planned. They watched as Filo fell to the first swing, and Winston and his crew rushed out of the locker and ran Raff and Kurt down.

Chloe and Paul, who'd run to the back of the locker in order to lure Raff inside, then made their way back to the doorway. Chloe's stun gun was in her hand and Paul had grabbed a baseball bat of his own that Winston had left for him. They reached the outside just as Winston and a woman named Lilly were standing above Raff and pounding away at him with their bats.

Then, from their right, a figure came running forward. It was the man in the shadows, and he had an automatic pistol in his hand. He started firing, releasing three very loud blasts into the night air. Chloe and Paul both ducked for cover inside the locker. There was a pause and then more shots followed by shouting.

"Everybody back off!" the gunman shouted. "Back off or someone else gets a bullet in the head!"

Paul peeked out from behind an overturned box to see the man help Raff to his feet. Two of the batmen were on the ground, and one of them was bleeding badly. He heard a car starting up and assumed this was Kurt, making his own escape. "Hold it right there!" the man with the gun shouted. "We're coming with you."

Raff and his guardian angel shambled out of Paul's line of sight. A few seconds later he heard car doors opening and closing and then the Cadillac kicked into gear and peeled out, headed for the front gate.

"Winston!" Chloe shouted from Paul's side. She ran out into the alleyway toward the bleeding figure. The gunman had shot Winston. Paul ran after her.

Winston's crew members were already at his side, pressing their hands against the wounds. He gurgled nonsense, but at least he was still breathing. They pulled the bandanna from around his head and saw a nasty wound along the side of his neck. The bullet hadn't hit anything vital, but even the grazing shot had torn out a large chunk of flesh. Another bullet had passed through his left bicep. The third shot was still inside him, just below his left shoulder blade. There was a chance it had penetrated his lung.

"We need to get him to a hospital!" cried Chloe, lifting Winston's head carefully off the pavement and cradling it in her hands. He breathed hard, in terrible pain.

"We're on it," said Lilly, pulling down her own bandanna and reaching for her two-way. "Help," she said into the handheld, her voice serious but calm. "Now! Now! Now!" From five rows over they heard an engine turn over and start.

Paul stood over the bloody tableau, dumbfounded. How had it gotten this bad? How had someone gotten shot? He replayed the last minute over and over again in his brain, all the while transfixed by the horror of Winston's blood seeping out onto the ground. The image of the stranger with the gun kept sticking in his head. The lighting was poor, the situation insane, but something about him was familiar. He wasn't a crew member, but…

A white, beat up Suburban hurtled around the corner and came to a screeching halt. It was more of Winston's crew, a man and a woman that Paul recognized from the drum circle on the beach. They leaped out of the truck and came running toward their fallen leader, the woman with a first aid kit clutched in her hands. They shoved Lilly and Chloe aside and started tending to their patient.

Chloe stood up and retreated from the scene. "You need to get him to a doctor," she said. "No bullshit."

The woman with the first-aid kit was using scissors to cut away Winston's clothing and expose his wounds. "I am a doctor," she snapped.

Lilly, who seemed to be in charge now that Winston was down, took Chloe by the arm and patiently walked her and Paul back toward the truck. "Kelly knows what she's doing," she said. Her presence and composure had a soothing effect on Paul. She seemed so certain of everything she said. "He'll make the call now. If we can treat him, we will. If we have to, we'll take him to the E.R."

"But…" Chloe started to say.

"We've got to discuss something else, though," Lilly continued without letting Chloe interrupt her. "What are you two going to do?"

"What do you mean?" asked Paul.

"We'll take you with us if you want." Lilly rubbed Chloe's shoulder with affection. "I know you and Win are close, and he told us to help you guys out. So if you want, you can come with us." Chloe didn't reply.

"Come with you where?" asked Paul.

"Into the wind. I've got to pull us out of this thing now—making sure Win's OK is all I care about. We can't help you get your money back right now. Maybe in a couple of weeks we can regroup."

"In a couple of weeks, Raff and the money will be long gone," Chloe said. "He knows where it is now, and if we don't get it fast, he'll get it himself, no problem."

"I'm telling you I can't help you on this, Chloe," Lilly insisted. "I'm sorry but…"

"No, I know, it's OK. You've done more…" she looked back at where Kelly was working on Winston's wounds. "Sacrificed more than I could have asked. But I can't let Raff get the payoff. Especially not after this."

"We don't have to do this, Chloe. It's just money," said Paul.

She turned on him. "It's not just money, Paul. It's your future. It's maybe the only future you have." She paused and then stepped forward and wrapped her arms around him in a fierce embrace. "I'm so sorry, Paul, but I don't know what will happen if we don't have that cash to work with."

"I don't understand," he said. "Isn't it enough we're alive after all that just happened?"

"Have you already forgotten? Why we're here? The cops are after you. Your credit is ruined. You're a wanted man. And maybe, with the whole crew behind us, those would've all been surmountable obstacles. But Raff's poisoned them against us. Kurt's presence here proves that. Without them helping me, I can't save you this time. We have to run and that takes money."

Paul thought about this. He was scared. Scared that she was right and worried about what that meant he had to do next. With everything coming apart around him, she was his only source of stability and support left. To see her scared and starting to come undone made it even worse. He thought about the times she'd already saved his ass; in the boardroom with his partners, in the restaurant with Frank, on the highway with that P.I….

"Christ!" he exclaimed. "Oh fuck."

"What?" Lilly and Chloe said together, looking around for some new danger.

"That guy with the gun. Fuck. That guy! I know that guy. It was the fucking private eye from the highway and that money pick-up."

"Are you sure?" asked Chloe.

"Yes. Absolutely sure now." And he was. Even in the bad light, he'd recognized the man's frame. Although he'd never gotten a good look at the shooter's face, he'd heard his voice, the same voice that had threatened him on the side of Highway 17.

"What the fuck was he doing here?" Chloe asked, of no one in particular. Her eyes were unfocused, her mind deep in thought, calculating this new piece of information's ramifications.

From over where Winston lay, they heard Dr. Kelly say in a loud voice, "OK, on three. One. Two. Three." They looked over to see four of Winston's crew lifting him and carrying him toward the truck. Lilly broke off from their conversation and ran over to help them.

"How's he doing?" she asked Kelly.

"It's not as bad as it could've been. Nothing vital hit. Two through and throughs and the other is lodged in his back. I think I can get it out, but I need better light and conditions. We need to go. Now." The others were already loading Winston into the back of the van.

"Ok, go," Lilly said. "I'll take the other car and meet you at the safe spot." Kelly nodded and then rushed back to the truck.

Paul and Chloe stood and watched the van disappear out of sight, following the same path Raff had retreated down just a few minutes before. "What's it going to be?" Lilly asked them. "You coming with me or not?"

Paul looked to Chloe for confirmation and they both silently agreed. "Not," he said. He wasn't ready to give up yet.

"OK," Lilly replied, a hint of sadness in her voice. "Good luck." She gave them one last look and then scooped her bat off the ground and started to jog off into the darkness.

"Lilly, wait a sec," Chloe shouted. "Can you do us one last favor?"

"Sure," she said, "What is it?"

"Can we switch cars?" Chloe asked.

"Why?"

"Raff bugged and put a tracker in ours, and I haven't deactivated either device yet. We need a clean vehicle."

Lilly thought about this for a moment. "Then he'll be able to track me, won't he?"

"Yeah, but he's not looking for you." Lilly didn't seem to buy this line of reasoning. "I know it's a pain in the ass, but we need to move fast and I don't have time to put that thing up on a lift and go over it. And I know you don't either, but…"

Lilly held up a hand to stop her. "No, it's OK." She pulled a key ring out of her pocket and tossed it to Chloe. "It's Win's car anyway. He'll be pissed if he finds out I didn't give it to you when you asked."

"Thanks, Lilly!" Chloe said, tossing Chloe her own keys. "I really appreciate it."

She took the keys and climbed into Chloe's car. From the open window she said, "Green Jetta, parked in the lot across the street." Then she tore off into the night.

Without looking back, Chloe and Paul set off at a run for the exit. They knew they didn't have much time.

When Filo finally regained consciousness hours later, he had no recollection of what had happened. Everybody had just disappeared. As he stumbled to his feet he noticed the pool of blood in the middle of the alleyway. With no idea whose it was or where his friends were, he ran, his head pounding. It took him another hour and a half to make it back to the main crew house. When he arrived, the locks had been changed and the place was stripped bare. The crew had gone.

Chapter 36

"Where are we going?" Paul asked a few minutes later. "The real storage locker is that way." He pointed toward a freeway onramp.

"We need a place to plan first. Besides, if he knows where it is, then he's got it covered. He'll have the place staked out."

"I knew we should've gotten the money first," he said.

"If we'd done that they would've caught us there instead of where we had reinforcements. Raff would have the money and we'd have our heads cracked." She pulled the car into a Denny's parking lot, shut the engine off and turned to face Paul.

"First let's talk about this private-eye fucker," she said. "You're sure it was him? I never got a good look at his face."

"Yeah, I'm sure. Abso-fucking-lutely. What I don't know is what it means. How did he get there? Why was he helping Raff?"

"I think he was always helping Raff."

"But he was with the CFO when I went to pick up the money. He's the guy who tackled me in the park. He can't have been working with Raff then?"

"Why not?" said Chloe. "Why couldn't he have been working with Raff all along?"

Paul had no answer for this startling suggestion. Could that be possible? Had he been planning this ever since then?

"Raff is the one who set up that whole Gondry con," Chloe said. "He put that whole thing together while we were away, and he was definitely the lead on that."

"Do you mean the whole con was a setup?"

"No, it was genuine. The payoff was certainly genuine and the whole crew worked that sting. Not even Raff could've fooled us all on something that big. Not even I could've done that. But the private eye was a late addition to the mix—he must've used some cover story to get close to the mark so he could be there at the exchange. That's why we were all so surprised when he showed up at the park."

Paul thought back over the debriefing. "Which finally makes sense of why Raff called me in at the last minute. He didn't need a fresh face and he wasn't trying to help me get into the crew. He was setting me up. Setting the whole thing up so that he could put pressure on me. He told the Private Eye where to find my car and put him on my trail."

"I don't even think he's a real private eye at all. He's just Raff's accomplice. His 'Winston' maybe. He knew I had someone in the life outside the crew. I always suspected that he did, too, but I could never find any hint of who it might be. This homicidal old fuck must be the guy. Raff's mentor in the biz."

"That can't be good for us," Paul said.

"Not good at all."

"So they've been after the money since the beginning. Just to split it between the two of them?" he asked.

"Looks like."

"Fuckers."

"Yep."

"It's really pretty brilliant," Chloe mused. "I have to say that if I wasn't so pissed I'd be impressed. The really clever thing is that he's managed to poison the whole crew against us. My own goddamned crew."

"Maybe he didn't get all of them," he said hopefully.

"It doesn't matter. Now that I know he got some of them, there's no way I can trust any of them. That's the brilliant part. He knows I won't risk it now, and all the while he'll win more of them over to his side." She frowned. "By the time it's safe to show my face—if that ever actually happens—I'll have no chance of winning them back."

"Unless we can prove he's the one who really betrayed them."

"Not fucking likely."

"But worth a shot, huh?"

"Maybe," she said. "But that's tomorrow's problem. Right now we've got to get the money before they break in and take it."

"The storage place my cousin used is actually pretty high tech. It's not the rat hole we just came from. All indoors. 24-hour security. Cameras.

The whole thing's only a few years old."

"They'll need to con their way in then," said Chloe. "At least that'll take them a little longer to put together." She thought for a while, running over scenarios in her mind. "What we need is for someone we can trust to go in there and get the cash out for us. Someone they won't recognize. But someone we can trust."

"Why not try disguises?" Paul suggested.

"Too risky. That's what they'll be looking for, especially now that they know we're on to them."

They both thought silently for a long while. The car started to become uncomfortably stuffy.

"This is the problem when all your friends turn against you," said Chloe. "You've got no one to pick up your stolen money for you in the middle of the night. Especially not in this neighborhood."

Paul looked out the rapidly fogging windows at the parking lot and street beyond. He in fact did know this neighborhood pretty well, which was unusual for him in San Jose.

"Actually I have a friend in this neighborhood," he said softly. "Or at least I used to."

"Really?" said Chloe. "Will he be happy to help us out?"

"Probably not. But maybe it's worth a try."

"Who're you thinking of?"

"You're not going to like it," he said.

"I haven't liked anything for three days. Who're you thinking of?"

"Greg."

Chapter 37

PAUL had met Greg in high school, when they'd both played in the same weekly Dungeons and Dragons game on Saturday afternoons. They'd hit it off almost immediately, which surprised many onlookers since outwardly they had almost nothing in common. Back then—the late '80s—Paul's image and fashion sense hovered somewhere between punk and goth, with lots of black leather and band T-shirts (although in retrospect he was the textbook example of a poseur). Greg was chubby and socially awkward but brilliant. Pretty much your stereotypical nerd, except for his love of water skiing and jet skis.

Below the surface, though, they had almost everything in common. They had both been fanatical Dr. Who fans as kids. They shared a passion for the same sci-fi and fantasy authors, from the comedy of Douglas Adams and Piers Anthony, to the hard sci-fi of Paul Anderson and Isaac Asimov, to the morbid and depressing fantasies of Stephen Donaldson and Michael Moorcock. They obsessed over the *X-Men* and read *The Dark Knight Returns* and *Watchmen* with mouths agape in awe. And of course they rejoiced in *Star Wars* and watched *Star Trek: The Next Generation* religiously. They were, in short, geeks of a feather.

But more than anything, they had in common a love of games. Their *Dungeons and Dragons* group became the center of their social lives, with every Saturday game stretching through the night and into the following Sunday evening. During the week they talked constantly about their adventures and their characters and various ways they could tweak or improve the rules to make their games better. In their most speculative midnight reveries, they plotted and planned the game company they would create if they had a chance, describing in every detail how they'd do things better.

After high school, they always stayed in touch, even as they went off to different colleges hundreds of miles apart. Greg studied computer systems engineering at Georgia Tech, where he knew more than most of the teachers and found he had a special talent for computer-chip design and engineering. Paul went to Oberlin College in Ohio, where he got a degree in fine arts and illustration. Every Christmas break and summer vacation the old D&D group would get together again, and the core group of five players stayed thick as thieves.

Seven years after graduating from college, Greg had started a chip-design company and sold it to another, much larger company, netting over twenty-million dollars for himself in the process. Paul had worked as an artist for various comic companies before self-publishing his own series, Metropolis 2.0, which became one of the better selling indie-comics of the late '90s. He didn't have anything resembling the kind of money Greg had made, but they were both successful and happy in their chosen careers.

The next step was obvious; a plan hatched over a series of excited phone calls that resulted in the foundation of Fear and Loading Games. Greg brought the money and some technical know how, and Paul brought the intellectual property and inspiration for their first game, based on his comic book. Greg's network of contacts in Silicon Valley made finding the other founding partners pretty easy. Evan, Jerry, and, of course, Frank soon joined their team. They incorporated, rented an office, and got to work making the next smash hit game.

That was three years ago now, and things hadn't quite worked out as Paul had expected. Two and a half years of working together had strained Paul's friendship with Greg. Paul found Greg to be strangely distant and yet oppressively controlling. Greg no doubt thought Paul was moody and lazy and hard to work with. They spent less and less time together socially, and by the end, Paul would've been hard-pressed to remember the last time the two old friends had seen a movie or had a meal together.

"And you're sure this is a good idea?" Chloe asked Paul for the fifth time. They were standing on the front porch of Greg's modest house in San Jose. For all his money, Greg was not the kind of guy to buy big expensive houses and cars just because he could. This was the same house he'd bought when he first moved out to San Jose. It had more room than he needed as it was, and since he spent most of his time at the office anyway, he saw no reason to upgrade.

"No," said Paul, "For the fifth time, I'm not sure this is a good idea at all. But it's definitely an idea."

"A bad idea," Chloe insisted.

"Do you have a better one?" he asked, tired of this conversation.

"I haven't had time to come up with one. I've been too busy trying to convince you that this plan is bullshit."

"Too late," Paul said and pressed the doorbell.

"This is fucking insane," Chloe said under her breath. She reached her hand into her shoulder bag. Paul knew that it was the stun gun, not the laptop that she was getting ready.

They heard footsteps from inside and then the door swung open. There was Greg, in shorts and a Fear and Loading T-shirt, a twenty-dollar bill in his hand. "You're not pizza," he said, confused at first glance.

"Nope," Paul agreed.

Recognition hit Greg like a ton of bricks. He reeled back from the door, saying "Jesus... Paul..."

"Hi, Greg. Can we come in?"

"What?" Greg stammered. "What are you doing here?" There was no fear, just utter surprise in his voice.

"I need to talk to you, Greg. About everything that's happened. I need to talk to you."

Greg stepped back from the doorway and held out an awkward arm, motioning them into the living room. "Oooookaaaaay," he drawled warily. The living room remained sparsely decorated, as always. Two fluffy Rooms to-Go couches facing Greg's one big splurge—a 66-inch plasma-screen TV and a top-end sound system. Chloe and Paul stood uncomfortably in the middle of the living room while Greg shut the door and then looked back at them with equal discomfort.

"So," Greg finally said, "Frank said he ran into you the other night." Paul recognized this as typical understatement for Greg.

"Yeah," said Paul. "That's what I wanted to talk to you about. It's not what everyone's saying it is."

"You didn't knock him out and tie him up in a closet?"

"I don't know anything about that, Greg, I swear. I was at that fund raiser thing, but I had nothing to do with Frank and whatever happened to him."

"Uh-huh," Greg replied. "That's not what Frank says."

"I'm going to go talk to him next," said Paul. "Try and get this straightened out. My face is all over the news and shit, and it's scaring the hell out of me."

Greg gestured toward Chloe. "Can't your lawyer here help you?"

Paul looked at Chloe for help, but her face was a stone mask. "I should explain that, too. She's my girlfriend, Greg. She's not really a lawyer. I just got her to help me out with that boardroom thing because…" he started to falter. "Because I didn't know who else to turn to, and I was kind of in shock and well…"

He looked up at Greg, hoping for some sign of empathy from his old friend, but he just stood there, looking as grave and inscrutable as Chloe did. "Listen, I'm really sorry about how all that went down. But you have to understand, Greg, I was so pissed and…"

Greg suddenly interrupted him. "You blackmailed me, Paul. You blackmailed all of us into paying you off. You read private e-mails, raided the company servers. How am I supposed to understand that kind of betrayal?"

Paul saw that Greg was getting angry and, in spite of himself, he felt his own gorge rising. "I wasn't the first person to do some betraying here. You betrayed me, Greg. You and Frank and all of them, you fired me without cause. Without warning. It was my fucking game, and you fucking fired me."

"We fired you because you were impossible to work with!" Greg retorted. "You were lazy and insufferable to talk to. You took the smallest criticism as a personal affront. Your design documentation was difficult to understand at best and you were never around to explain things when the programmers or artists had questions. You left me no choice, Paul."

"I was impossible to talk to?" Paul was near shouting. "Have you ever had a conversation with Frank where he didn't belittle you? Have you ever tried to get Evan to make a decision in less than three days? Has Jerry ever said the same thing to your face that he says behind your back? None of us were perfect there. You know that better than anyone."

Greg mulled this over for a minute, before responding. "You're right, Paul, they're hard to work with. But they're also something you ceased to be. They're indispensable. I need them all to finish the game. But you, you hadn't really added anything to the mix in over a year. Sure it was your idea and your comic. But what have you done for me lately?"

"Isn't that enough? There wouldn't even have been a game or a company if it weren't for me!"

"No, not at first there wouldn't have been. But I've got news for you. The company's still there, and it's doing fine without you, even better in many ways. You failed to make us need you, Paul, and once that happened, it was only a matter of time."

Deep down, Paul knew that everything Greg was saying was true. He'd known it long before they fired him, which was why he'd started coming in later and leaving earlier. No one really did need him there, and certainly no one wanted him. His place in the company had evaporated long before they'd made it official and fired him. Paul's head started to pound, a migraine-level headache coming on. He sat down on one of the couches, covering his face in his hands.

Chloe spoke up for the first time. "Greg, I'm really sorry for my part in all this." There was a quiver of fear in her voice. "I just wanted to help Greg out—he was so upset when you fired him and, well, I was angry for him. I'd never met any of you guys, and all I saw was someone I cared about who was in pain. I wanted to do right by him, and I'm sorry that meant doing wrong by you."

Greg really focused on Chloe for the first time since they'd shown up at his door. "How come I never heard Paul mention you before?"

"Well, you two weren't exactly close anymore by the time Paul and I met. I know you guys have been best friends forever, so it must be hard to have grown apart like this. Lord knows I know what that's like." A touch of sadness crept into Greg's features at the mention of their lost friendship. Chloe pressed the opening.

"You've been friends for years," she continued. "That's why we're here, because when I asked Paul who he trusted, who he could count on in a jam, he said 'Greg.' Without even thinking, he said he could trust you." Greg looked in surprise over at Paul, who still had his face down in his hands. She saw a hint of wetness in the corners of Greg's eyes. "And we're in a hell of a jam now. Way over our heads."

"Yeah," Greg said, turning back to look at Chloe. "I saw the news on TV."

"That's not what it seems. Not by a longshot," She moved over and sat down next to Paul, putting a comforting arm around him and squeezing him close. "It's complicated and hard to explain, but the short version is, I got us into some pretty nasty trouble. The guy who organized that fundraiser thing where Frank saw us? His name's Ralph Kryswiki, and he's an old acquaintance of mine and he asked us to help him out. That's all. We had no idea it was all a scam. But when things went wrong he blamed it all on Paul. He's just a scapegoat."

Greg moved into the center of the room and stared down at the two of them. "Is this true Paul?"

He finally looked up, rubbing his temples. "Yeah, Greg, it is. I don't know how this happened. I don't know what's going on, but this Ralph guy is really screwing with my life. Turns out he's some sort of con man, and now he knows everything about me. About my family. He's threatening to destroy my whole life."

Greg stared in silence, his expression aghast at what Paul was saying.

"I need your help Greg. This guy's watching every move I make, and I need your help."

"What can I do?" he asked. "Do you need money or something…?"

"No," said Paul. "No, you've given me more than enough money, Greg. I just need you to do me a favor. I need you to pick something up for me."

"Pick up what?"

"Do you remember that spring break when we went to New Orleans and stayed with my cousin?"

"Yeah," Greg said, an unconscious smile of remembrance crossing his features. "Sure, I remember that."

"Well, she lived out here before I moved to San Jose, you remember me telling you that?"

"Vaguely."

"Well, she left a bunch of stuff in a storage locker here in town when she moved. I've been using the locker too, and I need you to get something out of it for me."

"Why do you need me to get it?"

"This Ralph guy, he's all over us. Watching every move we make. I can't risk going there myself."

Greg started to look skeptical again, "Maybe you should just go to the police," he said.

"I will!" Paul said. "God knows I want to, but I need to get a few things sorted out and see a lawyer first. But I can't do that until tomorrow, and I'm afraid of what might happen if I don't get the bag out of there tonight."

"I know this sounds a little out of the ordinary," Chloe chimed in, "But we've got no one else we can turn to."

Greg regarded them both in turn, thinking things over. They just stared back at him, looking as helpless and sad as one could imagine, huddled together on the edge of Greg's couch. "What's in the bag?" he finally asked.

"Money," said Paul. "The money you paid me for my stock."

Greg had to laugh at that, although there wasn't a lot of humor in it. "You're kidding, right?"

"No, I'm serious," Paul pleaded. "I wouldn't be asking like this if I weren't serious."

"You want me to help you get back the money you extorted from me before someone else steals it from you?" Greg asked incredulously. "That takes some nerve."

"I know, Greg, I know. But at this point all I want to do is make sure this Ralph guy doesn't get it or get me arrested. That's all I care about—I just want my life back."

"Uh-huh," Greg said. His face was starting to set in stone again, and Paul knew he had to act fast.

"Listen, if you do this for me, you can take whatever you want from the bag. Leave me whatever it is you think I deserve. But please, I need your help on this."

Greg turned away and walked out of the living room, leaving Chloe and Paul alone and staring at each other in surprise. "I told you," Chloe whispered to him. But a moment later Greg came back with a pad of paper and a pen, which he tossed in Paul's lap.

"Write down the storage locker info and how you want me to get the bag to you," he said.

Relief flooded through Paul's body. "Do you mean it?" he said. "I really can't thank you enough."

Greg held out his hand for Paul to stop. "Hey," he said with a tight-lipped smile, "Just be good from now on, OK?"

Paul could only nod in agreement and, maybe, shame.

Chapter 38

"DO you not want this money?" Chloe asked, as they drove away from Greg's house. "Is that why you keep trying to give it away?"

"What the hell are you talking about?" he asked angrily.

"Telling him he could take whatever he wanted from the money, basically making it OK for him to take it all." She kept on talking before he could respond. "And before that, the thing that got us into this mess—telling the crew you'd give them the cash if your scam failed. If you hadn't done that..."

"If I hadn't done that, Raff would've found some other way to get at me!" Paul shouted. "He'd already had his gun-toting buddy try and shake me down before that, if you remember. And he'd already brought that guy into it before we got back from the beach!"

"Yeah," Chloe conceded, "OK, but..."

"And as for Greg," Paul said, "He doesn't care about the money. You've got to trust me; I've known this guy forever. He's got his own very strong views about what's right and wrong. He's not pissed about me stealing $850,000 from him; he's pissed at me for taking something he thinks I didn't deserve. I had to convince him that it wasn't about the money at all, that I was looking for forgiveness and help. If I'd tried to hide what was in the bag or tried to buy him off with just a portion of the cash, he'd have frozen up on us. Trust me, I know this guy."

"OK, OK, I'll grant you that this may have been the only way to play him. Fine. But..." Then she stopped herself and just concentrated on driving.

"But what?" Paul asked.

"Never mind. We've got to plan our next move now. If Greg is going to pick the bag up in an hour like he said he will, we need to get ready to give him some cover." They'd thought about telling Greg to wait for their signal that it was all clear, but decided that the less his actions seemed like part of some criminal enterprise, the more likely he was to cooperate. And so they'd let him choose his own time frame, which amounted to waiting until he'd finished his pizza and changed clothes. About an hour.

"How do we do that then?" Paul asked.

"We go in first, draw their attention."

"You mean draw their fire," Paul corrected.

"Hopefully not, but yeah, maybe. We can't let Greg just walk in there with them watching. They won't recognize him, but they might follow him anyway, just because of the timing of his visit. If they follow him home or run his plates and then figure out his connection to you, they'd move in on him."

"We don't even know if they really have someone watching the storage locker," Paul pointed out. "If it's just the three or four of them working together, they couldn't have the manpower."

"If they didn't before, they certainly do now. Since we beat up on Kurt he'll have helped Raff win the whole crew over. And even if he didn't bring them in, they've had plenty of time to get over there while we were dealing with Greg. No, there's definitely somebody watching the building now."

"So we just go in there and pretend to get the money? Again? We're going to use the same plan twice?"

"No," said Chloe, "This time it's different. This time we don't have any backup with baseball bats."

"Oh, well, then everything should work out peachy."

"Don't worry, I've got a plan," she turned and winked at him and grinned.

That wink had drawn him to her the day they met. It had pulled him into her world and trapped him there. It had a dozen different shades of meaning, from flirtation to warning. He'd seen every variation a hundred times since that first morning, but this was a new look. And suddenly he realized he knew her well enough to read its meaning without ever having seen it before.

"No you don't," Paul asserted.

The smile disappeared and she turned her head sharply back to the road. After a long while she said, "No. I don't."

The money's actual hiding place was in the two-story Store-Rite build-ing that had been built just four years earlier. It was a bitter orange and deep brown, with brightly lit picture windows breaking up the facade every twenty feet or so on the second floor. From the road you could see the steel doors of the storage lockers inside, illuminated under fluores-cent lighting that left no room for shadows.

The main entrance faced a parking lot that abutted the road. Anyone with a locker had twenty-four hour access. All they had to do was use their key and six-digit pass code to open the front door, sign in with the security guard on duty behind the desk and then proceed to the locker and use the same key and pass code again to open the door, all while being recorded on the internal security cameras. Paul had given Greg his key and code, so they had no way of even getting inside, much less into the actual locker.

Chloe drove by the building twice in a five-minute period, scarcely slowing down on either occasion. There had been no cars in the parking lot or even parked within view of the building on either occasion. If Raff and his crew were watching, they weren't out in the open.

"They've got to have a hidden camera set up," Chloe said. "They'll be watching from somewhere out of sight but nearby, waiting for us to come in and make a move."

"If they're smart, they wouldn't want to show themselves until after we went inside, or even until after we came out with the money, right?" Paul said.

"Exactly," she said. "Which means we have to find the camera and knock it out. Then they'll be blind for a moment, and they'll have to show their hand in order to figure out what's happening."

The area around the target building had hundreds of places to hide a camera: trees, doorways, roofs, windows, storm drains. If they started searching them all, they'd tip off whoever was watching.

Chloe drove by the location one last time and then parked in an of-fice building's lot two blocks away. She reached into the back of the car and pulled out her laptop and fired it up. She then drew out a black box the size of a pager and plugged it into one of the ports. "The one advantage of being betrayed by your friends is that you still all use the same equipment," she said.

"What's that?"

"The camera, wherever it is, is almost definitely one of Bee's. That means it's got its own power source, and it transmits whatever it's record-ing wirelessly to a receiver. This," she said, indicating the small black box, "is one of Bee's homemade receivers that I keep with my laptop. It's also good for eavesdropping on cell phone calls, so it's nice to have handy. I just have to find the right frequency and hope we're close enough to pick up the signal."

They both sat in silence and watched as Chloe tweaked with the display on her laptop. It automatically searched through the available frequencies and, after a few minutes, the screen lit up with a green-tinted night vision image of the storage facility front door.

"Sweet," said Paul.

"Super sweet," Chloe agreed. The image was from across the street and from a very low angle. "That's got to be hidden in the storm drain there. Either that or on the underside of a car or something, but there weren't any on the street." They kept looking for another five minutes, but their scan didn't pick up any more cameras that were broadcasting.

"Just one?" Paul asked.

"Looks like it," Chloe replied. "They're stretched thin as is, and they're in just as much of a rush as we are. Which is good, because it's an easy approach to block that camera. We might just be able to pull this off."

"OK," said Paul, "Greg will be here soon. Shall we?"

"Definitely. First, I need to get something from 7-11." Chloe threw the car into gear and headed back toward the street and the waiting camera.

Chapter 39

THE car screeched to a halt at the side of the road, its right front tire directly in front of the storm drain. Paul leaned out the passenger-side window and told Chloe to inch a foot forward just to be sure. He then looked down at the laptop screen and confirmed that the camera was completely blocked.

"Take the wheel and be ready," Chloe said as she swung the door open and raced across the deserted street, her shoulder bag bouncing at her side. Paul moved into the driver's seat and adjusted the mirrors so he could keep on eye out for the company they were expecting any minute. Chloe had guessed that whoever was watching would wait a minute or two and see if the obstruction cleared before sending someone to check it out in person.

He watched as Chloe reached the front door and started pounding on the glass. A quick scan around the street showed no one else. So far, so good. Unfortunately, Chloe seemed to be having a hard time convincing the guard to let her in. On the other side of the glass door, he was motioning her to clear off and had even moved his hand to his belt, just a few inches from his gun. Chloe gestured with a sweeping arm back toward the road and then brandished her cell phone. She was claiming an emergency of some sort.

They kept talking through the glass, but the guard refused to open the door. The conversation carried on for an infuriating two minutes and Paul started to shake his right leg in impatience. A pair of headlights appeared in the rearview mirror—a car pulling out from a side street about a block away. Paul tapped the horn lightly.

The security guard had given up and moved back to his desk where he picked up the phone. Ignoring him and the horn, Chloe tore open her shoulder bag and whipped out two large, brown paper shopping bags which they'd gotten at the 7-11 twenty minutes earlier. She opened these up and stood them on the ground in front of the door. The guard looked at her curiously, his hand actually seizing the handle of his gun. Chloe then took out a newspaper and started tearing out pages and crumpling them into balls.

Paul watched as the car behind him crept down the street at well under the speed limit. It wasn't the Cadillac from earlier that evening, but that didn't mean anything. With the headlights shining directly into his rear window, it was impossible for Paul to make out who was behind the wheel or even how many people were in the vehicle.

Back across the road, the security guard was yelling at Chloe from inside, while she finished stuffing balled-up pieces of newspaper into the shopping bags. Both bags now looked full. Possibly even full of money if you didn't know better. She slung her messenger bag over her shoulder again and took a shopping bag in each hand. She did a great job mimicking a weight that wasn't there.

The car now pulled even with Paul, less than a foot to his left. He couldn't help but look over. There were two people in the car, a man and a woman, neither of whom Paul recognized. From the passenger seat, the woman gave Paul a quick glance and a smile. The driver had his eyes fixed on Chloe across the street. He slowed his vehicle down even more, so that it was just barely cruising along at under five miles per hour.

Across the street Chloe stopped in her tracks and stared at the new arrivals. She and the driver locked eyes briefly and then he hit the accelerator, moving down the street and turning right at the first cross street. Chloe sprinted forward.

"Let's go!" she shouted. Paul was already prepared to do just that. As soon as Chloe clambered into the back seat, he took his foot off the brake and pulled into the street, making a wide U-Turn and heading back down the road in the opposite direction from where the mystery car had gone.

"Who was that?" Paul asked as he headed for the nearest freeway entrance, less than a quarter mile away.

"I'm not sure, friend's of Raff's, maybe? Passersby? I didn't recognize them."

Paul saw a pair of headlights appear in his rearview mirror, then another one. "Two cars back there," he said.

"Just get to the highway, and we'll shake them," she said.

"Looks like it worked," Paul said. Both cars were pulling closer to them. "They think we've got the money. Why didn't they try and grab you when you came out?"

"They probably didn't think I'd be able to get in and out with the cash as fast as I did. Whoever those two were, weren't prepared to make a grab. Probably not muscle, just another set of eyes."

"How many people do you think Raff's brought in on this damn thing?"

"I guess it's his mentor and his mentor's crew. Raff may have scared my old crew off entirely, just to clear the field and cut off my support." She was speaking fast and it took her a second to realize the full implications of what she'd just said. "Which means he might have been playing all of us from the beginning—not just you."

"Well," said Paul, "it's nice to have company."

They pulled onto Highway 880 heading north and poured on the speed. Both the cars followed suit. Paul merged into the right-hand lane. So did their new friends. They didn't appear too concerned about hiding their presence. One of them moved into the middle lane and started to accelerate, trying to come even next to Paul.

As they picked up speed, Paul suddenly jerked his wheel to the right. They cut across a patch of striped asphalt, narrowly missing a concrete barrier. He hit the brakes as they went into a tight, banked curve, exiting the highway as quickly as they'd gotten on.

Neither car reacted to the sudden change in time. The car in the middle lane shot north along the highway. The car still behind them hit its brakes hard, but still missed the turn off as it screeched to a halt in the emergency lane a few dozen yards past where Paul had turned.

"Fuck yeah!" Paul yelled. Chloe was laughing, patting him heartily on the shoulder.

"Just keep going," she said, watching through the rear windshield. "We need to keep them busy for a few hours so Greg can get in there without any trouble."

Paul took the first turn he could and then the next, winding his way through a maze of small office parks and warehouses. There wasn't any sign of pursuit, but he kept driving evasively for the next fifteen minutes, looking for someplace out of view from the road where they could park and regroup.

Eventually they settled on a half-full parking lot behind a complex of three office buildings. They must've run some sort of late-shift customer service or something there, so there was enough cover for them to get lost in but not so much in-and-out traffic as to worry about an employee noticing them. Most importantly, there was no sign of on-site security personnel.

Chloe moved up to the front seat and they sat and relaxed for a moment, catching their breath.

"Do you think they bought it?" Paul asked after a long while.

"Yeah," she said. "I really do. Which means they're shitting themselves right now. They think we're in the wind with the money. If that's true, they know there's no way they'll find us."

"But we're not free and clear yet."

"We might as well be," Chloe said with a chuckle. "Fuck, I can't believe we actually made this work."

"Yeah," Paul sighed. His voice was not nearly as full of joy and relief as hers was.

"What's wrong?" she asked.

"There's still the whole wanted by the police thing," he said.

"Oh, fuck that. What's the big deal there? No real money got stolen in the end. No one's going to care in a couple weeks. Trust me, they'll stop looking for you."

"But that won't clear my name. I'll still be wanted."

"So?" she asked.

"So? So?" He said, exasperation creeping into his voice. "So, I'll have to live my life as a fugitive."

"It's not that bad."

"The warrants won't just disappear."

"No," she interrupted. "I mean living as a fugitive. It's not that bad."

Paul looked at her incredulously. "Of course it is! How would you…" and then she pulled his head to hers and kissed him.

She broke the kiss just long enough to say "Trust me, I know" before kissing him once more. Their hands roamed over each other and Chloe started to nibble at his neck. "I've lived this way for ten years," she whispered. He moaned as she started caressing him through his pants. "It can be fun if you've got the right friends."

Paul didn't argue as she undid his pants, and she didn't argue when he pulled her shirt up over her head. He certainly didn't argue when she slipped the condom onto him and then climbed onto his lap. Right at that moment, as he slid into her, Paul felt like he had everything he'd ever wanted from life. Maybe she was right. Maybe this was the life for him.

Chapter 40

AS IS so often the case with men, after he'd orgasmed, Paul began to have second thoughts.

The car windows were completely fogged over, and they both sweated as they fumbled with trying to find and put their clothes back on. Chloe was talking about where they could go next and how they needed to get new ID's. Paul scarcely listened as all his problems washed back over him. He didn't want a new ID. He didn't want to live on a boat with Winston's crew (assuming the old hippie was even alive). On the other hand, he didn't have any better ideas. If only there was some other path they could figure out for themselves.

And that thought surprised him. He was thinking in terms of "us" not "I." Whatever happened next, he knew he wanted it to be with Chloe. Despite all the post-coital doubts about his immediate future, he had no doubt about how he felt about her. No doubt that whatever the next step was, it involved the two of them together.

He looked over to her in the passenger seat as she pulled her pants back on. She was expounding upon the merits of San Diego as a good hideaway option during the winter. He reached over and put his finger to her lips. She looked at him curiously.

"I love you, Chloe," he said, his heart in his throat.

"I love you too, Paul," she replied without a second's pause, as if it were the most obvious thing in the world. As if he was a moron to have ever thought otherwise.

"You do?" he asked.

She laughed and kissed him. Then kissed him again, harder. "Of course I do, didn't you know that? Why else would I do all this?"

He didn't know if he'd known it or not. But now -- now her phone was ringing.

They both looked at the phone, which had fallen on the floor of the back seat, in surprise. Chloe twisted around and picked it up, looking at the display screen. All it said was "Private Name, Private Number," which meant it was probably either a telemarketer or a crew member. She watched it ring for a moment before finally deciding to answer.

"Hello?" she asked. Paul couldn't make out the voice on the other end. "Bee?" she said in astonishment. "Where are you? Are you OK?"

Paul watched as Chloe's face turned from surprise and worry to intense resolve and concentration. "I don't know about that," she said. A long pause. "OK, OK, I trust you. You know I do." Another long pause. "Yes, yeah, fine. Yeah, I know the place. See you then."

"Is Bee OK?" Paul asked.

"I think so," she said. "But she says she needs help. She wants us to meet her."

"Oh Christ," said Paul. "That doesn't sound like a good fucking idea."

"No," Chloe agreed, "It doesn't. But we have to go."

"What if she's with Raff?"

"She's not," Chloe insisted. "She's not."

"Are you sure?"

"No," she said, her voice barely a whisper.

"Do you have a plan?"

"No."

They both stared at each other, although really they were staring past one another, thinking out all the possible dangers ahead of them. Paul realized that he couldn't even fathom what the dangers might actually turn out to be and so it was best to get on with it and find out first hand.

"Fine," said Paul. "But I'm driving."

They pulled into the parking lot of a ten-room motel in south San Jose, a largely Hispanic neighborhood that Paul, given his isolated techie existence, had never even driven through, much less stopped in. He consoled himself with the thought that it had been less than an hour since they lost their pursuers on the freeway and therefore whatever trap they might have set couldn't be too terribly complex.

Paul recognized one of the cars in the lot as Bee's small hatchback. The crew usually changed cars as easily as clothes, and it was a surprise to see that Bee was so openly advertising her presence to anyone who knew her. He wasn't sure what to make of that.

"What do you make of that?" he asked Chloe.

"I dunno. Other than the fact that Bee's probably actually in there." She pointed to room 8, which was the only one with a light on inside. "Just like she said she would be."

They'd spent the last ten minutes cruising the neighboring streets, scanning for other hidden cameras with Chloe's laptop and looking for any familiar cars or faces. Everything had come up clean. With no more precautions to take, they'd run out of excuses to not go in. Except, Paul thought, for the obvious excuse that it was a bad idea.

"Why're we doing this again?" he asked for the tenth time since they'd gotten Bee's call. She decided to ignore him this time. She pulled her stun gun from her bag and then leaned forward and tucked it into the back of her pants before pulling her shirt down over it. Paul backed the car into the space right in front of room 8, so they could make a quick escape if they needed to.

"I'll keep the motor running," he said as she opened the door.

"And your eyes open," she said, giving him a quick kiss on the cheek. "If I run into trouble, I'll call in the cavalry."

Paul held up his cell phone. "That's me, a cavalry of one. I'll have my horse saddled and ready to go," he said with a wan smile. She winked at him and went to the motel-room door.

He sat in the car and tried his best to look everywhere at once, but it wasn't working for him, so he concentrated on watching Chloe in the rearview mirror. She knocked lightly on the door and waited. After a few seconds, she put her hand on the doorknob and turned it herself. Paul got a glimpse of yellow light from inside but nothing else. She slipped into the room without opening the door all the way and then closed it behind her.

Paul sighed and scanned the quiet night around him. Across the street was a gas station and a small strip mall with several shops and a restaurant. All the signs were in Spanish, and all the businesses were closed. He tensed as a pickup truck passed by on the street, but it didn't even slow down and the driver never took his eyes off the road. He supposed Raff or the P.I. could be in any of the empty storefronts or in any of the adjacent motel rooms. For that matter, they could've been waiting inside with Bee and had Chloe in their clutches right now.

As the seconds ticked by without any sign from Chloe, another possibility crept unwanted into his head. What if Chloe was setting him up? Was it possible, even after everything that had happened? Was all this the most complicated con imaginable, a massive plot to steal his money? Given the fact that Winston had gotten shot earlier, that seemed impossible. Raff and Chloe were definitely at odds at this point, no doubt about that, but what about Bee and Chloe? Could they be planning something? Why else would Chloe risk coming here if not for the sake of some pre-arranged agreement with Bee?

His phone buzzed in his lap, starting him out of his reverie. He looked down at the face and saw Chloe's name. Huh?

"Hello?" he said.

"Act cool. Nonchalant," said Chloe, "But calmly get out of the car and come in here right now."

"Wh…"

"Right now," she insisted.

He turned the engine off and got out of the car, the phone still in his hand. He wondered if talking on the phone made him look more or less calm and decided he'd find out what was going on soon enough and so he kept his hand and the phone at his side. The motel room door opened easily and he stepped inside.

In the middle of the dingy room stood Bee and Chloe. The single queen sized bed was covered with electronics, including a laptop with its display open and facing the doorway. It took Paul a moment to understand what he was seeing on the screen.

"Shut the door," hissed Bee.

Paul reached behind him to knock the door shut, all the while keeping his eyes locked on the screen. There he saw an image of himself from a vantage point above and behind him, looking through the motel room door. There were cross-hairs on the back of his head. As the door slammed shut they moved and focused on the peephole.

"What the fuck," said Paul.

"It's a trap," said Chloe.

"Sorry," said Bee, meekly.

Chapter 41

"WHAT the fuck am I looking at?" Paul asked as he stared at the image of the motel room door on the computer monitor. The red, superimposed crosshairs were almost, but not quite, dead on the peephole. All three of them in the room were careful not to stand anywhere near the door.

"It's..." Bee started to explain. "It's a live feed from a camera across the street... I'm tapping into the signal from whoever's controlling it."

"And the crosshairs?" Paul asked.

"Well, I think it's because the camera's on a gun, but there's no way to be sure," she stared back at the screen. "It's really pretty clever if you think about it."

"Someone's pointing a remote controlled gun at us?" Paul didn't much care if it was clever or not.

"A rifle probably," Bee said distantly, her eyes locked on the screen.

"Oh my God," said Paul, stepping further away from the door.

Chloe gently gripped Bee by the shoulders and turned the small woman to face her. "Bee, listen to me, please. Is this Raff's gun camera? Is Raff controlling it?"

"I think maybe so," said Bee. "It's definitely my equipment he's using anyway. Stolen from the house when they cleared everything out earlier. So if it's not you guys then it's got to be Raff. Or maybe someone else." Her voice was distracted, distant. Paul thought she sounded like she was in shock, which didn't surprise him since he felt the same way himself.

"Why didn't he shoot us then?" Paul asked, panic working its way from his brain and into his voice. "If I was in his sights, why didn't he fucking shoot me?"

"Because he doesn't know if we've got the money with us," Chloe said. Amazingly, her voice was still calm.

"But now he's got us trapped in here, right?" Paul said as he looked around the tiny room. Bed, dresser, TV, bathroom. No rear exits. No other windows besides the one facing the front. No escape.

"Yeah, but he's right about one thing," Chloe said, "We don't have the money with us. If he wants that he's going to have to deal. We've got some leverage here. All we have to do is wait for him to contact us and then we'll talk our way out of this."

"Simple as that, huh?" Paul said.

"Simple as that," she assured him. "He'll call. Trust me, he won't want to come busting down that door until he knows more about what we've got in here." Chloe turned back to Bee and scanned the piles of electronics and black plastic cases that covered the bed and spilled out onto the floor. "What do we have here anyway, Bee?"

The engineer sat down on the bed amidst her equipment, like a child surrounded by her stuffed animals. "It's just everything that I could salvage when the word came down from Kurt to bug out of the house this afternoon."

"This afternoon?" said Chloe in surprise. "Not this evening?"

"No, this afternoon. After Raff and Kurt went to meet with you guys at the Great Mall, he called in and gave us the signal to bug out. We'd already half packed up everything anyway, once we saw Paul on TV. It was a madhouse getting everything together, and once it turned dark we moved out all the important stuff. I took everything I could fit into my car."

"Is there a fallback point?" Chloe asked

"We're supposed to call in to a number. Kurt and Raff said they'd set it up," Bee said. "But I don't think that's going to happen, do you? I don't think they're going to set up a fallback at all…" Bee's voice trailed off, and she looked around lovingly at her equipment. "They're all gone."

Paul looked at Chloe and asked, "What is she talking about?"

"The crew has bugged out from the house," Chloe said. "It's like an emergency procedure when everything just goes to shit. Everybody packs up anything that might be valuable or incriminating or even vaguely interesting to the police. Then they split up and go their separate ways. Everyone goes somewhere else and no one knows where anyone else is hiding. All they have is a number or a Website address or something

where they can check in for further instructions about how we're supposed to get back together."

"And Raff gave this order?"

"Sounds like it. And he had Kurt backing him up. Except of course
Kurt and Raff and Filo didn't bug out. They came after us instead, with
their friend and his gun."

Bee's attention snapped to Chloe when she heard this. "What?" she
asked.

Chloe cleared a space on the bed and sat down next to Bee, putting
a comforting hand on her friend's knee. "Raff tried to kill me and Paul
earlier. He's working with that private eye who attacked Paul on the
highway. He's the one who set up the whole thing from the beginning—
the one who invited Paul's old co-worker to the fundraiser. It was all a
set up."

Bee looked heart-stricken. "Why?" she asked. "Why would he turn on
you like that? Was it because of Paul?"

"He didn't turn on just me and Paul," Chloe insisted. "He betrayed
all of us. Look what he's done, Bee! He brought in the police and went
to an outsider for help in fucking the rest of us over."

Bee thought about this for a long time, while Chloe and Paul looked
on in awkward silence. She looked down at her hands, fidgeting with a
paper clip. When Chloe decided she wasn't going to say anything else,
she said, "Bee, is there anything here that can help us? Maybe a way to
jam the signal that's controlling the gun or something like that…"

But Bee didn't seem to have heard her. Instead of answering Chloe's
question she said, "To be fair, Chloe, you brought in an outsider first,
right?"

"Huh?" said Chloe. "You mean Paul?"

"Yes. He was supposed to be another mark, right? When you called
me from that Mexican restaurant and asked me to check his picture and
name. You said you had a live one. A live mark." Bee never looked up
from her hands as she said this. "That's what you said. You said I should
look up everything I could find on him as quick as possible and text you
if he was a good mark. And when I found out he was really the founder
of that game company, I did that. I told you he was a good mark."

It took Paul a minute to really understand what Bee was saying. She
was talking about the day he'd met Chloe at the Senor Goldstein's. The
day he'd been fired. He remembered Chloe talking on the phone. At the
time he'd thought she was calling into her bosses at the market research
firm she worked for, which seemed perfectly plausible under the circumstances. He hadn't thought about it since, but in retrospect he realized

that of course she was calling someone in the crew. And apparently that someone was Bee.

"Bee, come on, that's different," Chloe protested. "We need to focus on our big fucking problem of the moment." She pointed to the screen on the laptop. "That gun that's pointed right at us."

"All Raff wants is the money, right?" said Bee, her voice level and empty of emotion. "The money we were supposed to steal from Paul in the first place. Why not just give it to him? Just give him the money, and we'll call everyone back together and move back into the house and…"

"Bee, No!" Chloe shouted. "No. We're past that now. Raff has cut the crew loose because that was always his plan. He doesn't want to split the money with the rest of you; he wants it for himself, plain and simple. He tried to kill me. Do you fucking understand that? They shot at me and tried to kill me!"

"If we just gave him the money…" Bee tried to continue.

"No!" Chloe stood up. "You've got to trust me now, girl. Trust me. Raff is not your friend anymore. We have to concentrate on the problem at hand."

Paul could see how angry and frustrated Chloe was becoming, while Bee seemed more and more distant. Paul was getting pretty angry himself, although he was surprised how unsurprised he was that Chloe and everyone else had apparently been planning to steal from him since the beginning. Somewhere deep down he'd always assumed that was the case, which was why he'd hidden the money in the first place. Having it all out in the open was actually a relief.

He decided to jump in and see if maybe he could calm the situation down a bit. "Bee, I understand how you might blame me for screwing things up. My plan with the park and the fundraiser and all was pretty crazy, but you have to know that Raff did double-cross us. If you want a share of the money, I can cut you in when we get it. A full, equal share."

Bee finally looked up from fiddling with her paper clip and looked at Paul. "No, no," she said. "It's not your fault at all. It's my fault really. If you think about it, it really was all my mistake that caused this."

"What mistake are you talking about?" Paul asked. "It was Raff who…"

"It was my tracking device that failed," she said. Paul just looked at her in confusion.

"Oh Christ, not this again!" Chloe said, throwing her arms up in the air in disgust. "Are we really not past this yet?"

Bee ignored Chloe's outburst and focused her gaze even tighter on

Paul. "We put a tracking device on your car while you and Chloe were in the meeting with your old friends. It was working fine, but then something happened later. When you were at the bank. So when you left Chloe to go hide your money we had no way of tracking you. There was a car following you guys, too, but they got cut off in traffic." For the first time she smiled at him, a wan grin of resignation in the face of fate's cruel tricks. "You're really pretty lucky, you know."

"Yeah, I'm feeling lucky," Paul said, distractedly. So they had been tracking him after all. It only made sense. And it even made sense that Chloe had lied about it earlier when she'd said they didn't have a working tracking device. In a way that was actually true. He looked over at Chloe, wanting to let her know that it was OK, that he understood, but she avoided his gaze. Instead she decided to open up on Bee with both barrels.

"We fucking get it, OK?!?!" screamed Chloe. Bee flinched at the yelling and withdrew into herself. "We fucking very well get it! But as I keep trying to get through to you, we're past that! Well and truly fucking past that! Raff and his friend are out there and they've got guns pointed at us. And, boy oh fucking boy, is that bad news. Now, what the hell are we going to do about it?"

Bee sat there for a moment, silent. Then she exploded like a delayed bomb blast. She jumped up from the bed and shoved Chloe away from her. "Don't you talk to me like that! Don't you treat me like that!" She tried to shove Chloe again, but now that Chloe saw it coming, she easily fended off the smaller woman's attack. "This is your fault! You! You! You! I hate you!"

She shoved ineffectually at Chloe one last time and then turned around, snatched the laptop from the bed and retreated to the far corner of the room and crouched down, cradling the computer protectively.

Chloe stayed where she was but didn't stop yelling, "Then why the hell did you call us here? If it's all my fault, why call me crying and say you're in trouble? Huh?"

Bee wasn't crying now. Her eyes were dry and focused and very, very angry. "I wanted to see if we could work this out. See if we could come to an accord. I wanted to make everything like it was before he came into the house," she pointed at Paul.

"Fuck it, Bee! We're past that! I keep saying…" Chloe stopped in mid-sentence and then her voice was calm again. "You know what? Forget it. I'd rather let Raff shoot me than deal with anymore of this guilt bullshit."

She reached out to Paul, pulled him to her and kissed him hard on the lips and then looked back at Bee. "No, the con on Paul didn't work out and yes, as I told you weeks ago, I fell for him. I fell hard. And aren't I entitled? Why can't I fall in love with who I want?"

"But..." Bee started to protest, but Chloe wouldn't let her interrupt.

"And everything could've been great! You said yourself he was a promising crew member. You liked the comic con, and you liked the park prank. You voted for all of those, didn't you?"

"Yeah," Bee admitted, "But..."

"Weren't we all happy? Wasn't everything just the way you wanted it? And then what happened? Everything was going great until that miserable fuck Frank showed up at the fundraiser, right?"

"I guess," Bee whispered.

"Well, you remember those lists I had you e-mail me? Somebody had put Frank's name on those lists. Someone invited him to the party just so he'd recognize Paul. For the express purpose of blowing that con wide open, right?" Bee could only nod. "And that someone? That was Raff. It was fucking Raff, Bee. I can prove it."

"Why would he..." Bee stammered. "Why would he do that?"

"Why do we do anything, Bee?" Chloe sighed. "For the money."

"I don't...no..." Bee looked confused, hurt.

Paul thought back to his conversation with Raff and to what he'd said about people like Bee and him loving the crew not for the money, but for the lifestyle. He realized what a mistake he'd made with trying to buy her help. For her, it wasn't about the money.

"Bee, listen to me," Paul said. "I know you're upset at what happened, and I know you blame me and Chloe and I understand that. I understand that more than you know."

Chloe glanced at him skeptically, but he had Bee's attention. "What do you mean?" she asked.

"I was the only person who knew where my money was. I could've left at any time and gone and gotten my cash and just vanished. I could've gone back to Florida and drawn comic books and lived the good life for the next twenty years without worrying about anything. But I didn't. I stayed around. Why?"

"Because of Chloe?" Bee ventured.

"Sure, that was a part of it. But it's not like Chloe and I were really together all that much or even sleeping together for that matter. Yes, I love her, but I also loved all you guys, too. I loved living in that house, living in the world you all created for yourselves. We had everything we needed and anything we wanted and no one to tell us we couldn't have a good time or do drugs or have fun with our friends. It was, really, the first place that felt like home for me since I left my parents to go to college."

"I know what you mean," Bee said. He could see her eyes starting to tear up. "It was the only place that ever felt like home. The only family I ever had. The only one I liked, anyway." She started to sniffle. "And now it's all gone."

"It doesn't have to be," Paul reassured her. "We can build that again. You, me, and Chloe. And whoever else we can find. We can build it again. We will, I swear we will. Because that's what we all want. Because that's why I stuck around."

Chloe stepped in at this point, picking up on Paul's momentum. "He's right, Bee. Why do you think I came here when you called, even though I knew it might be a trap? Because I love you, Bee. Because we're family. And if we're going to rebuild, then we need to do it together. And we need to start now."

Bee started to cry in earnest now. She looked down at the computer in her lap and wiped away at the tears. She stared at the screen, apparently thinking about what they said. Paul and Chloe knew enough to let her figure things out for herself now.

Suddenly she looked up from the laptop. "OK, I'll help," she said. "But we need to hurry. Raff's here."

Chapter 42

"HERE as in here?" asked Paul with a hint of panic.

"As in at the door," said Bee.

Paul and Chloe both lunged toward the motel room door simultaneously. Being closer, Paul got there first and twisted the deadbolt shut, a second later whoever was on the outside tried to open the door.

"Hey," said Raff from outside. He knocked softly on the door. "Bee, it's me. Raff."

Chloe and Paul looked at each other in puzzlement and then at Bee, who was still staring at her computer screen. "I told him to come," she whispered. "He's expecting me to let him in."

Raff knocked again, this time louder. "Bee! Come on. Let me in!"

Chloe drew the stun gun from the back of her pants and showed Paul the she was ready with it. She nodded to him to go ahead and open the door while she retreated to the other side of the bed, where she crouched down out of sight. He wasn't sure this was a good idea, but it was a plan anyway. He moved to the door and, as quietly as possible, undid the deadbolt.

After it was unlocked, Bee waited a few long seconds before Chloe prodded her. Then she said, "Come in." Raff twisted the knob and started to swing the door open. Paul moved to the side, so he was hidden behind the door as Raff came in.

"Bee, what's going on?" Raff said as he stepped into the room. His left arm was in a makeshift sling and his face had a nasty purple bruise that covered his entire right cheek. He noticed Bee crouched in the corner and said, "Jesus, what're you doing down there? What's going on?"

He moved forward, leaving the door open with Paul still hiding behind it. Of course if he turned to the right even slightly he'd see that Paul was there. Paul wondered if maybe he should jump Raff now or wait for Chloe to make the first move.

"Just stay there," Bee said, her voice shaking. "Stay right where you are Raff."

Raff stopped and held up his one good hand in a gesture of surrender and peace. "It's OK, Bee. But we need to hurry. You said Chloe was coming here, right?"

"That's what I said," Bee whispered.

"What?" asked Raff.

"Yes, she's coming." Bee finally looked up from her screen. "But I need to know something first, Raff."

"Sure thing Bee, whatever you need to know."

"Why'd you do it?" she asked.

"Do what? Evacuate the house? I told you, with the cops coming down on Paul and him and Chloe running off, it was too dangerous to…"

"No," Bee said. "I mean why did you do it?" She looked back down at her laptop again. "Why did you add Paul's former partners to the list of invitees? Why did you get that Frank guy to come to the fundraiser?"

"What're you talking about, Bee? I didn't do…"

"I'm looking at the list right here, Raff. It's all right here on my computer. All five of those names are on the list, and they shouldn't be."

"I swear I don't know what you're talking about. Anyone could've put those names on the list. Hell, Paul probably put them there himself. You know how eager he was to prove he was one of us, even though he never really was." From behind Raff, Paul watched as the lanky man slipped his one good hand behind his back. Just where Chloe kept her stun gun, Raff had his extendable baton. At least it wasn't the damn gun, Paul thought. And then he remembered the P.I. and the camera across the street with the crosshairs.

Raff took a step toward Bee, still trying to talk his way out of this. "Why would I invite them there? Why would I bring the cops and all that trouble down on our crew? You know me, Bee. You've known me for almost two years. I'd never do that, would I?"

Bee never looked up from the laptop screen. "You'd do it for the money. To keep the money for yourself."

Raff took another step forward. He was even with the bed now, and in just a few feet he'd be able to see Chloe crouched behind it. The baton was at his side, held close along his leg so Bee couldn't see it.

"No way," Raff insisted. "There's no way I'd do that. I'm like you, Bee. I love this life. It's not the money, it's the life. Same for me as for you."

Bee finally broke her gaze away from the screen when she heard this. Paul wondered if Raff was getting through to her. He was glad he'd had a chance to use this tactic with her first. Still, Bee had always trusted Raff until today. Old loyalties might win out.

"No, Raff, not the same." Bee said. "Not the same at all. You ruined our family. Ruined it all." She then looked back down at the laptop's screen.

Raff's voice was smooth and calm as he stepped forward and raised the baton to strike. "That's just not true, Bee." The baton arced over his head as he moved quickly around the bed. "I'm your friend…"

If not for Chloe, he would have bashed Bee's head in then and there. Instead, Chloe lunged forward from her crouch and stabbed him in the chest with the stun gun, pressing him back against the flimsy motel wall with a crackle of electricity. Paul slammed the door shut and came charging forward as well, ready to subdue the stunned Raff.

Except Raff wasn't stunned. Braced against the wall, he kicked out at Chloe, catching her square in the stomach and doubling her over. He swung the baton down onto her back, sending her straight to her knees.

Paul kicked the motel room door closed and then slammed into him from the side. The two of them crashed down to the floor. Raff's baton wielding arm was trapped beneath both their bodies, and he cried out in pain as Paul landed hard on the broken left arm. "Fuuuuuuuck!" Raff screamed.

Chloe raised her head, wheezing for breath after having the wind knocked out of her. She saw Raff and Paul struggling on the floor a few feet away and crawled toward them, the stun gun still in her hand.

As Raff squirmed beneath him, Paul fought to pin the taller, stronger man to the ground. Raff managed to twist onto his back, freeing his good arm to swing at Paul with the baton. The blow glanced off his shoulder, but still hurt like a motherfucker. Now sitting astride Raff's torso, he grabbed at the baton arm with both hands.

Chloe looked for an opening, still amazed that Raff hadn't felt anything from the stun gun. As Paul grabbed Raff's arm, she saw a layer of black rubber beneath Raff's shirt—he was wearing a wetsuit. He really did know all Chloe's favorite tricks. She smiled and jabbed the stun gun into his neck. Raff instantly stopped resisting and started convulsing in pain.

Paul didn't have a chance to catch his breath before a booming thud came from the front door. Bee kept her eyes on her laptop. He and Chloe both turned to see what the noise was when the door flew open with a splintering thud. In the doorway stood the P.I., his gun pointed right at Paul.

"Hands up!" the P.I. shouted. "Drop everything, get off him right now or I'll shoot."

Before Chloe and Paul could move, the front of the P.I.'s head exploded with a wet plop. Blood and brains and skull fragments sprayed across the room and the man fell forward onto what was left of his face.

Bee finally looked up from her laptop screen.

Chapter 43

PAUL and Chloe looked over at Bee, shocked and horrified at what they'd just seen happen. Raff moaned underneath Paul, still unaware of what had befallen his comrade.

"What…?" Paul tried to say, although it came out more like "Wuuuuh"

"Did you hack their gun camera, Bee?" said Chloe, her voice somewhere between awe and skepticism.

Tears started to stream down Bee's face. She couldn't speak, but after a moment she shook her head vigorously no.

"Then why did they…" Suddenly realization dawned on Chloe. "That was never their camera, was it?"

Bee just shook her head again. No.

"You set this whole thing up?"

A tearful affirmative nod from Bee.

"Who were you planning to shoot?"

Bee struggled for words, but Chloe voiced her thoughts for her. "You were going to kill whoever destroyed your family, weren't you?"

Bee nodded, openly sobbing now.

"You did good, Bee" Chloe assure her with a calm voice. "You got the guy who screwed us all over. And if you hadn't, he probably would've shot us." Chloe's voice was comforting, almost motherly. "You did good, honey. But maybe you better shut that gun down now, just in case, OK?" Bee nodded again through her tears, grateful for both the approval and for being given a task to perform. She started typing on her laptop again.

Turning to Paul, Chloe said, "Shut the door and help me get him tied up, quick."

His shoulder still aching from the baton strike, Paul moaned as he got to his feet. The dead body of the P.I. still blocked the doorway. After a moment's inaction he grabbed the man's legs and pulled them through the door and then closed it behind him. He glanced outside but there was no one else out there, at least not that he could see.

Paul was surprised that he dealt with the dead body as easily as he did. He would have thought the mere sight of it would have made him helpless with disgust and horror. But since less than a minute earlier he'd been 99.9 percent sure that the man was going to shoot him dead, all he really felt was relief. He dimly imagined that the shock and alarm would set in pretty much any minute now.

"Wha happ'nnn?" Raff asked from the floor. Chloe was busy tying him up with a power cord she'd pulled free from a lamp. "Owww!" he shouted, as Chloe yanked his broken arm behind his back and tied his wrists together. She stuffed a towel into his mouth to shut him up and got up off the floor with a wince of pain.

"OK, the gun's shut down," Bee said in a soft, timid voice.

"Great," Chloe said. "Now I need you to start packing up. Pack all of this stuff up as fast as you can." She ripped another cord free from the room's other lamp. Now the only light came from the open bathroom door. "Paul, was there anyone else out there?"

"Not that I saw," he said.

"Good," she again bent over Raff, this time tying his legs together at the ankles. "I need you to take a towel, wet it down, and wipe every surface of the room for fingerprints. Everything, OK?"

Paul nodded and set to work. Bee was cramming her electronics into three big nylon bags and a milk crate. Testing her knots to make sure Raff was secure; Chloe took his baton, her stun gun and the dead man's pistol and stuffed them in her shoulder bag. Then she helped Bee pack.

"What name did you check in under?" she asked Bee.

"Suzy Wu," she said. Chloe's steady direction and the professional tone in her voice had gone a long way to calming Bee down. Paul found her to be a source of strength for himself as well, and wondered if it was this quality in particular that made her such a strong leader.

"Paid cash?" Chloe asked.

"Yeah, but secured with a false credit card."

"OK," Chloe said. "I'm going to step out and take a look around real quick. Make sure Raff's other friends aren't out there too. Then we're going to get out of here and not look back, OK?"

"OK," said Bee. "But I didn't see any other cars pull up when Raff got here."

"I've still got to check it out." She went to the window and pulled aside a corner of curtain to peer out into the parking lot. After about a minute of careful watching she let the curtain fall back, stepped over the dead body and opened the door just enough for her to squeeze out.

Paul and Bee both carried out their assignments in silence. Finished, they stared awkwardly at each other. Raff seemed unconscious on the floor, but Paul decided he was probably faking it. Now that he'd finished wiping the room down he was afraid to touch anything. Bee poked and prodded her pile of equipment, but it was all as packed as it was going to get.

"I really meant what I said," Paul finally announced, breaking the oppressive silence. Bee just looked at him with a sad, curious look on her face.

"I know Raff and I said the same thing—that the crew was a family for us. But for me it really was true. It is true, and I know it's probably even truer for you. I know that I'm really still kind of an outsider, but..." He paused, realizing that he was starting to babble. "I just wanted you to know. And thank you. Thank you for saving my life." He gestured toward the dead body. Neither of them wanted to look at it. Finally he concluded with, "And whatever happens next, I want the three of us to do it together, to stay together, to be a family."

Bee stared at him and started to turn watery. No, Paul realized. It was he himself who was tearing up now, turning everything in the dim room blurry with tears. Bee jumped up with surprising speed and clasped her small arms around Paul, holding him tight. He hugged her close. "Thank you," she said. "Thank you."

"No, thank you," Paul replied and gave her an affectionate kiss on the top of her head.

They stood like that for a few minutes, just comforting one another. Finally Chloe returned, slipping in quietly through the door. "What's this? I'm gone ten minutes and you're already with another woman?" They just smiled and held their arms out for her to join the hug.

"Yeah, yeah, ok." She gave them a perfunctory squeeze and then pulled away. "We all love each other. Blah, blah, blah. But we're not quiet finished here. We've still got that to deal with," she said, pointing to Raff.

"Why can't we leave him here like that?" Paul asked.

"Maybe we can," said Chloe, "But I need to talk to him first."

"About what?"

"We need to sort some things out," she said. She dug the stun gun out of her bag and then crouched down beside Raff before pulling the towel from his mouth. He opened his eyes then, giving up all pretense of being unconscious.

"Hey Chloe," he said. "How's it going?"

"Not bad," she said. "I'm afraid your friend over there got his head blown off."

"Yeah, I noticed." Raff craned his neck to catch a glimpse of his dead mentor. "I have to admit, I'm kind of pissed about that."

"Well, he did shoot my friend first."

"I guess that's true," Raff said. "Although that wouldn't have happened if…"

"Let's cut the blame game, Raff. We both know the score at this point and we both know who did what to who."

"To whom," he corrected.

"Whatever. Now we have to figure out what to do next."

"I figure you probably won't kill me, so that means you're going to leave me here, tied up, for the maid service to find."

"That's an option," Chloe said.

"Is there another option?" Raff asked.

"There is. We can cart your tied ass out of here and drop you off somewhere non-corpse adjacent, so at least you won't have to deal with the cops."

"Sounds good to me. What do you want in return?"

"Your promise that this over between us now. We each go our separate ways and never look back. No grudges, no vendettas."

"I can live with that," Raff said. "Anything else?"

"Yeah," Chloe said. "Forty-seven thousand, two hundred and eleven dollars and eighteen cents."

"Oh," Raff said. "You know about that, huh?"

"Know about you skimming money off the top of every job you ever helped the crew pull off? Yeah, I know all about that."

Raff laid his head back and looked up at the ceiling. "Let's see, we add my forty-seven thousand to the seventy-seven thousand you skimmed and you've got close to 120K, right?"

Chloe laughed. "I guess we both know a lot about each other, huh?"

"I guess so," he agreed. "You know, I'm really going to miss you, Chloe."

"You should've thought of that before you fucked me over."

"I did," he said, "But I decided I'd miss that money more."

"And now you get neither."

"But at least I get to be tied up in a ditch instead of in a room with a rotting corpse," he concluded.

"Way to look on the bright side," Chloe said. "Gimme the account number, password and routing info for the money, and there's a lovely ditch in your future."

"How can I refuse?" he said with a sigh.

"I can't believe we're letting him go," Paul said as he pulled their car out of the motel parking lot. There'd been a particularly anxious moment when Bee clambered up on the roof of the gas station and retrieved her remote controlled rifle, but no cars had passed by during that time. Now Bee's car was right behind theirs.

"We're going to dump him penniless in a ditch, for God's sake," Chloe said. "That's punishment enough."

"OK, OK," Paul said. "He only ruined my life. No big deal."

"Did you always whine this much?" she countered playfully.

"I only whine when it comes to anything to do with revenge or ditches," he said with a smile.

"I suppose I can live with that."

They drove on for a few miles. Chloe had a particular stretch of road in mind, one with muddy ditches that was far enough off the beaten path that Raff wouldn't receive help anytime soon, but not so far that he'd never be found.

"And I guess," Paul said, "that from a certain point of view Raff does have a legitimate grievance."

"I'm surprised to hear you of all people say that," Chloe said.

"Well, you did bring the crew in to try and steal my money from me, didn't you?" he said.

"Yeah, I meant to explain that," Chloe replied.

"And so from his point of view, fucked up as it is, you cheated him out of money he was due. And as you have repeatedly reminded me, you're all a bunch of fucking thieves."

"OK, Paul, I know what Bee and I said might've come as a shock, but I really…"

"No, it wasn't a shock at all," Paul said. "You think I didn't know you were after my money the whole time? Of course I did. What else would you want me for?"

"What?" said Chloe in surprise.

"I think the question you've got to be asking yourself right now is: who conned who?"

"What?" she repeated.

"I mean look at it from my point of view," he glanced over at her, flashing her a bright smile. "I got the girl and the money. Everything I ever wanted from this situation. OK, sure, I'm a wanted fugitive, but you said yourself that it's not so bad."

She cocked her head to the side and looked at him, as if seeing him in a new light.

"You know there's one possibility you never considered," Paul said.

"What's that?" she asked.

"Maybe it wasn't Raff who put my old partners on the invite list. Maybe it was me. Maybe I'm the one who set this whole thing up as a test to see which side you'd come down on. Mine or the crew's." For the first time since he'd met her, Paul believed that Chloe really was speechless.

"I mean, think back on it. Raff never really admitted to doing anything, did he? He never came out and said he put the names on the list. He never said he set me up." Out of the corner of his eye he could see that she was trying to remember everything Raff had said and done in the past two days.

"He didn't… ?" she said to herself.

"No, he sure didn't. I wonder why?"

"Wait," she said suddenly. "Yes, he did. He did admit it. I remember it distinctly."

"Are you sure?" Paul asked, barely containing his own laughter.

And then Chloe finally got it. "You're fucking with me, aren't you?" she asked. "You're fucking pulling my leg!"

The laughter finally burst out from him.

"You fuck!" she shouted, punching him playfully in the shoulder. "I can't believe you actually had me going there for a minute! You fuck!" she punched him again.

"Oww! Hey, I'm driving here!" They were both laughing now. She leaned over and kissed him on the cheek and gave his knee a squeeze.

"I guess I deserved that," she said.

"You did try to rob me blind," he pointed out.

"Sure." She snuggled up next to him, her head on his shoulder. "But that was before I got to know you."

Chapter 44

THEY'D left Raff in the ditch, as planned. After Bee used a cellular modem to confirm the bank transfer from his secret account, he cooperated fully and even jumped in (well, hopped in, given that his legs were still tied) of his own free will, depriving Paul of the joy of pushing him. Chloe said she'd call AAA and send them to him in twelve hours no matter what.

The next order of business was getting rid of Bee's car, which ended up parked on a side street in Santa Clara where it would likely remain unmolested until its registration expired in eight months. Even then, it wasn't in Bee's name, so it wouldn't lead the authorities anywhere. But on the off chance that the clerk at the motel remembered the car, they didn't want to risk leaving it anywhere near the scene of the crime. They cleaned it out and wiped it down for prints and let it be.

Lilly called Chloe and let her know that Winston was going to pull through. None of the wounds had been too serious for their in-crew doctor to handle. He was now resting and recuperating at an undisclosed location and eager to see Chloe. She sighed a great sigh of relief at this news, which Paul shared. Bee wanted to know who the heck they were talking about, so Chloe filled her in on the rough details.

Chloe had wanted to head straight over to Greg's and get the money, but Paul made them wait. The last thing they wanted to do was wake him up at 5 in the morning. Everything had to look calm and under control. Instead, they checked into a much nicer motel and, after stopping by Wal-Mart for clothes not stained with sweat and blood, they cleaned up and made themselves presentable.

Bee had been scarily quiet for the last few hours, but a hot shower and a clean shirt seemed to do some good. She wasn't her chipper old self yet, but she didn't look ready to burst into tears at any moment either. Chloe stayed by her side almost constantly throughout this period, giving her encouraging hugs and friendly touches to keep her spirits up. Paul felt a little awkward showing that kind of affection with Bee and so left it all to Chloe.

By 7:30 a.m. Chloe was ready to head over to Greg's again, but Paul still insisted it was too early. "Those guys never come into work before 10 or 11. There's no way he's awake yet. Let's get some pancakes." Bee thought this a grand idea, and Chloe gave in, although he could tell she was getting a little anxious to get on the road.

In a quiet corner of Hobbee's, they ate pancakes and blueberry coffeecake and chatted quietly about what to do next.

"Between what I've saved up and Paul's money, we've got close to million bucks," Chloe said. "That's enough to get set up anywhere we want."

"I've got about eight thousand in cash," Bee said. "I'd have more if I didn't buy so much cool gear."

"But all that equipment's great," Paul assured her. "That's gotta be worth a lot."

"I'm not going to sell it!" she said defensively. "Besides, I made most of that myself."

"I know, I know," Paul said calmly. "I just meant that since we've already got all that gear of yours, we're already ahead of the game when it comes to setting up our own crew."

"Oh," said Bee, smiling sheepishly. "That's a good point." She turned to Chloe now. "Do you think we'll be able to find any of the others? Like Popper maybe? Or Max?"

"I don't know," Chloe said. "Maybe. But we should still get far away from the Bay Area first and then see what we can do. That number Raff left you all is no good, so there's no surefire way to find them."

Bee didn't like this answer very much, but she seemed resigned to it. "Yeah, that's about what I figured. Still, we should try."

"Definitely," Chloe said.

"So where should we go then?" Paul asked.

"Portland's cool," Bee chimed in. "Or Seattle. They're both tech heavy areas and full of cool people. We could probably find as many targets there as here, maybe more."

"Too cold," Paul said. "Too rainy. I had a job interview up there once and just two days of that weather depressed me for a week."

"I've always thought New York would be a great spot," Chloe suggested. "That many people with egos that big, the whole city is ripe for the taking."

"Maybe we could con Donald Trump," Paul joked.

Chloe threw her arm around his neck and drew him into a headlock. "Didn't you learn anything about flashy, public cons?" She teased.

"Ok, ok," he said. "Uncle! I've learned my lesson."

"How 'bout you, Paul," she said as she released him. "What do you wanna do?"

He thought back to the day she'd helped him change his life forever. "Didn't we have this conversation once before?" he asked.

"I guess we did." She smiled. "Although I wasn't paying much attention at the time because I wasn't planning on letting you keep any of the money."

"Ha, ha," he said. "Very funny. Well, now you have to listen."

"I'm all ears," she said.

"Me too," agreed Bee. "Besides, I missed it the first time."

Paul settled back into his seat and looked at both of them. "I'd like to go back to Florida. No snow, no winter, no techie bullshit."

"But plenty of mosquitoes, humidity and alligators," Chloe said.

"And old people," he reminded her. "Never forget the old people."

"It's a possibility, I suppose," Chloe said. "Although you know you can't see your family, right, or any of your old friends? Or even your hometown, for that matter."

"Yeah, yeah, I know," he said. "But it's home anyway, or closer to it. We could go anywhere, really. The other coast maybe."

"I've never been to Florida," Bee said. "Heck, I've never been east of Las Vegas. It sounds like fun."

"You mentioned Key West once. Would that be OK?" Chloe asked.

"Key West would be great!" Paul said. "I love it there! Why do you ask?"

"I've got some contacts in that area. We might be able to get something up and running pretty quick."

Paul mulled this possibility over. "It sounds great and all, Chloe, but I'm not thrilled about the idea of surviving by conning old people out of their retirement money or whatever."

"Ahhh, old people are easy marks, no challenge or fun in that," replied Chloe. "Besides, I liked the direction you went with your con."

"You mean totally screwing up and getting the media and cops involved?"

"Not so much that part," said Chloe. "More the Robin Hood aspect. You know, more like the kinds of actions Winston and his crew pull."

"I admit, they were part of the inspiration for my scheme."

"You were just trying to impress me so you could get in my pants, weren't you?" she asked with a wink.

"It worked, didn't it?"

"I guess it did," she said. "So, Key West then?"

"Sounds like a plan!" Paul said, his voice as happy as it'd been in a long time, both at the prospect of going home and at the fact that Chloe had remembered what he'd told her about Key West. "Bee, does that work for you?" he asked.

"Sure," she said. "As long as they've got DSL down there."

"They do, they do," Paul assured her. "All the comforts of home, I promise you."

"Plus mosquitoes and alligators," Chloe pointed out.

"And sharks," Paul said. "But those are the comforts of home as far as I'm concerned."

Chloe stood up and tossed two twenty-dollar bills on the table. "Fine. Let's get started then. And that means finally going to get your money."

They pulled up into Greg's driveway, and Paul got out of the car by himself. "Let me handle this alone, in case he wants to talk in private or something."

"OK," said Chloe. "But if you run into trouble, don't be afraid to call in the cavalry."

"Thanks," he said, "But I should be fine."

He walked up to the front door and, as he approached, he noticed the black bag he'd stuffed his money into sitting beside the door, a piece of paper taped to it. This was a safe neighborhood and all, but still, it didn't strike Paul as particularly smart to leave that much money sitting outside like that. Maybe being rich really had screwed with Greg's sense of proportion.

Paul plucked the note from the bag and unfolded it.

"Paul, here's your bag. I took out what I thought was fair, as you suggested, and returned you some of the stuff you left in your office. Good luck—Greg."

He put the note in his pocket and opened the bag. Despite himself, he smiled at what he saw.

The bag was heavy and he grunted as he tossed it into the back seat of the car next to Bee. "That was fast," said Chloe, "What did he say?"

"Nothing," said Paul. "He just left the bag on the porch."

"Really? That's mighty trusting of…" Chloe's voice trailed off and she twisted around in her seat and said to Bee. "Open it up. Count it."

Bee unzipped the bag and just stared, dumbfounded. "It's just a bunch of comic books," she said as she pawed through the bag's contents. "There's no money here at all!"

Chloe slowly turned to face Paul. He looked at her expression of frozen anger and cut her off before she could start yelling. "He did leave me a check," he said, easing an envelope he'd found in the bag.

"For how much?" Chloe said, very slowly.

"Exactly what he agreed to," Paul said, handing her the envelope.

She tore it open and read the figure. "$12,640" she said, her voice much calmer than she actually was.

"Two months' severance," Paul said, "just what he promised when he fired me."

"Fuck! Fuck! Fuck!" Chloe shouted, slamming her fists against the steering wheel. "I fucking knew it! Fuck!"

Paul and Bee both gaped at her, too scared to say anything that might set her off even more. "Fuck," she said again, her voice quieter. "Fuck." She took a deep breath. Then another one. Then a third. Then, without a word she threw the car into reverse and pulled back out of the driveway.

"Where are we going?" Paul asked.

"Where do you think?" she said.

"Chloe, we can't go after Greg. There's no way…"

"Who said anything about Greg? I thought you wanted to go to Key West?"

"But without…"

She stopped the car in the middle of the road with a screech and whipped around to face Paul. She grabbed his head and pulled him into a hard, almost painful kiss.

"It's not about the money anymore," she said. "Remember?"

"Yeah," Paul said, momentarily caught breathless.

"Besides," Chloe said with a grin. "We've still got over a hundred grand between us. That's more than enough for two sexy ladies and a comics geek to make their way in the world, don't you think?"

"Absolutely!" Bee said.

"I'm not a geek," Paul started to protest.

Chloe patted him on the knee affectionately. "I know you don't want to admit it, honey, but yes, you are," she teased as she hit the accelerator again and pointed the car toward Highway 101 South. "I love you, but you're definitely a geek."

The End

Geek Mafia Q and A with Author Rick Dakan

"Questions are a burden to others. Answers are a prison for one's own self."

- The Prisoner

Interviewer: How did you start writing?
Rick Dakan: Sort of by accident. In college I never thought of myself as a writer. The first inkling I had that I might have some facility for it came in an upper level American History class. We'd all turned in our first papers and the professor came in the next week and just laid into us for being such crappy writers. He devoted the whole lecture to explaining some basics of good writing. Then he handed back our papers and I'd gotten an "A" minus and he stopped to say it was one of the few well written papers he'd gotten. Sometimes all it takes is something like that to give you that boost of confidence and get you going.

My first published book, *Dark Kingdom of Jade*, was co-written with Mark Friedman. It was for a role-playing game called Wraith: The Oblivion. It was a brand new role-playing game at the time, and Mark knew the editor in charge a little through an online writing group. We just cold pitched her the idea for the book and she liked it. Then, much to our surprise, we had to write the damn thing. I was really rough back then, but Mark was a good editor as well as a writer and that's how things started. I was in grad school at the time, supposedly working on my Master's Thesis in Ancient History, so I signed up for a writing class that was supposed to help you improve your thesis. Instead I used a lot of the workshop time with pieces from Dark Kingdom of Jade.

After that I did a whole string of role-playing game books for games like *Conspiracy X*, *Deadlands*, *Kult*, and *Dungeons and Dragons*, and on and on. Which is good, because grad school really wasn't working out. Walking out of Ohio State and never looking back was one of the happier days of my life. Afterwards, I did the freelance game writer thing for about five or six years. The pay was low, but the deadlines were tight. It taught me to write fast or die. It was a great crucible to hone my skills and, more importantly, my work ethic. I may have been living on $13k a year, but at least I was earning it all by writing.

What made you decide to write Geek Mafia?
Well, I got fired from the videogame company I helped start, Cryptic Studios. That's the short and bitter answer, although it's not quite the whole story. I'd been working freelance for a year and a half after leaving Cryptic, still working for them on *City of Heroes* and writing and publishing the comic book of the same name. But I was getting sick of the work and they were getting sick of me, so with the writing on the wall and my girlfriend recently gone back to California, I was moping around the house one day when I pulled down one of my favorite books from the shelf, *Perdido Street Station* by China Mievelle. I flipped it over and had my Caesar at the tomb of Alexander The Great moment. There was this awesome book and the author was not only bald like me, but the same age and similar radical politics. I had always been working towards a day when I could just write fiction, and I realized that while I was waiting around other people were out there doing it. People just like me. And the title and some of the plot elements had already been floating in my brain for a while, as had the idea of writing something about what I went through with Cryptic. The flash of insight came then to put the two together, which, in retrospect, is insanely obvious.

How much of Geek Mafia is drawn from your own personal experiences?
All of it and none of it. I've never been part of a criminal conspiracy and I've never committed any of the crimes portrayed in this book (as far as you know). Certainly all the characters are purely fictional. But pieces of them are inspired by both my own life and other true-life stories.

At the same time, many of the settings and some of the events closely mirror my own experiences living in Silicon Valley and working in the videogame industry. I was an inexperienced game designer who moved out to San Jose with nothing but a great idea and a friend willing to invest money in it. And my partners did indeed fire me in a way a lot like what's shown in the book, very much to my utter surprise when it happened. And I really did harbor a burning desire for revenge there for a while. So I wrote this book instead.

But, while *Geek Mafia's* genesis was in my own experiences the characters and story soon took on a life of their own. Even as the story spun off into a tale much more interesting and exciting than anything that's ever happened to me, all the little details remain true to what Silicon Valley was like while I lived there. People who live there will recognize all the locations and the general vibe of both the place and the computer game industry.

In your mind, who are geeks?
First of all, geeks are people who become obsessed with things that aren't widely seen as "cool." Moreover, the objects of their obsession require a bit of smarts to fully appreciate. Comic books, video games, audio equipment, even cars all produce geeks. And of course, computers. A geek looks at one or more of these things and sees more than just a box for checking e-mail or a storybook with bright pictures. The true geek sees all the possibilities in that thing – and those possibilities become the basis for the obsession.

In *Geek Mafia* we have characters who are definitely criminals. They're stealing and extorting money from people, just like the traditional Mob. But they're doing it through the lens of their geek world-view. They not only see the possibilities in comics and computers and games, they see the possibility to make a quick and dirty buck.

What about the technology and the cons? Where did those ideas come from?
Well, from my head mostly, but also all inspired by real technology and people and places. For example, my brother works for a company that grades comic books, and that's what inspired me to come up with the idea for the comic con. Now, those guys he works with have read the book and loved it, but they won't confirm or deny that a con like that would work. All the other technology used is, as far as I can tell anyway, realistic and accurate. There's one little question about how much fake blood you could store in a giant coffee cup and still carry it around, but other than that, I think it's all really possible. And making things really possible was important to me, since I wanted to ground what was otherwise a pretty far out story into the world we all actually live in. If none of this actually happened, at least it could have.

In Geek Mafia, Chloe and her criminal crew live an "off the grid" or "underground" lifestyle. Is that based on any particular research you've done or life experiences you've had?

More than anything, this is a bit of wishful thinking on my part. I find the idea of living underground and dropping out of mainstream society very seductive. I think the central theme of *Geek Mafia* is really that you're responsible for creating your own life and your own fate. Chloe and her crew are the most extreme embodiment of that idea. They do what they want and live in total freedom – and that freedom comes with a lot of danger and excitement and, ultimately, deceit. And Paul finds that way of living compelling, but also very frightening. I'm not quite brave enough to do it myself, and so I write about it and maybe I'll find my way there through my books.

I was inspired by the great documentary, *The Weather Underground*, which came out in 2003. I didn't know anything about the Weathermen or their activities and I was just startled at what they managed to get away with for the decade or so they were underground. I don't necessarily agree with all their actions and tactics, but I do admire their commitment to their cause and beliefs. After I saw that, I started reading more about them and looking for information about other groups or individuals who've survived and even prospered outside of normal societal constraints. That led me in particular to Hakim Bey and his essays on *Temporal Autonomous Zones* and *Pirate Utopias*, both of which I found definitely inspirational. I suppose that I hope *Geek Mafia* itself can be seen as contributing to this line of literary exploration and maybe, if I'm real lucky, it'll allow me to live out the dream in some way myself.

Who does Geek Mafia appeal to? Does it fit into any particular genre?

The simple answer is that *Geek Mafia* is a kind of thriller/crime novel that appeals to people like me. Or, put another way, it's for people like the characters in the book – geeks of all stripes and creeds. First and foremost it's a ripping yarn about conmen and pranks and creative crimes, all of which have a very wide audience. Paul and Chloe and the other people that inhabit the novel live in a world that'll be familiar to fans of science fiction stories, comic books, and of course gamers. But not because it's a sci-fi setting, but rather because it's the kind of world fans of those genres live in every day. The book itself is set right in the heart of Silicon Valley, the source of so much cutting edge entertainment, software, and general geeky goodness. One reader said it was a story for Gen X grown up and in its 30's. Certainly there's that element to it – the idea of having responsibilities and accomplishments and then having to act when it all comes falling apart around you. My main character Paul just deals with his problems in a way much more exciting and dangerous than most of us would ever dare.

It's been received very well by people I have since come to know in the hacker community, which is a real badge of honor for me. I made a tour of hacker conventions all over the country and in Germany in 2006 and made a lot of amazing friends and learned some cool and some downright scary stuff about hacking which you'll see in the next few *Geek Mafia* books. I'm just really pleased with how well the book has gone over.

Part of the plot of Geek Mafia centers around talk radio and right-wing politics. Without giving too much away, what role does politics play in Geek Mafia?
Well, politics plays an important role in the story as the plot unfolds, but *Geek Mafia* is not a fundamentally political story. Having said that, there are of course political geeks out there – myself included. Like anything that's equal parts opinion and arcane knowledge, the world of politics attracts plenty of nerds. I spend a large portion of every day reading political blogs and listening to news and talk podcasts and there was a time when I was writing the book that I listened to a TON of talk radio, and some of that experience/interest has made it into the book.

If there is an overt political stance to *Geek Mafia*, it's certainly not one that's represented by either major political party. The characters themselves are, if anything anarchists for the most part, and I did do a fair amount of research into anarchist philosophies and thinkers like Bakunin, Proudhon, and Chomsky. I think, for a lot of people, these ideas go hand in hand with the "off the grid" or "underground" lifestyle that my characters aspire to. But they're not hard core revolutionaries – they're fun-loving and occasionally very dangerous criminals. For them – to paraphrase Clausewitz – politics is just crime carried out by other means. Or, in my case, plot and characterization carried out by other memes.

Is Geek Mafia a stand alone novel or part of an ongoing series?
Definitely part of an ongoing series. In fact, the second book. *Geek*

Mafia: Mile Zero, is out now. I'd already started on a completely unrelated novel while I was editing Geek Mafia – but the more time I spent in this world and with these characters, the more stories popped into my head. I knew that a sequel had to happen and hopefully another two or three after that. And once I came to that point, I didn't want to write anything else, so I dove right into the next book. The third book is all plotted out now and I'm going to start writing it very soon. I have a general idea what the fourth book will be like too.

Why did you decide to release Geek Mafia under the Creative Commons copyright regime?
I first heard about Creative Commons when one sci-fi author Cory Doctrow released his latest book, *Someone Comes to Town, Someone Leaves Town* (which is great by the way). I poked around the CreativeCommons.org Website and I really liked what I saw. I'm all in favor of authors and artists having protection for their works, but I do think that modern day, corporate controlled copyrights and patents have gotten overly restrictive. As a writer, what I want most is for people to read and like my stories. Anything I can do to make that easier for people just makes sense for me. Creative Commons allows me to distribute electronic copies of *Geek Mafia* while still retaining the rights to be the only guy who makes money off the book. And eventually, I can allow it to pass into the public domain – something most creations these days will never do as long as big corporations keep lobbying Congress to have the reversion deadlines extended. And last, but not least, Creative Commons is just a such a perfect fit for the kinds of themes and characters that *Geek Mafia* deals with – it's what my main characters, Chloe and Paul, would want me to do.

ALSO AVAILABLE FROM PM FICTION

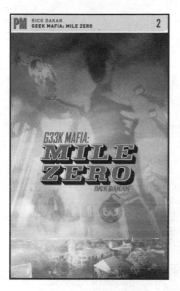

Geek Mafia: Mile Zero
PB ISBN: 978-1-6048-6002-3
$15.95

Key West–southernmost point in the United States, Mile Zero on Highway 1; and as far as you can run away from your past troubles without swimming to Cuba.

Key West–originally Cayo Huesos or Isle of Bones, for centuries a refuge for pirates, wreckers, writers, scoundrels, drunks, and tourists. Now home to a Crew of techno geek con artists who've turned it into their own private hunting ground.

Paul and Chloe have the run of the sun-drenched island, free to play and scam far from the enemies they left behind in Silicon Valley. But that doesn't mean they can't bring a little high tech know-how to the paradise. They and their new Crew have covered the island with their own private Big Brother style network–hidden cameras, FID sensors, and a web of informers that tip them off about every crime committed and tourist trapped on the island.

But will all the gadgets and games be enough when not one but three rival crews of con artists come to hold a top-secret gang summit? And when one of them is murdered, who will solve the crime?

Inspired by author Rick Dakan's own eventful experiences in the video game and comic book industries, the Geek Mafia series satisfies the hunger in all of us to buck the system, take revenge on corporate America, and live a life of excitement and adventure.

"The story is gripping as anything, and the characters are likable and funny and charming. I adore caper stories, and this stands with the best of them, a geeky version of The Sting.*" –Cory Doctorow*

PM

PM Press was founded in 2007 as an independent publisher with offices
in the US and UK, and a veteran staff boasting a wealth of experience in
print and online publishing. Operating our own printing press enables us
to print and distribute short as well as large run projects, timely texts and
out of print classics.

We seek to create radical and stimulating fiction and non-fiction books,
pamphlets, t-shirts, visual and audio materials to entertain, educate and
inspire you. We aim to distribute these through every available channel with
every available technology. Whether that means you are seeing anarchist
classics at our bookfair stalls, reading our latest vegan cookbook at the café
over (your third) microbrew, downloading geeky fiction e-books, or digging
new music and timely videos from our website.

PM Press is always on the lookout for talented and skilled volunteers,
artists, activists and writers to work with. If you have a great idea or can
contribute in some way, please get in touch.

PM Press
PO Box 23912
Oakland, CA 94623
www.pmpress.org